PENGUIN BOOKS

PUSHCART PRIZE, XIII

The Pushcart Prize series has been awarded *Publishers Weekly*'s Carey-Thomas Award for distinguished publishing and editions have been named Outstanding Book of the Year by *The New York Times Book Review*.

THE PUSHCART PRIZE XIII

BEST OF THE SMALL PRESSES

*Edited by
Bill Henderson
with the
Pushcart Prize
editors.
Introduction by
Richard Ford.
Poetry editors:
Philip Booth
and Jay Meek.*

PENGUIN BOOKS

PENGUIN BOOKS
Published by the Penguin Group
Viking Penguin Inc., 40 West 23rd Street,
New York, New York 10010, U.S.A.
Penguin Books Ltd, 27 Wrights Lane,
London W8 5TZ, England
Penguin Books Australia Ltd, Ringwood,
Victoria, Australia
Penguin Books Canada Ltd, 2801 John Street,
Markham, Ontario, Canada L3R 1B4
Penguin Books (N.Z.) Ltd, 182–190 Wairau Road,
Auckland 10, New Zealand

Penguin Books Ltd, Registered Offices:
Harmondsworth, Middlesex, England

First published in the United States of America by
Pushcart Press 1988
Published in Penguin Books 1989

10   9   8   7   6   5   4   3   2   1

Note: Nominations for this series are invited from any small,
independent, literary book press or magazine in the world.
Up to six nominations—tear sheets or copies selected from
work published in the calendar year—are accepted by our
October 15 deadline each year. Write to Pushcart Press, P.O.
Box 380, Wainscott, NY 11975 for more information.

Library of Congress Card number: 76–58675
ISBN: 0 14 01.1699 0
ISSN: 0149–7863

Printed in the United States of America
Set in Baskerville

Acknowledgments

Introduction © 1988 Richard Ford
"Icarus Descending" © 1987 Antaeus
"Entrepreneurs" © 1987 The Quarterly
"Where The Sea Used To Be" © 1987 The Paris Review
"Happiness of the Garden Variety" © 1987 Shenandoah
"Girls" © 1987 Milkweed Chronicle
"Johnnieruth" © 1987 Seal Press
"Wonderland" © 1987 The Iowa Review
"The Blue Baby" © 1987 TriQuarterly
"Hector Composes A Circular Letter. . . . " © 1987 Missouri Review
"What Is It Then Between Us?" © 1987 The Ontario Review
"After Yitzl" © 1987 The Georgia Review
"The Era of Great Numbers" © 1987 Epoch
"Life Moves Outside" © 1987 Burning Deck Press
"The Golden Robe" © 1987 Fiction International
"What The Shadow Knows" © 1987 Exquisite Corpse
"Star, Tree, Hand" © 1987 New England Review/Bread Loaf Quarterly
"Andantino" © 1987 Western Humanities Review
"A Note In Memoriam: Terrence Des Pres" © 1987 TriQuarterly
"Atlas of Civilization" © 1987 Parnassus: Poetry In Review
"Redneck Secrets" © 1987 Graywolf Press
"Learning from Chekhov" © 1987 Western Humanities Review
"Literary Talk" © 1987 The Threepenny Review
"Exorcising Beckett" © 1987 The Paris Review
"Excellent Things In Women" © 1987 Raritan A Quarterly Review
"Flip Cards" © 1987 The Georgia Review
"Birds of Paradise: A Memoir" © 1987 MSS
"The Woman Poet: Her Dilemma" © 1987 The American Poetry Review
"To Charlotte Bronte" © 1987 The American Scholar
"Dim Man, Dim Child" © 1987 Ironwood
"Approaching August" © 1987 Northern Lights
"The Dogwood Tree" © 1987 Poetry
"My Son and I Go See Horses" © 1987 The American Poetry Review
"December Journal" © 1987 The Paris Review
"The Rise of the Sunday School Movement" © 1987 North American Review
"Henry James and Hester Street" © 1987 Salmagundi
"Send Pictures, You Said" © 1987 Five Fingers Review
"Tenderness" © 1987 Poetry
"The Guest Ellen At the Supper for Street People" © 1987 Raritan A Quarterly Review
"Talking to God" © 1987 North Dakota Quarterly
"Justice Without Passion" © 1987 ZYZZYVA
"Between Flights" © 1987 Poetry Northwest
"Cheer" © 1987 Ironwood
"Mother Teresa" © 1987 Raccoon
"Tu Do Street" © 1987 Indiana Review
"Elegy for Robert Winner (1930–1986)" © 1987 The Quarterly
"Heron" © 1987 Ploughshares
"20–200 on 737" © 1987 The Threepenny Review
"Eagle Poem" © 1987 Streetfare Journal
"Epithalamium" © 1987 Open Places
"Leaves That Grow Inward" © 1987 Ironwood
"May, 1968" © 1987 Poetry
"Box" © 1987 American Poetry Review
"Making A Great Space Small" © 1987 Quarry West
"What She Had Believed All Her Life" © 1987 Ironwood
"A Little Death" © 1987 Crazyhorse
"Bird Watching" © 1987 Field

This book is in memory of
Terrence Des Pres (1939–1987)

A NOTE IN MEMORIAM: TERRENCE DES PRES

by REGINALD GIBBONS

from *TriQuarterly*

TERRENCE DES PRES, born on December 26, 1939, died accidentally on November 16, 1987.

One might want to grieve well enough and then go on to the next thing that needs to be done. The trouble with following that advice, for this writer, is that Des Pres was one of those very ones to whom I turned frequently for companionship in both the pleasure and the responsibility of figuring out what it was, exactly, that next needed doing—at least in the circumscribed (and to both of us compelling, even unrenounceable) world of writing. So this brief memorial is offered in personal tribute to Des Pres.

To me he seemed a great spirit, a great conscience, a great lover of poetry for its most potent utterances rather than its most ingrained or wispy, for its signs of trouble rather than its more polished airs. Brilliant but modest, restless and edgy, mordant, intense, reticently loving, angry, generous and always ready to laugh whether with delight or out of grim or bitter rue, he was a great and encouraging companion not only when once in a while we could meet here or there, but also and always in the mind, as a fellow-spirit whom I sensed was there, thinking, walking-with-thought ahead into these times.

He had been struck, I think, into a permanent grief over the horrors of violence against persons in this century, he made no secret of it, and he said to me more than once that he would never get over having gone through the writing of *The Survivor: An Anatomy of Life in the Death Camps*. I did not distrust that sentiment; I do not consider it to have been expressed, as some would have expressed it, out of a perverse pride in his own suffering. On the contrary, I thought it the measure of a knowledge and compassion greater than I could have welcomed in myself, for fear of it, but which he had discovered in himself and had no choice but to accept. And he never placed his own premonitions, nightmares, obsessions, before the suffering of those whose lives and deaths, whose living against death, he had studied.

Born or raised into such uncommon sensitivity—I don't know which—he was what he was, and would confess his temperament and gifts as a kind of weakness. And perhaps others who knew him would agree that this made him seem to live at twice the rate we did, burning furiously through thought and feeling in his restless, winning way; tiring of thinking on dark things, certainly, but willing to return to them for more thought, as well as unable not to. He had the authority—not wanted, and almost unwitting—of one who knows too much, and for whom that knowledge is an obstacle, a boulder, needing to be leapt over again and again and again. Or perhaps he was, I feel now, a sort of Sisyphus—not condemned out of fault, but out of vulnerability, out of conscience, to roll that rock ahead of him always. Some persons have to do that and he was one. But what was perhaps most inspiring about him was that with all his knowledge of the suffering of others, he was himself productive, energetic, excited by his reading of poetry. At the time of his death, I think he had never been happier.

But he himself was, until he died, a survivor—of early, irrevocable loss. And if he accepted a long turn pushing that stone, studying the survival of others for whom the *word* was life-saving, he later got past that stone with the extraordinary chapters of *Praises and Dispraises*, a book which looks back to Hannah Arendt's *Men in Dark Times*, but chooses only poets for its subjects. And he was already at work on a new book—taking notes and thinking his way into it—about flight; about, as I remember him mentioning it only a few weeks ago, not only the technological reality of flight, but its cultural function as a ceaselessly sought activity both real and symbolic, as we Americans keep flying away from troubles we seem to have no way of solving: nuclear weaponry and all the rest. This was a brilliant opening into which Des Pres could have driven all his alertness and intellectual power. All of his work was of a rare and invaluable kind that one cannot imagine anyone else ever accomplishing in his stead; so his absence now as a writer will not be filled any more than his absence as a person.

When we last talked, by telephone, he and I were looking forward to many different things—the publication of *Thomas McGrath: Life and the Poem* (*TQ* #70), which we had edited together; the realization of the hopes of others whom we loved; meeting in Chicago in a few weeks. But now he is dead. If there are vocations or missions for any of us at all, and I think there are, then there was certainly such for Terrence Des Pres, but he did not live long enough to carry his vocation to all the places where he wanted to exercise it. And because his vocation was lived in the literary realm, the disappointments and modest triumphs of which I think I understand—a realm always in need of such writers as Des Pres—I feel beyond my own grief a loss to what common cause we can make, as writers and readers, for sanity and reason, for compassion and passionate opposition to all that is cruel and irrational, violent and besotted with self-righteousness and untruth. That common cause is what he and the work he completed will stand for, now. A keener savoring, a higher valuing, than Terrence's, of the language of poetry, when it tangles and untangles such matters, exists in no one. I hope we will remember his work and his name.

Editor's Note: "Self/Landscape/Grid" by Terrence Des Pres was the lead essay in *Pushcart Prize IX*. His essay "Poetry in Dark Times" appeared in *Pushcart Prize VII*.

THE
PEOPLE WHO HELPED

FOUNDING EDITORS—*Anaïs Nin (1903–1977), Buckminster Fuller (1895–1983),Charles Newman, Daniel Halpern, Gordon Lish, Harry Smith, Hugh Fox, Ishmael Reed, Joyce Carol Oates, Len Fulton, Leonard Randolph, Leslie Fiedler, Nona Balakian, Paul Bowles, Paul Engle, Ralph Ellison, Reynolds Price, Rhoda Schwartz, Richard Morris, Ted Wilentz, Tom Montag, William Phillips, Poetry editor: H. L. Van Brunt.*

EDITORS—*Walter Abish, Ai, Elliott Anderson, John Ashbery, Russell Banks, Robert Bly, Robert Boyers, Harold Brodkey, Joseph Brodsky,Wesley Brown, Hayden Carruth, Raymond Carver, Frank Conroy, Malcolm Cowley, Paula Deitz, Steve Dixon, Andre Dubus, M. D. Elevitch, Loris Essary, Ellen Ferber, Carolyn Forché, Stuart Freibert, Jon Galassi, Tess Gallagher, Louis Gallo, George Garrett, Reginald Gibbons, Jack Gilbert, Louise Glück, David Godine, Jorie Graham, Linda Gregg, Barbara Grossman, Donald Hall, Michael Harper, Robert Hass, DeWitt Henry, J. R. Humphreys, David Ignatow, John Irving, June Jordan, Edmund Keeley, Karen Kennerly, Galway Kinnell, Carolyn Kizer, Jerzy Kosinski, Richard Kostelanetz, Seymour Krim, Maxine Kumin, Stanley Kunitz, James Laughlin, Seymour Lawrence, Naomi Lazard, Herb Leibowitz, Denise Levertov, Philip Levine, Stanley Lindberg, Thomas Lux, Mary MacArthur, Thomas McGrath, Daniel Menaker, Frederick Morgan, Cynthia Ozick, Jayne Anne Phillips, Robert Phillips, George Plimpton, Stanley Plumly, Eugene Redmond, Ed Sanders, Teo Savory, Grace Schulman, Harvey Shapiro, Leslie Silko, Charles Simic,*

Dave Smith, William Stafford, Gerald Stern, David St. John, Bill and Pat Strachan, Ron Sukenick, Anne Tyler, John Updike, Sam Vaughan, David Wagoner, Derek Walcott, Ellen Wilbur, David Wilk, David Wojahn, Bill Zavatsky.

CONTRIBUTING EDITORS FOR THIS EDITION—John Allman, Philip Appleman, James Atlas, Bo Ball, Jim Barnes, Barbara Bedway, John Berger, Martha Bergland, Linda Bierds, Norbert Blei, Michael Blumenthal, Rosellen Brown, Christopher Buckley, Richard Burgin, Michael Dennis Browne, Kathy Callaway, Henry Carlile, Kelly Cherry, Naomi Clark, Robert Cohen, Peter Cooley, Stephen Corey, Douglas Crase, Philip Dacey, John Daniel, Barbara Thompson Davis, Susan Strayer Deal, Rita Dove, Mark Doty, John Drury, Stuart Dybek, Carol Emshwiller, Louise Erdrich, Jane Flanders, H. E. Francis, Barry Goldensohn, Kenneth Gangemi, Gary Gildner, Patricia Goedicke, Thom Gunn, Patrick Worth Gray, O. B. Hardison Jr., Amy Hempel, Don Hendrie Jr., Garrett Kaoru Hongo, James Baker Hall, Patricia Henley, Brenda Hillman, Edward Hirsch, Susan Howe, Andrew Hudgins, Lynda Hull, Colette Inez, Elizabeth Inness-Brown, Richard Jackson, Josephine Jacobsen, Harold Jaffe, Laura Jensen, Elizabeth Jolley, August Kleinzahler, Dorianne Laux, Gerry Locklin, Phillip Lopate, David Madden, Dan Masterson, Cleopatra Mathis, William Matthews, D. R. MacDonald, Robert McBrearty, Jean McGarry, Joe-Anne McLaughlin, Wesley McNair, Sandra McPherson, Lisel Mueller, Joan Murray, Susan Mitchell, Leonard Nathan, Sheila Nickerson, Fae Myenne Ng, Lucia Perillo, Mary Peterson, Michael Palmer, Jonathan Penner, Robert Pinsky, Joe Ashby Porter, C. E. Poverman, Tony Quagliano, Bin Ramke, Donald Revell, Pattiann Rogers, William Pitt Root, Vern Rutsala, Michael Ryan, Sherod Santos, Leslie Scalapino, Lloyd Schwartz, Lynne Sharon Schwartz, Bob Shacochis, Arthur Smith, Jim Simmerman, Tom Sleigh, Elizabeth Spencer, Elizabeth Spires, Maura Stanton, Pamela Stewart, Mary Tall Mountain, Susan Tichy, Bill Tremblay, Lee Upton, Sara Vogan, Marilyn Waniek, Michael Waters, Gordon Weaver, Bruce Weigl, Susan Welch, Anita Wilkins, C. K. Williams, Harold Witt, Christina Zawadiwsky, Pat Zelver.

EUROPEAN EDITORS—Kirby and Liz Williams, Lily Frances

MANAGING EDITOR—Hannah Turner

ROVING EDITOR—*Helen Handley*

FICTION EDITOR—*Genie D. Chipps*

ESSAYS EDITOR—*Anthony Brandt*

POETRY EDITORS—*Philip Booth, Jay Meek*

EDITOR AND PUBLISHER—*Bill Henderson*

CONTENTS

XVIII

INTRODUCTION

by RICHARD FORD

AT MY PARTICULAR AGE, which is forty-four (neither exactly young or exactly old is how that feels) almost every partisan argument aimed at proving some general truth about the world—even the publishing world—seems to resolve itself—in my mind, anyway—into what I think of as nice, existential equilibrium: almost nothing seems to be generally true, almost nothing generally false; so that the best anyone can do is, find his own way, reveal it as such, and go on hopefully. Counsel is of course what's needed. Though real counsel, in the way Walter Benjamin meant it—useful words about human life—is hard to come by and was to him almost exclusively a virtue of *told stories*, something we don't have much anymore, and therefore a category I see good reason to expand so as to include short stories, poems and even essays—all of them forms wherein the writer, working at his or her highest achievement, invites, as Benjamin says, the righteous man to encounter himself.

What follows here are fifty-six such pieces of highly-achieved writing, the most prizable that could be gathered and selected over the past year from hundreds of America's small presses, published writing which, but for the *Pushcart* series, might suffer to be little read, but ought not. What's been chosen is from *Antaeus*, The Graywolf Press, *The Ontario Review*, *Western Humanities Review*, and also writing from less easily findable journals; *Five Fingers*, *Raccoon*, *The Milkweed Chronicle*, Burning Deck. I cannot say that counsel will always be available in each and every selection, at least not the precise counsel each of us needs. But much that's good is here, and it is hopeful that we find it other than where conventional wisdom and literary fashion would tell us it only lies. The righteous man can and probably always should encounter himself far from his obvious and most public haunts. How else can his righteousness seem tried, or ever persuade others?

Inasmuch as the act of publishing is, of course, the second and unsaid concern of this volume—publishing that's done by writers, and that done by publishers of every coat and hat size—it is on this subject that I will briefly introduce these poems, stories and essays of my contemporaries. Being a writer, I have, of course plenty of excellent opinions about publishing; and having been a writer of one sort or other for twenty years, I also have a catalog of unflattering publishing experience, some of which I will now make public in at least the *spirit* of counsel, and if that should fail, in the hope of offering mild consolation.

When I got out of school, in 1970, ready to begin being a writer, there seemed to hold sway in this country a kind of conventional wisdom regarding writing, and particularly getting started writing; a protocol for getting work (stories, in my case) published into the world and eventually read by real readers.* I'm no longer sure that such a protocol exists in the minds of young writers today. I do not even know why we thought what we thought. But we thought it, acted on it. And for some people it worked out fine, while for others—me—it didn't.

Wisdom was that for young writers there was a particular "publishing world" out there, a world divided into hemispheres. One hemisphere was the sub-world of small presses, literary magazines, university reviews. And the other, more brilliant, upper half was the world of large-circulation, widely-read, money-paying, famous-making magazines printed on slick pages, and not in Baton Rouge or Bowling Green, but in New York and Boston. The Big Time this was.

What we—or at least I—understood about this world was that I needed to "break into it." There was a "level" I could empirically find by sending my stories out—literary magazines were where one started—and either getting them back or having them approved and published. Good stories were to be found there, and mine would stand a chance. Once I did that, broke into print, I could try to "move up" to better, more widely-read and distributed magazines—there was a floating sense of which magazines were

*Readers are people you don't know or aren't related to.

better than others. My work, my name would begin to get around. I would see some action. Acceptance would be a word I'd hear more. Money would rarely change hands, but I was not in this for money (and, truly, I wasn't). All of this would go along for a while, years perhaps, while I got better, while I had more work published, while my name on a manuscript began to be associated with good writing; and until by some act of providence a story of mine would get "taken" upwards by an editor from the other world, the one where all the bright lights were turned on. And then I would be someplace. That would be the *it* heard often in the phrase, "you've made *it*."

The trouble was, this progression didn't work for me. It worked for others well enough. Some of the finest and most widely read and admirable writers writing today have gone up through these ranks, their good stories published, their readership solidly banked by their earliest admirers. And some writers, of course, simply ignored this whole ladder-and-rung business altogether, sent stories to *The New Yorker* or *The Atlantic,* got the good word straight away, hit the ground running and have never looked back. Though much maligned now by spoil-sports, early and great success must've been very sweet. I'd have handled mine admirably, I'm sure. In any case, all formulas for creating one's writing life break down once the first term is established: I write a story.

I, however, could not get my stories published. I sent them to many—very many—of the magazines represented in this very volume. I kept a log, a little notebook in which I had lined off little boxes, inside which I wrote where this story was sent and when, when it came back, where it went next. Somebody—I forget who, now—told me this is what I should do. I needed to be orderly. Systematic. It was serious business I was up to. The strangling horror that a story would be accepted at two or perhaps three magazines at once, the embarrassment, and bad editorial blood this would cause to flow, could all be avoided this way. Meanwhile, the system, my logging in dates and destinations like a shipping clerk, would give me something to do while I awaited my own good news, offer solace when there wasn't good news. And there wasn't.

I was persistent. I kept my stories out. I furrowed my brow over levels. Maybe *The Cimarron Review* was just too good for me at this point. I should send a story to a magazine with a less resolute name. I remember one called *The Fur-Bearing Trout,* where I was chattily turned down by an editor who said he didn't like short stories longer than eight pages, though they need not be about fish.

I pulled strings—any ones I thought I had. To *Sumac*, a magazine in Michigan, I wrote that I was a graduate of Michigan State. That seemed cagey. To a magazine in Mississippi I bragged I was a native. No dice. I got my friend whom *The Cimarron Review* actively admired and regularly published to recommend me. No again. I even got an old teacher who had once taught Willie Morris, now editor at *Harper's*, to middleman a story to *Harper's*—shooting, once, for the moon. No.

Once a man named Nick Crome (I hope he's happy, wherever he is) asked me to revise a story I'd sent to his magazine, *TransPacific*. Though when I eagerly did and returned it, he ignored my new version, yet asked me to badger my local library (which happened to be the Chicago Public Library) into subscribing and inserting his magazine on its shelves. I admit it—I wrote him promptly and suggested where he ought best insert his magazine, whereupon he dispatched to me a three-page, single-spaced letter full of invective and threat in which he periodically used the red half of his ribbon for emphasis, and in which he called me "sonny," "sport," "ace," "junior," a "simpleton," a "sorry, petulant fool," and an "ignorant motherfucker." Though in his behalf he also wrote this to me: "I devote most of my waking hours to the attempt to promote the careers of people like you, ace. I do this not only by publishing them—but by writing every one personally, so they know there's a real person here, who knows who they are and who does read what they write. . . . My wife, who is acting now as the business manager tells me you're not a subscriber. That's ok—relatively few care about preserving the means by which young writers in America find publication—shit now, junior, they just want to get PUBLISHED!!!!!" PUBLISHED was one of the words typed in red.

Seasoning, I think this is called. Dues paying. Rope-learning. Getting my feet wet. Starting at the bottom. I was doing this. Only nobody liked my stories.

Finally a call came from a friend in California. A magazine, he said, in New Zealand was interested in new American writing. Maybe I could send something there. New Zealand, I thought, gazing out my window at an unpromising winter sky. A nice place. English spoken there. Yes. I would. And sure enough the editors took my story, even asked for another, which I sent and they agreed to publish soon. And for a time in the winter of 1971, I thought very, very fondly about New Zealand, about what good people were there. Readers. People willing to give you a chance. Careless of trends, vogues, reputations. It was summer there, then. I thought of Mr. Peggotty sailing off to Australia: "We will begin a new life over theer," is how he put it. Exuberant. Valiant. I considered a move.

First, though, I fastidiously entered the titles of my two stories and their new "homes" into the here-to-fore empty space on my curriculum vita reserved for publications. New Zealand. It seemed farther away there on that page than when the happy letters had arrived. I wondered what someone would think who saw these entries, what sort of writer they'd think I was, what form of wild desperation inhabited me that I needed to send my stories all the way there. Would they realize the North American serial rights for each story were still intact, and I could still publish the story stateside if I wanted to? Or if someone else wanted to? And who would ever read these stories? The editors—all good fellows—liked them, paid them compliments. But no one else ever weighed in with praise or complaint or notice of any kind. All was quiet. And in a month I decided not to move to New Zealand. Not yet. It wasn't going anyplace, after all. But neither was I.

I went back to circulating my stories. *Epoch, The North American Review, The Red Clay Reader, The New American Review*— where I'd read some writers whose names I knew. Phillip Roth, William Gass. I quit writing cagey cover letters. My own "production," though, was beginning to slow. I'd written eight or so stories, I was twenty-seven years old, and I was becoming confused about my "style." My log book was filled up. A student journal at a small Ohio college agreed to print a story, but one I'd written three years ago! When I was just starting school! The editor loved it "If you can write like this," I remember his letter saying, "you should be writing for the *slicks*." Only I couldn't write like that anymore. I'd "developed" beyond this. Maybe I shouldn't have. What did he know?

It all got me down. That much I can tell you. Stories would whistle back into my mailbox just ahead of a dark mistral. I'd read the enclosed letters, check to see if the story was still clean and enough-undented by paper clips to send out again, gulp down some bearable bitterness, then just quit for the day. Usually I'd have a drink about ten forty-five in the morning and take a long walk until my wife got off work and there was something new to take heart from.

And then, unsuddenly, I just quit writing stories, " . . . gagged by the silence of others," as Sartre says. I was discouraged. But I do not think I was disillusioned. Even then I knew that a life, even a short one like mine, once dedicated to literature was not a wasted life. I was merely a failure at what I was doing. And along with failure's other dull commissions comes—as should be—the time to think things over. Failure may not always inspire one's best decisions, but one's profoundest convictions do often arise nearby.

And so, in the late winter of 1971, in Chicago, I took an account of the world and, as it says in Dickens, my "personal history, adventures, experience and observation" of it.

There is a koan often audible among avante gardistes and inside the better, more progressive graduate writing programs, which asks: is it not usually the case that you can tell a good story by the fact that very few people like it? Considering, however, who were the few who liked my stories, I did not feel I had the full assurance of even that befuddling wisdom. And in any case, I wanted people to like my stories. More importantly, I wanted people to read them, even if they couldn't like them. I believed—or I came to believe that winter—that writers, the ones I cared about, and even myself, wrote to be read; not to aggrandize themselves in cringing elitism, not to please or psychoanalyze themselves by getting closer to their feelings, and not, indeed, just to be published and to fill that empty space on a resumé. Writers wrote, I thought, not even to appeal to a particular readership, but to discover and bring to precious language the most important things they were capable of, and to reveal that to others with the hope that it will commit an effect on them— please them, teach them, console them. Reach them.

I, it was plain, wasn't succeeding here. Nobody was reading my stories because, I decided, they simply weren't very good, not good enough, anyway. Maybe I knew it in my back-brain; maybe I just trusted the editors who sent them all back to me. But I knew it. It's true I've always trusted rejection more than acceptance (at the time I'd had a whole lot more experience with rejection). But it's also true that I came to believe that no good writing would go unpublished. Perhaps this was a free and blind act of writer's faith, but if so, it seemed to me collateralized by the abundant evidence that so much awful writing—even if not mine—routinely found its "home" in public print.

Past these first principles of belief, certain practical matters became apparent to me. I did not write very fast. I wrote hard, but at my pace I would never get the proper amount of low-level publishing experience to move up through the ranks. Too few at-bats, you could say. Moreover, I didn't like the whole major league/minor league premise of that conventional wisdom I'd inherited. I read the magazines I'd been submitting to, as well as the ones I wished I could, and I couldn't see evidence that the premise worked very well. Plenty of terrible stories were popping up in both leagues. There was reason to believe, in fact, that not a lot of really excellent writing got done, or probably ever did. That, of course, is still the case, though it doesn't discourage anyone, nor should it.

Even more to the point, I began to resent what seemed to me the unprovable premise that there existed *any* useful structure or scheme of ascendable rungs whose rule was that my stories weren't good enough at first but might be better later on; and that I should have patience and go on surrendering myself to its clankings. What I felt was that I wanted my stories to be great stories, as good as could be written. And now. And if they weren't (and they weren't) that was my own business, my problem, not the concern of some system for orderly advancement in the literary arts, some wisdom kept presumptuously active by wretched, grad-student magistrates sitting before piles of mss., or else some already bellied-up writer who'd changed boats middle-course and become an "editor." I had hard thoughts that winter. But I meant my failings to be my own affair.

Some people, I guess, thrive by deferring to unknown and presumably higher authority, to the benevolence of vast, indistinct institutions. And of course, it's never a simple matter when your life requires submitting to the judgment of others. We all accommodate that. But most of the writers I have respected and still respect seem to me not so adept at discerning and respecting underlying design, but actually spend all their efforts trying to invent designs anew. What was out there, I thought eighteen years ago, and think even more this minute, is not a structure for writers to surrender to, but fidgety, dodgy chaos. And our privileged task is to force it, calm it to our wills.

What I did, then, with all this fresh-in-mind was to put my stories away in their tabbed folders, fattened by the various drafts and revisions and rejection notices that lodged with them, and dedicate myself to writing a novel, which I assumed would take years, and did. Not that I advise this strategy for anyone else. My belief about starting novels and particularly the first one, is that you treat the impulse like the impulse to marry: solemnly, and with the proviso that if you can talk yourself out of it you should. And if you can't then there's no advice to give.

But I needed to get better—much, much better at what I was doing, and in ways I don't even want to think about now. A novel would take those years; I could go more slowly; there was more to work on, get better at. No demoralizing rejections would crash into my mailbox every morning. One might eventually come, but it was far off. And in trade for this easement, this slow-going, this sumptuous usage of my time and youth, I'd have a novel, maybe, when all was over—a not inconsiderable achievement. It was a bargain I was only too happy to enter.

Thinking back on 1971 now, I am even more convinced than I could've been then. Failure at publishing stories where I wanted and tried vigorously to publish them turned me back to my work and away from the thin solace of publication. "Success," which I've always calibrated in readers, was withheld, and I somehow was encouraged—even if it felt different at the time. And it did feel different.

I dignify my decision now by believing that publication of those first stories might've just plain shot me in the foot by conferring approval—of some kind—on work I wanted to be good but that wasn't very good. When I look around in literary book stores now, and in the back ad-pages of magazines, it seems that with patience and resourcefulness *every* writer can find a publisher for everything that's written—good, bad, indifferent. And while I won't wag a finger at publishing too fast, or publishing your buddies, or publishing the famous because they're thought to be "lightning rods of the culture" (as a famous editor recently admitted), or even just publishing a magazine that nobody but the editors and their parents will ever read—a young Joyce might always be lurking, and anyway who cares—I have written enough stories myself that "aren't right for us," or that "showed promise," or that "would surely find a home elsewhere," so as to feel sovereignty over this one opinion: publishing work that's no good probably isn't a very good idea for writers and publishers alike, no matter where along the literary ladder they happen to be clinging. For writers, it's hard when no one likes your work and hard in another way when things begin finally to break your way, but it's best to try and set your own high standards for what's good and what isn't—even if, God knows, you happen to have written the stuff yourself.

Finally, small presses, literary magazines, university reviews, which by all means have not been the sole subject of this preface, do still have a place in my writing life. On occasion they have been willing to publish what—by my own standards—have been stories as good as I can write after years of trying. I do not, however, any longer believe in such a thing as a "small press world." All magazines and presses exist discretely, doing this or that independent of each other, excellently or with dismaying mediocrity. I don't believe, either and in the same spirit, that small presses or literary journals are "where it's at" for writing in this country, any more than I believe *The New Yorker* or *Esquire* are. I've never been convinced or seen evidence that the audiences for quarterlies with 1,800 readers were any more perceptive or appreciative or forgiving than other putative audiences, or that their editors were any more open-minded, generally willing to take risks, less capricious, less victims of cronyism, or had their ears more finely tuned to excellent work than anybody else who sets up as a public literary arbiter. True, those slick magazines are run to the tune of profits. Money. But one fellow's profit is likely to be another man's principle. Who's to say whose god is meaner, coarser?

Where it's really *at* for literature in this country is where it's always been, of course—with writers, and only there. And while I have no doubt that gauged by volume, small presses, literary magazines, modest reviews of all size and paper quality publish a larger amount of writing I would not want to read than I could find by looking in any other general direction, it is also simply indisputable and to the good of any writer writing and any reader with the time and need to turn toward literature—which after all, is what's contained in this volume, the thirteenth in the *Pushcart Prize* series—that more good poems, good essays, good stories are to be found in these magazines, these journals, and from these presses than in any other place on the planet. And that's a lot to say. And quite enough.

THE
PUSHCART PRIZE XIII:
BEST OF THE
SMALL PRESSES

WHERE THE SEA
USED TO BE

fiction by RICK BASS

from THE PARIS REVIEW

THEY MET before midnight at the house of the richest man in Mississippi, and left shortly with a dark old leather country doctor's satchel that was bulging with money, bulging as if trying to breathe, swollen like a dying fish's gills: they were unable to even shut it all the way. There wasn't a moon, and they had to drive slowly, because one of the dogs was sick, and the old man had to urinate every forty minutes, and the truck was old, because they did not want to appear conspicuous. They had coffee in Starkville, urinated in Columbus, and crossed over the state line of Alabama at dawn. The sun was orange and promising as they came down through the tall pines; no traffic was out on the road yet, and there was smoke in only a few of the chimneys, rising slow and straight. It was October.

"I like to be traveling at this time of day," Harry told Jack. Harry had slept between his stops, the entire drive. Soft fog was out over the lowest meadows; Holsteins, and Angus, grazed. It had rained in the night, lightly, before their arrival: that smell was in the air. The road was black and narrow, and wound down through the heavy trees and there was greenness, in the small meadows: cleared by hand, and mule, all stumps burned, the meadows had field stones stacked around their boundaries. There were old tool sheds.

"You can rip up those old nasty barns and make picture frames of 'em," Harry told Jack, and laughed. "People in the city'll pay money for those things." He eyed the occasional ancient sheds with a

3

steady, labored look as they passed each one, pausing in his heavy breathing, not even hawking phlegm, so that Jack was alarmed into picturing them driving out into the field, hooking up to the porch or a window frame with a rope, and driving off, pulling the scatter of wood and building down like dominoes. Stacking the wood in the back of the truck. Driving on, deeper into the heart of Alabama, to enter, to take. Harry was seventy-two, the boss. The peace and freshness of the morning made Jack not mind anything. His life was set before him. The dogs awoke and began tumbling about in the back: jawing, yipping, fighting. The poor one feeling better.

The orange sun rose above the hills as they reached the Vernon city limits: trees, dark green, pines. Harry said he was hungry. They were on an expense account. He ate six eggs and three biscuits. Jack fed and watered the dogs, and scratched their ears. Dudley had said the dogs would be as valuable as the satchel. People still thought Dudley could find oil. It was the last hurrah.

The dogs had been purchased late the afternoon before from the Animal Rescue League, and were along because there was a man who was already working up in north Alabama, a man named Wallis Featherston, who had worked in a menial job for Dudley Estes for several years, but who was now on his own, taking small bits and pieces of leases and then telling his ideas to other, larger companies, larger than even Old Dudley—companies that Dudley wanted someday to equal: Shell, Phillips, Texaco—who would go in and buy the remaining leases in the prospect, and drill the wells, and Wallis would be able to participate for a percent or two or three. It was said that Wallis was getting his leases very cheaply, because he was country, like the people he was leasing from—bone raw and country, rusty and gravel, a people of cold winters, rainy springs, and hard farming—and Wallis had a dog that rode around with him everywhere. Wallis had a plane, too; he flew around, looking at things.

So they, Old Dudley, had decided to go with what worked. Old Dudley was sixty years old, a billionaire, and for some reason was chasing this ex-clerk: trying to catch up with him and pass him. Wallis was twenty-eight, and slept in a field, in his sleeping bag, or in the truck when it rained. He hadn't participated in a dry hole yet. He'd hit on thirteen straight wells. He had named his dog Dudley.

Jack ordered ham for breakfast. The sausages and hams were good, up in these hills. The farmers wore overalls and straw hats

4

and were nasal, and still used mules, red championship ones from Tennessee. The country was too tough for tractors. There were also sawmills, a few.

Jack smiled at one of the waitresses. None of the girls were pretty, and they all looked the same, like a hundred plain sisters. He would find one, though, an outsider, passing through, like himself. She would be smitten with the promise of youth and his existence There was a heavy chain around the satchel, padlocked. The key to the lock was on a necklace over Jack's chest. The key against his skin felt like a woman's hand, sometimes; the heat. It made him dizzy. He wanted to do good, for Dudley. He wanted to do so good. The dogs barked, and played, outside. People went to the window, and asked what kind they were.

Wallis sat out in the field where he camped, with his maps in his lap, checking leases. A woman brought him some lunch: chicken, cream corn, biscuits, all of it still hot. It was in a straw basket with a cloth over the top. People were discovering the basin: it hadn't been drilled for over seventy years. The day was bright, and there was newness; you could smell oil in the air, too. No one knew where it was coming from—there were no wells in the area, hunters had never found any seeps along the creeks—but it had the heady smell of live oil, black. Dudley had drilled eight dry holes in the little valley. Wallis loved to lunch there often. He had saved the dog Dudley from being killed by a bird hunter: speechless, furious at the dog's ineptitude, his inability to point birds, the man had been aiming his gun at the dog when Wallis, out walking, came up on them. Wallis bought the dog for all the money he had in his pocket, a dollar and sixty-seven cents, and named him Dudley, because he couldn't hunt.

"It's a hot summer," Wallis said aloud, to himself. It was mid-October. Coldness seemed it would never come, in the days. Everything tasted good, in the warmth. He shut his eyes. There had to be some trick; he had to be missing something. He was too happy. There was very much the urge to be cautious: to suspect a pratfall.

He flew: long, lazy circles around the towns, over the woods, flying low and slow: peeling an apple as he flew, sometimes. Looking for the thing, the thing no one else knew to look for yet, though he knew they would find it, and rip it into shreds. He considered falling in love.

He sat on the porch of people's houses, and discussed leisurely the business of finding oil. He scratched his dog's ears, and talked hunting. He ate dinner; he took their leases, writing a personal check, and became friends with the people. His jeans and shirts were always clean. He didn't worry about his happiness too much. It was always there. He could count on it. In the years 1902, 1903, and then again in 1917, there had been some wells drilled in the basin. Then nothing: for years, and years. Now they were coming back. His heart had been broken, like anyone else's, so very long ago, and unfairly. It didn't matter. He didn't even think of her name, anymore. It didn't even matter, now.

The basin was an ancient, mysterious, buried dry sea: scooped out deep into the old earth, over three hundred million years ago, and then filled slowly with sand, from an old ocean, waves lapping at empty shores—an Age of Sharks, thousands of varieties of sharks in the warm waters in those days—empty, beautiful, hundreds of miles of empty beaches, a few plants, windy days, warmth, no one to see anything, the most mysterious sea that ever was—and then, slowly, the sea had left again, and the dunes, the bays, the beaches, were covered up, by millions and millions of years: swamps, first, then deserts, then mountains, then river country, carrying parts of the mountains back down to the same sea, older, further south . . . The basin and its history lay hidden, and no one ever knew it was there, and the oil and gas from all its lives and warmth were only two thousand feet below the green and growing things of the present. It had been ten thousand feet below, at one time, but erosion and time were stripping back down, coming back closer to it, as if trying to get back to the old beaches and those times.

The woods were full of pine trees. The hills were steep: they stretched up into the Appalachians, they were the foothills, crumpled, of the Appalachians. The people were terribly wiry and most of them had never seen a beach. Wallis had helped discover the basin's existence. When he walked through the woods, and it was quiet, he tried to imagine the sound the old waves had made: miles and miles of empty beach: nothing there, nor would there be, ever.

6

Doomed, and sealed. A beach missing something, but beautiful. Pine straw beneath his feet.

A late night, in one of the three little restaurants in Vernon: Harry and Jack, eating again, dessert and coffee, the only ones in the place, save for waitresses: near closing time. Going over some leases to be looked at the next day. The money bag, chained to the table, at their feet.

"Get what you can," said Harry, eyes merry, leaning forward over his stomach: waiting, for Jack to join in, and finish the singsong phrase he'd made up.

"Can what you get," said Jack tiredly.

Harry laughed and leaned back, a howl. "Poison the rest!" he cried. Tears came to his eyes. Old Dudley's strategy was less than brilliant, in the new basin, but effective: if they leased everything that was available, then surely some of it would contain oil, far enough down. Harry thought Wallis' string of successful wells, of having never participated in a dry hole, was a little dainty, a little foppish.

"These little piss-ant two-and three-acre leases," he growled. "Shit almighty, a man can't make a living off those things. Shit almighty he can't even buy groceries on them. He can just barely get his money back, so he can go out and buy another two acres." They had tied up over a thousand acres belonging to a family called the Stanfords that afternoon, for ten years—they would probably never drill it—and another hundred and fifty from the Woodvilles, for five years.

Harry ordered another piece of pie. "A man that won't take a risk on what he believes in, and sink it all on one well—a man like that, that can't take a big lease, has got a short hooter."

He cut into the second piece of pie, breathing hard.

Wallis lived in the field, and liked it: the smells. He rolled his maps out on the hood. Only on the very hardest of freezing nights, in the winters, or sometimes for a day or two, in the middle of a drought, breaking summer, would he come into town and get a room at Mrs. Brown's Motel. He didn't have much money. There was some good income from the few wells he was in, but he turned it all back into still more leases. Mrs. Brown let him use her typewriter when he was ready to finalize a lease. Neither of them ever had money. Mrs. Brown was sixty-five and her husband had been killed in a mugging one night at the motel desk: four sad years ago. The car that got away had Illinois plates and they never saw it again. Mrs. Brown had a gas well on her land that Wallis had helped get drilled. The rooms were $16.50 a night.

She let him keep Dudley in his room. It was her only concession. She was violently cheerful. She lived in the motel office, had a small kitchen and folding sofa bed back there, a television and a coffee maker, and it was almost as if she was waiting for the muggers to return.

"Evening," Wallis would say, when he came into the office. (Bells would jangle, hanging over the threshold: a warning signal.)

"Right," Mrs. Brown would say. The grief had made her grim, and she smiled like a skeleton. If she tried to speak even an entire sentence it would dissolve and there would be tears. She had loved him beyond what was healthy. He had been a normal man; there had been no call for that excess of love. Wallis was a little wary, uneasy, sometimes, around Mrs. Brown. But he liked her.

"Cold," Wallis would say, grinning at her.

"Single digits," she would say, the lower lip trembling between the two words: the challenging smile, leading with her chin. Daring anyone to say she was not happy. Wallis was a little too sad to talk to her for very long.

Harry and Jack always stayed there. They took showers too long, and used up all the hot water. Anyone staying in the motel could hear Harry's wet coughs, violent hacks. Wallis would read, Dudley's head in his lap and sometimes his thoughts would drift, and he'd wonder, wonder hard, about Jack: picturing himself—briefly, only for a few almost unimaginable seconds—the way one sometimes imagines being in jail—holed up in that room with Harry. And for what reason, any reason.

The coughs would burst out into the night: almost exactly when the ringing from the last one had just disappeared, thinned away to nothing, and the beautiful night silence and clarity of Alabama blackness was beginning to build back up—smoke, up in the hills above town, from old chimneys; yellow blazes of windowlight, comfortably and widely scattered over the hills, some hills larger than others—only then would the next cough, like something expelled, blat out. It was on one of these sleepless nights that Wallis realized Harry was dying.

He tried to picture Dudley, the other Dudley, at the funeral, but could not. He knew that Harry had family. Doubtless they pictured him a hero: gone for weeks at a time, on the great hunt, seeking out the biggest riches, never knowing he was only executing: a gear, a wire, a small switch on a wall in a closet. The wind blew hard, over the motel. Dudley slept soundly. Wallis lay on his back with his hands behind his head, sadly, and listened to Harry cough. He had a little more respect for Jack, but there was still no understanding. The winds got harder, limbs and branches began to land on the roof, and finally, the sounds of the coughs were carried away and lost quickly in a place where no one would hear them, ever, or at all.

Wallis dreamed about what it was like, to be out there when the well was tested, and the proof, terrible, powerful, smelling good and very hot, came rushing up the hole: proving that you had been right.

The town was too small. He couldn't avoid them all the time; they had to run into each other, now and again. Dinner, dusk, at the cafeteria with the buffet, on Wednesday nights. Tables near each other: Harry, speaking across two tables.

"Why'd you leave Dudley, boy?" he asked, pausing with his mouth full. There were field peas and grits and all sorts of things in it. The waitress blanched and left that area of the room. Jack looked down at his plate and clenched his jaws. He wanted girls, oil, money, respect. He'd do anything for it: sell himself to Dudley, live with Harry. He played with his cornbread, vaguely, scooted it a-round on his plate, and leaned slightly forward to hear Wallis better.

"I learned how to find oil," Wallis said. He could have been saying he had learned how to tie his shoelace. It didn't seem to hold any intrigue for him, it was clear, and that puzzled Jack.

Harry was mesmerized by oil, and thought all geologists were witches, shamans, fakes. He could only believe that which was in him.

Jack looked at Wallis and could feel the thing different in Wallis, but didn't know it had a name. There was confusion. Wallis seemed pretty much like a loser, to Jack. Wallis would lose, thought Jack. But the chain around his neck felt heavy: as heavy as if the entire satchel was hanging from it when he looked at Wallis.

Harry paid for Jack's meal: he told Wallis he'd have to get his own, being competition and all. They laughed, going out the door. Wallis finished his tea.

9

There was a pretty girl in town. Her name was Sara. She'd lived in the valley all her life: lived it above the oil, all the time. She was twenty and wanted to go places. She looked at the money truck a little too long, when it rumbled down the roads, raising dust—the odd young man with the necklace and the old man, and two hounds they never seemed to pay attention to—but also, she laughed at it, after it was gone: after it had passed her by. They had already drilled on her land. Harry Reeves' old puppeteer, Dudley, had drilled on her parents' land—a German family, the Geohegans—a tremendous landholder, they owned over eight thousand acres—and the well had been dry. They drove past her, every time, now. She laughed at them after they were gone. She hoped they would stop. She went down to see Wallis: everyone knew where he camped. This in the summer. Her hair was soft.

"How many wells have you drilled?" she asked him, after she drove up and got out. He was sitting on the wing of the plane, looking at his notes. Wallis knew who she was, and where she was from, and about her parents' well. He didn't think it should have been dry, and he knew that the rest of the lease was oil. He sat quietly on the wing of his plane and considered the nuances of revenge. He bit into an apple. She handed him a piece of cheese she had brought, boldly, like a student having come for a good grade—she held it far out away from her, for him to take—he accepted it, sliced it with his knife, looked up at her with the sun behind her—and he handed her a piece back. He did not have enough money to lease all of the Geohegan's land. He had found too much oil, this time. He did not know her name, only who she was.

"Thirteen," said Wallis. He decided to keep it quiet, about the oil beneath her. To wait until he could afford to drill the whole thing. To sting Dudley. It would be a big well: the biggest in the county, the most the old sea could give.

"Thirteen?" she said, softly. Her hair was blonde, down in a braid. She had on a light blue dress. There were faint freckles on her nose. Thirteen wells did not seem like a lot. "I've never drilled a dry hole," Wallis said. It was funny, he thought, for him to say that. It made the apple taste bad.

They finished the cheese. He reached into his truck and got a thermos: shared some warm water with her. She brushed her hair back, as if the wind was in it, and watched him. Lamar County, in the state of Alabama. There were bears in her woods. Her parents raised chickens, and had many cattle. It was unbelievable that he had a plane. She didn't think she'd look at the money truck, anymore.

He had mapping to do that day. She stood back, and watched him take off: bumping along down the long wide open field; when he was hazy in the distance, the plane left the ground. She shielded her eyes. He disappeared over the hill.

Dudley, in the warm cockpit, lifted his head and looked at Wallis steadily as the plane flew, gaining altitude. He could tell what was coming.

When they were far above the earth, Wallis banked the plane and then rose up into a steep climbing stall, after the engine was warm, pointing the plane straight at the sun, as he did every day, at least once: the propeller's revolutions becoming weaker and softer, more futile, as the engine strained against the pull of the rocks and mountains and rivers below it: the persistent, wavering squall of the stall horn: hard shuddering, and then the plane, five thousand feet up by now, peeling off to the side, unable to go any higher that quickly—the nose was pulled abruptly down, as if following an anchor tossed from the window, and went into a spinning dive, like a ride at the fair, straight at the ground, which was visible far below in patches through the clouds, and pencils and erasers and dust flying past their ears, the press of force on their bodies. Dudley was strapped in as always. His long ears hung out at right angles, as if in space.

When the last clouds were cleared, Wallis pushed the yoke in sharply, about half its length, and pressed one rudder pedal in, to stop the spinning. The plane pulled smoothly out of the dive, and was flying flat and straight. Things that were struck to the ceiling rained back down again. They were going to live. Wallis could do other things with an airplane, too. It didn't charge him, or thrill: he did it to stay sharp—so that when there was a thunderhead or wind shear or he got trapped between trees and a power line, too near a radio antenna's guy wires, he would be able to get out: have the ability to get out.

Farmers and others below who saw him, practicing far out over the larger, wooded hills that rolled up, folding, into the Appalachians like waves of forest, said he was witching: that there was a device or machine in the nose of his plane, that could smell oil. Whenever he passed over a large stretch of it, it pulled the plane down towards it, into a dive.

Wallis was a hero, and risking his life for them. He ate free, at some of the restaurants, on slow evenings when no one else was in the cafe. They began to feel badly, sometimes, taking the money from Harry Reeves and Jack: bargaining, dickering. Wishing maybe they could lease to Wallis.

People waved at him and Dudley, when they saw them driving, and yet he remained a mystery, unlike other things in the country. Their lives were simple and straight and were crops and the grocery store, and ever, pleasurably, hatefully, always with emotion, the weather, but he was outside these things.

"He's got to be that way," an old man said, spitting, when they talked about him at the gas station. "He's looking for the hardest thing to find in the world. Shit, hit's buried: hit's invisible."

Head nodding. They looked up at the sky. He was looking for the invisible thing. He could see things they couldn't.

Another time, in a restaurant: breakfast, the three of them in the same room. Early, foggy. He looked at Jack, when Jack turned slightly away from him, checking out, paying the cashier. There was no way on earth Jack could *like* Harry, or even tolerate him, or Dudley either. It was very obvious, even to Wallis, who rarely watched people, that Jack was being a fake, a turd, a brown nose, for some later motive. Everyone knew, it had to be a natural fact and feeling, that it was better to belong to yourself, and have one acre in a drilling well, than to belong to another man, even if that man had a hundred, a thousand wells, or the whole county. This had to be common knowledge, a fact of existence, didn't it? How could one breathe, and not know this? The girl that had left him had done it because she accused him of never being himself.

Jack turned and was looking back at Wallis. Wallis realized this, but could not turn away. His mouth was slightly open, even: staring. He looked and looked at Jack, frowning with his eyes, trying to get a handle on it but unable to, trying to see beyond, like the old ocean he could see from the sky—but not this. Finally Jack said, "Damn," and turned away, shaking his head, and left the restaurant, behind Harry, who was carrying the satchel. Wallis watched him go; he gave them a minute to be gone before leaving himself: woodsmoke, when

12

he stepped outside, and the smell of bacon. He rolled his collar up and felt good.

Later that day, flying, he forgot to pull the carburetor heat switch, coming down through some clouds. The plane looked different to him, too, the mountains as well. He had to put down in a field, and got out and walked around. The ground felt different, too. His legs were shaky. He called Dudley and they walked a little ways off from the plane and he lay down in the middle of the field in the sun on his back and closed his eyes and felt wind, sun, the ground below him. He lay with his back to the ground as a wrestler would, pinning it: he thought what a short distance two thousand feet was, and tried to imagine the oil beneath him, straining to get out, but was unable to: the sun confused him, with its warmth, and brightness. He dozed, and did not work, the rest of that afternoon. His life meant something. He was his own man, belonged to no one, he had never drilled a dry hole, and he had saved a dog from being killed. There was a balance sheet and as long as one did not go below zero, it seemed a victory.

He was terrified of going below that zero: of belonging to someone else. It seemed that everything bad would follow from that. You would catch emphysema. You would have to wear a chain around your neck. You would have sold yourself, and by the very act of doing it once—though he was sure those who did it told themselves otherwise, that it was only for a little while—you would never, ever be able to buy yourself back. Because there wouldn't be anything left to buy. Not even if you went a little fraction of an inch below that zero. The sea would move in: the old times would be buried.

He fed Dudley, scratched his ears, ate apples in the sunlight and in the plane as he flew, and held on for dear life.

He and Jack and Harry were somehow yet again in the same restaurant at the same time, even though it was north of town several miles. Bad luck, thought Wallis, the third time in a month, but also he was not much concerned. He had bought twenty-seven acres in section thirteen that day, for a tenth of what it usually cost: that was how he'd been able to afford such a large amount. The reason he had gotten it so cheaply was that Old Dudley had drilled a well there several years ago, and had thought it dry, and had plugged it. Wallis had never owned twenty-seven acres in a prospect before. He was almost dizzy. Too, it would be fun, to embarrass Old

13

Dudley—to go in and drill a place that Dudley had left, and find oil. The statement would be stark and obvious: Dudley could not find oil on that twenty-seven acres, Wallis could, therefore Wallis was a better geologist.

He didn't need to be nice to Dudley. He would try hard to stay away from the very natural feeling of revenge because he knew it was a trap, like going below the zero—he had found so much oil for Old Dudley, when he worked for him, unrewarded—and it would cut him up, and beat him, even if it did sound fun and good— questing for vengeance—but neither did he have to be nice to him. If revenge happened, it happened. It was good. He could belch in Old Dudley's company if he wished and not excuse himself.

He had escaped Old Dudley, and his life mattered. The salt and pepper shakers on the tables seemed to have significance and clarity. He watched Jack and Harry muddle along through the buffet: pausing, asking questions of the chef, frowning, rubbing their chins: reaching (Harry, fatly) slowly and hesitantly for this dish, and that: pie, beans, chicken—leaning over and reaching as if controlled by strings from above. The air tasted like spring water to Wallis. He got a bowl of oatmeal, a piece of cold melon, and a Coke. He sat at the far end of the restaurant, his back to them—and their backs to his—and ate. The melon was fresh; the oatmeal was hot.

He left a tip and walked out the door. It was good, to be able to just stand up and take four steps and be out the door: not having to turn around, or look back, or pass by them. He drove out to the field with the windows down and took his sleeping bag out and unrolled it on the ground and got in it.

The stars were like Christmas. The night was cold. The twenty-seven acres on his lease application in the glove box made his toes still want to dance around in the bottom of the sleeping bag. He supposed that he was getting close to revenge and that was different from flying around eating apples and looking for oil but also there was the wild and primal goodness of the feeling, visceral, of having scored a killing punch, of having entered , for the first time, something loved: something about it made him want to do it again, and maybe even again and again. He lay awake for a very long time, pleased with himself, and was enormously happy. The stars seemed to encourage him as if they were on his side. He knew Dudley wasn't sleeping beneath them.

14

It got much colder. New Year's Eve saw zero; the next day, twelve below and windy. Sara and Wallis lay in bed at the Brown Motel with the lights off and the curtains open. Dudley slept at the foot of the bed: a beautiful, steady breathing. There were stars, more than ever. He held her tightly, for Wallis. They watched the stars for a while, and then she rolled over on top of him and made love to him. She looked at his face the whole time. There were blankets over them. The room was cold. The bed rocked, steadily; Dudley stirred in his sleep once. She was imagining that she was atop one of the pumping jacks that went down with the rods and then came back up with a rushing swab of oil. In the cold weather, the oil sometimes steamed.

He tried hard, very hard, to love her. He felt, the way he felt all things, just a time in the air, that it was time for him to be in love. That he needed to be in love.

After, he closed his eyes and pulled her to him, and put her head up under his chin: kept his eyes closed. It would happen. He would find love. They would find the Big Well, he would somehow get the money together to drill it himself—not paying for one percent, or three percent, but the whole one hundred percent, start to middle to finish—he did like *that* idea—and then he would try. There would be a house in the woods, with Dudley the hound that couldn't hunt, and they'd have a child, and Wallis would work very hard at loving her the way he thought it *should* be, the pure way, the way he found oil. If only he could love her the way he looked for oil, it would be perfect. He'd try.

Around midnight, there began a fierce, jagged coughing in the night, coming through the cinder blocks from about three rooms down. Wallis listened to the sound of Old Dudley running a young man and an old one down to their deaths. Sara awoke, not knowing where she was, reaching for a lamp.

"What's that?"

"Harry and Jack," he said tiredly.

"Is there oil on my land?" she said, suddenly. She had his shoulders in her hands: she was over him again. He looked away: at the dark wall, and listened to Harry's coughs, vertical now—waddle-pacing the room, an old death stagger—Jack probably with his head under both pillows. It was possible that he couldn't love anyone. He knew there were people like that.

15

"Maybe," he said, getting up angrily, leaving her grasp and pulling a pair of underwear on: Dudley rising, startled, at his heels, not knowing this routine, but with him. They went quickly out the door—Sara sitting up, pulling the blankets around her, looking at the empty door—and barefooted, shivering violently already from the weather's strength, Wallis hurried across the gravel and reached Harry's door and began kicking on it: backing off and hitting it with his heel. There wasn't any moon. The wind carried the thumps of his kicks quickly off. The door shook. A light came on: Jack's face through the crack of the door, the chain beneath his chin like the chinstrap on a football helmet.

Wallis put his face in the crack so that he was an inch away from Jack's startled eyes.

"Shut that shit up or kill the old man," he said. Dudley growled, and raised his hackles: he stood as big as a wolf. Leaves blew in through the cracked open door.

"I . . . I . . . I'm sorry," Jack said.

"It keeps Mrs. Brown awake," Wallis said. The sound of the "k's" on his words was like death. Jack could see the squareness and hardness of his teeth, and the thing that was in the bottom of him, in the bottom, far bottom, of everyone.

"We'll . . . he'll stop," Jack said.

"I'm going to cut his throat out, tonight, if he doesn't," Wallis hissed. "I'll either come through the door or the window. There'll be blood all over the sheets."

He walked hurriedly back to his room, and barely made it before he could walk no farther. Sara cried out loudly when he got in bed; it was as if a block of ice had been slid in with her.

"Yes, there's oil under your land," he said. He was shuddering as if seized by a current.

She came back to him: moved back in closer, held his coolness, tentatively, then all the way: pulled him to her yet again.

"Oh, baby," she said, eyes shut: her body, to him.

"Oh, baby," he repeated: trying it out.

He was numb. He warmed slowly.

When he awoke in the morning, he felt thicker, heavier, and later in the day realized it was because he was now carrying two things, anger and revenge. Logic, and having worked for Dudley—having seen everything done the *wrong* way—told him that the angrier he got, at not being able to fall in love with Sara, the less he was going to be able to—but he had exploded at Jack and Harry, and now, walking, he still felt as if it was building up again. He felt as if he was oil, far below the ground, trapped in a thin layer of rock. He felt that when the drilling bit did hit his formation, and just pierced the very top of it, he would come out: blowing, all of it, a fire, a roar. That he would burn down whatever it was that had touched him. He bent down and scratched Dudley's ears, dizzy. The day was clear and cold: the light was pretty. It seemed—no, he knew—that you could only do one thing well: to do it the right and best way, there could be nothing else. His old boss was too good at making money, whether off of other people's woes or not, to be a good geologist. Wallis was too good at what he did, feeling what used to be, to make money. He knew about the old ocean. He could see it, and felt he had lived on it. He had its number.

He wondered if he could drill a dry hole: if he could stop wanting to find oil.

He wondered if she was worth it.

She came driving up just as he was climbing in the plane that afternoon—jeans, tennis shoes, a heavy old blue sweater and a parka: her hair, in the sun. She hugged him, standing under the high wing of the plane to do so. Her face felt cool and smooth, like love was supposed to. She smelled good, and he wanted her.

Surely, thought Wallis, if love was not capable for him with this girl, then it could not exist, for him.

He took her up. He was jittery: flushed, a little, as when he first realized he was tracking oil. (When he actually found it, pinpointed it, mapped and contained it, he was cool—anticlimactic, by that point—but the first scent—the turn of the head, the question—that was the rush.)

She took her parka off. She took her shirt off. The sun was warm, up high, in the cockpit.

"Show me you're a very good pilot," she said. She was laughing. Her eyes were laughing. It happened to everyone: it could happen to any one. It was the most common thing in the world. She had come out to see him.

They were a mile above the earth. They made slow, graceful love: he let her hold the yoke, work the pedals, some, as they flew, and made love. It alarmed him, a little, to not be able to see in front of him. He liked her in the bed, and its softness, better. He also knew that the bed would never again be the same for her. It did feel good.

17

He closed his eyes as long as he dared. When she began to cry out he took the yoke and began to climb slowly into the sun.

She wanted to fly over her farm, her parents' farm. She wanted to drop her bra into the woods, to see if she could then find it. She didn't wear underwear.

"What will happen if it hits someone?" she asked.

"It'll kill them," he said, truthfully. She was poised at the little crack of the window, ready to open it, holding the bra in one hand like a thing soiled. She looked at him, surprised and then laughed: the thought of it. And now the excitement: the risk. Quickly, she shoved the window open—the fast suck of wind, she had to push hard to open it and keep it open—and tossed the bra out, this time like a cheer. He watched her watch it. Her back was still bare and had goose pimples. Her waist was narrow, with faint gold hairs in the base, and her back broadened as it rose. She was totally engrossed, watching the bra get smaller and smaller. He banked into a tight holding turn, like water spiraling around in a drain, so that she could keep watching. He watched her, in his plane. He had found love, his first time out, since the last time. It was no different from anything else in the world, he decided.

Harry and Jack, with binoculars, on a hill deep in the woods, the highest point in the country, watched them circle.

"He just threw something out," Jack said.

"It's a marker," Harry said. He began to cough: bending over. He straightened up. "I've seen 'em do it a million times." He turned to Jack in earnest: believing himself, almost, as he went along. "It's for when the woods are too thick or dense to survey. He's marking where the oil is. They do it in Texas all the time."

Jack watched them circle, and nodded. They would try to find the marker.

Seventeen acres, from the Fellowship Church of Vernon. Sixty-eight acres, from a serviceman in Germany: a quiet, simple letter, explaining what he was about, what he wanted to do—to go in and drill where Dudley had missed. He got the lease for free. He began to go back and search all of Old Dudley's plugged wells. About half of them seemed, to him, to be good. He took Sara with him often. They climbed to two miles in the plane. She wanted to laugh and cry both: there was so much to be seen. They climbed to three miles, until the engine faltered and their heads felt light and it was

18

hard to breathe—Dudley on the floor, head under his paws, confused—and looked briefly, when there were no clouds, at the big roll of Appalachians: it was easy to see where the sea had ended. The area below them was, quite obviously—from three miles up—the old beach. Beaches. A hundred miles of it, curving and snaking all around, like a serpent, like a thing still, even that day, alive: it seemed to move as they watched it.

Haze, and the sweep of the earth, curving away over the edge, its lovely roundness: they had left the earth. Three minutes, four minutes, as long as they dared—five—the sky a rich heavy purple, a color never seen—and then the slow ride down, that took forever: both of them suddenly aware of the frailty of the little plane; the lightness, and thinness, of the wings, light canvas wrapped around a hollow aluminum frame. The thinness of the thing that kept them aloft.

"When he crashes, we go in and top his leases," said Harry. The plane had disappeared from view, even to the plastic drug store binoculars. "We pay the landowners, beforehand, to lease to us, exclusively, the first day his leases run out."

Jack nodded. It was what he was being taught. The leases were for three years. Harry and Jack tied up the land with five year leases, but for some reason Wallis never asked for more than three years. Jack counted: both he and Wallis would be thirty-one, then. He looked at Harry's folds of fat, his face, mouth open—a wetness, saliva—as Harry looked heavenward through the little glasses, and was jealous, that Wallis owned his own leases. The richest man in the state of Mississippi—a king, the king of the poorest state, in money, in education, in anything—was using them to chase a poor young pilot in love across the county, to learn what he was doing. With an old, dying, coughing fat man leading the chase. It made Wallis seem like some kind of magic. It made Old Dudley's terrible money and power seem less.

Wallis started to work late, at nights. He got a key from the Probate Judge, so that he could lock up when he was through: midnight, one A.M. A peanut butter sandwich for supper, around seven: the great ledger record-books open, like biblical testaments, showing years and years of dizzying history; mortgages, leases, foreclosures, dry holes and producers: he chewed his sandwich, slowly, and read them, and looked in all the right books. Dudley sat up on top of the counter and watched him, waited patiently. Wallis was looking for all the leases on old wells that Old Dudley had plugged without testing. He was going to stop looking for oil, purely, and restrict himself to looking only for oil beneath places where Old Dudley had missed it. It would be like slapping his face with gloves: satisfying.

It had been a new feeling for him, the other day, an unexpected one, taking the twenty-seven acre lease that Old Dudley had dropped, several years ago. It was a surprise, and wonderful and new, much as flying and loving had been for Sara. He wanted to do it some more. In fact, it was all he wanted to do.

Sara came up to the courthouse with him once, sat on the counter with Dudley and drank a beer swinging her legs and watched, but it was far too slow for her.

When he could no longer keep his eyes open, he would call to Dudley, who would leap down from the counter, and he would shut off the lights and lock up, and drive back out to the pasture. Sometimes he would build a little fire, and fix some coffee, and go over what he had found. It was a lonely life. Dudley would sit and watch him, and wait for whatever was going to happen next. Some nights there was the sound of coyotes; geese, owls, too. The air was fresh.

They flew more and more: everywhere. They did it five hundred feet above the ground: they went lower. They skimmed along over the tops of trees: scattering birds, doves in roost. Sara got to be a fair pilot.

"Can you find oil down on the Coast?" she asked him.

Wallis grinned, shook his head, looking at her. "Nope," he said "Just up here." His greatness was limited. He thought later how it was odd that he had never asked himself that question. There had never been a desire to look anywhere else. Why would a man want to go into a country he was not familiar with, knew nothing about?

He showed her stalls, spins, figure-eights. She was delighted one day when he rolled; she clapped her hands. He started leaving Dudley in the truck. More aerobatics, less mapping. Dudley drilled on one of his prospects, one that Wallis had been able to muscle into by buying two acres on the edge of it (and then twenty acres beyond that—in case the edge proved someday to be the middle—which it often did). They went out to visit the well: Sara, her hair long and clean, static against her sweater, on his arm, flushed, elsewhere, in her mind: having just flown.

Old Dudley was out at the well, too, which was very unusual: Wallis had never seen him on a location, as long as he'd known him. There was word that he hadn't been out to one in ten years.

Harry and Jack knew nothing about geology, and were off eating or leasing. Old Dudley had his chauffeur and stretched limousine, both of which had been flown over from England. There was red mud from the thick hills all over the limousine's brilliant blackness.

Wallis smiled, gave a little wave, then smiled wider. He was free.

Dudley smiled, gave his little embarrassed half-nod—a tip of the head, almost like a bird beginning to feed—when he recognized Wallis, in jeans and boots. Dudley had on a black business suit, and an overcoat, and Wallis felt good, that Old Dudley was acknowledging his freedom. He could read Old Dudley, had learned him like a fascinating book, had studied the locations where he had drilled, and knew why he did things—and he was confused, then, when Old Dudley turned his look to Sara, and almost smiled, as if relieved at something. As if he knew some sly and childish secret which he would not tell Wallis but would keep to himself, and be made happy by it. He turned and began walking, with his chauffeur, over to the well: roughnecks, up on the derrick floor, looking down, shirtless, muddy, ragged: a few of them wrestling with the drill pipe. A clear blue sky, a warming day.

Wallis' dog bolted: a blur at the edge of the cleared location was a rabbit.

"Yo! Dudley! Get back here!" Wallis shouted. Old Dudley's shoulders stopped, and he half-turned: an expression of genuine surprise, and then disappointment, to see that Wallis was running after a dog. He turned back around and continued walking. The well turned out to be oil: the largest discovery ever found in the basin.

Old Dudley stopped by Wallis's and Sara's truck on the way out: the dog, muddy, bounding happily around in the back of the truck, barking at him, at the strange long car. Old Dudley rolled his window down so that he could speak to Wallis.

"Maybe we should plug it?" He looked somehow a way that Wallis had never seen him. Wallis leaned slightly closer, curious: never afraid, though the sense of power was thick and heavy, malignant, like a bad odor.

"I beg your pardon?" The well had metered out at 1200 barrels per day.

Old Dudley chuckled: it escaped, and was a high quick chuckle, so that it was almost a giggle. He quickly covered his mouth with his hand, as if trying to rub it away.

"I mean, that's a lot of oil: we don't want to glut the market, or anything. Perhaps we should shut it in, until prices are more economical, more worth our while." Dudley's father had been a farmer, and poor all his life. This time Old Dudley didn't giggle, and looked straight and hard and striking at Wallis, but Wallis was free, his jeans felt good on his legs, and he liked the smell of the old truck. He knew that it had to be impressing Sara beyond end, to tingling, for the richest man in Mississippi to be carrying on this conversation with him for such a long and earnest time. Wallis shrugged, and held up his hands. It truly did not matter.

"Why not?" he said. "It's your well."

Old Dudley's face was leaning a little too far out: the anger, if it had been that, had to come back in. He looked tricked, betrayed.

"I mean, for twenty or thirty years," he said. But he was not good at cruelty. He was only good at making money.

Wallis smiled, shrugged.

Old Dudley watched him for a minute, unable to believe it was sincere, but then he did: the girl, the dog, the truck. He smiled at Wallis, no longer angry, but thoughtful, nodded to Sara—the tip of an imaginary hat, it seemed—and even glanced at the dog, as he was being driven off, after the window had rolled back up. The well began selling oil that afternoon.

On the drive home, Old Dudley thought about purity, and even intensity: how it used to be, when it truly didn't matter whether a well was shut in, after being discovered, and not produced—how finding it had been the good and only thing. He was a businessman now, but had been a scientist, in school, and had been impressed with the knowledge that purity could never last, that nothing could ever last: that everything was changing, always. He had made his choice early and had not bothered to waste the energy—for it would have been wasted—trying to preserve it, the purity. He was sixty and had ten or fifteen years of life left and what he was interested in now, after so many years, what he was wishing, was that perhaps he had retained a little bit of it after all, and its intensity, because he had all the success he needed.

Though he had seen Wallis's leasing activity, on the scouting reports, and was alarmed, slightly, at what it looked like he was doing. As if even his success—not physically, but emotionally— might be spirited from him.

He thought that Wallis would fall back: that he would lose his purity, too.

He had hundreds of employees to think about and hundreds of business concerns, most of them larger and many of them more critical and pressing than what had over the years gotten to be a sideline, his oil activity, particularly in the Black Warrior Basin, but on the drive home, it was Wallis, and purity, and Wallis's truck, dog and girl that he thought about, all the way: thumb and forefinger holding his chin: tenement houses, ragged, and scraggly winter cotton remains, and drooping telephone lines whizzing past. Tinted windows: conditioned air. An old black woman, in an apron, coming out onto her porch and staring, as his limousine passed. The chauffeur, up in front of him, so far up in front of him that an intercom was necessary, to communicate. He looked away from the chauffeur, back out the window again, at the delta, and thought about Wallis. He knew that he couldn't have picked a better girl to do it, but also Wallis was no fool, was finding oil, was on to something, and still had the dog and truck.

Harry Reeves died on a Sunday afternoon, while driving the money truck: a grim picture it made, him collapsed over the wheel, heart squeezed out by fat, finally, as the truck and dogs thundered down the mountain off of Little Hell's Creek Road and toward town—Jack, trying to steer, trying to pull Harry's deadness—with one hand—off of the wheel—his foot jabbing empty space in the vicinity of the brake, getting tangled up with Harry's dead legs, polyester double-knit . . . The truck glanced the curb, outside of town, and rolled, spilling dogs, Harry, the spare tire, lug wrench, and the money satchel: Jack held on to the steering wheel and stayed in the truck.

There was no one else around. He got out, amongst the broken glass and hissing—one dog was dead, curled up in the wrong shape, and Harry was stretched out, dead like an actor—the other dog was injured, and was trying to reach around and lick its hind leg, or bite it—and like the last person on earth, with a raw and stinging patch on his forehead, Jack began walking in circles, around the truck, methodically, gathering up all of Dudley's money: caught in tufts of grass, tumbling across the road, some blown up against Harry, like seaweed against a whale's carcass . . . Two thousand feet above the darkness of underground, oil in places, and a sealed, Paleozoic ocean, a silent beach, two hundred and fifty million years of silence, he walked, alone, picking up money. He wondered if he would get fired. It hadn't been his fault: it had been Harry, that had wrecked the truck. He wondered what he would do, for a living, if he lost his job. The richest man in Mississippi: he was working for the richest man in Mississippi.

Wallis was having fried chicken at the Geohegan's when he heard the news. The operator had called to tell Mrs. Geohegan: the harsh, shrill clang of mountain phone, that made the walls tremble, that made the silverware in his hand tingle. He looked out the window down over the large pasture and motionless cattle, and into the wooded creek, and out further into blue haze and treetops. The chicken was good. The gravy was rich, and had pepper in it. He and Sara and Dudley had played tag, out in the yard, before lunch. He paused, digesting what he was hearing of the conversation between Mrs. Geohegan and the operator, tasting the food, and was relieved to feel sorrow, and a stillness, like being in the woods, alone late in the afternoon, that Harry was gone. He had been worried by his quest for vengeance, and was hoping—knowing that Harry would die—that when he did, the news would not please him.

That night, under the stars, colder than usual for March—a night wind—again, as ever, with his hands behind his head, looking up—dreaming he was on the beach, the old beach, the one he knew better than anyone else and was born two hundred and fifty million years too late to see, to know, to walk on—to skip across, barefooted, splashing in the shallows—warm tidal channels, back dunes, sea oats—he thought about what he would do if he did not look for oil, up in this country. He tried, faithfully, to think of Sara's kisses: of her eyes, looking up at him when he talked about oil: the shine in them, like that of her hair. A magic child. It bothered him that he could not fall in love with her. Perhaps if he could find one more oil well, a big one, the biggest ever . . . there had to be a release in it, eventually.

He was trapped into succeeding, he thought. Maybe if he drilled a dry hole he could be normal.

He went to the funeral. Jack's dog was bandaged, looking silly, sitting in the cab of a new blue truck: watching the funeral with a bandage around its waist and head. Wallis went over to the rolled-down window, and stuck his hand in, and let the dog lick it. Jack came over and asked if Wallis could do him a favor: if he could take care of the dog. . . .

"Yes," said Wallis, without looking up. He watched the dog lick his hand. The dog was desperate to be loved. The dog was desperate to love. He thought about Old Dudley, coming out to test that well. He thought about a prospect in the eastern portion of the county. The sun and windiness of spring was making him feel light and drawn away. It seemed that every day he could see the old beach more and more clearly: where the dunes were, which ones would hold oil and which wouldn't long after they had died, and were buried: what the waves had looked like, what the view down the beach had been—the long, straight stretches, and too, the bends, and deep parts, offshore . . . he was the only inhabitant in the world, and it was a beach before men, and he liked it: he felt . . . loved. As if the beach had chosen him, for its loneliness. How could he drill a dry hole, when he knew the old empty beach so well?

He flew. The trees and creeks, cemeteries and hills, didn't bother him. He was seeing his old land. He now only made weak, stabbing attempts at loving Sara. She flew with him: they did it, and afterwards, he was looking out the window again; sometimes, and without guilt, even, he would look out even as it was going on, the love. She wanted to go to Atlanta one weekend, having never been, and he took her. It didn't matter. He found three more wells: small, small interests, but they belonged to him.

She wanted to go to New Orleans, and they stayed in a room high up over the city and smelling of old rich times and with mirrors on the ceiling, above the bed. He felt detached, far from his shore. They walked down to the river, where it went into the sea, at night: a cool breeze lifted off of it and came at them. This was his old ocean, cowardly, on the retreat, now: some three hundred miles south of where it had once been, in its greatness, inland, when it was brave: the great advance into a place and country where it had never been before, and might never return to. He looked out at the river, going into the Gulf, and tried to feel close to it, knowing it was the same, but it wasn't. It didn't have that bravery his had had. She looked at him, questioningly, and took his arm, and they went to eat. She was starting to fall in love with him.

She moved in with him: they bought a cabin, on land up above the field where he used to sleep. The austerity and church-going of the hills' people bent, for them, and didn't mind, very much: Wallis was becoming a champion, and some things seemed right. When he went out to get into his plane, there were often people standing around it, a lot of children, watching, waiting: wanting to know where he was going, that day. What part of the country he was going to check.

When he took leases, and did courthouse work—his news had spread—there were businessmen, undertakers and monstrous insurance salesmen, seeds of bad earth, and leeches, like Dudley only without money, who followed him: like puppies, like gulls over a field being furrowed, they tracked him, anticipated, and battled savagely and wretchedly for the small pieces that, like Wallis, they could afford: two acres, fifteen acres, one acre. They used him, and then sat back fatly, smiling, and waited, hopefully, for a well to be drilled on their lease. Not understanding, not knowing—where the oil was.

He made four more wells, the next month: twenty in a row. No one had ever made more than four in a row.

Sara still wanted him to drill on her land.

"I can't afford to take your parents' lease," he said, "and with that much land, it's unfair to even consider a free lease, even if they would give it. I can't drill it, not yet, not now." He was getting better at the love-making: he seemed to be growing into it. He brought her things, when she was in the bathtub: a cool wet washcloth, to press to her forehead; a mint; a stick of gum. He was surprised to find that he liked to watch her chew gum.

"But there is oil under my land, right?" she asked. Pausing, washing under an arm.

"Right," he said. "A lot of it."

He wanted to touch her face, but drew back. The bathroom seemed empty: hollow. A thing was missing.

The twenty-first well, gas, from the very borehole of a well from which Dudley had walked away, three years ago: much gas. A ring, for her finger—not wedding, just friendship—but it felt good, when he held that hand, and they rolled, or walked or sat. Woodpeckers hammering in the woods, above their house. The scold of a blue jay. His picture was in a newspaper, then two magazines. He kissed her in the day, without even wanting to undress her.

Old Dudley heard that they were living together and was pleased. A little.

Once, on a farm far back in the hills, farther than he had ever been before—a glint of sun on a lake, late in the afternoon, had pulled him there: the plane peeling away, flying him there in short minutes—so far back up into the hills that perhaps it was not even his sea he was feeling—he touched down, and got out, and walked around, all day, feeling something and seeing things but not knowing what was going on. And Jack, in the new money truck, saw him go down, and drove out in that direction, drove all morning, and found where his plane had landed—a gravel road, wide but not very—and Jack went all up and down the side roads, with the satchel, leasing for pennies from people who had never seen a drilling rig. And Wallis was unable to get even a few small leases before Jack and Old Dudley got all of them. A well was drilled, and it was dry.

Wallis did not leave his territory anymore. He stayed on the ground he knew, and Jack decried him, told all, proud of nothing. "He was going to lease it, but I stepped in and took the leases before he could and it was dry. He was going to drill a dry hole."

Old Dudley drove up, one day, in the summer, in the limousine. The sun had come out about an hour earlier, as if turned on by a curtain: suddenly. Sara fixed him coffee. Old Dudley had a proposition. Wallis had to think about it overnight, before saying no.

Sara didn't say anything. She didn't know what was right, what was wrong. She wasn't sure if she even wanted the well drilled any more. Old Dudley could have done it.

Her mother came out one day and brought them chicken. Dudley the hound had dug a place out on the side of the cabin where he would curl up and lie down. She petted his back, scratched his ears. He played with the other dog, who was healed. The two dogs sat in the sun and jawed like bears in a stream. The light on their coats and in their eyes was startling, up on the hill, back in the trees, coming down through the leaves. When he drove home in the truck, in the evenings, if he was going back to the courthouse, he would have supper first. She would listen for his plane, in the afternoons. It did not make sense, but she could hear it even before the dogs could.

Two more of Old Dudley's failures turned into successes, for Wallis: one, a small well, the other, a rushing oil well. He took more leases, with the money. He bought Sara a dress, that looked beautiful on her.

Old Dudley bought Jack a plane. It amused the townspeople. They started giving their leases to Wallis for free: if he would only drill on them. Old Dudley turned sixty-two. He hired a man who was fifty-five to work for him: a geologist, to do the same thing that Wallis was doing, only on fancier, larger maps. In the fall, Wallis drilled his first well: number thirty-four, that he had been involved in, but this one, finally, all his. There was so much gas when he drilled into it that it blew the drill pipe out of the hole, caught on fire, and burned the rig down: a man was killed. Old Dudley came in and leased around him, and began making smaller, weaker wells. Wallis didn't have any money again.

Sara kissed him, the night it happened, held him with the lights off, and thought about her parents' farm. She hadn't ever had money before. No one in the county had. She didn't know if it was important or not.

Jack flew, clumsily, nervously, and dropped flaggings out the window, randomly, trying to make it appear he knew what he was doing, remembering Harry Reeves' wisdom. Shakily, he told Old Dudley that he thought he had it figured, and that he thought he knew where they should drill. He'd seen a creek, water bubbling out of a spring: it had to be a fault. They had a rig on it the next week: it made a good little oil well. Jack bought a suit and a gold pocketwatch, and watch chain. Even though Old Dudley didn't wear one.

When it rained, Wallis worked in the courthouse, or drove: looked at the trees, and the way they grew. But it wasn't as clear. He couldn't see it all at once. There was no money for a while, only leases, and he paid debts with the dollars coming in from his fractions in his good wells.

"I don't mind being poor," Sara said one evening, mending a shirt. "But I don't want to have any chickens around the house. Every family in this county has chickens, damn it, leaving feathers and bad smell underfoot, and I don't like the sound they make, either." She stamped her foot. There had been no talk of chickens, ever before—Wallis didn't want any chickens, either—and he was surprised. It had been five weeks since the rig burned.

"If ever there was a sound of being poor, it's the cackle of chickens," she said. Her parents had always had chickens around the house, even after they were not poor anymore. She was very near tears. He got up and put his hand on her forehead, and stroked her hair.

"No chickens," he said, cheerfully. "All right! No chickens!"

She had to laugh, to keep from crying. He made her laugh often. She had thought she wanted to go places.

She didn't ask him about her parents' land anymore. She thought, sometimes, about the mirrors in New Orleans—how down looked up, and up, down: everything reversed, from the way it really felt.

They played games.

"I want to learn how to swim," she said.

He smiled. "When I drill again, next time, and hit, we'll build a swimming pool inside the cabin. We'll heat it. It'll be right next to the kitchen, and we'll add on a room for it."

"I can come straight in from grocery shopping in the winter, set the groceries down on the table, slip out of my clothes, walk down some steps, and dive into the water," she said.

"Nekkid," said Wallis.

"There'll be steam coming up off the water," she said.

They smiled. She tried to picture him working for Old Dudley, as he had, for six years, but could not. They laughed, and joked about Jack flying the little plane. He was clumsy. He bounced the plane like a basketball, on landings. He got lost, often, and all the various towns in the area had at one time or another seen him flying a circle around their water tower, sometimes several times in the same day, trying to find out where he was.

Old Dudley was trying to go back and re-lease all his old acreage, as just a blanket policy: to halt the embarrassment. But there was too much of it, and many people wouldn't lease, to him or anyone, until they had talked to Wallis: to see if he wanted it, even for a lower price. They didn't want Dudley to drill any more dry holes on their land. The money truck had lost almost all of its charm except to the absolute and very poorest, most desperate few.

Everyone had come from miles, to watch Wallis's rig burn down. The glow had been visible in eight counties. The earth had shaken, around the location.

Jack wrote a lot of checks, for Dudley's leases. There was no longer a need to wear the key on a chain around his neck. But he kept it there anyway, out of habit, and for power.

Springs were beautiful. It rained, and shimmered hot, too, in the summers. Eventually, as Wallis began to pay more and more attention to Sara, he drilled a few dry holes. Old Dudley grew old and feeble, lost his teeth and went into a nursing home: his lawyers declared him incapable, and took his business away, gave it to his children. Jack crashed, one day, still looking: still dropping white handkerchiefs out the window of the plane, still pretending to see. Wallis and Sara got married, in the field. Mrs. Brown died, and the motel closed up, and became vacant: weeds, and vines. Wallis drilled; Wallis leased. He held on for dear life, to two things, not one, himself and another human being, and did not let go, and never went under zero, not for a day, not for an hour.

Sometimes, they would fly down to the coast, near Mobile, and land the plane on a lonely stretch of beach, and get out and walk along the shore, in winter: no one else out. He would lean slightly forward, listening to the slow, steady lapping of waves, dying into the shore. He would hold Sara's hand. If she tried to speak, while he was listening, imagining, he would raise a finger to his lips. The only reason he could have two passions, rather than one, was because he had never ruined the first. It hadn't ever been sold, when asked for. She watched him watch the beach, the ocean, and considered his success.

Nominated by H. E. Francis and The Paris Review

EXCELLENT THINGS
IN WOMEN

by SARA SULERI

from RARITAN A QUARTERLY REVIEW

LEAVING Pakistan was, of course, tantamount to giving up the company of women. I can only tell this to someone like Anita, knowing that she will understand, as we go perambulating through the grimness of New Haven and feeding on the pleasures of our conversational way. Dale, who lives in Boston, would also understand. She will one day write a book about the stern and secretive life of breast feeding, and is partial to fantasies that culminate in an abundance of resolution. And Fawzi, with a grimace of recognition, knows because she knows the impulse to forget.

To a stranger or an acquaintance, however, some vestigial remoteness obliges me to explain that my reference is to a place where the concept of woman was not really part of an available vocabulary: we were too busy for that concept, just living, and conducting precise negotiations with what it meant to be a sister or a child or a wife or a mother or a servant. By this point of course I am damned by my own discourse, and doubly damned when I add that yes, once in a while we naturally thought of ourselves as women, but only in some perfunctory biological way that we happened on, perchance. Or else it was a hugely practical joke, we thought, hidden somewhere among our clothes. But formulating that sentence is about as hopeless as attempting to locate the luminous qualities of an Islamic landscape, which can on occasion generate such esthetically pleasing moments of life. My audience is lost, and angry to be lost, and

31

both of us must find some token of exchange for this failed conversation. I try to put the subject down and change its clothes, but before I know it, it has sprinted off evilly in the direction of ocular evidence. It goads me into saying, with the defiance of a plea, you did not deal with Dadi.

Dadi, my father's mother, was born in Meerut toward the end of the last century. She was married at sixteen and widowed in her thirties, and in her later years could never exactly recall how many children she had borne. When India was partitioned in August 1947, she moved her thin, pure Urdu into the Punjab of Pakistan and waited for the return of her eldest son, my father. He had gone careening off to a place called Inglestan, or England, fired by one of the several enthusiasms made available by the proliferating talk of independence. Dadi was peeved. She had long since dispensed with any loyalties larger than the pitiless give-and-take of people who are forced to live in the same place, and she resented independence for the distances it made. She was not among those who, on the fourteenth of August, unfurled flags and festivities against the backdrop of people fleeing and cities burning. About that era she would only say, looking up sour and cryptic over the edge of her Koran, and I was also burned. She was, but that was years later.

By the time I knew her, Dadi, with her flair for drama, had allowed life to sit so heavily upon her back that her spine wilted and froze into a perfect curve, and so it was in the posture of a shrimp that she went scuttling through the day. She either scuttled, or did not: it all depended on the nature of her fight with the devil. There were days when she so hated him that all she could do was lie out straight and tiny on her bed, uttering the most awful imprecations. Sometimes, to my mother's great distress, she could only berate Satan in full eloquence after she had clambered on top of the dining room table and lain there like a little moldering centerpiece. Satan was to blame: he had after all made her older son linger long enough in Inglestan to give up his rightful wife, a relative, and take up instead with a white-legged woman. He'd taken her only daughter Ayesha when Ayesha lay in childbirth. And he'd sent her youngest son to Swaziland, or Switzerland: her thin hand waved away such sophistries of name.

God she loved, understanding him better than anyone. Her favorite days were those when she could circumvent both the gardener and my father, all in the solemn service of her God. She'd steal a knife and weedle her way to the nearest sapling in the garden, some sprightly poplar, or a eucalyptus newly planted. She'd squat, she'd hack it down, and then she would peel its bark away until she had a walking stick, all white and virgin and her own. It drove my father into tears of rage. He must have bought her a dozen walking sticks, one for each of our trips to the mountains, but it was like assembling a row of briar pipes for one who will not smoke. For Dadi had different aims. Armed with implements of her own creation, she would creep down the driveway unperceived to stop cars and people on the street, to give them all the gossip that she had on God.

Food, too, could move her to intensities. Her eyesight always took a sharp turn for the worse over meals, so that she could point hazily at a perfectly ordinary potato and murmur with an Adamic reverence, what *is* it, what *is* it called. With some shortness of manner, one of us would describe and catalog the items on the table. *Alu ka bhartha,* Dadi repeated with wonderment and joy. Yes, Saira begum, you can put some here. Not too much, she'd add pleadingly. For ritual had it that the more she demurred, the more she expected her plate to be piled with an amplitude that her own politeness would never allow. The ritual happened three times a day.

We pondered on it but never quite determined whether food or God constituted her most profound delight. Obvious problems, however, occurred on occasions which brought the two together. One was the Muslim festival called Eid, which celebrates the seductions of the Abraham story in a remarkably literal way. In Pakistan, at least, people buy sheep or goats and fatten them up for weeks with all sorts of delectables. Then, on the appointed day they're chopped, in place of sons, and neighbors graciously exchange silver trays heaped with raw and quivering meat. After Eid prayers the men come home, the animal is cooked, and shortly thereafter, they rush out of the kitchen steaming plates of grilled lung and liver, of a freshness quite superlative.

It was a freshness to which my Welsh mother did not immediately take. She observed the custom but located in it a conundrum that allowed for no ready solution. For, liberal to an extravagant degree on thoughts abstract, she found herself to be remarkably slow and squeamish on particular things. Chopping up animals for God was one. She could not quite locate the metaphor, and was therefore a little uneasy. My father, the writer, quite agreed, for he was so civilized in those days.

Dadi didn't agree. She pined for choppable things. Once she made the mistake of buying a baby goat and bringing him home months in advance of Eid. She wanted to guarantee the texture of his festive flesh by a daily feeding of tender peas and ghee, or clarified butter. Ifat and Shahid and I greeted a goat into the family with boisterous rapture, and soon after, he ravished us completely when we found him nonchalantly at the clothesline, eating up Shahid's pajamas. Of course there was no fight: the little goat was our delight, and even Dadi knew there was no killing him. He became my brother's and my sister's and my first pet, and he grew huge, a big and grinning thing.

Years after, Dadi had her will. We were all old enough, she must have thought, to make the house sprawl out, abstracted, into a multitude of secrets. That was true, but still we all noticed one another's secretive ways. So my sisters and I just shook our heads when the day before Eid our Dadi disappeared. We hid the fact from my father, who at this time of life had begun to equate petulance with extreme vociferation. So we went about our jobs and were Islamic for a day. We waited to sight moons on the wrong occasions and we watched the food come into lavishment. Dried dates change shape when they are soaked in milk, and carrots rich and strange can turn magically sweet when deftly covered with green nutty shavings and smatterings of silver.

Dusk was sweet as we sat out, the day's work done, in an evening garden. Lahore spread like peace around us. My father spoke, and when Papa talked it was of Pakistan. But we were glad, then, at being audience to that familiar conversation, till his voice looked up, and failed. There was Dadi making her return, and she was prodigal. Like a question mark interested only in its own conclusions, her body crawled through the gates. Our guests were spellbound; then they looked away. For Dadi, moving in her eerie crab formations chose to ignore the hangman's rope she firmly held. And behind her in the gloaming minced, hugely affable, a goat.

That goat was still smiling the following day, when Dadi's victory meant that the butcher came and went just as he should, on Eid. Goat was killed and cooked: a scrawny beast that required much cooking and never melted into tenderness, he muscularly winked and glistened on our plates as we sat eating him on Eid. Dadi ate, that is: Papa had taken his mortification to some distant corner of the house: Ifat refused to chew on hemp: Tillat and Irfan still gulped their baby sobs over such a slaughter. Honestly, said Mamma, honestly. For Dadi had successfully cut through tissues of festivity just as the butcher slit the goat, but there was something else that she was eating with that meat. I saw it in her concentration. I know that she was making God talk to her as to Abraham, and see what she could do—for him—to sons. God didn't dare, and she ate on, alone.

Of those middle years it is hard to say whether Dadi was literally left alone or whether a quality of being apart and absorbed was always emanated by her bodily presence. In the winter, I see her alone, painstakingly dragging her straw mat out to the courtyard at the back of the house, and following the rich course of the afternoon sun. With her would go her Koran, a metal basin in which she could wash her hands, and her ridiculously heavy-spouted watering pot that was made of brass. None of us, according to Dadi, was quite pure enough to transport these particular items: the rest of the paraphernalia we could carry out. These were baskets of her writing and sewing materials and her bottle of most pungent and Dadi-like bitter oils, which she'd coat on the papery skin that held her brittle bones. And in the summer, when the night created an illusion of possible coolness, and all held their breath while waiting for a thin and intermittent breeze, Dadi would be on the roof, alone. Her summer bed was a wooden frame latticed with a sweetly smelling rope, much aerated at the foot of the bed. She'd lie there all night, until the wild monsoons would wake the lightest and the soundest sleeper into a rapturous welcome of rain.

In Pakistan, of course, there is no spring but just a rapid elision from winter into summer, which is somewhat analogous to the absence of a recognizable loneliness from the behavior of that climate. In a similar fashion it is quite hard to distinguish between Dadi with people and Dadi alone. She was just impossibly unable to remain unnoticed. In the winter, when she was not writing or reading, she would sew for her delight tiny and magical reticules out of old silks and fragments that she had saved, palm-sized cloth bags that would unravel into the precision of secret and more secret pockets. But none of them did she ever need to hide, for something of Dadi always remained intact, however much we sought to open her. Her discourse, for example, was too impervious to allow for penetration, so that when one or two of us remonstrated with her in a single hour she never bothered to distinguish her replies. Instead, generic and prophetic, she would pronounce, the world takes on a single face. Must you, Dadi, I'd begin, to be halted then by her great complaint: "the world takes on a single face."

It did. And often it was a countenance of some delight, for Dadi also loved the accidental jostle with things belligerent. As she went perambulating through the house, suddenly she'd hear Shahid, her first grandson, telling me or one of my sisters that we were vile, we were disgusting women. And Dadi, who never addressed anyone of us without first conferring the title of lady, so we were Teellat begum, Nuzhat begum, Iffatt begum, Saira begum, would halt in reprimand and tell her grandson never to call her granddaughters women. What else shall I call them, men? Shahid yelled. Men, said Dadi, men. There is more goodness in a woman's little finger than in the benighted mind of man. Hear, hear, Dadi, *hanh hanh*, Dadi, my sisters cried. For men, said Dadi, shaking the name off her fingertips like some unwanted water, live as though they were un-suckled things. And heaven, she grimly added, is the thing Mohammed says (peace be upon him) lies beneath the feet of women! But he was a man, Shahid still would rage, if he weren't laughing, as all of us were laughing, while Dadi sat among us like a belle or a May queen.

Toward the end of the middle years my father stopped speaking to his mother, and the atmosphere at home appreciably improved. They secretly hit upon novel histrionics that took the place of their daily battle. Instead they chose the curious way of silent things: twice a day, Dadi would leave her room and walk the long length of the corridor to my father's room. There she just peered around the door, as though to check if he were real. Each time she peered, my father would interrupt whatever adult thing he may have been doing in order to enact a silent paroxysm, an elaborate facial pantomime of revulsion and affront. At teatime in particular, when Papa would want the world to congregate in his room for tea, Dadi came to peer her ghostly peer. Shortly thereafter conversation was bound to fracture, for we could not drown the fact that Dadi, invigorated by an outcast's strength, was sitting in the dining room and chanting an appeal: God give me tea, God give me tea.

At about this time Dadi stopped smelling old and smelled instead of something equivalent to death. It would have been easy to notice if she had been dying, but instead she managed the change as a certain gradation into subtlety, just as her annoying little stove could shift its hanging odors away from smoke and into ash. During the middle years there had been something more defined about her being, which sat in the world as solely its own context. But Pakistan was increasingly complicating the question of context, as though history, like a pestilence, was insisting that nothing could have definition outside relations to its own fevered sleep. So it was simple for my father to ignore the letters that Dadi had begun to write to him every other day, in her fine wavering script, letters of advice about the house or the children or the servants. Or she transcribed her complaint: Oh my son, Zia. Do you think your son, Shahid, upon whom God bestowed a thousand blessings, should be permitted to lift up his grandmother's chair and carry it into the courtyard, when his grandmother is seated in it? She had cackled in a combination of delight and virgin joy when Shahid had so transported her, but that little crackling sound she omitted from her letter. She ended it, and all her notes, with her single endearment. It was a phrase to halt and arrest when Dadi actually uttered it: her solitary piece of tenderness was an injunction, really, to her world. Keep on living, she would say.

Between that phrase and the great Dadi conflagration comes the era of the trying times. They began in the winter war of 1971, when East Pakistan became Bangladesh and Indira Gandhi hailed the demise of the two-nation theory. Ifat's husband was off fighting and we spent the war together with her father-in-law, the brigadier, in the pink house on the hill. It was an ideal location for anti-aircraft guns, so there was a bevy of soldiers and weaponry installed upon our roof. During each air raid the brigadier would stride purposefully into the garden and bark commands at them, as though the success of the war rested upon his stiff upper lip. Then Dacca fell, and General Yahya came on television to resign the presidency and accede defeat. Drunk, by God, barked the brigadier as we sat watching, drunk.

The following morning General Yahya's mistress came to mourn with us over breakfast, lumbering in with swathes of overscented silk. The brigadier lit an English cigarette—he was frequently known to avow that Pakistani cigarettes gave him a cuff—and bit on his moustache. Yes, he barked, these are trying times. Oh yes, Gul, Yahya's mistress wailed, these are such trying times. She gulped on her own eloquence, her breakfast bosom quaked, and then resumed authority over that dangling sentence. It is so trying, she continued, I find it so trying, it is trying to us all, to live in these trying, trying times. Ifat's eyes met mine in complete accord: mistress transmogrified to muse; Bhutto returned from the U.N. to put Yahya under house arrest and become the first elected president of Pakistan; Ifat's husband went to India as a war prisoner for two years; my father lost his newspaper. We had entered the era of the trying times.

Dadi didn't notice the war, just as she didn't really notice the proliferation of her great-grandchildren, for Ifat and Nuzzi conceived at the drop of a hat and kept popping babies out for our delight. Tillat and I felt favored at this vicarious taste of motherhood: we learned to become that enviable personage, a khala, mother's sister, and when our married sisters came to visit with their entourage, we reveled in the exercise of khala-love. I once asked Dadi how many sisters she had had. She looked up with the oceanic gray of her cataracted eyes and answered, I forget.

The children helped, because we needed distraction, there being then in Pakistan a slightly musty taste of defeat to all our activities. The children gave us something, but they also took away: they initiated a slight displacement of my mother, for her grandchildren would not speak any English, and she could not read them stories as of old. Urdu always remained a shyness on her tongue, and as the babies came and went she let something of her influence imperceptibly recede, as though she occupied an increasingly private air space. Her eldest son was now in England, so Mamma found herself living in the classic posture of an Indian woman, who sends away her sons and runs the risk of seeing them then succumb to the great alternatives represented by the West. It was a position that preoccupied her, and without my really noticing what was happening, she quietly handed over many of her wifely duties to her two remaining daughters, to Tillat and to me. In the summer, once the ferocity of the afternoon sun had died down, it was her pleasure to go out into the garden on her own. There she would stand, absorbed and abstracted, watering the driveway and breathing in the heady smell of water on hot dust. I'd watch her often, from my room upstairs. She looked like a girl.

We were aware of something, of a reconfiguration in the air, but could not exactly phrase where it would lead us. Dadi now spoke mainly to herself, and even the audience provided by the deity had dropped away. Somehow there was not a proper balance between the way things came and the way they went, as Halima the cleaning woman knew full well when she looked at me intently, asking a question that had no question in it: Do I grieve, or do I celebrate? Halima had given birth to her latest son the night her older child had died in screams of meningitis; once heard, never to be forgotten. She came back to work a week later, and we were talking as we put away the family's winter clothes into vast metal trunks. For in England, they would call it spring.

We felt a quickening urgency of change drown our sense of regular direction, as though something was bound to happen soon, but not knowing what it was that was making history nervous. And so we were not really that surprised when we found ourselves living through the summer of the trials by fire. That summer's climax came when Dadi went up in a little ball of flames. But somehow sequentially related were my mother's trip to England, to tend to her dying mother, the night I beat up Tillat, and the evening I nearly castrated my little brother, runt of the litter, serious-eyed Irfan.

It was an accident on both our parts. I was in the kitchen, so it must have been a Sunday when Allah Ditta, the cook, took the evening off. He was a mean-spirited man with an incongruously delicate touch when it came to making food. On Sunday at midday he would bluster one of us into the kitchen and show us what he had prepared for the evening meal, leaving strict and belligerent instructions about what would happen if we overheated this or dared brown that. So I was in the kitchen heating up some food, when Farni came back from playing hockey with that ominous asthmatic rattle in his throat. He, the youngest, had been my parents' gravest infant: in adolescence he remained a gentle invalid. Of course he pretended otherwise, and was loud and raucous, but it never worked.

Tillat and I immediately turned on him with the bullying litany that actually is quite soothing, the invariable female reproach to the returning male. He was to do what he hated, and stave off his disease by sitting over a bowl of camphor and boiling water, inhaling its acrid fumes. I insisted that he sit on the cook's little stool in the kitchen, holding the bowl of water on his lap, so that I could cook and Farni could not cheat and I could time each minute he should sit there thus confined. We seated him and flounced a towel on his reluctant head. The kitchen jointly reeked of cumin and camphor, and he sat skinny and penitent and swathed for half a minute before begging to be done. I slammed down the carving knife and screamed *Irfan* with such ferocity that he jumped literally and figuratively quite out of his skin. The bowl of water emptied onto him, and with a gurgling cry he leapt up, tearing at his steaming clothes. He clutched at his groin, and everywhere he touched the skin slid off, so that between his fingers his penis easily unsheathed, a blanched and fiery grape. What's happening, screamed Papa from his room; what's happening, echoed Dadi's wail from the opposite end of the house. What was happening was that I was holding Farni's shoulders, trying to stop him jumping up and down, but I was jumping too, while Tillat just stood there frozen, frowning at his poor ravaged grapes.

This was June, and the white heat of summer. We spent the next few days laying ice on Farni's wounds: half the time I was allowed to stay with him, until the doctors suddenly remembered I was a woman and hurried me out when his body made crazy spastic reactions to its burns. Once things grew calmer and we were alone, Irfan looked away and said, I hope I didn't shock you, Sara. And I was so taken by tenderness for his bony convalescent body that it took me years to realize that yes, something female in me had been deeply shocked.

Mamma knew nothing of this, of course. We kept it from her so that she could concentrate on what took her back to the rocky coastline of Wales, and to places she had not really revisited since she was a girl. She sat waiting with her mother, who was blind now and of a fine translucency, and both of them knew that they were waiting for her death. It was a peculiar posture for Mamma to maintain, but her quiet letters spoke mainly of the sharp astringent light that made the sea wind feel so brisk in Wales, and so many worlds away from the daily omnipresent weight of a summer in Lahore. And there, one afternoon, walking childless among the brambles and the furze, Mamma realized that her childhood was distinctly lost. It was not that I wanted to feel more familiar, she later told me, or that I was more used to feeling unfamiliar in Lahore. It's just that familiarity isn't important, really, she murmured absently, it really doesn't matter at all.

When Mamma was ready to return she wired us her plans, and my father read the cable, kissed it, then put it in his pocket. I watched him and felt startled, as we all did on the occasions when our parents' lives seemed to drop away before our eyes, leaving them youthfully engrossed in the illusion of knowledge conferred by love. We were so used to conceiving of them as parents moving in and out of hectic days that it always amused us, and touched us secretly, when they made quaint and punctilious returns to the amorous bond that had initiated the unlikely lives through which we knew them.

That summer, while my mother was away, Tillat and I experienced a new bond of powerlessness, which is the white and shaking rage of sexual jealousy in parenthood. I had always behaved toward her as a belligerent surrogate parent, but she was growing beyond that scope, and in her girlhood asking me for a formal acknowledgment of equality that I was loath to give. My reluctance was rooted in a helpless fear of what the world could do to her, for I was young and ignorant enough not to see that what I could do was worse. She went out one evening, when my father was off on one of his many trips. The house was gaping emptily, and Tillat was very late. Allah Ditta had gone home, and Dadi and Irfan were sleeping; I read, and thought, and walked up and down the garden, and Tillat was very very late. When she came back she wore that strange sheath of complacency and guilt which pleasure puts on faces very young. It smote an outrage in my heart until despite all resolutions to the contrary I heard my hiss: and where were you? Her returning look was both fearful and preening at the same time, so that the next thing to be smitten was her face. Don't, Sara, Tillat said in her superior way, physical violence is so degrading. To you, maybe, I answered, and hit her once again.

It made a sorrowful bond between us, for we both felt complicit in the shamefulness that had made me seem righteous, when I had felt simply jealous, which we tacitly agreed was a more legitimate thing to be. But we had lost something, a certain protective aura, some unspoken myth asserting that love between sisters at least was sexually innocent. Now we had to fold that vain belief away and stand in slightly more naked relation to our affection. Till then we had associated such violence with all that was outside us, as though, somehow, the more historical process fractured, the more whole we would be. But now we were losing a sense of the differentiated identities of history and ourselves, and were guiltily aware that we had known it all along, our part in the construction of unreality.

By this time, Dadi's burns were slowly learning how to heal. It was she who had given the summer its strange pace by nearly burning herself alive at its inception. On an early April night Dadi awoke, seized by a desperate need for tea. It was three in the morning and the household was asleep, so she could do the great forbidden thing of creeping into Allah Ditta's kitchen and taking charge, like pixies in the night. As all of us were so bored with predicting, one of her many cotton garments took to fire that truant night. But Dadi deserves credit for her resourceful voice, which wavered out for witness to her burning death. By the time Tillat awoke and found her, she was a little flaming ball: *Dadi*, said Tillat in the reproach of sleep, and beat her quiet with a blanket. In the morning we discovered Dadi's torso had been quite consumed and nothing recognizable remained, from collarbone to groin. The doctors bade us to some decent mourning.

But Dadi had different plans. She lived through her sojourn at the hospital: she weathered her return. And then after six weeks at home she angrily refused to be lugged daily to the doctor's to get her dressings changed, as though she were a chunk of meat: Saira begum will do it, she announced. And thus developed my great intimacy with the fluid properties of human flesh. By the time Mamma left for England, Dadi's left breast was still coagulate and raw. When Farni got his burns she was growing pink and livid tightropes, strung from hip to hip in a flaming advertisement of life. And in the days when Tillat and I were wrestling, Dadi's vanished nipples started to congeal and turn their cavities into triumphant little loveknots.

I learned about the specialization of beauty from that body. There were times like love when I felt only disappointment to carefully ease the dressings off and find again a piece of flesh that would not knit, happier in the texture of a stubborn glue. But then, on some more exhilarating day, I'd peel like an onion all her bandages away and suddenly discover I was looking down at some literal tenacity, and was bemused at all the freshly withered shapes she could create. Each new striation was a triumph to itself, and when Dadi's hairless groin solidified again, and sent firm signals that abdomen must do the same, I could have wept with glee.

During her immolation, Dadi's diet underwent some curious changes. At first her consciousness teetered too much for her to pray, but then as she grew stronger it took us a while to notice what was missing: she had forgotten prayer. It left her life as firmly as tobacco can leave the lives of only the most passionate smokers, and I don't know if she ever prayed again. At about this time, however, with the heavy-handed inevitability that characterized his relation to his mother, my father took to prayer. I came home one afternoon and looked for him in all the usual places, but he wasn't to be found. Finally I came across Tillat and asked her where Papa was. Praying, she said. *Praying?* I said. Praying, she said, and I felt most embarrassed. For us it was rather as though we had come upon the children playing some forbidden, titillating game, and decided it was wisest to ignore it calmly. In an unspoken way, though, I think we dimly knew we were about to witness Islam's departure from the land of Pakistan. The men would take it to the streets and make it vociferate, but the great romance between religion and the populace, the embrace that engendered Pakistan, was done. So Papa prayed, with the desperate ardor of a lover trying to converse life back into a finished love.

And that was a change, when Dadi sewed herself together again and forgot to put back prayer into its proper pocket, for God could now leave the home and soon would join the government. Papa prayed and fasted and went on pilgrimage and read the Koran aloud with the most peculiar locutions. Occasionally we also caught him in nocturnal altercations that made him sound suspiciously like Dadi: we looked askance, but did not say a thing. And my mother was quite admirable. She behaved as though she always knew she'd wed a swaying, chanting thing, or that to register surprise would be an impoliteness to existence. Her expression reminded me somewhat of the time when Ifat was eight, and Mamma was urging her recalcitrance into some goodly task. Ifat postponed, and Mamma, always nifty with appropriate fables, quoted meaningfully: "I'll do it myself, said the little red hen." Ifat looked up with bright affection. Good little red hen, she murmured. Then a glance crossed my mother's face, a look between a slight smile and a quick rejection of eloquent response, something like a woman looking down, and then away.

She looked like that at my father's sudden hungering for God, which was added to the growing number of subjects about which we, my mother and her daughters, silently decided we had no conversation. We knew that there was something other than trying times ahead and would far rather hold our breath than speculate about what other surprises the era held up its capacious sleeve. Tillat and I decided to quash our dread of waiting around for change by changing for ourselves, before destiny took the time to come our way. I moved to America and Tillat to Kuwait and marriage. To both intentions my mother said, I see, and helped us in our preparations: she knew by now her son would not return and was not unprepared to extend the courtesy of waiting to her daughters, too. We left, and Islam predictably took to the streets, threatening and shaking Bhutto's empire. Mamma and Dadi remained the only women in the house, the one untalking, the other unpraying.

Dadi behaved abysmally at my mother's funeral, they told me, and made them all annoyed. She set up loud and unnecessary lamentations in the dining room, somewhat like an heir apparent, as though this death had reinstated her as mother of the house. While Ifat and Nuzzi and Tillat wandered frozen eyed, dealing with the roses and the ice, Dadi demanded an irritating amount of attention, stretching out supine and crying out, your mother has betrayed your father; she has left him; she has gone. Food from respectful mourners poured in, cauldron after cauldron, and Dadi rediscovered a voracious appetite.

Years later, I was somewhat sorry that I heard this tale because it made me take affront. When I went back to Pakistan, I was too peeved with Dadi to find out how she was. Instead I heard Ifat tell me about standing there in the hospital, watching the doctors suddenly pump upon my mother's heart—I'd seen it on television, she gravely said, I knew it was the end. Mamma's students from the university had found the rickshaw driver who had knocked her down, pummeled him nearly to death, and camped out in our garden, sobbing wildly, all in hordes.

By this time Bhutto was in prison and awaiting trial, and General Zulu was presiding over the Islamization of Pakistan. But we had no time to notice. My mother was buried at the nerve center of Lahore, a wild and dusty place, and my father immediately made arrangements to buy the plot of land next to her grave: we are ready when you are, Shahid sang. Her tombstone bore some pretty Urdu poetry and a completely fictitious place of birth, because there were some

44

details my father tended to forget. Honestly, it would have moved his wife to say.

So I was angry with Dadi at that time, and I didn't stop to see her. I saw my mother's grave and then came back to America, and hardly reacted when, six months from then, my father called from London and mentioned that Dadi was now dead. It happened in the same week that Bhutto finally was hanged, and our imaginations were consumed by that public and historical dying. Pakistan made rapid provisions not to talk about the thing that had been done, and somehow accidentally Dadi must have been mislaid into that larger decision, because she too ceased to be a mentioned thing. My father tried to get back in time for the funeral, but he was so busy talking Bhutto-talk in England that he missed his flight. Luckily, Irfani was at home and saw Dadi to her grave.

Bhutto's hanging had the effect of making Pakistan feel quite unreliable, particularly to itself. There was a new secretiveness its landscape learned, quite unusual for a formerly loquacious place. It accounts for the fact that I have never seen my grandmother's grave, and neither have my sisters. I think we would have tried, had we been together, despite the free-floating anarchy in the air that—like the heroin trade—made the world suspicious and afraid. Now there was no longer any need to wait for change because change was all there was, and we had quite forgotten the flavor of an era that stayed in place long enough to gain a name. One morning I awoke to see that, during the course of the night, my mind had completely ejected the names of all the streets in Pakistan, as though to assure that I could not return, or that if I did, it would be returning to a loss. Overnight the country had grown absentminded, and patches of amnesia hung over the hollows of the land like fog.

But I think we would have mourned Dadi in our belated way, except that the coming year saw Ifat killed in the consuming rush of change and disbanded the company of women for all times. It was a curious day in March, two years after my mother died, when the weight of that anniversary made us all disconsolate for her quietude. I'll speak to Ifat, though, I thought to myself in America. But in Pakistan someone had different ideas for that sister of mine and thwarted all my plans. When she went walking out that warm March night a car came by and trampeled her into the ground, and then it vanished strangely. By the time I reached Lahore, a tall and slender mound had usurped the grave space where my father hoped to lie, next to the more moderate shape that was his wife. Children take over everything.

So worn by repetition we stood by Ifat's grave and took note of the narcissi, still alive, that she must have put upon my mother's on the day that she had died. It made us impatient, in a way, as though we had to decide there was never anything quite as farcical as grief, and that it had to be eliminated from our diets for good. It cut away, of course, our intimacy with Pakistan, where history is synonymous with grief and always most at home in the attitudes of grieving. Our congregation in Lahore was brief, and then we swiftly returned to a more geographic reality. We are lost, Sara, Shahid said to me on the phone from England. Yes, Shahid, I firmly said, we're lost.

Today, I'd be less emphatic. Ifat and Mamma must have honeycombed and crumbled now, in the comfortable way that overtakes bedfellows. And somehow it seems apt and heartening that Dadi, being what she was, was never given the pomposities that enter the most well meaning of farewells, but seeped instead into the nooks and crannies of our forgetfulness. She fell between two stools of grief, which is quite appropriate, since she was greatest when her life was at its most unreal. Anyway, she was always outside our ken, an anecdotal thing, neither more nor less. And so some sweet reassurance of reality accompanies my discourse when I claim that when Dadi died, we all forgot to grieve.

For to be lost is just a minute's respite, after all, like a train that cannot help but stop at way stations, in order to stage a pretend version of the journey's end. Dying, we saw, was simply change taken to points of mocking extremity; it wasn't a thing to lose us but to find us out, and catch us where we least wanted to be caught. In Pakistan, Bhutto became rapidly obsolete after a few successions of bumper harvests, and none of us can fight the ways that the names Mamma and Ifat have become archaisms and quaintnesses on our lips.

Now I live in New Haven and feel quite happy with my life. I miss of course the absence of woman, and grow increasingly nostalgic for a world where the modulations of age are as recognized and welcomed as the shift from season into season. But that's a hazard that has to come along, since I have made myself an inhabitant of a population which democratically insists that everyone from twenty-nine to fifty-six roughly occupies the same space of age. When I teach topics in third world literature, much time is lost in trying to explain that such a place is not locatable, except as a discourse of convenience. It is like pretending that history or home is real and not located precisely where you're sitting, I hear my voice quite idiotically say. And then it happens. A face, puzzled and attentive and belonging to my gender, raises its intelligence to ask why, since I am teaching third world writing, I haven't given equal space to women writers on my syllabus. I look up, the horse's mouth, a foolish thing to be. Unequal images battle in my mind for precedence—there's imperial Ifat, there's Mamma in the garden and Halima the cleaning woman is there too, there's uncanny Dadi with her goat. Against all my own odds I know what I must say. Because, I'll answer slowly, there are no women in the third world.

Nominated by Raritan A Quarterly Review

MAY, 1968

by SHARON OLDS

from POETRY

The Dean of the University said
the neighborhood people could not cross campus
until the students gave up the buildings
so we lay down in the street,
we said The cops will enter this gate
over our bodies. Spine-down on the cobbles—
hard bed, like a carton of eggs—
I saw the buildings of New York City
from dirt level, they soared up and stopped,
chopped off cleanly—beyond them the sky
black and neither sour nor sweet, the
night air over the island.
The mounted police moved near us
delicately. Flat out on our backs
we sang, and then I began to count,
12, 13, 14, 15, I
counted again, 15, 16, one
month since the day on that deserted beach when we
used nothing, 17, 18, my
mouth fell open, my hair in the soil,
if my period did not come tonight
I was pregnant. I looked up at the sole of the
cop's shoe, I looked up at the
horse's belly, its genitals—if they
took me to Women's Detention and did the
exam on me, jammed the unwashed

48

speculum high inside me, the guard's
three fingers—supine on Broadway, I looked
up into the horse's tail like a
dark filthed comet. All week, I had
wanted to get arrested, longed to
give myself away. I lay in the
tar, one brain in my head and another
tiny brain at the base of my tail and I
stared at the world, good-luck iron
arc of the gelding's shoe, the cop's
baton, the deep curve of the animal's
belly, the buildings streaming up
away from the earth. I knew I should get up and
leave, stand up to muzzle level, to the
height of the soft velvet nostrils and
walk away, turn my back on my
friends and danger, but I was a coward so I
lay there looking up at the sky,
black vault arched above us, I
lay there gazing up at God, at his
underbelly, till it turned deep blue and then
silvery, colorless, *Give me this one
night*, I said, *and I'll give this child
the rest of my life*, the horses' heads
drooping, dipping, until they slept in a
dark circle around my body and my daughter.

nominated by Kathy Callaway, Naomi Clark, Joyce Carol Oates,
Lucia Perillo, Christina Zawadiwsky

GIRLS

fiction by TESS GALLAGHER

from MILKWEED CHRONICLE

ADA HAD INVITED HERSELF ALONG on the four-hour drive to
Corvallis with her daughter, Billie, for one reason: she intended to
see if her girlhood friend, Esther Cox, was still living. When Billie
had let drop she was going to Corvallis, Ada had decided. "I'm
coming too," she said. Billie frowned, but she didn't say no.

"Should I wear my red coat or my black coat?" she'd asked Billie.
"Why don't I pack a few sandwiches." Billie had told her to wear the
red coat and said not to bother about sandwiches; she didn't like to
eat and drive. Ada packed sandwiches anyway.

Billie had on the leather gloves she used when she drove her
Mercedes. When she wasn't smoking cigarettes, she was fiddling
with the radio, trying to find a station. Finally, she settled on some
flute music. This sounded fine to Ada. "Keep it there, honey," she
said.

"Esther was like a sister to me, an older sister," Ada said. "I don't
know anyone I was closer to. We did the cooking and housekeeping
for two cousins who owned mansions next door to one another—the
Conants was their name. Esther and I saw each other every day. We
even spent our evenings together. It was like that for nearly four
years." Ada leaned back in her seat and stole a look at the speed-
ometer: 75 miles an hour.

"It's like a soap opera," Billie said. "I can't keep the names straight or who did what when." She brought her eyes up to the rearview mirror as if she were afraid someone was going to overtake her.

Ada wished she could make her stories interesting for Billie and make it clear who the people were and how they had fit into her life. But it was a big effort and sometimes it drove her to silence. "Never mind," she'd say. "Those people are dead and gone. I don't know why I brought them up." But Esther was different. Esther was important.

Billie pushed in the lighter and took a cigarette from the pack on the dash. "What are you going to talk to this person about after all these years?" she said. Ada considered this for a minute. "One thing I want to know is what happened to Florita White and Georgie Ganz," Ada said. "They worked up the street from us and they were from Mansfield, where Esther and I were from. We were all farm girls trying to make a go of it in the city." Ada remembered a story about Florita. Florita, who was unmarried, had been living with a man, something just not done in those days. When she washed and dried her panties she said she always put a towel over them on the line so Basil, her man, couldn't see them. But that was all Ada could remember Florita saying. There had to be more to the story, but Ada couldn't remember. She was glad she hadn't said anything to Billie.

"You might just end up staring at each other," Billie said.

"Don't you worry," Ada said. "We'll have plenty to say." That was the trouble with Billie, Ada thought. Since she'd gone into business, if you weren't *talking* business you weren't talking. Billie owned thirty llamas—ugly creatures, Ada thought. She could smell the llama wool Billie had brought along in the back seat for the demonstration she planned to give. Ada had already heard Billie's spiel on llamas. There were a lot of advantages to llamas, according to Billie. For one thing, llamas always did their job in the same place. For another, someone wanting to go into the back country could break a llama in two hours to lead and carry a load. Ada was half inclined to think Billie cared more about llamas than she did about people. But then Billie had never gotten much out of people, and she *had* made it on llamas.

"Esther worked like a mule to raise three children," Ada said.

"Why are you telling me about this woman?" Billie said, as if she'd suddenly been accused of something. She lit another cigarette

51

and turned on her signal light. Then she moved over into the passing lane. The car sped effortlessly down the freeway.

Ada straightened herself in the seat and took out a handkerchief to fan the smoke away from her face. What could she say? That she had never had a friend like Esther in all the years since? Billie would say something like: *If she was so important then why haven't you seen her in forty-three years?* That was true enough, too; Ada couldn't explain it. She tried to stop the conversation right where it was.

"Anyway, I doubt if she's still living," Ada said, trying to sound unconcerned. But even as she said this Ada wanted more than ever to find Esther Cox alive. How had they lost track? She'd last heard from Esther after Ada's youngest son had been killed in a car crash twenty years ago. Twenty years. Then she thought of one more thing about Esther, and she said it.

"The last time I saw Esther she made fudge for me," Ada said. "You'll see, Billie. She'll whip up a batch this time too. She always made good fudge." She caught Billie looking at her, maybe wondering for a moment who her mother had been and what fudge had to do with anything. But Ada didn't care. She was remembering how she and Esther had bobbed each other's hair one night, and then gone to the town square to stroll and admire themselves in the store windows.

In the hotel room, Ada hunted up the phone book.

"Mother, take off your coat and stay awhile," Billie said as she sat down in a chair and put her feet up on the bed.

Ada was going through the *C*'s, her heart rushing with hope and dread as she skimmed the columns of names. "She's here! My God, Esther's in the book." She got up and then sat back down on the bed. "Esther. She's in the book!"

"Why don't you call her and get it over with," Billie said. She was flossing her teeth, still wearing her gloves.

"You dial it," Ada said. "I'm shaking too much."

Billie dropped the floss into a waste basket and pulled off her gloves. Then she took Ada's place on the bed next to the phone and dialed the number her mother read to her. Someone answered and Billie asked to speak to Esther Cox. Ada braced herself. Maybe Esther was dead after all. She kept her eyes on Billie's face, looking for signs. Finally Billie began to speak into the phone. "Esther? Esther Cox?" she said. "There's someone here who wants to talk to you." Billie handed Ada the phone and Ada sat on the bed next to her daughter.

"Honey?" Ada said. "Esther? This is Ada Gilman."

"Do I know you?" said the voice on the other end of the line.

Ada was stunned for a moment. It *had* been a very long time, yes. Ada's children were grown. Her husband was dead. Her hair had turned white. "We used to work in Springfield, Missouri, when we were girls," Ada said. "I came to see you after my first baby was born, in 1943." She waited a moment and when Esther still did not say anything, Ada felt a stab of panic. "Is this Esther Cox?" she asked.

"Yes it is," the voice said. Then it said, "Why don't you come over, why don't you? I'm sorry I can't remember you right off. Maybe if I saw you."

"I'll be right over, honey," Ada said. But as she gave the phone to Billie she felt her excitement swerving toward disappointment. There had been no warm welcome—no recognition, really, at all. Ada felt as if something had been stolen from her. She listened dully as Billie took down directions to Esther's house. When Billie hung up, Ada made a show of good spirits.

"I'll help you carry things in from the car," she said. She could see Billie wasn't happy about having to drive her anywhere just yet. After all, they'd just gotten out of the car.

Billie shook her head. She was checking her schedule with one hand and reaching for her cigarettes with the other. "We don't have much time. We'll have to go right now."

The street they turned onto had campers parked in the front yards, and boats on trailers were drawn up beside the carports. Dogs began to bark and pull on their chains as they drove down the street.

"Chartreuse. What kind of a color is that to paint a house?" Billie said. They pulled up in front of the house and she turned off the ignition. They didn't say anything for a minute. Then Billie said, "Maybe I should wait in the car."

The house had a dirty canvas over the garage opening, and an accumulation of junk reached from the porch onto the lawn. There were sheets instead of curtains hung across some of the windows. A pickup truck sat in the driveway with its rear axles on blocks. Esther's picture window looked out onto this. Ada stared at the house, wondering what had brought her friend to such a desperate-looking place.

"She'll want to see how you turned out," Ada told Billie. "You can't stay in the car." She was nearly floored by Billie's suggestion. She was trying to keep up her good spirits, but she was shocked and afraid of what she might find inside.

They walked up to the front door. Ada rang the bell and, in a minute, when no one answered, she rang the bell again. Then the door opened and an old, small woman wearing pink slacks and a green sweater looked out.

"I was lying down, girls. Come in, come in," the woman said. Despite the woman's age and appearance, Ada knew it was Esther. She wanted to hug her, but she didn't know if she should. Esther had barely looked at her when she let them in. This was an awful situation, Ada thought. To have come this far and then to be greeted as if she were just anyone. As if she were a stranger.

A rust-colored couch faced the picture window. Esther sat down on it and patted the place beside her. "Sit down here and tell me where I knew you," she said. "Who did you say you were again?"

"God, woman, don't you know me?" Ada said, bending down and taking Esther's hand in hers. She was standing in front of the couch. "I can't believe it. Esther, it's me. It's Ada." She held her face before the woman and waited. Why wouldn't Esther embrace her? Why was she just sitting there? Esther simply stared at her.

"Kid, I wished I did, but I just don't remember you," Esther said. "I don't have a glimmer." She looked down, seemingly ashamed and bewildered by some failure she couldn't account for.

Billie hovered near the door as if she might have to leave for the car at any moment. Ada dropped the woman's hand and sat down next to her on the couch. She felt as if she had tumbled over a cliff and that there was nothing left now but to fall. How could she have been so insignificant as to have been forgotten? she wondered. She was angry and hurt and she wished Billie *had* stayed in the car and not been witness to this humiliation.

"I had a stroke," Esther said and looked at Ada. There was such apology in her voice that Ada immediately felt ashamed of herself for her thoughts. "It happened better than a year ago," she said. Then she said, "I don't know everything, but I still know a lot." She laughed, as if she'd had to laugh at herself often lately. There was an awkward silence as Ada tried to take this in. Strokes happened often enough at their age so she shouldn't be surprised at this turn of events. Still, it was something she hadn't considered: she felt better and worse at the same time.

"Is this your girl? Sit down, honey," Esther said and indicated a chair by the window stacked with magazines and newspapers. "Push that stuff onto the floor and sit down."

"This is my baby," Ada said, trying to show some enthusiasm. "This is Billie."

Billie let loose a tight smile in Esther's direction and cleared a place to sit. Then she took off her gloves and put them on the window sill next to a candle holder. She crossed her legs, lit a cigarette and gazed out the window in the direction of her Mercedes. "We can't stay too long," she said.

"Billie's giving a talk on business," Ada explained, leaving out just what kind of business it was. "She was coming to Corvallis, so I rode along. I wanted to see you."

"I raise llamas," Billie said, and turned back into the room to see what effect this would have.

"That's nice. That's real nice," Esther said. But Ada doubted she knew a llama from a goat.

"Now don't tell me you can't remember the Conants—those cousins in Springfield we worked for," Ada said.

"Oh, I surely do remember them," Esther said. She was wearing glasses that she held to her face by tilting her head up. From time to time she pushed the bridge of the glasses with her finger. "I've still got a letter in my scrapbook. A recommendation from Mrs. Conant."

"Then you must remember Coley Starber and how we loaned him Mrs. Leslie Conant's sterling silver," Ada said, her hopes rising, as if she'd located the scent and now meant to follow it until she discovered herself lodged in Esther's mind. Billie had picked up a magazine and was leafing through it. From time to time she pursed her lips and let out a stream of smoke.

"Coley," Esther said and stared a moment. "Oh, yes, I remember when he gave the silver back. I counted it to see if it was all there. But, honey, I don't remember you." She shook her head helplessly. "I'm sorry. No telling what else I've forgot."

Ada wondered how it could be that she was missing in Esther's memory when Coley Starber, someone incidental to their lives, had been remembered. It didn't seem fair.

"Mom said you were going to make some fudge," Billie said, holding the magazine under the long ash of her cigarette. "Mom's got a sweet tooth."

"Use that candle holder," Esther told Billie, and Billie flicked the ash into the frosted candle holder.

Ada glared at Billie. She shouldn't have mentioned the fudge. Esther was looking at Ada with a bemused, interested air. "I told Billie how we used to make fudge every chance we got," Ada said.

"And what did we do with all this fudge?" Esther asked.

"We ate it," Ada said.

"We ate it!" Esther said and clapped her hands together. "We *ate* all the fudge." Esther repeated the words to Billie as if she were letting her in on a secret. But Billie was staring at Esther's ankles. Ada looked down and saw that Esther was in her stocking feet, and that the legs themselves were swollen and painful-looking where the pantleg had worked up while Esther sat on the couch.

"What's making you swell up like that?" Billie said. Ada knew Billie was capable of saying anything, but she never thought she'd hear her say a thing like this. Such behavior was the result of business, she felt sure.

"I had an operation," Esther said, as if Billie hadn't said anything at all out of line. Esther glanced toward a doorway that led to the back of the house. Then she raised up her sweater and pulled down the waistband of her slacks to show a long violet-looking scar which ran vertically up her abdomen. "I healed good though, didn't I?" she said. Esther lowered her sweater, then clasped her hands in her lap.

Before Ada had time to take this in, she heard a thumping sound from the hallway. A man appeared in the doorway of the living room. His legs bowed at an odd angle and he used a cane. The longer Ada looked at him, the more things she found wrong. One of his eyes seemed fixed on something not in this room, or in any other for that matter. He took a few more steps and extended his hand. Ada reached out to him. The man's hand didn't have much squeeze to it. Billie stood up and inclined her head. She was holding her cigarette in front of her with one hand and had picked up her purse with the other so as not to have to shake hands. Ada didn't blame her. The man was a fright.

"I'm Jason," the man said. "I've had two operations on my legs, so I'm not able to get around very easy. Sit down," he said to Billie. Jason leaned forward against his cane and braced himself. She saw that Jason's interest had settled on Billie. Good, Ada thought. Billie considered herself a woman of the world. Surely she could handle this.

Ada turned to Esther, and began to inquire after each of her other children, while she searched for a way to bring things back to that time in Springfield. Esther asked Ada to hand down a photograph album from a shelf behind the couch, and they began to go over the pictures.

"This arthritis hit me when I was forty." Jason said to Billie.

"I guess you take drugs for the pain," Billie said. "I hear they've got some good drugs now."

Ada looked down at the album in her lap. In the album there were children and babies and couples. Some of the couples had children next to them. Ada stared at the photos. Many of the faces were young, then you turned a page and the same faces were old. Esther seemed to remember everyone in the album. But she still didn't remember Ada. She was talking to Ada as to a friend, but Ada felt as if the ghost of her old self hovered in her mind waiting for a sign from Esther so that she could step forward again and be recognized.

"But that wouldn't interest you," Esther was saying as she flipped a page. Suddenly she shut the book and gazed intently at Ada.

"I don't know who you are," Esther said. "But I like you. Why don't you stay the night?" Ada looked over at Billie, who'd heard the invitation.

"Go ahead, Mother," Billie said, a little too eagerly. "I can come for you tomorrow around two o'clock, after the luncheon."

Ada looked at Jason, who was staring out the picture window toward the Mercedes. Maybe she should just give up on getting Esther to remember her and go back to the hotel and watch TV. But the moment she thought this, something unyielding rose up in her. She was determined to discover some moment when her image would suddenly appear before Esther from that lost time. Only then could they be together again as the friends they had once been, and that was what she had come for.

"You'll have to bring my things in from the car," Ada said at last.

"I wish I could help," Jason said to Billie, "but I can't. Fact is, I got to go and lay down again," he said to the room at large. Then he turned and moved slowly down the hallway. Billie opened the door and went out to the car. In a minute she came back with Ada's overnight bag.

"Have a nice time, Mom," she said. "I mean that." She set the bag inside the door. "I'll see you tomorrow." Ada knew she was glad to be heading back to the world of buying and selling, of tax shelters and the multiple uses of the llama. In a minute she heard Billie start up the Mercedes and heard it leave the drive.

The room seemed sparsely furnished now that she and Esther were alone. She could see a table leg just inside the door of a room that was probably the dining room. On the far wall was a large picture of an autumn landscape done in gold and brown.

"Look around, why don't you," Esther said, and raised herself off the couch. "It's a miracle, but I own this house."

They walked into the kitchen. The counter space was taken up with canned goods, stacks of dishes of every kind, and things Ada wouldn't expect to find in a kitchen—things like gallon cans of paint. It was as if someone were afraid they wouldn't be able to get to a store and had laid in extra supplies of everything.

"I do the cooking," Esther said. "Everything's frozen but some wieners. Are wieners okay?"

"Oh, yes," Ada said. "But I'm not hungry just yet."

"I'm not either," Esther said. "I was just thinking ahead because I've got to put these feet up. Come back to the bedroom with me."

Ada thought this an odd suggestion, but she followed Esther down the hallway to a room with a rumpled bed and a chrome kitchen chair near the foot of the bed. There was a dresser with some medicine containers on it. Ada helped Esther get settled on the bed. She took one of the pillows and placed it under Esther's legs at the ankles. She was glad she could do this for her. But then she didn't know what to do next, or what to say. She wanted the past and not this person for whom she was just an interesting stranger. Ada sat down in the chair and looked at Esther.

"What ever became of Georgie Ganz and Florita White?" she asked Esther, because she had to say something.

"Ada—that's your name, isn't it? Ada, I don't know who you're talking about," Esther said. "I wish I did, but I don't."

"That's all right," Ada said. She brightened a little. It made her feel better that Georgie and Florita had also been forgotten. A shadow cast by the house next door had fallen into the room. Ada thought the sun must be going down. She felt she ought to be doing something, changing the course of events for her friend in some small but important way.

"Let me rub your feet," Ada said suddenly and raised herself from the chair. "Okay?" She moved over to the bed and began to massage Esther's feet.

"That feels good, honey," Esther said. "I haven't had anybody do that for me in years."

"Reminds me of that almond cream we used to rub on each other's feet after we'd served at a party all night," Ada said. The feet seemed feverish to her fingers. She saw that the veins were enlarged and angry-looking as she eased her hands over an ankle and up onto the leg.

After a little while, Esther said, "Honey, why don't you lie down with me on the bed. That way we can really talk."

At first Ada couldn't comprehend what Esther had said to her. She said she didn't mind rubbing Esther's feet. She said she wasn't tired enough to lie down. But Esther insisted.

"We can talk better that way," Esther said. "Come lay down beside me."

Ada realized she still had on her coat. She took it off and put it over the back of the chair. Then she took off her shoes and went to lie down next to Esther.

"Now this is better, isn't it?" Esther said, when Ada was settled. She patted Ada's hand. "I can close my eyes now and rest." In a minute, she closed her eyes. And then they began to talk.

"Do you know about that preacher who was sweet on me back in Mansfield?" Esther asked. Ada thought for a minute and then remembered and said she did. "I didn't tell that to too many, I feel sure," Esther said. This admission caused Ada to feel for a moment that her friend knew she was someone special. There was that, at least. Ada realized she'd been holding her breath. She relaxed a little and felt a current of satisfaction, something just short of recognition, pass between them.

"I must have told you all my secrets," Esther said quietly, her eyes still closed.

"You did!" Ada said, rising up a little. "We used to tell each other everything."

"Everything," Esther said, as if she were sinking into a place of agreement where remembering and forgetting didn't matter. Then there was a loud noise from the hall, and the sound of male voices at the door. Finally the front door closed, and Esther put her arm across Ada's arm and sighed.

"Good. He's gone," Esther said. "I wait all day for them to come and take him away. His friends, so called. He'll come home drunk, and he won't have a dime. They've all got nothing better to do."

"That must be an awful worry," Ada said. "It must be a heartache."

"Heartache?" Esther said, and then she made a weary sound. "You don't know the start of it, honey. 'You need me, Mom,' he says to me, 'and I need you.' I told him if he stopped drinking I'd will him my house so he'd always have a place to live. But he won't stop. I know he won't. He can't.

"You know what he did?" Esther asked and raised up a little on her pillow. "He just looked at me when I said that about willing him the house. I don't think he'd realized until then that I wasn't always going to be here," Esther said. "Poor fellow, he can't help himself. But girl, he'd drink it up if I left it to him."

Ada felt that the past had drifted away, and she couldn't think how to get back to that carefree time in Springfield. "It's a shame," she murmured. And then she thought of something to tell Esther that she hadn't admitted to anyone. "My husband nearly drank us out of house and home, too. He would have if I hadn't fought him tooth and nail. It's been five years since he died. Five peaceful years." She was relieved to hear herself admit this, but somehow ashamed too.

"Well, I haven't made it to the peaceful part yet," Esther said. "Jason has always lived with me. He'll never leave me. Where could he go?"

"He doesn't abuse you, does he?" Ada said. *Abuse* was a word she'd heard on the television and radio a lot these days, and it seemed all-purpose enough not to offend Esther.

"If you mean does he hit me, no he doesn't," Esther said. "But I sorrow over him. I do."

Ada had done her share of sorrowing too. She closed her eyes and let her hand rest on Esther's arm. Neither of them said anything for a while. The house was still. She caught the faint medicinal smell of ointment and rubbing alcohol. She wished she could say something to ease what Esther had to bear, but she couldn't think of anything that didn't sound like what Billie might call "sappy."

"What's going to become of Jason?" Ada said finally. But when she asked this she was really thinking of herself and of her friend.

"I'm not going to know," Esther said. "Memory's going to fall entirely away from me when I die, and I'm going to be spared that." She seemed, Ada thought, to be actually looking forward to death and the shutting down of all memory. Ada was startled by this admission.

Esther got up from the bed. "Don't mind me, honey. You stay comfortable. I have to go to the bathroom. It's these water pills."

After Esther left the room Ada raised up in bed as if she had awakened from the labyrinth of a strange dream. What was she doing here, she wondered, on this woman's bed in a city far from her own home? What business of hers was this woman's troubles? In Springfield, Esther had always told Ada how pretty she was and what beautiful hair she had, how nicely it took a wave. They had tried on each other's clothes and shared letters from home. But this was something else. This was the future and she had come here alone. There was no one to whom she could turn and say without the least vanity, "I was pretty, wasn't I?" She sat on the side of the bed and waited for the moment to pass. But it was like an echo that wouldn't stop calling her. Then she heard from outside the house the merry, untroubled laughter of some girls. It must be dark out by now, she thought. It must be night. She got up from the bed, went to the window and pulled back the sheet that served as a curtain. A car was pulling away from the house next door. The lights brushed the room as it moved past. In a moment, she went back to the bed and lay down again.

For supper Esther gave her wieners, and green beans fixed the way they'd had them back home, with bacon drippings. Then she took her to the spare room, which was next to Jason's room. They had to move some boxes off the bed. Esther fluffed up the pillows and put down an extra blanket. Then she moved over to the doorway.

"If you need anything, if you have any bad dreams, you just call me, honey," she said. "Sometimes I dream I'm wearing a dress but it's on backwards and I'm coming downstairs, and there's a whole room full of people looking up at me," she said. "I'm glad you're here. I am. Good night. Good night, Ada."

"Good night, Esther," Ada said. But Esther went on standing there in the doorway.

Ada looked at her and wished she could dream them both back to a calm summer night in Springfield. She would open her window and call across the alley to her friend, "You awake?" and Esther would hear her and come to the screen and they would say wild and hopeless things like, Why don't we go to California and try out for the movies? Crazy things like that. But Ada didn't remind Esther of this. She lay there alone in their past and looked at Esther, at her old face and her old hands coming out of the sleeves of her robe, and she wanted to yell at her to get out, shut the door, don't come back! She hadn't come here to strike up a friendship with this old scarecrow of a woman. But then Esther did something. She came over to the bed and pulled the covers over Ada's shoulders and patted her cheek.

"There now, dear," she said. "I'm just down the hall if you need me." And then she turned and went out of the room.

Sometime before daylight Ada heard a scraping sound in the hall. Then something fell loudly to the floor. But in a while the scraping sound started again and someone entered the room next to hers and shut the door. It was Jason, she supposed. Jason had come home, and he was drunk and only a few feet away. She had seen her own husband like this plenty of times, had felt herself forgotten, obliterated, time after time. She lay there rigid and felt the weight of the covers against her throat. Suddenly, it was as if she were suffocating. She felt her mouth open and a name came out of it. "Esther! Esther!" she cried. And in a few moments her door opened and her friend came in and leaned over her.

"What is it, honey?" Esther said, and turned the lamp on next to the bed.

"I'm afraid," Ada said, and she put out her hand and took hold of Esther's sleeve. "Don't leave," she said. Esther waited a minute. Then she turned off the light and got into bed beside Ada. Ada turned on her side, facing the wall, and Esther's arm went around her shoulder.

The next day Billie came to the house a little early. Ada had just finished helping Esther wash her hair.

"I want you to take some pictures of us," Ada said to Billie. "Esther and me." She dug into her purse and took out the Kodak she'd carried for just this purpose. Billie seemed in a hurry to get on the road now that the conference was over.

"I was a real hit last night," Billie said to Ada as if she'd missed seeing her daughter at her best. Little tufts of llama wool clung to

Billie's suit jacket as she took the camera from Ada and tried to figure out where the lens was and how to snap the picture. Ada felt sure she hadn't missed anything, but she understood Billie's wanting her to know she'd done well at something. That made sense to her now.

"Let's go out in the yard," Billie said.

"My hair's still wet," Esther said. She was standing in front of a mirror near the kitchen rubbing her hair with a towel, but the hair sprang out in tight spirals all over her head.

"You look all right," Ada said. "You look fine, honey."

"You'd say anything to make a girl feel good," Esther said.

"No, I wouldn't," Ada said. She stood behind Esther and, looking in the mirror, dabbed her own nose with powder. They could be two young women readying themselves to go out, Ada thought. They might meet some young men while they were out, and they might not. In any case, they'd take each other's arm and stroll until dusk. Someone—Ada didn't know who—might pass and admire them.

Billie had them stand in front of the picture window. They put their arms around each other. Esther was shorter and leaned her head onto Ada's shoulder. She even smiled. Ada had the sensation that the picture had already been taken somewhere in her past. She was sure it had.

"Did you get it?" Ada said as Billie advanced the film and moved closer for another shot.

"I'm just covering myself," Billie said, squatting down on the lawn and aiming the camera like a professional. "You'll kill me if these don't turn out." She snapped a few more shots from the driveway, then handed the camera back to her mother.

Ada followed her friend into the house to collect her belongings and say goodbye. Esther wrapped a towel around her head while Ada gathered her coat, purse, and overnight bag.

"Honey, I'm so sorry I never remembered you," Esther said.

Ada believed Esther when she said this. *Sorry* was the word a person had to use when there was no way to change a situation. Still, she wished they could have changed it.

"I remembered *you*, that's the main thing," Ada said. But a miserable feeling came over her, and it was all she could do to speak. Somehow the kindness and intimacy they'd shared as girls had lived on in them. But Esther, no matter how much she might want to, couldn't remember Ada, and give it back to her, except as a stranger.

"God, kid, I hate to see you go," Esther said. Her eyes filled. It seemed to Ada that they might both be wiped from the face of the earth by this parting. They embraced and clung to each other a moment. Ada patted Esther's thin back, and then moved hurriedly toward the door.

"Tell me all about your night," Billie said, as Ada slid into the passenger's seat. But Ada knew this was really the last thing on Billie's mind. And anyhow, it all seemed so far from anything Ada had ever experienced that she didn't know where to begin.

"Honey, I just want to be still for a while," Ada said. She didn't care whether Billie smoked or how fast she drove. She knew that eventually she would tell Billie how she had tried to make Esther remember her, and how she had failed. But the important things— the way Esther had come to her when she'd called out, and how, earlier, they'd lain side by side—this would be hers. She wouldn't say anything to Billie about these things. She couldn't. She doubted she ever would. She looked out at the countryside that flew past the window in a green blur. It went on and on, a wall of forest that crowded the edge of the roadway. Then there was a gap in the color and she found herself looking at downed trees and stumps where an entire hillside of forest had been cut away. Her hand went to her face as if she had been slapped. But then she saw it was green again, and she let her hand drop to her lap.

Nominated by Jim Simmerman and Pat Zelver

DECEMBER JOURNAL

by CHARLES WRIGHT

from THE PARIS REVIEW

God is not offered to the senses,
                              St. Augustine tells us,
The artificer is not his work, but is his art:
Nothing is good if it can be better.
But all these oak trees look fine to me,
                              this Virginia cedar
Is true to its own order
And ghosts a unity beyond its single number.
This morning's hard frost, whose force is nowhere
    absent, is nowhere present.
The undulants cleanse themselves in the riverbed,
The mud-striders persevere,
                              the exceptions provide.

I keep coming back to the visible.
                              I keep coming back
To what it leads me into,
The hymn in the hymnal,
The object, sequence and consequence.
By being exactly what it is,
It is that other, inviolate self we yearn for,
Itself and more than itself,
                              the word inside the word.

It is the tree and what the tree stands in for, the
    blank,
The far side of the last equation.

———————

Black and brown of December,
                        umber and burnt orange
Under the spoked trees, front yard
Pollocked from edge-feeder to edge run,
Central Virginia beyond the ridgeline spun with
    a back light
Into indefinition,
                 charcoal and tan, damp green . . .
Entangled in the lust of the eye,
                 we carry this world with us wherever we go,
Even into the next one:
Abstraction, the highest form, is the highest good:
Everything's beautiful that stays in its due order,
Every existing thing can be praised
                   when compared with nothingness.

———————

The seasons roll from my tongue—
Autumn, winter, the *integer vitae* of all that's in vain,
Roll unredeemed.
               Rain falls. The utmost
Humps out to the end of nothing's branch, crooks there like
    an inch-worm,
And fingers the emptiness.
December drips through my nerves,
                 a drumming of secondary things
That spells my name right,
            heartbeat
Of slow, steady consonants.
Trash cans weigh up with water beside the curb,
Leaves flatten themselves against the ground
                   and take cover.

How are we capable of so much love
                                for things that must fall away?
How can we utter our mild retractions and still keep
Our wasting affection for this world?
                                Augustine says
This is what we desire,
The soul itself instinctively desires it.
                                He's right, of course,
No matter how due and exacting the penance is.
The rain stops, the seasons wheel
Like stars in their bright courses:
                                the cogitation of the wise
Will bind you and take you where you will not want to go.
Mimic the juniper, have mercy.

The tongue cannot live up to the heart:
Raise the eyes of your affection to its affection
and let its equivalents
                                ripen in your body.
Love what you don't understand yet, and bring it to you.

From somewhere we never see comes everything that we do
        see.
What is important devolves
                                from the immanence of infinitude
In whatever our hands touch—
The other world is here, just under our fingertips.

Nominated by Edward Hirsch, Garrett Kaoru Hongo, and Sherod Santos

20–200 ON 737

by HEATHER MCHUGH

from THE THREEPENNY REVIEW

Here and now is clear so we
can't see it (what we know too well
we notice least). In airplanes, chance
encounters want to know, so what
are your poems about? They're about

their business and their father's business
and their monkey's uncle, just about
undone, about themselves, and not about
being about, of of. This answer
drives them back to the snack tray every time.

One Phil Fenstermacher, for example, turns up
perfectly clear in my memory, perfectly attentive to
his Piedmont Vache Qui Rit (that saddest cheese)—and let us now
commiserate with that engagement, for it takes what might
be years to open life's array

of incidental parcels—mysteries of red strips, tips and strings—
the tricks of tampons, band-aids, perforated notches on
detergent boxes, spatial reasoning milk carton quiz and subtle
eschatologies of toilet paper—O,
it's endless. Mister Fenstermacher is relieved

to fill his mind with the immediate
and masterable challenge of the cheese, after our brief

and chastening foray into the social arts. We part
before we part; indeed
we part before we meet. (I sense the French

philosophers nearby—I hope not in the cockpit—
furious about an act of metaphor, they rock
the plane and all the singers in it (contrary to popular
belief, the vehicle is one, the tenors many)—they intone

we're sunk, we're sunk, in our little container, our
story of starting and stopping.) Whose story
is it anyway? Out of my mouth
whose words emerge? Who's the self the self
surpasses? Look at your glasses, someone
whispers. Maybe the world is speckled

by your carelessness. Look at your glasses,
if you want to see. (Who says? It's night, we're not alone,
the town down there grows huge, one tiny runway will
engulf us. Is the whisperer Phil Fenstermacher, getting
a last word in before

the craft alights?) I look at my glasses.
I see what he means. They're a sight.

nominated by The Threepenny Review

CHEER

by LAURA JENSEN

from IRONWOOD

The nights are restless, days
are noise right into night.

That was not what I wanted
ever to say. I waited

until the day said *cheer*.
That moment, *cheer*, I had begun

picking a few things up
and was running a bath

and the thought
was the robin's song

the clay birds in the chimes
on the porch, saying *cheer up*.

It all came together, every part
so intimate and right

that the song is a song
without words. I waited some more

and remembered Marilyn Monroe
who died alone, a suicide.

                    *

Trim.

Rick-rac.
Lace
with a ribbon
latticed.

Just lace.
Edging
made with a ruffle.
Braid.

Quilting.
Smocking.

Lace daisy.
Child
needs the emblem
appliqued.

Make it all
small.
Doll
needs its soul

said
and decorated.
And
embroidered.

                    *

My little friends
were blonde
or dark and some
were remarkable in their
cleanliness, brushed
so that was their essence.

The fairness of us
was unmistakable.
Marilyn Monroe—
all of us knew she was
beautiful. A girl named
Marilyn had the same
name as she.
We knew her, she
was like one of us
and any of us
could believe. She made it
seem real, and fun.
We may look at old photos,
almost a photo
of someone we knew,
although we were not
someone she knew, and say
she was so pretty, so
small, her hair like a
beautiful flower, why—
and the pictures stay,
a loveliness about us.

But Katherine Hepburn
is still just
as lovely, Greta Garbo
is still just
so in the photos,
they are still lovely,
their names are still
lovely to us.

*

We may say,
I suppose, and I suppose.
And, what happened?
Someone should have
eased her, we say, when. Was she
cheated, did someone

cheat her? Did we?
We suppose, and we suppose
and that loveliness did
not stay alive
to stay with us, just
the loveliness alive.
But the child
she was, complete
and completed?

What was
does not have to be
what had to happen.

                    *

A leaf flies off
the tree.
It hits the house
like a rubber glove.

Little frail thing
that is a house—
please do not fall
during the winter.

I go and put on socks.

Yellow light
falls through the trees.

nominated by Sandra McPherson, and Pamela Stewart

HERON

by DAN MASTERSON

from PLOUGHSHARES

Late August, and the pond is holding
the summer's heat close to shore
where leaf-litter has begun to form;
even out at the center of things
there are pockets of warmth
deep beneath a canoe short-roped
to a slab of scrap iron heaved into place
once again on a scrub-topped boulder
barely covered by water.

The swimmer is up from his dive,
settling flatout aside the makeshift anchor,
far from the potbelly smoke
drifting from his empty cabin losing
itself in the high peaks
of the Adirondacks, the noon sun
drying him out full length.

He stands, then hunkers down
on the rock, rubbing himself hard
with open hands, his hair running
what feels like snowmelt down
across his shoulders as he searches
the vacant sky, the disturbed water
coming from the inlet.

It is another ending, the last
swim of the season, the day
before he takes his place
in the downstate office waiting
for his return, the long year
ahead, only a small framed picture
on a desk: this place
he is trying not to leave.

Something low to the water comes fast,
gliding, making its way toward the rock,
dipping, leading the wind, arriving
overhead too soon, stalling
the right wing to turn abruptly,
tilting into the sun, circling the boulder
and its naked swimmer: little more
than bones spattered with meat,
bland and bunched, trying
to become part rock, part air.

It seems to stop, casting
a huge ragged cross in shadow, its
body stretched, wings straining
their six-foot span against the glare
mostly gone except at the webbing of wings,
the connecting flesh, the membrane
where the tertial feathers become
scapular, and the swimmer

Sees through it, the translucent window
of tissue, fascia wrinkled yet clear, light
streaming through ligaments and veins, an arm's
reach away, the hoarse guttural squawk
leaving the mandibles, loose plumage emblazoned
with feathers long and ruffled, bald legs
set rigid as a clean-plucked tail, unblinking
eyes, caught in passing, a blur
of underbelly, the crook of neck tucked
for flight, a single flex of wings
lifting the Great Blue atop the wind,

Tipping the swimmer over the side, drawing
him toward the shadow skimming off
to the shallows, sending him deep, his arms
folded to his thighs like wings,
legs rigid, feet fluttering him on
through the reeds, hands coming forward
to pull him into the dark corridor
he is making, his chest closing
like a bag of air caught in a fist;
time left to rise into sunlight,
but the need slacking off as his face
feels the slim stalks reaching
for the surface long unbroken, almost still.

Nominated by John Allman

ICARUS DESCENDING

fiction by MARJORIE SANDOR

from ANTAEUS

GREGORY IS IN THE arena five minutes, and in those five minutes every man old enough to have a grown son has stopped by to offer him a friendly word of advice. It's been three months since he left his house, but everywhere the same story. Whether he's on construction, or carnival, or state fair crew, up they come, a little astonished but mostly wise, offering instruction in their specialties: stage-building, tightrope and net repair, light setup. He holds his face perfectly still, refuses to look them in the eye, but up they come, not hesitating at all, as if he's waved them over from a great distance. Now an older man climbs down from the light booth, his legs slow on the rungs. It's August, and the arena air is heavy with fairground dust and humidity, yet the man wears a cardigan, as if to say that where he works, there's another, cooler atmosphere.

"Hello, son," says the man. "Shouldn't you be in school?"

"I'm not as young as I look," says Gregory.

The man smiles, and Gregory knows he has failed.

At dinner he takes a corner window seat, but the man finds him. His name is Matt and he is head light technician for the Wild Bill Carnival of Omaha, which has the concession at the state fair this year. Matt confesses to Gregory that he is not a very good light technician, especially since developing acrophobia. "I lost a boy in Vietnam," he says, making the motion with his hands of a plane going down.

"Wrong profession for an acrophobic," he says, laughing. "I'm glad you showed up. Maybe I can gracefully retire." Matt's hands, which earlier that day had been long and heavy and capable on the

77

dimmer board, tremble. It's the small things that give him away, Gregory thinks. Pickles, olives, peas. Matt lifts his fork and they scatter. Gregory wants to tell him to take a rest, but the older man grips his fork and scoops up the strays so violently that Gregory looks away.

"Now go," Matt says. "And let everybody get acquainted with you."

In his duffel bag, Gregory still has the two letters, one from Caltech and one from MIT, both of which begin, *We are pleased to tell you*. They were in the mailbox the day he left, and have been in the duffel since he boarded a bus in the Los Angeles Greyhound terminal. He had taken a window seat on the bus so he could watch the landscape empty itself and start over. He watched it turn into straight roads running outward in spokes, evenness running on forever into places nobody could see; into fields that were fans, always opening; and where there were no mountains closing in a valley, no oceans to come to and say, "Well, I guess we're here," as if they had reached the end of the last frontier. He has saved the letters just in case his father finds him. He pictures their meeting to consist solely of his father stopping in the center of the fairground midway, squinting in the dust and glare, and himself wordlessly pulling out the two letters, an actor in slow motion.

Try putting down on paper why you left, someone suggested to him on the bus. An English teacher moving east. It will make you feel better. But he can't. When he thinks of his father, he can barely see him: he is always standing in a darkened room, backlit by the faint light that comes from a hallway lamp. He is slender and pale and looks young for his age, except for the faint purple shadows under his eyes and beneath his fingernails, as if the ink he used for his blueprints has gotten permanently imbedded in his flesh. For years he had come into Gregory's room at night to stand beside the bed, barely breathing while he thought Gregory slept. Gregory, under the covers, kept his eyes closed and imagined what his father was wearing: tweed suit, trench coat, long chestnut-colored shoes with the pattern of tiny holes. He felt his father not breathing and thought, while my father is not breathing, I should not be breathing either.

After a moment, his father would exhale. Then he would whisper an inexplicable phrase. "You are dreaming this, my son," he would

78

say. "There is no one in your room, and never was." He always left suddenly, the cool air, the firm, accountable smell of ink and metal compass going with him.

Gregory lengthened, went long and gangly and tall as his father, though not so pale. He had a rosy skin that seemed always to have a flush beneath it, which a girl named Liz loved. At night he hauled her up through his window and they stared at each other's arms and faces and hair in the faint yellow of the streetlight. They made it a game, touching each other tentatively until they heard the sound of feet coming down the hall. Then Liz ran to the window, Gregory holding her wrists till the last second. She laughed, twisting lightly out of his grip, knowing exactly when to drop to the grass. One night Gregory went so far as to take off his shirt, and lift her blouse over her arms. He was breathless, and could not help tingling with the thought of his father accidentally seeing them. He slowed his motions, letting his fingers get stupid on her bra strap, and when they heard the steps coming down the hall, they could not move apart fast enough. He stood over them, and did not seem to see the girl. She scrambled to the window and out, not wanting to see what a man so calm and cool-skinned might do. Gregory and his father stood face to face, identical in height, and Gregory's father said nothing. He was not wearing a trench coat, but a bathrobe so loose that it might at any moment come undone. He made no effort to cover himself, and seemed to Gregory to be holding his breath as he had all the nights of Gregory's childhood.

"Dad," he said. "Get out of my room. You're dreaming this, because there's no one in my room, and never was."

His father did not answer, only trembled as if he were a fragile vase with a faltering blue light inside. After he left, Gregory waited ten minutes, until he knew he would never catch his breath if he stayed. Outside, the spring air surrounded the house, harsh and soft at once, like a girl twisting out of his grip. He packed his jeans and shirt, and the two letters. Then he gripped the white sill, like Liz, and let himself drop.

After Matt dismisses him from dinner, Gregory does as he is told. He sits on his trailer step so that people can get acquainted with him. He doesn't mind: he's good at being looked at. He's good at holding still and feeling how it is with the people doing the looking. They look at his clothes, his hair, his mouth: waiting to see what he will give away. Meanwhile, he looks slightly to the side and down, to the feet as they pass, to the height of the dust kicked up. A little high means that person is sick to death of newcomers, and wants to tell him so. A little low is timid, with favors to ask. No dust at all isn't what you'd think, isn't obliteration. It's a kind of power: the kind someone gets when he decides he's invisible.

By the time dinner is over and the men have walked by, it's the women's turn. They walk past in twos and threes, each with a different step than she had as she came toward him. Each skirt sways more deliberately from side to side, as if it will swing just so far before heading back the other way. Some walk too carefully, and Gregory closes his eyes to prevent them from tripping on some little twig in front of him.

The last one out is alone: a small, narrow, nervous person with a crop of brown hair she must have cut herself, in a bad mood. She takes long strides that end in abrupt stops, as if she's being yanked in by reins. Gregory takes this as a sign of a certain kind of courage: abrupt, and probably undependable. She is brave now, though. She pushes back her bangs with her small hands, and sits down next to him. She lights a cigarette and offers one to him. He takes it, and lights it from hers, so that she can see he isn't shy.

"So," she says, "what do you think of Nebraska?"

"I'm *from* Nebraska," he says, thinking of the fanning-out roads and fields.

"Is that supposed to be a joke?" she says.

"Not that I know of. Why?"

"Because you're smiling," she says, putting out her cigarette. "I hate it when people smile like they have some secret and you're supposed to guess what it is."

"Don't you have a secret?" Gregory asks her.

She closes her eyes a moment, then stands up to leave.

Gregory is thinking, here's a secret. I am going to close my eyes and pretend that I know you, and that your name is Liz.

Gregory has a system for falling asleep. He pictures the workshop in their garage, and his father's back to him, hunched intent over a project at his drafting table. Gregory starts at one end of the garage and works his way across, recalling the name on each cabinet and drawer, each labeled in a precise, back-slanted hand. *The handwriting of a genius*, Gregory once said, and his mother smiled, her hand to her mouth. Once Gregory has finished counting, and has remembered each name, he waits for his father's daily question.

"In what situation," asks his father, "is it possible for a person to hang on to the live wire of a cable and not be electrocuted?"

Gregory smiles: it takes him no time at all to answer.

"In the situation of not being grounded," he says. "If you are suspended in the air, with nothing metal on you, and you don't touch anything but the hot wire, you're safe."

"Good answer," says his father, "good and quick." Then he frowns. "Of course, we'll keep this theoretical, won't we, son?"

"Theoretical is your father's favorite word," says Gregory's mother, leaving the garage.

If this doesn't work, Gregory pictures his bedroom, not the way it was when he left, but when he was younger. There are pictures on the wall of a dog, a cat, and a rudimentary building, too primitive to show promise. He closes his eyes and holds still, waiting for the door to open, for the smell of ink on paper, of book dust to enter. He smells the ruler and compass, chill metal in the night air. His father is here, two feet from him and no more, and the silence between them is warm, regular, good. His father stands, and he lies, and in silent agreement they each pretend they are not breathing, knowing that one might overwhelm the other. Gregory, lying in his trailer bed, narrows his face back to what it must have been when he was nine or ten, narrowing it until he hears his father exhale.

"You're a good boy," his father says. "You'd never make your old man look bad, would you?"

In the morning it turns out that the brave girl is a trick rider, a bareback artist. She rides an Arabian around the ring, and when the horse rears up, the two of them are one, indistinguishable from one another from up in the light booth or on a catwalk. Sometimes a second horse comes into the ring, and she plants a foot on each, raising her small, muscular arms over her head. She never looks back, never to the side, no matter what position she's in. She sits, or stands, or does a front flip and lands with her feet exactly seven inches apart on the horse's back. All the time she looks in whatever direction is straight ahead for her.

It also turns out that she has a lover, or at least her lover thinks she does. He is a follow-spot operator with dark hair and a laugh too powerful and erratic for the tiny light booth, where he leans in the afternoon over the panels with Matt and Gregory. He is leaning heavily, gazing down into the arena where the girl practices alone, and there is an imbalance to his weight that makes Gregory think he might fall into the ring if the glass walls weren't there to prevent it. He flicks the dimmer switches aimlessly, and Matt's small, compact body twitches slightly. Then the younger man turns from the panel and cocks his head at Gregory.

"You ever worked in an arena this size?" he asks, still looking down into the ring.

"Sure," says Gregory.

"In this line of work," says the man, "there's no such thing as sure. Watch out for yourself."

Then he's gone, out across the upper catwalk to a place Gregory can't see from the booth. The moment he leaves, the little room seems sized right again, and cooler.

Matt is at his best up here. His hands rest on the dimmer switches comfortably: the hands of a professional, loving the surfaces he has made dependable. Squinting across space, he brings up red and brings down blue, crossing fire into ice on the girl below. His feet are planted straight ahead and flat, like the feet of people riding on a jet or a boat, as if straight and flat makes the surface seem more like solid earth. In two days Gregory has not seen Matt on a catwalk. He stays inside the booth, ordering Gregory or someone else out to make repairs. Now a blue burns out high up, near center. Gregory grabs a new bulb and gel.

"I'll go up with you," says Matt. He's behind Gregory, shivering as he puts one foot onto the ladder. "Frank has a little test for newcomers," he says. "Especially the ones that go for Annie."

"Who's Annie?" Gregory asks.

Matt sighs, his face lit to lavender as he gazes down into the ring. "Innocence is bliss," he says.

"I think the phrase is ignorance," corrects Gregory. "I like tests, anyway. You stay here and watch."

"All right," says Matt. "But if anything seems funny at all, jump."

"Jump?"

Matt is grinning now, both feet back inside the booth. "Jump," he says. "You're not acrophobic, too?"

It isn't until Gregory is in the middle of the high catwalk under the burned-out bulb that he sees something shimmering between himself and Annie. If it had been anyone other than Matt who told him, he would not have believed in the net: it is as faint as stars when you stare directly at them. He takes out the old bulb, clamps in a new one, slides the new blue gel across the lightbox. Some cords dangle loose near by, and he pulls a length of duct tape from his belt loop. *Never let a stray cord stay stray,* was his father's line, said with his back furled safely over the drafting table away from Gregory. Here's a problem, a test, his father would say, and Gregory, high above the ring, is waiting, when he glances up and sees Matt waving at him from the booth. He starts to wave back and Matt shakes his head, pointing upward. It's a light tree, unhinged at one end and swinging toward Gregory, the colored gels all flying toward him like a row of bright geese. He can lie down flat and they will miss him, but here is the test. He spreads his arms, feels the air rush above and below, marveling at the searing heat that passes through his arms and belly, belly and arms not knowing there's a net to catch them. Flying, he thinks, this is what it would be like to not be grounded.

Frank and Annie stand beside the net.

"Now I can say it," Annie is whispering, her voice tight and small as a drum. "Now I can say that I hate—"

The gels flutter down over Gregory in the net, red and green and blue. They make a falling curtain, shutting everything out.

Annie is waiting for him at five-thirty, when he reaches his trailer.

"Want to walk?" she asks, pointing toward the north end of the fairgrounds, where Gregory sees a long line of trees that could be a park, or a river, he can't tell.

He doesn't pay attention to the direction she takes him. He concentrates on the swing of her arms, the light, nervous step that is just enough like Liz's. They leave the midway in a hot wind, the dust racing up and down the booth corridor, hurling up cinders and curled leaves and sawdust. They pass the dart booths and the ping-pong-in-the-fishbowl booths, and a ride called Bob's Sleds, where a man named Bob sits listening to an old Buddy Holly tune while counting his ticket rolls for tomorrow's opening. They pass the heavy red and white boxes labeled DANGER/HIGH VOLTAGE, next to the Ferris wheel. It's running now, with nobody on it, and the boxes hum, not knowing. Red and white, they draw the eye:

they are alive and asking for attention the way heights and water do. Gregory and Annie cross the parking lot and enter the grove of trees. She sighs and raises her arms the way she does when she is free and triumphant on a horse. Through the trees Gregory sees the reflections of windows, a square of trimmed lawn, and a redwood deck where a man stands, hands on his hips, looking out.

"He's sick," Annie says. "He could have killed you."

"The net was there," says Gregory. "It was just a test."

She looks at him. "It isn't always," she says, and he isn't sure which she means, the net or the test. The late-afternoon light coming through the trees is weak on her arms; it is not a performer's light. Under it her wrists are fragile, light freckles appear, and her elbows are bony under the rolled-up sleeves of a man's flannel shirt. She looks comfortable and glad to be wearing it, even though it probably comes from a man who frightened her. Gregory runs his finger along its edge, along her forearm to her wrist. She draws her breath in sharply and averts her face from his.

"I know what you're thinking," he says. "You're thinking that if you can't see him, he can't see you. Like that game, Olly, Olly Oxen Free."

Her eyelids shut more tightly, barely letting the tears out.

Gregory doesn't want anything, except not to move. Daylight has passed, has been replaced by the faint blue from a backyard lamp. Blue is the color of new love, he thinks, the color that shines in on forbidden places, backyards, bedrooms, shining in on smooth, small limbs before anything happens. It is movement that makes things go wrong, a false move of an arm or leg, a mouth opening when it is perfect, closed. Branches are smart, he thinks. They finger the air over our heads, splitting it infinite and graceful, without striving, as if to say that if you don't touch earth, there can never be an end to you. It is something he would like to tell his father when they meet again. *Dad*, he would say, *I learned something for both of us*, and hold out his hand as if something, an offering, lay upon it. In the grove, Annie has fallen asleep, and he leans over her, watching the shadows finger her cheek, holding his fingers slightly above her face, sure that if he leans more they will touch the glass of a window, or the fiber of a net. He is leaning slow, suspended, when she opens her eyes.

"Oh God," she says. "Somebody's here."

Gregory knows he is supposed to stand up, but he can't shake himself out of his dream. It is like one of his father's tests: how do you let go of perfection, fast and easy? A girl is tumbling, crying, leaving him again, and he is supposed to rise and answer. The man before him is not wearing a trench coat, his hair is not neat and curled back over his collar, nor does the good smell of ink accompany him. He is wearing a bathrobe and slippers, and beneath its skirt Gregory can see a pale slant of flesh, and hair.

"No," he cries, "No!" And he is suddenly taller than the man. He sees a forehead close to his own, a forehead not broad, not intelligent, but narrow and throbbing in one place with a pulse so small it can be hidden and brought out. "Go away," he cries, and the pulse settles, small and tense and contained. He remembers his mother's hand coming up to her mouth. *Theoretical is his favorite word.*

"You're in the wrong backyard," says the man. "I'll give you till the count of three—"

"Dad," cries Gregory. "Can I wake up now?"

The man cocks his head and smiles. "Well," he says. "What do you think?"

It's a question Gregory can't answer right away. He looks all around, at the branches of the trees, at the ground between them, at the fine dust covering the ground, which if he waits long enough will rise and tell him what lies just beyond words. His turning is like a prayer, and when he finishes, he is alone.

It is already hot, and Gregory's alarm clock, set for seven, has been shut off. The sheets are gritty with small stones and twigs, and someone is knocking on the trailer door: four times and a pause, four times and a pause. It is a broad-daylight knock, the kind that won't acknowledge it's connected to the night before, the kind that forces you to answer in your best day voice, "Yes, I'm awake."

After a few minutes Gregory looks out the small upper window. A man is walking away, already too far to recognize in the early morning glare. On the floor is a note. "Somebody here to see you," it says. All he can think is that his father would not leave a note like that. His father would sign his name, and explain.

It is the first day, and the parking lot is full. The stock-car races have begun, all of them at once, it seems, their engines blurring into one enormous roar that to someone far away might sound comforting, like water, or wind in the branches of a tree. Already the dust is rising and swirling on the midway, and Bob is at his station, helping families into little ice blue sleds, his *Origins of Rock 'n Roll* at full blast. The families are obedient, stepping into the little sleds, and for a moment only the dust moves, and the small Swiss flags over the ride station, and Bob moving among the families like a man among mannikins. He pulls back the lever and the cars jerk forward, the children's and the parents' heads jerking forward with them, while the rest of their bodies stay still. Hair flutters back, like the flags, as the sleds gain speed around the curves.

People move around this country, Gregory thinks, walking down the midway. People he knew will grow up and settle in towns far away, and bring their children to the fair on a Sunday, on a hot August Sunday just like this. He will recognize them first, but wait for them to turn to him and say, *Hey, aren't you the one who left—?* It is on a day like this, when the heat is stifling, making everything hold its breath, that, walking down the midway he will see a tall, slim man in a professorial tweed jacket, stooping to throw a skidball. His aim will be precisely taken, and he will barely miss, then turn to make sure that no one has seen.

With five minutes to go till showtime Gregory climbs the ladder to the light booth and joins Matt at the panel. Matt nods, headphones on, his lips pursed in concentration.

"Was somebody looking for me?" Gregory asks.

Matt shrugs. "Houselights down, reds 4, 5, blues 2 and 8, up. Frank, take Annie on the follow-spot."

Gregory pulls the dimmer switches smoothly as Annie leads the riders into the ring. She's standing up on the Arabian, arms in the air in magenta warmth, the combination of his reds and blues and Frank's powerful spot. She doesn't know or care whose light is on her, Gregory thinks. Her head is high, not looking at anyone, as if at some point, earlier in her life, she had made a deal never to look anywhere but straight ahead.

"I don't believe it," says Matt. "Number four just went out, the whole tree. Frank said they were brand-new bulbs, for God's sake."

"It's okay," says Gregory, already up. "I'll fix them, one at a time, so nobody notices."

"You stay right where you are," Matt answers, wagging his head. "Right after the first show we'll switch off the circuit breaker and let them cool. Then you can go be a hero."

Gregory is digging in the box for replacement bulbs.

"I know what not to touch," he says, and is out of the booth before Matt can say anything else.

Up on the highest catwalk, Gregory marvels at the glare and the heat, at the blues and reds full on his hands; the performers have no idea how hot the lights get. He wonders if his father ever felt something like this in his work, if he ever, when he was young, had the chance to climb this high above a scene. He looks down at the horses and riders spinning around the ring. He can tell Annie because she is first, and because her figure is straighter, more controlled, than the others. She's lying on her back now, looking up, and around and around she goes, bound to the running horse, letting something other than her own motion carry her. That's not something Gregory could do. He wants to wave to her and shout, *Annie catch me, I'm coming down, not bound to anything*. But he knows she doesn't see him, that she is looking at some point between them that he can't see, feeling only the spine of the horse and maybe something else, the spinning of a planet with nothing above or below it. That's her art. The ring is a wide sea and she has learned how to float, how to stay afloat for hours.

Gregory has brought his gloves just in case, but he knows, he knew back in the booth, that this bank of bulbs cannot be too hot. They had all burned out instantly. He peels back the blue gels and the extra bits of duct tape, leaning out slightly from the catwalk.

Matt is on the headphones: "For Pete's sake get off the catwalk," he says. "Use the bracing cable or you'll fry yourself silly."

"Don't worry," says Gregory. "I will if I need to."

The gel is between his teeth now, slightly warm, like the smooth surface of a stone, or a pond on a nice day. He puts in a new bulb but nothing happens.

"Terrific," says Matt. "It's a fuse. Come on back."

"I've got an extra," Gregory answers. "While I'm at it—"

Annie does a front flip and the crowd applauds. She's got her arms flung out again, triumphant, actually smiling at them.

The bracing harness hangs near by. Gregory takes off the headphones and places them on the catwalk. *There can't be anything metal on you*, he thinks. *If you're not grounded, and if you don't touch the neutral wire when you touch the hot, you'll be safe.* He steps into the harness: it swings, goes taut, holds him. Below, Annie is on her back again, going around for the finale. The crowd is on its feet, the faces so small that Gregory can't tell if they're watching her, or if someone who knows where to look has seen the harness and pointed to the boy swinging high over their heads.

Matt looks old from where Gregory is; from above, his face is no longer washed in lavender, but a dark, mottled purple from the mix of blue and red. He is not watching Gregory, but staring down at his light board like a man in church, looking down for something he has lost. Gregory wants to hold him in his mind like that, up high in his little glass booth, struggling to be a good technician when something else is swelling in him, forcing itself to the surface.

Gregory is ready now. He hauls himself along toward the cable where the fuse connection is, but he can't seem to get close enough. It's peculiar: what else is the harness for if not to repair the fuse or wire along this line of cable? Then he sees the problem. The cable hooks nearest him are empty; the cables have been moved over two feet, just far enough so a person in the harness could not reach them. For a moment the name *Frank* occurs to Gregory, then vanishes. Big and dark and erratic, Frank is oddly necessary and incidental, like a messenger in a play who is not important in himself, only for what he bears.

Gregory remembers everything his father taught him now: bits of questions on physics, engineering, house-building, and how to answer a question quickly and accurately. How his father kept things neatly labeled and theoretical, kept everything clear between them in daylight so that no one, not even Gregory, could label his hidden, trembling self. In sorrow and love Gregory pulls himself out of the harness, looking down one more time, but the lights are so brilliant that he cannot tell whether the shimmering beneath him is the net, or a reflection of the glittering human activity below. He squints out across the arena, filled with the perfect, certain sensation of knowledge he has only known in dreams: that his father is in the audience, and watching him.

Below, Annie rides on her back, and her lips, though Gregory cannot see them, are opening and closing in warning. A surge of adrenalin washes through him as he realizes that it is at last his turn to perform for her, and for his father. He lifts one foot out of the harness and reaches for the hot wire, feeling, miraculously, only a small tickle of electricity. Dad, he thinks, it is true, and he grips the hot cable with both hands now, the fuse forgotten. It is true, he thinks, and now it is my turn to ask a question. If you were me, what would you do? Go back to the catwalk, or take the descent; slow, free, and full of possibility?

nominated by Stanley Lindberg

ENTREPRENEURS

fiction by CHRIS SPAIN

from THE QUARTERLY

Harold READS the musts. He is on must number 4, going backward from 25. Must number 4 is you must get started. Harold reads while I row. I interrupt Harold reading the musts and I say to him, "You know what the last thing they said before they vaporated was?"

"I know," says Harold.

Harold was reading the musts when they vaporated. We were out on *My Toot-Toot*, dragging a sea anchor and barracuda bait and listening to Cocoa Beach Countdown radio, this being the number tenth time we had been out on account of all the times they had called it off. We were wrapped in army surplus and leaning back and drinking 7-Eleven coffees. Harold was on must number 1. Must number 1 is you must develop the ability to see the needs and wants of others. This must had had us stumped for months. It still had us stumped when the water started rattling and we cranked our heads back to watch the thing punch a hole through the sky. When it blew, we were what you might call awed.

"Fourth of July," said Harold.

I said, "I don't think that's what it's supposed to do."

Myrtle keeps her finger, what she calls her "too small a tragedy to keep," in a jar. She holds her hand, the still whole one, dangled over the side into the warmth of the Gulf Stream. At her feet is a burlap bag full of unwanted needs and wants, and seawall stones to drag it down. Harold takes a break from reading the musts. What is left to hear is the sound of the oar wood blistering my fingers. I say, "You know what them and Tylenol and a walrus got in common?"

"We know," says Harold.

Our very first thought was honorable. We thought we would motor over there and, if they were still alive, save them. Our very second thought was that with all that machinery dropping out of the sky it would be dangerous to motor over there, and that maybe our very first thought, though honorable, was stupid. Our very third thought was that that thundering shower of tech was a primo example of the needs and wants of others. Stupid or not, we were laying down a wake before the big pieces hit the water.

The twenty-four musts are on the back of *The Start-up Entrepreneur,* a book Harold permanently borrowed from the library on wheels when the librarian was inside the 7-Eleven buying a burrito. On the front of the book it says, "How you can succeed in building your own company into a major enterprise starting from scratch." Harold figured with that information we were halfway to rich already.

Where we are halfway to now is a burial at sea. Harold is reading the musts by flashlight light, while I row by the light of the moon.

"You know why they only sent up one colored, don't ya?" I ask Harold.

"I know," he says.

We got underneath it before the little pieces finished precipitating out of the sky. There was a white cloud still hanging to mark where it had happened. It was feathery like dove dust, what is left on the air when the dove never sees you and you shotgun him point-blank. The little pieces fluttered down on us, and when they hit the water they sounded like belly flop.

Once we cornered must number 1 in our heads, we figured we had must number 2 cold. Must number 2 is you must find a market gap. Our thinking was that the market gap in right-stuff-gone-wrong was about as wide as you could get. We would have a corner on the market of the market gap.

When we found the stain on the water we throttled back to look. We were not prepared for search-and-rescue. We had barracuda poles, a gaffing hook, and a landing net. I hung the net over the side while Harold zigzagged through the ruin of what looked a moon picnic turned loose. It turned out we were floating right on their pantry. The net came back with space food for a week and wet wipes. Harold had a hunger and jumped right on the tubified eggs and was going for seconds when I evoked must number 13 or 14, telling him he was eating our inventory.

While I row, it comes to me that rowing is a strange way to get somewhere, because it puts your back to where you are going. If Columbus had had to row, he probably never would have done it.

"You hear why they're sending the next one up the Fourth of July?" I ask Harold.

"I heard," says Harold.

"You practically invented that one yourself, you co-me-di-an," I tell him.

We about had the boat full of souvenirs when a chopper whomp-whomped down on us. Leaning out the door was a kid with a kid-looking-for-his-lost-dog look on his face. The bladed air on *my* face took me back so hard that I nearly fell in the water.

"I'm having some kind of violent reaction to that Huey," I told Harold.

"We're here to save you!" megaphoned down the kid.

I was puking over the side already.

"Tell him to go away," I said between pukes.

The chopper settled into its hover.

"Fuck off!" yelled Harold, and he went after the chopper with the gaffing hook.

The kid's face went to ununderstanding.

"But a terrible thing has happened!" yelled the kid.

"It is true," I said.

"Are the rest dead?" asked the kid.

"There is no rest," said Harold.

The kid leaned back in the chopper, and then he leaned back out.

"Are you astronauts?" he asked us.

"Entrepreneurs," said Harold.

The kid looked as if he had just found his dog on the highway, made into motor meat.

I take a break from rowing and say to Harold, "You hear what they had for breakfast?"
"I heard," says Harold.

We were headed for Miller Time with our load of bits and pieces when we saw a school of minnows circling on a floating something. It was a finger. A ring finger with a ring on it.
We netted it and wrapped it in a wet wipe.

Must number 7 is you must use the telephone constantly for acquiring all kinds of information. The only phone we had was the pay phone outside our 7-Eleven. Harold, then a believer in all musts, started saving silver.
I asked him. "But who are we going to call?"
"The people with the information," said Harold.

They were waiting for us when we made port. They confiscated everything. We said we were bringing it to them anyway, that we just wanted to help. The Cocoa Beach *Bay Times* ran the story, saying: "Local fishermen help retrieve remains of space heroes." There was a picture of us holding up pieces of bits and pieces—an ambulance had already come to pick up the finger—and they even printed what I said about the fishing, which was that I did not think this terrible tragedy would have an effect on it, that in fact it might make it better, what with all the fish nosing up to see what all the banging was about, and that our boat was available for a scenes-of-the-aftermath charter.

"You hear what they weather-forecasted?" I ask Harold.
"For tonight?" says Harold.
"No," I say. "It's another joke. What they weather-forecasted the morning of?"
"I heard," says Harold.

The next day they declared our water off-limits to us and everybody else. They closed the ocean for twenty miles, which is about nineteen miles farther out than we can convince anybody to go on *My Toot-Toot*. We were seriously shored, our economy shot to hell.

Must number 16 is you must develop tenacity and perseverance to survive days and nights of anxiety.

We were halfway through our first night of anxiety, drinking beers and hand-grenading the empty cans over the side, when we had our collective fourth thought. What we thought was that a wooden boat like *My Toot-Toot*, without the motor, wouldn't show up on their radar screens. What we thought was that we would do some night fishing, junk fishing, casting for the bottom.

Before we got used to being celebrated for saving the only piece of space hero that got saved, they figured out it was no astronaut finger we had fished. It was a finger from a Palm Bay woman. It was Myrtle's, who we didn't know yet. She had come back from work that morning because she wasn't feeling right, and she found her husband doing it with the Twiggy from across the street. Myrtle tried to take her wedding ring off and throw it at them, but her finger was too fat and the ring would not come off. Her husband said to her, "You big ugly thing, can you blame me?"

I say to Harold, "You hear they found that schoolteacher's husband rowing around out here?"
Harold doesn't answer.
"He was rowing around out here just like we are," I say.
Harold still doesn't answer.
"Don't you want to know what he was looking for?" I ask.
"No," says Harold.

In the late afternoons we would wait for the winter dark to come down fast, and then we would unslip *My Toot-Toot* and row her to under where the thing had thundered and stormed itself to pieces. We rigged our poles with speaker magnets that we popped out of Harold's mongo-woofers and dangled them on the deep. It was fishing-booth fishing. We pulled up an ocean full of needs and wants, and a rusty hook with a fish jaw still hanging on.

Harold reads must number 26. Must number 26 we made up. Must number 26 is if musts number 1 through 25 don't work.

Her husband called her Myrtle Bitch, after Myrtle Beach, South Carolina, where they had driven to for their honeymoon. Myrtle tried dish soap, sewing-machine oil, and WD-40 that she found in the garage. But the ring stayed on. She says she felt as if her whole self were being strangled by that ring. She left the house not knowing where she was headed. She ended up at the docks, so weak from no air in her head that she had to lean on a piling for help. Then she heard the same rattling on the water that we were hearing, and she looked up to watch it soar. For those seconds she forgot the heaviness of her body, and she soared also.

Must number 6 is you must start small. We advertised on telephone poles. Our sign said: OWN HISTORY. *If you witnessed this event, you'll need and want a souvenir to remember your memories with. Grand opening tonight!* We set up a tent on the beach.

After our ungrand grand opening, Harold decided there had to be a more elemental must that came before must number 1. Now the first must is must number 0, which is that you must hit someone before they hit you. We learned must number 0 the hard way.

When the thing blew, Myrtle lost all the balance she had left. She had a pain in her chest that she said came from deeper than where earthquakes come from, and she thought she might fault open. Beside her on the dock was a kid skipping school so he could watch the men he wanted to be sky their machine. He had been scaling a little bait fish, but now his jaw was hanging unhinged and his scaling knife was hanging in his hand. Myrtle grabbed his knife, put her ring finger to the wooden piling, put the knife to the ring finger, and good-bye ring and finger.

The day after we heard the news that we weren't heroes anymore for saving the only piece of space hero that got saved, a sheriff came by to tell us that by marine salvage law the ring was ours. He said he would have to give the finger back to Myrtle. We told him to give the ring back to her, too.

Myrtle left a message at the 7-Eleven that she wanted us to come to St. Luke's to see her. We bought a flower. They had her strapped down. The finger, which was hers, and the ring, which by marine law was ours, were in a specimen jar on the nightstand. She thanked us for saving the finger, and then she said she wanted us to throw it back.

"Back where?" we asked.

"If the fish is too small, you throw it back, don't you?" said Myrtle.

We said that was mostly true.

"Just think of it as too small a tragedy to keep," she said. "And throw it back."

We left her leaning hard on her straps so as to smell the flower.

Our grand opening turned out not to be. They called us frauds and said that what we had was nothing but dumpster trash. Then they turned patriot on us, said we were disrespectful, defiling the dead, et cetera, and that this was no joke. I asked them if they had heard the walrus and Tylenol one. Harold asided to me that the mood of America in general and this crowd in particular would make it difficult for them to appreciate the punch line.

I think he was right.

I stop rowing when we are under where it all rained down. Myrtle said she wanted her finger buried with all the rest of the truth. The truth is, we do not know how to do a burial at sea. We drop the seawall stones in the bag full of unwanted needs and wants, Myrtle's finger, too, and let it go.

"What do we say?" says Harold.

"I've never done this," I say.

Myrtle doesn't know, either. Above us, astronaut footprints all over her face, is the moon.

Failed entrepreneurs, Harold and I sat on a driftwood to do our where-did-we-go-wrong thinking. When we finally saw it through our raccooned-by-patriot eyes, we saw it so clear that it knocked us to the sand. What we saw was that we had identified the needs and wants all wrong. What people want is to see other people get blown to shit. What they need is to see what dead looks like. It makes them feel more here, seeing others not here.

We tested our new understanding of needs and wants on the four-way stoplight in front of the 7-Eleven. It didn't take any time at all.

A red Chevy slammed an old Ford pickup, then a Volvo piled on. The local television and both newspapers sent people. But when they discovered that the signal box had been rewired for go-green all the way around, it made the Miami news. The announcers shook their heads and said, Who could be so coldhearted, and how lucky because it could have been a school bus full of children. They did not say it would have made a better story if it had been a school bus full of children.

We went back to St. Luke's to pick up Myrtle's finger. We were throwing everything else back, we figured why not that, too. We couldn't leave her. We asked her if she wanted a career of giving people what they needed, what they wanted. It made perfect sense to Myrtle.

I turn my back on accident, tragedy, mayhem, and disaster, and lean into the oars. We are off to give you what you need and want, what you are looking for.

"You know what the last thing they said before they vaporated was?" I ask Harold.

"I already said I knew," says Harold.

"I mean for real," I say.

"You mean on the recording?" asks Harold.

"After that," I tell him.

"Would you look at this," says Myrtle.

We look at Myrtle.

"That is the last thing which they said," she says.

nominated by Lily Francis

EXORCISING BECKETT

by LAWRENCE SHAINBERG

from THE PARIS REVIEW

I MET BECKETT in 1981, when I sent him, with no introduction, a book I'd written, and to my astonishment, he read the book and replied almost at once. Six weeks later, his note having emboldened me to seek a meeting, our paths crossed in London, and he invited me to sit in on the rehearsals of *Endgame* which he was then conducting with a group of American actors for a Dublin opening in May.

It was a happy time for him. Away from his desk, where his work, he said (I've never heard him say otherwise), was not going well at all, he was exploring a work which, though he'd written it thirty years before, remained among his favorites. The American group, called the San Quentin Theatre Workshop because they had discovered his work—through a visiting production of *Waiting for Godot*—while inmates at San Quentin, was particularly close to his heart, and working in London he was accessible to the close-knit family that collects so often where he or his work appears. Among those who came to watch were Billie Whitelaw, Irene Worth, Nicole Williamson, Alan Schneider, Israel Horowitz, Siobhan O'Casey (Sean's daughter), three writers with Beckett books in progress, two editors who'd published him and one who wanted to, and an impressive collection of madmen and Beckett freaks who had learned of his presence via the grapevine. One lady, in her early twenties, came to ask if Beckett minded that she'd named her dog after him (Beckett: "Don't worry about me. What about the dog?"), and a wild-eyed madman from Scotland brought flowers and gifts for

Beckett and everyone in the cast and a four-page letter entitled "Beckett's Cancer, Part Three," which begged him to accept the gifts as "a sincere token of my deep and long-suffering love for you," while remembering that "I also hold a profound and comprehensive loathing for you, in response to all the terrible corruption and suffering which you have seen fit to inflict upon my entirely innocent personality."

The intimacy and enthusiasm with which Beckett greeted his friends as well as newcomers like myself—acting for all the world as if I'd done him an enormous favor to come—was a great surprise for me, one of many ways in which our meetings would force me to reconsider the conception of him which I had formed during the twenty years I'd been reading and, let's be honest about it, worshiping him. Who would expect the great master of grief and disenchantment to be so expansive, so relaxed in company? Well, as it turned out, almost everyone who knew him. My surprise was founded not in his uncharacteristic behavior but in the erroneous, often bizarre misunderstandings that had gathered about him in my mind. Certainly, if there's one particular legacy that I take from our meetings it is the way in which those misunderstandings were first revealed and then corrected. In effect, Beckett's presence destroyed the Beckett myth for me, replacing it with something at once larger and more ordinary. Even today I haven't entirely understood what this correction meant to me, but it's safe to say that the paradoxical effects of Beckett incarnate—inspiring and disheartening, terrifying, reassuring, and humbling in the extreme—are nowhere at odds with the work that drew me to him in the first place.

The first surprise was the book to which he responded. Because it was journalism—an investigation of the world of neurosurgery—I had been almost embarrassed to send it, believing that he of all people would not be interested in the sort of information I'd collected. No, what I imagined he'd really appreciate was the novel that had led me to neurosurgery, a book to which I had now returned, which dealt with brain damage and presented it with an ambiguity and dark humor that, as I saw it, clearly signaled both his influence and my ambition to go beyond it. As it turned out, I had things exactly backward. For the novel, the first two chapters of which he read in London, he had little enthusiasm, but the nonfiction book continued to interest him. Whenever I saw him, he questioned me about neurosurgery, asking, for example, exactly how close I had stood to the brain while observing surgery, or how much pain a craniotomy entailed, or, one day during lunch at rehearsals: "How is the skull removed?" and "Where do they put the skull bone while they're working inside?" Though I'd often heard it said of him that he read nothing written after 1950, he remembered the names of the patients I'd mentioned and inquired as to their condition, and more than once he expressed his admiration for the surgeons. Later he did confess to me that he read very little, finding what he called "the intake" more and more "excruciating," but I doubt that he ever lost his interest in certain kinds of information, especially those which concerned the human brain. "I have long believed," he'd written me in his first response to my book, "that here in the end is the writer's best chance, gazing into the synaptic chasm."

Seventy-four years old, he was very frail in those days, even more gaunt and wizened than his photos had led me to expect, but neither age nor frailty interfered with his sense of humor. When I asked him how he was doing one morning at the theatre, he replied with a great display of exhaustion and what I took to be a sly sort of gleam in his eye, "No improvement." Another day, with an almost theatrical sigh, "A little wobbly." How can we be surprised that on the subject of his age he was not only unintimidated but challenged, even inspired? Not five minutes into our first conversation he brought us round to the matter: "I always thought old age would be a writer's best chance. Whenever I read the late work of Goethe or W. B. Yeats I had the impertinence to identify with it. Now, my memory's gone, all the old fluency's disappeared. I don't write a single sentence without saying to myself, 'It's a lie!' So I know I was right. It's the best chance I've ever had." Two years later—and older—he explored the same thoughts again in Paris. "It's a paradox, but with old age, the more the possibilities diminish, the better chance you have. With diminished concentration, loss of memory, obscured intelligence—what you, for example, might call 'brain damage'—the more chance there is for saying something closest to what one really is. Even though everything seems inexpressible, there remains the need to express. A child needs to make a sand castle even though it makes no sense. In old age, with only a few grains of sand, one has the greatest possibility." Of course, he knew that this was not a new project for him, only a more extreme version of the one he'd always set himself, what he'd laid out so clearly in his famous line from The Unnamable: " . . . it will be the silence, where I am, I don't know, I'll never know, in the silence you don't know, you must go on, I can't go on, I'll go on." It was always here, in "the clash," as he put it to me once, "between can't and must" that he took his stand. "How is it that a man who is completely blind, completely deaf, must see and hear? It's this impossible paradox which interests me. The unseeable, the unbearable, the inexpressible." Such thoughts of course were as familiar to me as they would be to any attentive reader of Beckett, but it was always amazing to hear how passionately—and innocently—he articulated them. Given the pain in his voice, the furrowed, struggling concentration of his face, it was impossible to believe that he wasn't unearthing these thoughts for the first time. Absurd as it sounds, they seemed less familiar to him than to me. And it was no small shock to realize this. To encounter, I mean, the author of some of the greatest work in our language, and find him, at seventy-four, discovering his vision in your presence. His excitement alone was riveting, but for me the greatest shock was to see how intensely he continued to work on the issues that had preoccupied him all his life. So much so that it didn't matter where he was or who he was with, whether he was literally "at work" or in a situation that begged for small talk. I don't think I ever had a conversation with him in which I wasn't, at some point, struck by an almost naive realization of his sincerity, as if reminding myself that he was not playing the role one expected him to play, but simply pursuing the questions most important to him. Is it possible that no one surprises us more than someone who is (especially when our expectations have been hyperbolic) exactly what we expect? It was as if a voice in me said, "My God, he's serious!" or, "So he's meant it all along!" And this is where my misunderstandings became somewhat embarrassing. Why on earth should he have surprised me? What did it say of my own sense of writing and reading or the culture from which I'd come that integrity in a writer—for this was after all the simple fact that he was demonstrating—should have struck me as so extraordinary?

Something else he said that first night in London was familiar to me from one of his published interviews, but he said this too as if he'd just come upon it, and hearing it now, I felt that I understood, for the first time, that aspect of his work which interested me the most. I'm speaking of its intimacy and immediacy, the uncanny sense that he's writing not only in a literary but an existential present tense, or more precisely, as John Pilling calls it in his book

Samuel Beckett, an imperfect tense. The present tense of course is no rare phenomenon in modern, or for that matter, classical fiction, but unlike most writers who write *in* the present, Beckett writes *from* the present and remains constantly vulnerable to it. It is a difference of which he is acutely aware, one which distinguishes him even from a writer he admires as much as he does Kafka. As he said in a 1961 interview, "Kafka's form is classic, it goes on like a steamroller, almost serene. It seems to be threatened all the time, but the consternation is in the form. In my work there is consternation behind the form, not in the form." It is for this reason that Beckett himself is present in his work to a degree that, as I see it, no other writer managed before him. In most of his published conversations, especially when he was younger and not (as later) embarrassed to speak didactically, he takes the position that such exposure is central to the work that he considers interesting. "If anything new and exciting is going on today, it is the attempt to let Being into art." As he began to evolve a means by which to accommodate such belief, he made us realize not only the degree to which Being had been kept out of art but *why* it had been kept out, how such exclusion is, even now, the *raison d'être* of most art, and how the game changes, the stakes rising exponentially, once we let it in. Invaded by real time, narrative time acquires an energy and a fragility and, not incidentally, a truth which undermines whatever complacency or passivity the reader—not to mention the writer—has brought to the work, the assumption that enduring forms are to be offered, that certain propositions will rise above the flux, that "pain-killers," which Hamm seeks in vain throughout *Endgame,* will be provided. In effect, the narrative illusion is no longer safe from the narrator's reality. "Being," as he said once, "is constantly putting form in danger," and the essence of his work is its willingness to risk such danger. Listen to the danger he risks in this sentence from *Molloy:* "A and C I never saw again. But perhaps I shall see them again. But shall I be able to recognize them? And am I sure I never saw them again?"

The untrustworthy narrator, of course, had preceded Beckett by at least a couple of centuries, but his "imperfect" tense deprives Molloy of the great conceit that most authors have traditionally granted their narrators—a consistent, dependable memory. In effect, a brain that is neither damaged, in that it doesn't suffer from amnesia, nor normal, in that it is consistent, confident of the information it contains, and immune to the assaults that time and environment mount on its continuities. But Beckett's books are not *about* uncertainty any more than they're *about* consternation. Like their author, like the Being which has invaded them, they are themselves uncertain, not only in their conclusions but their point of view. Form is offered, because as he has so often remarked, that is an obligation before which one is helpless, but any pretense that it will endure is constantly shown to be just that, pretense and nothing more. A game the author can no longer play and doesn't dare relinquish. "I know of no form," he said, "that does not violate the nature of Being in the most unbearable manner." Simply stated, what he brought to narrative fiction and drama was a level of reality that dwarfed all others that had preceded it. And because the act of writing—i.e., his own level of reality, at the moment of composition—is never outside his frame of reference, he exposes himself to the reader as no writer has before him. When Molloy changes his mind it's because Beckett has changed his mind as well, when the narrative is inconsistent it's not an esthetic trick but an accurate reflection of the mind from which that narrative springs. Finally, what Molloy doesn't know Beckett doesn't know either. And this is why, though they speak of Joyce or Proust or other masters in terms of genius, so many writers will speak of Beckett in terms of courage. One almost has to be a writer to know what courage it takes to stand so naked before one's reader or, more important, before oneself, to relinquish the protection offered by separation from the narrative, the security and order which, in all likelihood, were what drew one to writing in the first place.

That evening, speaking of *Molloy* and the work that followed it, he told me that, returning to Dublin after the war, he'd found that his mother had contracted Parkinson's Disease. "Her face was a mask, completely unrecognizable. Looking at her, I had a sudden realization that all the work I'd done before was on the wrong track. I guess you'd have to call it a revelation. Strong word, I know, but so it was. I simply understood that there was no sense adding to the store of information, gathering knowledge. The whole attempt at knowledge, it seemed to me, had come to nothing. It was all haywire. What I had to do was investigate not-knowing, not-perceiving, the whole world of incompleteness." In the wake of this insight, writing in

French ("Perhaps because French was not my mother tongue, because I had no facility in it, no spontaneity") while still in his mother's house, he had begun *Molloy* (the first line of which is "I am in my mother's room"), thus commencing what was to be the most prolific period of his life. Within the first three paragraphs of his chronicle, Molloy says "I don't know" six times, "perhaps" and "I've forgotten" twice, and "I don't understand" once. He doesn't know how he came to be in his mother's room, and he doesn't know how to write anymore, and he doesn't know why he writes when he manages to do so, and he doesn't know whether his mother was dead when he came to her room or died later, and he doesn't know whether or not he has a son. In other words, he is not an awful lot different from any other writer in the anxiety of composition, considering the alternative roads offered up by his imagination, trying to discern a theme among the chaos of messages offered by his brain, testing his language to see what sort of relief it can offer. Thus, Molloy and his creator are joined from the first, and the latter—unlike most of his colleagues, who have been taught, even if they're writing about their own ignorance and uncertainty, that the strength of their work consists in their ability to say the opposite—is saying "I don't know" with every word he utters. The whole of the narrative is therefore time-dependent, neurologically and psychologically suspect and contingent on the movement of the narrator's mind. And since knowledge, by definition, requires a subject and an object, a knower and a known, two points separated on the temporal continuum, Beckett's "I don't know" has short-circuited the fundamental dualism upon which all narrative, and for that matter, all language, has before him been constructed. If the two points cannot be separated on the continuum, what is left? No time, only the present tense. And if you must speak at this instant, using words which are by definition object-dependent, how do you do so? Finally, what is left to know if knowledge itself has been, at its very root, discredited? Without an object, what will words describe or subjugate? If subject and object are joined, how can there be hope or memory or order? What is hoped for, what is remembered, what is ordered? What is Self if knower and known are not separated by self-consciousness?

Those are the questions that Beckett has dealt with throughout his life. And before we call them esoteric or obtuse, esthetic, philosophical or literary, we'd do well to remember that they're not much different from the questions many of us consider, consciously or not, in the course of an ordinary unhysterical day, the questions which, before Molloy and his successors, had been excluded, at least on the surface, from most of the books we read. As Beckett wrote once to Alan Schneider, "The confusion is not my invention . . . It is all around us and our only chance is to let it in. The only chance of renovation is to open our eyes and see the mess . . . There will be new form, and . . . this form will be of such a type that it admits the chaos and does not try to say that it is really something else."

At the time of his visit with his mother, Beckett was thirty-nine years old, which is to say the same age as Krapp, who deals with a similar revelation in his tape-recorded journals and ends (this knowledge, after all, being no more durable than any other) by rejecting it: "What a fool I was to take that for a vision!" That evening, however, as we sat in his hotel room, there was no rejection in Beckett's mind. In the next three years, he told me, he wrote *Molloy, Malone Dies, The Unnamable, Stories and Texts for Nothing,* and—in three months, with almost no revision of the first draft—*Waiting for Godot.* The last, he added, was "pure recreation." The novels, especially *The Unnamable,* had taken him to a point where there were no limits, and *Godot* was a conscious attempt to reestablish them. "I wanted walls I could touch, rules I had to follow." I asked if his revelation—the understanding, as he'd put it, that all his previous work had been a lie—had depressed him. "No, I was very excited! There was no effort in the writing. I worked all day and went out to the cafes at night."

He was visibly excited by the memory, but it wasn't long before his mood shifted, and his excitement gave way to sadness and nostalgia. The contrast between the days he had remembered and the difficulty he was having now—"racking my brains," as he put it, "to see if I can go a little farther"—was all too evident. Sighing loudly, he put his long fingers over his eyes, then shook his head. "If only it could be like that again."

So this is the other side of his equation, one which I, like many of his admirers, have a tendency to forget. The enthusiasm he had but moments before expressed for his diminishments did not protect him from the suffering those diminishments had caused. Let us remember that this is a man who once called writing "disimproving the silence." Why should he miss such futile work when it deserts him? So easy, it is, to become infatuated with the way he embraces his ignorance and absurdity, so hard to remember that when he does so he isn't posturing or for that matter "writing," that what keeps his comedy alive is the pain and despair from which it is won. The sincerity of writers who work with pain and impotence is always threatened by the vitality the work itself engenders, but Beckett has never succumbed to either side of this paradox. He has never, that is to say, put his work ahead of his experience. Unlike so many of us, who found in the Beckett vision—"Nothing is funnier than unhappiness," says Nell in *Endgame*—a comic esthetic which had us, a whole generation of writers, I think, collecting images of absurdity as if mining precious ore, he has gazed with no pleasure whatsoever at the endless parade of light and dark. For all the bleakness of *Endgame*, it remains his belief, as one of the actors who did the play in Germany recalls, that "Hamm says no to nothingness." Exploit absurdity though he does, there is no sign, in his work or his conversation, that he finds life less absurd for having done so. Though he has often said that his real work began when he "gave up hope for meaning," he hates hopelessness and longs for meaning as much as anyone who has never read *Molloy* or seen *Endgame*.

One of our less happy exchanges occurred because of my tendency to forget this. In other words, my tendency to underestimate his integrity. This was three years later, on a cold, rainy morning in Paris, when he was talking, yet again, about the difficulties he was having in his work. "The fact is, I don't know what I'm doing. I can't even bring myself to open the exercise book. My hand goes out to it, then draws back as if on its own." As I say, he often spoke like this, sounding less like a man who'd been writing for sixty years than one who'd just begun, but he was unusually depressed that morning, and the more he talked, the more depressed I became myself. No question about it, one had to have a powerful equanimity that his grief might leave it intact. When he was inside his suffering, the force of it spreading out from him could feel like a tidal wave. The more I listened to him that morning, the more it occurred to me that he sounded exactly like Molloy. Who else but Molloy could speak with such authority about paralysis and bewilderment, in other words, a condition absolutely antithetical to authority itself? At first I kept such thoughts to myself, but finally, unable to resist, I passed them along to him, adding excitedly that, if I were forced to choose my favorite of all Beckett lines, it would be Molloy's: "If there's one question I dread, to which I've never been able to invent a satisfactory reply, it's the question, 'What am I doing?' " So complete was my excitement that for a moment I expected him to share it. Why not? It seemed to me that I'd come upon the perfect antidote to his despair in words of his own invention. It took but a single glance from him—the only anger I ever saw in his eyes—to show me how naive I'd been, how silly to think that Molloy's point of view would offer him the giddy freedom it had so often offered me. "Yes," he muttered, "that's my line, isn't it?" Not for Beckett the pleasures of Beckett. As Henry James once said in a somewhat different context: "My job is to write those little things, not read them."

One of the people who hung around rehearsals was a puppeteer who cast his puppets in Beckett plays. At a cast party one night he gave a performance of *Act Without Words* which demonstrated, with particular force, the consistency of Beckett's paradox and the relentlessness with which he maintains it. For those who aren't familiar with it, *Act Without Words* is a silent, almost Keatonesque litany about the futility of hope. A man sits beside a barren tree in what seems to be a desert, a blistering sun overhead. Suddenly, offstage, a whistle is heard and a glass of water descends, but when the man reaches for it, it rises until it's just out of reach. He strains for it, but it rises to elude him once again. Finally he gives up and resumes his position beneath the tree. Almost at once the whistle sounds again, and a stool descends to rekindle his hope. In a flurry of excitement, he mounts, stretches, grasps, and watches the water rise beyond his reach again. A succession of whistles and offerings follow, each arousing his hope and dashing it until at last he ceases to respond. The whistle continues to sound but he gives no sign of hearing it. Like so much Beckett, it's the bleakest possible vision rendered in comedy nearly slapstick, and that evening, with the author and a number of children in the audience and an ingenious three-foot-tall puppet in the lead, it had us all, children included, laughing as if Keaton himself were performing it. When the performance ended, Beckett congratulated the puppeteer and his wife, who had assisted him, offering—with his usual diffidence and politeness—but a single criticism. "The whistle isn't shrill enough."

As it happened, the puppeteer's wife was a Buddhist, a follower of the path to which Beckett himself paid homage in his early book on Proust, when he wrote, "the wisdom of all the sages, from

Brahma to Leopardi . . . consists not in the satisfaction but the ablation of desire." As a devotee and a Beckett admirer, this woman was understandably anxious to confirm what she, like many people, took to be his sympathies with her religion. In fact, not a few critical opinions had been mustered, over the years, concerning his debt to Buddhism, Taoism, Zen, the Noh theatre, all of it received—as it was now received from the puppeteer's wife—with curiosity and appreciation and absolute denial by the man it presumed to explain. "I know nothing about Buddhism," he said. "If it's present in the play, it is unbeknownst to me." Once this had been asserted, however, there remained the possibility of unconscious predilection, innate Buddhism, so to speak, so the woman had another question, which had stirred in her mind, she said, since the first time she'd seen the play. "When all is said and done, isn't this man, having given up hope, finally liberated?" Beckett looked at her with a pained expression. He'd had his share of drink that night, but not enough to make him forget his vision or push him beyond his profound distaste for hurting anyone's feelings. "Oh, no," he said quietly. "He's *finished*."

I don't want to dwell on it, but I had a personal stake in this exchange. For years I'd been studying Zen and its particular form of sitting meditation, and I'd always been struck by the parallels between the practice and Beckett's work. In fact, to me, as to the woman who questioned him that evening, it seemed quite impossible that he didn't have some explicit knowledge, perhaps even direct experience, of Zen, and I had asked him about it that very first night at his hotel. He answered me as he answered her: he knew nothing of Zen at all. Of course, he said, he'd heard Zen stories and loved them for their "concreteness," but other than that he was ignorant on the subject. Ignorant, but not uninterested. "What do you do in such places?" he asked. I told him that mostly we looked at the wall. "Oh," he said, "you don't have to know anything about Zen to do that. I've been doing it for fifty years." (When Hamm asks Clov what he does in his kitchen, Clov replies: "I look at the wall." "The wall!" snaps Hamm. "And what do you see on your wall? . . . naked bodies?" Replies Clov, "I see my light dying.") For all his experience with wall-gazing, however, Beckett found it extraordinary that people would seek it out of their own free will. Why, he asked, did people do it? Were they seeking tranquillity? Solutions? And finally, as with neurosurgery: "Does it hurt?" I answered with growing discomfort. Even though I remained convinced that the concerns of his work were identical with those of Zen, there was something embarrassing about discussing it with him, bringing self-consciousness to bear, I mean, where its absence was the point. This is not the place for a discussion of Zen, but since it deals, as Beckett does, with the separation of subject and object ("No direct contact is possible between subject and object," he wrote in his book on Proust, "because they are automatically separated by the subject's consciousness of perception . . . "), the problems of Self, of Being and Non-being, of consciousness and perception, all the means by which one is distanced or removed from the present tense, it finds in Beckett's work a mirror as perfect as any in its own literature or scripture.

This in itself is no great revelation. It's not terribly difficult to find Zen in almost any great work of art. The particular problem, however, what made my questions seem—to me at least—especially absurd, is that such points—like many where Beckett is concerned—lose more than they gain in the course of articulation. To point out the Zen in Beckett is to make him seem didactic or, even worse, therapeutic, and nothing could betray his vision more. For that matter, the converse is also true. Remarking the Beckett in Zen betrays Zen to the same extent and for the same reasons. It is there that their true commonality lies, their mutual devotion to the immediate and the concrete, the Truth which becomes less True if made an object of description, *the Being which form excludes*. As Beckett put it once, responding to one of the endless interpretations his work has inspired, "My work is a matter of fundamental sounds. Hamm as stated, Clov as stated . . . That's all I can manage, more than I could. If people get headaches among the overtones, they'll have to furnish their own aspirin."

So I did finally give up the questions, and though he always asked me about Zen when we met—"Are you still looking at the wall?"—I don't think he held it against me. His last word on the matter came by mail, and maybe it was the best. In a fit of despair I had written him once about what seemed to me an absolute, insoluble conflict between meditation and writing. "What is it about looking at the wall that makes the writing seem obsolete?" Two weeks later, when I'd almost forgotten my question, I received this reply, which I quote in its entirety:

Dear Larry, When I start looking at walls, I begin to see the writing. From which even my own is a relief.

As ever,

Sam

Rehearsals lasted three weeks and took place in a cavernous building, once used by the BBC, called the Riverside Studios. Since it was located in a section of London with which I was not familiar, Beckett invited me that first morning to meet him at his hotel and ride out in the taxi he shared with his cast. Only three of his actors were present that day—Rick Cluchey, Bud Thorpe, and Alan Mandell, (Hamm and Clov and Nagg respectively)—the fourth, Nell, being Cluchey's wife, Teresita, who was home with their son, Louis Beckett Cluchey, and would come to the theatre in the afternoon. The group had an interesting history, and it owed Beckett a lot more than this production, for which he was taking no pay or royalties. Its origins dated to 1957 when Cluchey, serving a life sentence for kidnapping and robbery at San Quentin, had seen a visiting production of *Waiting for Godot* and found in it an inspiration that had completely transformed his life. Though he'd never been in a theatre—"not even," he said, "to rob one"—he saw to the heart of a play which at the time was baffling more sophisticated audiences. "Who knew more about waiting than people like us?" Within a month of this performance, Cluchey and several other inmates had organized a drama group which developed a Beckett cycle— *Endgame, Waiting for Godot,* and *Krapp's Last Tape*—that they continued, in Europe and the United States, after their parole. Though Cluchey was the only survivor of that original workshop, the present production traced its roots to those days at San Quentin and the support which Beckett had offered the group when word of their work had reached him. Another irony was that Mandell, who was playing Nagg in this production, had appeared with the San Francisco Actor's Workshop in the original production at San Quentin. By now Beckett seemed to regard Rick and Teri and their son, his namesake, as part of his family, and the current production was as much a gift to them as a matter of personal or professional necessity. Not that this was uncharacteristic. In those days much of his work was being done as a gift to specific people. He'd written *A Piece of Monologue* for David Warrilow, and in the next few years he'd write

110

Rockaby for Billie Whitelaw and *Ohio Impromptu* for S. E. Gontarski, a professor at Georgia Tech, who was editor of the *Journal of Beckett Studies*. When I met him later in Paris he was struggling to write a promised piece for Cluchey at a time when he had, he said, no interest in work at all. In my opinion, this was not merely because he took no promise lightly or because at this point in his life he valued especially this sort of impetus, though both of course were true, but because the old demarcations, between the work and the life, writing and speaking, solitude and social discourse, were no longer available to him. If his ordinary social exchanges were less intense or single-minded than his work it was certainly not apparent to me. I never received a note from him that didn't fit on a 3 x 5 index card, but (as the above-mentioned note on Zen illustrates) there wasn't one, however lighthearted, that wasn't clearly Beckett writing. Obviously, this was not because of any particular intimacy between us, but because, private though he was, and fiercely self-protective, he seemed to approach every chance as if it might be his last. You only had to watch his face when he talked—or wait out one of those two or three minute silences while he pondered a question you'd asked—to know that language was much too costly and precarious for him to use mindlessly or as a means of filling gaps

Wearing a maroon polo sweater, grey flannel pants, a navy blue jacket, no socks, and brown suede sneaker-like shoes, he was dressed, as Cluchey told me later, much the same as he'd been every time they'd met for the past fifteen years. As the taxi edged through London's morning rush hour, he lit up one of the cheroots he smoked and observed to no one in particular that he was still unhappy with the wheelchair they'd found for Hamm to use in this production. Amazing how often his speech echoed his work. "We need a proper wheelchair!" Hamm cries. "With big wheels. Bicycle wheels!" One evening, when I asked him if he was tired, his answer—theatrically delivered—was a quote from Clov: " 'Yes, tired of all our goings on.' " And a few days later, when a transit strike brought London to a standstill, and one of the actors suggested that rehearsals might not go on, he lifted a finger in the air and announced with obvious self-mockery, "Ah, but we must go on!" I'm not sure what sort of wheelchair he wanted but several were tried in the next few days until one was found that he accepted. He was also unhappy with the percussion theme he was trying to establish, two pairs of knocks or scrapes which recur throughout the play—when

Nagg, for example, knocks on Nell's ashcan to rouse her, when Hamm taps the wall to assure himself of its solidity, or when Clov climbs the two steps of his ladder with four specific scrapes of his slippers. For Beckett, these sounds were a primary musical motif, a fundamental continuity. It was crucial that they echo each other. "Alan," he said, "first thing this morning, I want to rehearse your knock." Most discussions I was to hear about the play were like this, dealing in sound or props or other tangibles, with little or no mention of motivation, and none at all of meaning. Very seldom did anyone question him on intellectual or psychological ground, and when they did, he usually brought the conversation back to the concrete, the specific. When I asked him once about the significance of the ashcans which Nagg and Nell inhabit, he said, "It was the easiest way to get them on and off stage." And when Mandell inquired, that morning in the taxi, about the meaning of the four names in the play—four names which have been subject to all sorts of critical speculation, Beckett explained that Nagg and Clov were from "noggle" and "clou," the German and French for nail, Nell from the English "nail" and Hamm from the English "hammer." Thus, the percussion motif again: a hammer and three nails. Cluchey remembered that when Beckett directed him in Germany in *Krapp's Last Tape* a similar music had been developed around the words "Ah well," which recur four times in the play, and with the sound of Krapp's slippers scraping across the stage. "Sam was obsessed with the sound of the slippers. First we tried sandpapering the soles, then layering them with pieces of metal, then brand new solid leather soles. Finally, still not satisfied, he appeared one day with his own slippers. 'I've been wearing these for twenty years,' he said. 'If they don't do it, nothing will.' " More and more, as rehearsals went on, it would become apparent that music—"The highest art form," he said to me once. "It's never condemned to explicitness"— was his principal referent. His directions to actors were frequently couched in musical terms. "More emphasis there . . . it's a crescendo," or, "The more speed we get here, the more value we'll find in the pause." When Hamm directs Clov to check on Nagg in his garbage can—"Go and see did he hear me. Both times."—Beckett said, "Don't play that line realistically. There's music there, you know." As Billie Whitelaw has noted, his hands rose and fell and swept from side to side, forming arcs like a conductor's as he watched his actors and shaped the rhythm of their lines. You could see his lips move, his jaws expanding and contracting, as he mouthed the words they spoke. Finally, his direction, like his texts, seemed a process of reduction, stripping away, reaching for "fundamental sound," transcending meaning, escaping the literary and the conceptual in order to establish a concrete immediate reality, beyond the known, beyond the idea, which the audience would be forced to experience directly, without mediation of intellect.

What Beckett said once of Joyce—"his work is not about something. It is something"—was certainly true of this production. The problem, of course, what Beckett's work can neither escape nor forget, is that words are never pure in their concreteness, never free of their referents. To quote Marcel Duchamp, himself a great friend and chess partner of Beckett's, "Everything that man has handled has a tendency to secrete meaning." And such secretion, because he is too honest to deny it, is the other side of Beckett's equation, the counterweight to his music that keeps his work not only meaningful, but (maniacally) inconclusive and symmetrical, its grief and rage always balanced with its comedy, its yearning for expression constantly humbled by its conviction that the Truth can only be betrayed by language. Rest assured that no Beckett character stands on a rug that cannot be pulled out from under him. When Didi seeks solace after Godot has disappointed them again—"We are not saints, but at least we have kept our appointment. How many people can say as much?"—Vladimir wastes no time in restoring him to his futility: "Billions."

But more than anyone else it is Hamm who gets to the heart of the matter, when he cries out to Clov in a fit of dismay, "Clov! We're not beginning to . . . to . . . mean something?"

"Mean something!" Clov cries. "You and I, mean something. Ah that's a good one!"

"I wonder. If a rational being came back to earth, wouldn't he be liable to get ideas into his head if he observed us long enough? 'Ah good, now, I see what it is, yes, now I understand what they're at!' And without going so far as that, we ourselves . . . we ourselves . . . at certain moments . . . to think perhaps it won't all have been for nothing!"

As promised, Nagg's knock was the first order of business after we reached the theatre. This is the point in the play where Nagg has made his second appearance, head rising above the rim of the ash-can with a biscuit in his mouth, while Hamm and Clov—indulging in one of their habitual fencing matches—are discussing their garden ("Did your seeds come up?" "No." "Did you scratch the ground to see if they have sprouted?" "They haven't sprouted." "Perhaps it's too early." "If they were going to sprout they would have sprouted. They'll never sprout!"). A moment later, Clov having made an exit, and Hamm drifted off into a reverie, Nagg leans over to rouse Nell, tapping four times—two pairs—on the lid of her bin. Beckett demonstrated the sound he wanted, using his bony knuckle on the lid, and after Mandell had tried it six or seven times—not "Tap, tap, tap, tap," or "Tap . . . tap . . . tap . . . tap," but "tap, tap . . . tap, tap"—appeared to be satisfied. "Let's work from here," he said. Since Teri had not arrived, he climbed into the can himself and took Nells' part, curling his bony fingers over the edge of the can, edging his head above the rim, and asking, in a shaky falsetto that captured Nell better than anyone I'd ever heard in the part: "What is it, my pet? Time for love?"

As they worked through the scene, I got my first hint of the way in which this *Endgame* would differ from others I'd seen. So much so that, despite the fact that I'd seen six or seven different productions of the play, I would soon be convinced that I'd never seen it before. Certainly, though I'd always thought *Endgame* my favorite play, I realized that I had never really understood it or appreciated the maniacal logic with which it pursues its ambiguities. Here, as elsewhere, Beckett pressed for speed and close to flat enunciation. His principal goal, which he never realized, was to compress the play so that it ran in less than ninety minutes. After the above line, the next three were bracketed for speed, then a carefully measured pause established before the next section—three more lines—began. "Kiss me," Nagg begs. "We can't," says Nell. "Try," says Nagg. And then, in another pause, they crane their necks in vain to reach each other from their respective garbage cans. The next section was but a single line in length (Nell: "Why this farce, day after day?"), the next four, the next seven, and so on. Each was a measure, clearly defined, like a jazz riff, subordinated to the rhythm of the whole. Gesture was treated like sound, another form of punctuation. Beckett was absolutely specific about its shape—the manner in which, for example, Nagg and Nell's fingers curled above the rim of their cans—and where it occurred in the text. "Keep these gestures small," he said to Cluchey, when they reached a later monologue. "Save the big one for 'All that loveliness!' " He wanted

114

the dialogue crisp and precise but not too realistic. It seemed to me he yearned to stylize the play as much as possible, underline its theatricality, so that the actors, as in most of his plays, would be seen as clearly acting, clearly playing the roles they're doomed to play forever. The text, of course, supports such artifice, the actors often addressing each other in language which reminds us that they're on stage. "That's an aside, fool," says Hamm to Clov. "Have you never heard an aside before?" Or Clov, after his last soliloquy, pausing at the edge of the stage: "This is what they call . . . making an exit." Despite this, Beckett wanted theatrical flourish kept to a minimum. It seemed to me that he stiffened the movement, carving it like a sculptor, stripping it of anything superfluous or superficial. "Less color please," he said to Alan while they were doing Nagg and Nell together, "if we keep it flat, they'll get it better." And later, to Thorpe: "Bud, you don't have to move so much. Only the upper torso. Don't worry, They'll get it. Remember: you don't even want to be out here. You'd rather be alone, in your kitchen."

Though the play was thirty years old for him, and he believed that his memory had deteriorated, his memory of the script was flawless and his alertness to its detail unwavering. "That's not 'upon.' It's 'on.'" He corrected "one week" with "a week," "crawlin'" with "crawling." When Cluchey said to Thorpe, "Cover me with a sheet," Beckett snapped: "*The* sheet, Rick, *the* sheet." And when Clov delivered the line, "There are no more navigators," he corrected, "There's a pause before navigators." He made changes as they went along—"On 'Good God' let's leave out the 'good'"—sometimes cutting whole sections, but had no interest in publishing a revised version of the play. For all the fact that he was "wobbly," he seemed stronger than anyone else on the set, rarely sitting while he worked and never losing his concentration. As so many actors and actresses have noted, he delivered his own lines better than anyone else, and this was his principal mode of direction. When dealing with certain particular lines, he often turned away from the cast and stood at the edge of the stage, facing the wall, working out gestures in pantomime. For those of us who were watching rehearsals, it was no small thing to see him go off like this and then hear him, when he'd got what he wanted, deliver his own lines in his mellifluous Irish pronunciation, his voice, for all its softness, projecting with force to the seats at the back of the theatre:

115

" 'They said to me, That's love, yes, yes, not a doubt, now you see how easy it is. They said to me, That's friendship, yes, yes, no question, you've found it. They said to me, Here's the place, stop, raise your head and look at all that beauty. That order! They said to me, Come now, you're not a brute beast, think upon these things and you'll see how all becomes clear. And simple! They said to me, What skilled attention they get, all these dying of their wounds.' "

To say the least, such moments produced an uncanny resonance. Unself-conscious, perfectly in character, one felt that he was not only reading the lines but writing them, discovering them now as he'd discovered them thirty years before. That we, as audience, had somehow become his first witness, present at the birth of his articulations. If his own present tense—the act of writing—had always been his subject, what could be more natural or inevitable than showing us this, the thoughts and meaning "secreted" and rejected, the words giving form, the form dissolving in the silence that ensued. For that was the message one finally took from such recitations, the elusiveness of the meanings he had established, the sense of the play as aging with him, unable to arrest the flow of time and absolutely resolved against pretending otherwise. Why should Hamm and Clov be spared the awareness of Molloy: "It is in the tranquility of decomposition that I remember the long confused emotion which was my life."

Perhaps it was for this reason, that he was never far removed from what he'd written, that if an actor inquired about a line, his answers could seem almost naive. When Cluchey asked him why Hamm, after begging Clov to give him his stuffed dog, throws it to the ground, Beckett explained. "He doesn't like the feel of it." And when he was asked for help in delivering the line "I'll tell you the combination of the larder if you promise to finish me," he advised, "Just think, you'll tell him the combination if he'll promise to kill you." Despite—or because of—such responses, all four members of the cast would later describe the experience of his direction in language that was often explicitly spiritual. "What he offered me," said Cluchey, "was a standard of absolute authority. He gave my life a spiritual quotient." And Thorpe: "When we rehearsed, the concentration was so deep that I lost all sense of myself. I felt completely

116

empty, like a skeleton, the words coming through me without thought of the script. I'm not a religious person, but it seemed a religious experience to me. Why? Maybe because it was order carried to its ultimate possibility. If you lost your concentration, veered off track for any reason, it was as if you'd sinned." Extreme though such descriptions are, I doubt that anyone who watched these rehearsals would find in them the least trace of exaggeration. More than intense, the atmosphere was almost unbearably internalized, self-contained to the point of circularity. In part, obviously, this was because we were watching an author work on his own text. In addition to this, however, the text itself—because *Endgame* is finally nothing but theatre, repetition, a series of ritualized games that the actors are doomed to play forever—was precisely about the work that we were watching. When Clov asks Hamm. "What keeps me here?" Hamm replies, "The dialogue." Or earlier, when Hamm is asking him about his father, "You've asked me these questions millions of times." Says Hamm, "I love the old questions . . . ah, the old questions, the old answers, there's nothing like them!" If the play is finally about nothing but itself, the opportunity to see it repeated, again and again for two weeks, offered a chance to see Beckett's intention realized on a scale at once profound and literal, charged with energy but at the same time boring, deadening, infuriating. (A fact of which Beckett was hardly unaware. While they were working on the line, "This is not much fun," he advised Cluchey, "I think it would be dangerous to have any pause after that line. We don't want to give people time to agree with you.") To use his own percussion metaphor, watching these rehearsals was to offer one's head up for *Endgame's* cadence to be hammered into it. Finally, after two weeks of rehearsal, the play became musical to a hypnotic extent, less a theatrical than a meditative experience in that one could not ascribe to it any meaning or intention beyond its own concrete and immediate reality. In effect, the more one saw of it, the less it contained. To this day the lines appear in my mind without reason, like dreams or memory-traces, but the play itself, when I saw it in Dublin, seemed an anti-climax, the goal itself insignificant beside the process that had produced it. If *Waiting for Godot* is, as Vivian Mercier has written, "a play in which nothing happens, twice," it might be said of *Endgame* that it is an endless rehearsal for an opening night that never comes. And therefore that its true realization was the rehearsals we saw rather than its formal production later in Dublin.

Could this be why, one reason at least, Beckett did not accompany his cast to Ireland or, for that matter, why he has never attended his own plays in the theatre?

He left London the day after rehearsals ended, and I did not see him again until the following spring in Paris. At our first meeting, he seemed a totally different person, distant and inaccessible, physically depleted, extremely thin, his eyes more deeply set and his face more heavily lined than ever. He spoke from such distance and with such difficulty that I was reminded again of Molloy, who describes conversation as "unspeakably painful," explaining that he hears words "a first time, then a second, and often even a third, as pure sounds, free of all meaning." We met in the coffee shop of a new hotel, one of those massive gray skyscrapers that in recent years have so disfigured the Paris skyline. Not far from his apartment, it was his favorite meeting place because it offered a perfect anonymity. He wasn't recognized during this or any subsequent meeting I had with him there. Early on in our conversation, I got a taste of his ferocious self-protection, which was much more pronounced here, of course, where he lived, than it had been in London. "How long will you be here?" he said. "Three weeks," I said. "Good," he said. "I want to see you *once* more." Given his politeness, it was easy to forget how impossible his life would have been had he not been disciplined about his schedule, how many people must have sought him out as I had sought him out myself. What was always amazing to me was how skillful he was in letting one know, where one ranked in his priorities. Couching his decision in courtesy and gentleness, he seemed totally vulnerable, almost passive, but his softness masked a relentless will and determination. He left one so disarmed that it was difficult to ask anything of him, much less seek more time than he had offered. Though he promptly answered every letter I wrote him, it was three years before he gave me his home address, so that I would not have to write him in care of his publisher, and he has never given me a phone number, always arranging that he will call me when I come to town. Why not? Rick Cluchey told me that whenever Beckett went to Germany a documentary film crew followed him around without his permission, using a telephoto lens to film him from a distance.

As it turned out, however, there was another reason for his distance now. In London, the only unpleasant moment between us had occurred when, caught up in the excitement of rehearsals, I'd asked if I could write about him. Though his refusal, again, had been polite ("Unless of course you want to write about the work . . . ") and I had expressed considerable regret about asking him, it would soon become clear that he had not forgotten. Even if he had, the speed with which I was firing questions at him now, nervously pressing all the issues I had accumulated since I'd seen him last, would have put him on his guard. Beckett is legendary, of course, for his hatred of interviews, his careful avoidance of media and its invasions (*The Paris Review* has tried for years, with no success, to interview him for its "Writers at Work" series), and the next time we met, he made it clear that before we continued he must know what I was after. "Listen, I've got to get this off my chest. You're not interviewing me, are you?"

We had just sat down at a restaurant to which he had invited me. The only restaurant he ever frequented, it was a classic bistro on the edge of Montparnasse where he kept his own wine in the cellar and the waiters knew his habits so well that they always took him to the same table and brought him, without his having to order, the dish he ate—filet of sole and french fries—whenever he went there. Though I had my notebook in my pocket and upon leaving him would, as always, rush to take down everything I could remember about our conversation, I assured him that I was certainly not interviewing him and had no intention of writing about him. At this point in time, there was nothing but truth in my disclaimer. (And I might add that he obviously trusted me on this score, since he gave me permission to publish this article, and as far as I can see, has never held it against me.) Since I was not yet even dimly conscious of the ambiguous, somewhat belligerent forces that led to this memoir, the notes I took were for myself alone, as I saw it, a result of the emotion I felt when I left him and the impulse, common if not entirely handsome in a writer, to preserve what had transpired between us. Taking me at my word, Beckett relaxed, poured the wine, and watched with pleasure as I ate while he picked at his food like a child who hated the dinner table. "You're not hungry?" I said. "No," he said. "I guess I'm not too interested in food anymore." And later, when I asked if he'd ever eaten in any of the Japanese restaurants that were just beginning to open in Paris: "No. But I hear they make good rice."

Considering how thin he was, I wasn't surprised to hear that the desire for food—like almost all other desires, I believe, except those which involved his work—was a matter of indifference to him. What did surprise me, as the wine allowed us to speak of things more commonplace, was the view of his domestic situation—evenings at home with his wife, and such—which emerged during the course of the evening. He told me that he'd been married for forty years, that he and his wife had had just two addresses during all their time in Paris, that it had sometimes been difficult for them—"many near-ruptures, as a matter of fact"—but that the marriage had grown easier as they'd got older. "Of course," he added, "I do have my own door." Since I'd always thought of him as the ultimate solitary, isolated as Krapp and as cynical about sex as Molloy, I confessed that I couldn't imagine him in a situation so connubial. "Why should you find it difficult?" he said with some surprise. In fact, he seemed rather pleased with his marriage, extremely grateful that it had lasted. It was one more correction for me, and more important, I think, one more illustration of the symmetry and tension, the dialectic he maintains between his various dichotomies. Just as "can't" and "must" persist with equal force in his mind, the limitations of language no more deniable than the urgent need to articulate, the extreme loneliness which he's explored throughout his life—the utter skepticism and despair about relationships in general and sexuality in particular—has had as its counterpoint a marriage which has lasted forty years. But lest one suspect that the continuity and comfort of marriage had tilted the scales so far that the dream of succession had taken root in his mind, "No," he replied, when I asked if he'd ever wanted children, "that's one thing I'm proud of."

For all my conviction that I did not intend to write about him, I always felt a certain amount of shame when I took up my notebook after I left him. For that matter, I am not entirely without shame about what I'm writing now. One does not transcribe a man like Beckett without its feeling like a betrayal. What makes me persist? More than anything, I believe, it is something I began to realize after our meetings in Paris—that the shame I felt in relation to him had not begun with my furtive attempts to preserve him in my notebook, but rather had been a constant in our relationship long before I'd met him. To put it simply, it began to strike me that Beckett had been, since the moment I discovered *Molloy*, as much a source of inhibition as inspiration. For all the pleasure it had given me, my first reading of the trilogy had almost paralyzed me (as indeed it had paralyzed any number of other writers I knew), leaving me traumatized with shame and embarrassment about my own work. It wasn't merely that, in contrast to his, my language seemed inauthentic and ephemeral, but that he made the usual narrative games—the insulated past tense, the omniscient narrator, form which excluded reference to itself, biographical information—seem, as he put it in *Watt*, "solution clapped on problem like a snuffer on a candle." More than any other writer I knew, Beckett's work seemed to point to that which lay beyond it. It was as if, though its means were Relative, its goals were Absolute, its characters beyond time precisely because (again and again) they seemed to age before our eyes. And such accomplishment was not, it seemed to me, simply a matter of talent or genius but of a totally different approach to writing, a connection between his life and his work which I could covet but never achieve. It was this union—the joining, if you like, of "being" and "form"—that I envied in him and that caused me finally to feel that the very thought of Beckett, not to mention the presence of one of his sentences in my mind, made writing impossible. And once again: it was not merely a matter of talent. I could read Joyce or Proust or Faulkner without such problems, and I had no lack of appreciation for them. It was just that they were clearly *writers*, while Beckett was something else, a sort of meta-writer who, even as he wrote, transcended the act of writing.

Oddly enough, if there was anyone else I knew who stood in such relation to his work, it was Muhammad Ali, who seemed to laugh at boxing even as he took it to higher levels of perfection, who not only defeated but humiliated his opponents, establishing such possession of their minds that he won many fights before the first round began, because he stood outside the game in which his adversary was enclosed. One cannot play a game unless one believes in it, but Ali managed such belief without the attachment to which it usually leads. Say that he found the cusp that separates belief from attachment, concentration from fixation, and on the other hand, play from frivolity, spontaneity from formlessness. And it seems to me that Beckett has done the same. No writer has lived who took language more seriously, but none has been more eloquent about its limitations and absurdities. Like Ali, he shows us where we are imprisoned. The danger is that, in doing so, he will imprison us in his example. If some fighters tried, playing the clown, to imitate Ali, and ended by making fools of themselves in addition to being defeated, writers with Beckett too much in mind can sound worse than the weakest student in a freshman writing class. After reading Joyce or Proust, one can feel embarrassed about one's lack of music or intelligence, but in the wake of one of Beckett's convoluted, self-mocking sentences, one can freeze with horror at the thought of any form that suggests "Once upon a time," anything in fact which departs from the absolute present. But if you take that too far you lose your work in the ultimate swamp, the belief that you can capture both your subject and your object in the instant of composition: "Here I am, sitting at my desk, writing 'Here I am, sitting at my desk.' "

None of this of course is historically unprecedented. Every generation of artists has to do battle with its predecessors, and each such battle has its own unique configurations. What made it so vivid for me was that now, twenty years after that first reading, his presence affected me much as his work had. Happy though I felt to see him, however amazing I found our time together, I always left him with an acute sense that I'd come up short, failed him somehow, as if the moment had passed before I had awakened to it. As if my conversational and psychological habits had stood between us. Or more to the point, as if the *form* of my social habit had violated the nature of his *Being* in much the same way that literary form, as he'd concluded years before, violated the being it excluded. Sitting across from me in the cafe, his eyes fierce in their concentration, his silence so completely unapologetic, he seemed to occupy, according to my reverential opinion, a present tense—*this* space, *this* moment in time—which I could merely observe from afar. Despite—no, because of—his humility, his uncertainty, the "impotence" which, as he'd once put it, his work had set out to "exploit,"* he manifested for me, as for years he had for Rick Cluchey, a kind of ultimate authority, a sense of knowledge very near to Absolute. Neither egoism nor self-confidence—the opposite, in fact, of both—such knowledge seemed a by-product of suffering, the pain that was so evident on his face, an earned if not entirely welcome result of having explored and survived an emptiness that people of less courage, if they acknowledged it at all, considered by means of intellect alone.

*"The kind of work I do," he explained to Israel Schenker in a *New York Times* interview in 1966, before he'd closed the door to media, "is one in which I'm not master of my material. The more Joyce knew the more he could. He's tending toward omniscience and omnipotence as an artist. I'm working with impotence, ignorance. I don't think impotence has been exploited in the past."

Exaggerated and romantic though all this seems, I'm sure it's not entirely unjustified. Beckett is indeed an extraordinary being, a man who has travelled in realms that most people don't want to hear about, much less explore. A true writer, an artist who pursues his vision so courageously and with such disregard for easy gratification that his work becomes, in the purest sense, a spiritual practice. What my responses showed, however, my idealization of him and the self-criticism it evoked, was that such authority was nothing if not a hazardous experience. Like all great wisdom, it could bring out the best or the worst in you, challenge or intimidate you, toughen you or make you self-effacing. Finally, if you were a writer, it could inspire you to listen to your own voice or trap you into years of imitating his. Like Joyce or Proust, or for that matter, any other great artist one adopts as a teacher, Beckett is an almost impossible act to follow, but more so than most, I think, because his work is so subjective, so seductive in the permissions it grants, because his apparent freedom from plot and character and his first person present tense can draw you into a swamp in which art and self-indulgence begin to seem identical. It is so easy to think that he opens the gates for anything you're feeling or thinking at the moment you sit down at your desk. How many writers could I count who had books like mine, the one I'd shown him, the one he'd criticized because the voice was "not believable," which would not be written until the Beckett had been removed from them? The great irony is that, for all his rejection of authority and knowledge— precisely because of such rejection, in fact—Beckett is almost too much an authority, he knows too much that one must discover on one's own. If you aren't to go on imitating him, you either face the fact that there is nothing you really need to say and find yourself another vocation, or you dig for something truer in yourself, something you don't know, at the bottom of all you do. In other words, you start where he started, after meeting his mother in Dublin. The trouble is that, since most of such digging, if you're an ordinary mortal, is surely doomed to fail, it can seem as if he's taken you out of the game you're capable of playing and signed you up in one for which you've neither the courage, the talent, nor the appetite. Finally, his greatest danger—and his greatest gift—may be his simple reminder that writing is not about reiteration.

But of course there is also the other side to it, one which has explicitly to do with the nature of his vision, the "being" he allows into the work, the void he's faced, the negation he's endured, the grief he's not only experienced but transformed with his imagination. "Yes, the confusion of my ideas on the subject of death," says Molloy, "was such that I sometimes wondered, believe me or not, if it wasn't a state of being even worse than life. So I found it natural not to rush into it and, when I forgot myself to the point of trying, to stop in time." Once we'd got over our laughter and exhilaration, how were we to deal with such a statement? For Beckett, such negation had fueled the work, but for many who presumed to be his successors, it had often become an easy, a facile nihilism, less a game you lost than one you refused to play. Indeed, for some of us, true disciples, it could become one you were ashamed to play. As if, having finally been enlightened as to the absurdity of life, you were too wise to persist at its illusions, too wise to allow enthusiasm, occupy space, to feed the body you knew to be disintegrating. In effect, if you misread him well enough, Beckett could turn you into a sort of literary anorexic, make you too cool or hip, too scared, too detached and disenchanted, to take, by writing, the only food that nourished you. But the irony is that he himself, as he'd shown me in London, in our very first conversation, is anything but anorexic. That's obvious, isn't it? This man who writes, in *Molloy,* "you would do better, at least no worse, to obliterate texts than to blacken margins, to fill in the holes of words till all is blank and flat and the whole ghastly business looks like what it is, senseless, speechless, issueless misery," has published six novels and fourteen plays during his lifetime, not to mention a great body of short prose, poetry, criticism, a number of television and radio plays, and a filmscript. Just fifteen pages later in *Molloy* he writes, "Not to want to say, not to know what you want to say, and never to stop saying, or hardly ever, that is the thing to keep in mind, even in the heat of composition." Much as he can recognize the tyranny of hope or meaning, he cannot deny that there is hope and meaning within such recognition, and he cannot pretend that this hope and meaning is any less exciting or more enduring than the others. It's all part of the equation, however absurd, of being alive, and he's never rejected that condition for its alternative. After all, when Nell says "Nothing's funnier than unhappiness," we laugh at that statement, and—if only for an instant—are less unhappy as we do so. In a sense Beckett is the great poet of negation, but what is poetry for him can easily become, if we use him incorrectly, if we make him too much an authority or if we underestimate the integrity of his paradox, a negation so extreme and absolute that it threatens the very source of one's energy and strength.

Of course, it's not easy to speak of these things. It's always possible that his greatest gift, not only to those of us he's challenged, but the readers we might have enlisted, is the silence toward which he's pressed us. If you can't accept his example, and allow Being into your work, why add your lies to the ocean of print which is drowning the world already? In my opinion, most writers deal with his challenge in one of two ways. Either they ignore his example, go on—as I had, for example, in writing journalism—making forms that exclude Being, accepting the role of explainer, describer, or they try—as I was trying with my novel—to play his game despite the astronomical odds against any possibility of success. For those who take the latter path, the entry of Being into the form often means the entry of self-consciousness, writing about writing about writing. Too late we discover that Beckett, Molloy, Malone, *et al*, though they may be mad, haven't a trace of neurosis or narcissism about them, that their present tense is shaped and objectified by an inherently classical, concrete mind, a sense of self which differs radically from our own. In effect, that the present tense which becomes, inevitably, an imperfect tense for them, remains a merely present—a merely reductive, a totally self-absorbed—tense for us. If you can't take the leap from present to imperfect, you remain rooted in the present. An honorable intention, of course, but if you're honest about it, you have to admit that writing and being in the present are not necessarily compatible, that in fact you're always flirting with contradiction and dishonesty. Tantalized by what amounts to a desire to write and not-write simultaneously, you may be equally loyal to form and being, but you may also be a mother who would keep her child forever in her womb. It's the sort of game in which defeat can lead to farce that's not only hypocritical but blasphemous toward the master one has pretended to revere.

These are just a few of the reasons, I think, I took notes when I left him, and despite my disclaimer, am writing about him now. Why? Perhaps because Beckett himself, as I said earlier, freed me from the Beckett myth. Not entirely for sure, but enough at least to help me resume a voice that differed from the one he once inspired in me. Not for nothing did he show me that he enjoyed my journalism. "Look here, Larry," he said to me once in London, "your line is witnessing." By which I understand him to have meant: take your object and be done with it. Be content to write what you know without acknowledging every moment that you don't. So here I am, witnessing him. Maybe this is all just rationalization, but getting him down like this may be the best homage and the best revenge, the only weapon I have against the attack he mounted on my mind. I can't forget him, and I can't think of anything else to do with his example but reject it. Just as Buddhists say about their own ultimate authority, "If you meet the Buddha on the road, kill him," I say of Beckett that a writer can only proceed from him by recognizing that he is now, having taken his work to all of its ultimate conclusions, utterly emptied of possibility. As Hamm says, "All is absolute. The bigger a man is, the fuller he is . . . and the emptier."

The next time we saw each other, a year later in Paris, our conversation continued, where it had begun and where it had been left, with the difficulties of writing. Because my work (the same novel) was going as badly as his, there wasn't a whole lot of joy in the air. For a moment, in fact, it became a sort of sparring match between us, agony versus agony, but then, remembering whom I was in the ring with and how much he outweighed me, I backed off. "It's not a good time at all," he sighed, "I walk the streets trying to see what's in my mind. It's all confusion. Life is all confusion. A blizzard. It must be like this for the newborn. Not much difference I think between this blizzard and that. Between the two, what do you have? Wind machines or some such. I can't write anything, but I must." He paused a moment, then suddenly brightened, once again repeating a famous Beckett line as if he'd just come upon it, "Yes, that's it! Can't and must! That's my situation!"

He spoke of a sentence that haunted him. "It won't go away, and it won't go farther: 'One night, as he sat, with his head on his hands, he saw himself rise, and go.' " Except for this, however, there was nothing. "It's like the situation I spoke of in my book on Proust. 'Not just hope is gone, but desire.' " When I reminded him—quoting the line I mentioned earlier ("The wisdom of all the sages . . . consists not in the satisfaction but the ablation of desire.")—that according to the book he'd remembered, the loss of desire was not an entirely unwelcome development, he replied, "Well, yes, but the writing was the only thing that made life bearable." Sighing as if in tremendous pain, he seemed to drift off for a moment. "Funny to complain about silence when one has aspired to it for so long. Words are the only thing for me and there's not enough of them. Now, it's as if I'm just living in a void, waiting. Even my country house is lonely when I'm not writing."

Occasionally, when he talked like this, there was an odd sense, absurd as it seems, that he was asking for help, even perhaps advice, but this time was different. Now seventy-eight years old, he appeared to have reached a sort of bottom-line exhaustion. He seemed smaller to me, the lines in his forehead more deeply etched, like a grid. Every gesture seemed difficult, every word a struggle. His blue eyes were shy, gentle, youthful as ever, but incredibly pained and sorrowful. I told him that sometimes I found it amazing that he went on. "Yes," he replied, "often I think it's time I put an end to it. That's all through the new work. But then again . . . there are also times when I think, maybe it's time to begin." He said there had always been so much more in the work than he'd suspected was there, and then added, in what seemed an almost unconscious afterthought, a phrase I've never forgotten, which may have summed up his work as well or better than any other: "Ambiguities infirmed as they're put down . . ."

"Which is more painful," I asked him, "writing or not writing?"

"They're both painful, but the pain is different."

He spoke a little about the different sorts of pain—the pain of being unable to write, the pain of writing itself, and—as bad as any—the pain of finishing what he'd begun. I said, "If the work is so painful when one does it and so painful when it's done, why on earth does anyone do it?"

This was one of those questions that caused him, as I've mentioned already, to disappear behind his hand, covering his eyes and bending his head toward the table for what must have been two full minutes. Then, just when I'd begun to suspect that he'd fallen asleep, he raised his head and, with an air of relief, as if he'd finally resolved a lifelong dilemma, whispered, "The fashioning, that's what it is for me, I think. The pleasure in making a satisfactory object." He explained that the main excitement in writing had always been technical for him, a combination of "metaphysics and technique." "A problem is there and I have to solve it. *Godot*, for example, began with an image—of a tree and an empty stage—and proceeded from there. That's why, when people ask me who Godot is, I can't tell them. It's all gone."

127

"Why metaphysics?" I said.

"Because," he said, "you've got your own experience. You've got to draw on that."

He tried to describe the work he wanted to do now. "It has to do with a fugitive 'I' [or perhaps he meant 'eye']. It's an embarrassment of pronouns. I'm searching for the non-pronounial."

"Non-pronounial?"

"Yes. It seems a betrayal to say 'he' or 'she.' "

The problem of pronouns, first person versus third, which had been so much explored and illuminated throughout his work, was also the one he addressed in mine. That morning, as always, he was extremely solicitous, asking me question after question about the progress of my novel. Though the book continued to defy me, so much so that I'd begun to wonder if brain damage, as I wanted to approach it, might not be beyond the limits of art, he seemed to know exactly what I wanted to do. It wasn't surprising, of course, that the man who'd once described tears as "liquified brain" should be familiar with the subject of brain damage, but his questions were so explicit that it was difficult to believe that he hadn't considered, and rejected, the very book I wanted to write. The chapters I'd shown him in London had been written in the first person, which he had considered a mistake. "I know it's impertinent to say this, please forgive me . . . but this book, in my opinion, will never work in the first person." When I told him, here at the cafe, that I had now moved it to the third person, he nodded, but he knew that problems of point of view were never resolved with pronouns alone. "Still," he said, returning to the point he'd made when we met in London, "you need a witness, right?"

He excused himself from the table—"pardon my bladder"—but when he returned it was clear that he'd taken my book with him. "Well, do you see the end of it?"

"No," I said, "not at all."

He sighed. "It's really very difficult, isn't it?"

He sipped his coffee, then homed in on the principal issue in my book as in so much contemporary fiction—the need for objectivity and knowledge in conjunction with the need for the intimacy and immediacy of a naked subjectivity. "You need a witness and you need the first person, that's the problem, isn't it? One thing that might help . . . you might have a look at an early book of mine, perhaps you know it, *Mercier and Camier*. I had a similar problem

128

there. It begins, 'I know what happened with Mercier and Camier because I was there with them all the time.' "

After I returned from Paris, I looked at *Mercier and Camier* again but found no place for his solution in the problems I had set myself. Still, I wrote an entire version of my novel in the third person, and I can say without a doubt that there were very few days I didn't feel him looking over my shoulder, whispering, "It's really very difficult, isn't it?" or when things were going worse, commenting on me as Nagg comments on Hamm, "What does that mean? That means nothing!" Halfway through, I knew it wasn't working, suspecting strongly that my only hope, despite what Beckett had said, was in the first person, but I pushed on. Certainly, it wasn't merely his recommendation that kept me going in that direction, but how can I pretend it didn't matter? When finally—a year and a half and an entire manuscript later—I turned it around and started over, in the first person, I could not, though I wrote him more than one letter about the book, bring myself to mention it to him. To my mind, the book worked, not only because it was in the first person, but because I had finally succeeded in weaning myself from him. Given all this, I felt no small trepidation when I sent him the manuscript but, as before, he read the book at once and replied with generosity and enthusiasm. There was no sign of his original disappointment and none of his position *vis-à-vis* my point of view. His note, as always, was confined to a 3 x 5 index card, and his scrawl, which had grown progressively worse in the years that I'd corresponded with him, was not completely legible. To my chagrin, in fact, its most important sentence was only half-accessible to me. After offering his compliments and appreciation, he concluded with a sentence that drifted off into a hopeless hieroglyphics after beginning with "And on with you now from . . ."

After "from" was a word which looked like "this," but might have been "thus" or "phis," a word which looked like "new" but might have been "man" or "ran," a word which looked like "thought" or "bought" or "sought," and finally a word which looked like "anew." "And on with you now from this new thought anew"? It didn't sound like Beckett at all. I asked several friends to have a look but none could read his writing any better than I. What absurd apocryphy that a note from Beckett should conclude, "And on with you now from [illegible] [illegible] [illegible]." Finally, unable to stand it any longer, I wrote to ask if, by some chance (after all, more than three weeks had passed since he'd written the note) he could remember what he'd written. Again he answered promptly, ending our dialogue, as I will end this memoir, with a note that was characteristic, not only in its economy and content, but in what it says about his (failing?) memory and the attitude with which he approached his correspondence:

Dear Larry,
   I believe I wrote, 'And on with you now from this new nought anew.'
As ever,
Sam.

nominated by Edward Hirsch

THE RISE OF THE SUNDAY SCHOOL MOVEMENT

by GERALD COSTANZO

from THE NORTH AMERICAN REVIEW

> *"I am not a healer. Jesus is the healer. I am only the little girl who opens the door and says 'Come in'."*
>
> —Aimee Semple McPherson

I *had* wanted my daughter
to become an evangelist—

Sister Lizabeth Adrienne—

not to relive my life in hers,
nor for desire after the great abstraction

in lieu of the bits of carpentry
I've managed. No, like anyone
I just longed for a little pomp amid
all of this circumstance.
A progeny who could shout *Sweet*

131

Beautiful Jesus and mean it.
To have borne
a pillar in the rise
of the Sunday School Movement,
or one of the overdue

Northern Crusades. One who could
espy the dance halls of Venice,
California with the true conviction
of a Sunday afternoon; who could bathe
in the sea at Carmel and not

disappear for three weeks
in Mexico with her married lover;
who'd never be transported
back from the lost, paraded
in a throne of white

wicker from her private train car
to overdose on tablets
of the newest redemption.
The way I figured it
I'd be sitting at a corner table

in the Desdemona Club
nursing a brew. She'd be up
there on the large-screen TV next
to the bar, having taken over Billy
Graham's Asian Tour after his terrible

swift heart attack in China. The petite
brunette beauty from America!
She'd be singing *Lord,*
We Need Thee Every Hour as
the afflicted clutched at the hem

of her flowing dress. Maybe
I'd kneel among them, then
and there. Begin

to believe as we're able to believe
what reaches us by satellite—
bow down as she gave us
the beauteous word, all of us praising,
loving her, adoring the celestial
melody, possessed by our irrevocable
conversions.

nominated by Vern Rutsala

APPROACHING AUGUST

by SANDRA ALCOSSER

from NORTHERN LIGHTS

Night takes on its own elegance.
The catenary curve of snakes,
the breathing, pentagonal-shaped
flowers, the shadblow pliant
and black with berries. Orion
rises in the east, over
fat green gardens, and all meanness
is forgiven.

We canoe the river
in the amethyst hour before dark.
Twenty-five billion beats to each heart.
Two passengers fish, two paddle
past the chalk caves, the banks
of aster, the flood plains dense
with white tail and beaver.

We are lost near midnight, a moonless
summer evening, midseason in our senses,
midlife. The sky overhead like glitter ice.
The water round swollen cottonwoods
pulls like tresses and torn paper.

Today I had a letter from France.
"What a truly civilized nation," my friend wrote
as she drank her morning coffee with thick cream

in a country cafe near Avignon. "To my right
a man in a black tuxedo sips raspberry liqueur
and soda."

And here on the same latitude we lie back at dawn
on the caving bank of the Bitterroot.
A shadow slips through the silver grasses.
And then a moth.
And then the moon.

nominated by William Pitt Root

EPITHALAMIUM

by LESLIE ADRIENNE MILLER

from OPEN PLACES

I have seen them introduce the silver
twisted bits, spikes and wires into the mouths
of horses with the skill and care
the young learn in love. There is little
or no philosophy to this act. The horse will
take the bit. The girl will rise over him
like a moon because she is beautiful
and he does not care if she can or cannot stay.
I've watched these girls for days in the barn,
passing their knowing fingers over the bodies
of the animals, chiding the neurotic
and most beautiful one called Incomparable
who rocks for hours against his stall, silent
and closed as an autistic child. I have seen
the smallest girl stand before a chest
wide and hard as a truck bumper, and shove
the creature off balance for some slight
misconduct. She is intimate with every
muscle and bone that longs to crush her;
she will marry the back of the beast
because it is the only way to be with him in this world.

When it is my turn to ride, the young flutter
around me as if I am going to ascend.
They towel my boots and stirrup irons,
say I am happy, he is happy, if we leave

136

the ground for a moment, it will be joy
that throws his head, joy that rings
the silver bits and chains, throws the clods
of earth above the dreaming bleachers.
It is part of the art for horse and rider
to move out looking haughty and pained
as martyrs. I look down at the meaty shoulders
that take us forward, two creatures
pursued by something we can't stop to think about—
what we have in common now is our wish to exceed
time, that scream or storm behind us
far more complicated than death. I can almost
believe we are ahead of it, seeing ourselves
with those eyes that are not the heart's eyes,
not the soul's eyes or even the intellect's,
but the eyes in our flesh that see,
without mirror or word, that beauty lifts itself
ever so slightly and moves ahead of its own end.

nominated by Edward Hirsch and Joan Murray

JOHNNIERUTH

fiction by BECKY BIRTHA

from LOVER'S CHOICE (Seal Press)

SUMMERTIME. Nighttime. Talk about steam heat. This whole city get like the bathroom when somebody in there taking a shower with the door shut. Nights like that, can't nobody sleep. Everybody be outside, sitting on they steps or else dragging half they furniture out on the sidewalk—kitchen chairs, card tables—even bringing TVs outside.

Womenfolks, mostly. All the grown women around my way look just the same. They all big—stout. They got big bosoms and big hips and fat legs, and they always wearing runover house-shoes, and them shapeless, flowered numbers with the buttons down the front. Cept on Sunday. Sunday morning they all turn into glamour girls, in them big hats and long gloves, with they skinny high heels and they skinny selves in them tight girdles—wouldn't nobody ever know what they look like the rest of the time.

When I was a little kid I didn't wanna grow up, cause I never wanted to look like them ladies. I heard Miz Jenkins down the street one time say she don't mind being fat cause that way her husband don't get so jealous. She say it's more than one way to keep a man. Me, I don't have me no intentions of keeping no man. I never understood why they was in so much demand anyway, when it seem like all a woman can depend on em for is making sure she keep on having babies.

We got enough children in my neighborhood. In the summertime, even the little kids allowed to stay up till eleven or twelve o'clock at night—playing in the street and hollering and carrying

138

on—don't never seem to get tired. Don't nobody care, long as they don't fight.

Me—I don't hang around no front steps no more. Hot nights like that, I get out my ten speed and I be gone.

That's what I like to do more than anything else in the whole world. Feel that wind in my face keeping me cool as a air conditioner, shooting along like a snowball. My bike light as a kite. I can really get up some speed.

All the guys around my way got ten speed bikes. Some of the girls got em too, but they don't ride em at night. They pedal around during the day, but at nighttime they just hang around out front, watching babies and running they mouth. I didn't get my Peugeot to be no conversation piece.

My mama don't like me to ride at night. I tried to point out to her that she ain't never said nothing to my brothers, and Vincent a year younger than me. (And Langston two years older, in case "old" is the problem.) She say, "That's different, Johnnieruth. You're a girl." Now I wanna know how is anybody gonna know that. I'm skinny as a knifeblade turned sideways, and all I ever wear is blue jeans and a Wrangler jacket. But if I bring that up, she liable to get started in on how come I can't be more of a young lady, and fourteen is old enough to start taking more pride in my appearance, and she gonna be ashamed to admit I'm her daughter.

I just tell her that my bike be moving so fast can't nobody hardly see me, and couldn't catch me if they did. Mama complain to her friends how I'm wild and she can't do nothing with me. She know I'm gonna do what I want no matter what she say. But she know I ain't getting in no trouble, neither.

Like some of the boys I know stole they bikes, but I didn't do nothing like that. I'd been saving my money ever since I can remember, every time I could get a nickel or a dime outta anybody.

When I was a little kid, it was hard to get money. Seem like the only time they ever give you any was on Sunday morning, and then you had to put it in the offering. I used to hate to do that. In fact, I used to hate everything about Sunday morning. I had to wear all them ruffly dresses—that shiny slippery stuff in the wintertime that got to make a noise every time you move your ass a inch on them hard old benches. And that scratchy starchy stuff in the summertime with all them scratchy crinolines. Had to carry a pocketbook and wear them shiny shoes. And the church we went to was all the way

139

over on Summit Avenue, so the whole damn neighborhood could get a good look. At least all the other kids'd be dressed the same way. The boys think they slick cause they get to wear pants, but they still got to wear a white shirt and a tie; and them dumb hats they wear can't hide them baldheaded haircuts, cause they got to take the hats off in church.

There was one Sunday when I musta been around eight. I remember it was before my sister Corletta was born, cause right around then was when I put my foot down about the whole sanctimonious routine. Anyway, I was dragging my feet along Twenty-fifth Street in back of Mama and Vincent and them, when I spied this lady. I only seen her that one time, but I still remember just how she look. She don't look like nobody I ever seen before. I *know* she don't live around here. She real skinny. But she ain't no real young woman, either. She could be old as my mama. She ain't nobody's mama—I'm sure. And she ain't wearing Sunday clothes. She got on blue jeans and a man's blue working shirt, with the tail hanging out. She got patches on her blue jeans, and she still got her chin stuck out like she some kinda African royalty. She ain't carrying no shiny pocketbook. It don't look like she care if she got any money or not, or who know it, if she don't. She ain't wearing no house-shoes, or stockings or high heels neither.

Mama always speak to everybody, but when she pass by this lady she make like she ain't even seen her. But I get me a real good look, and the lady stare right back at me. She got a funny look on her face, almost like she think she know me from some place. After she pass on by, I had to turn around to get another look, even though Mama say that ain't polite. And you know what? She was turning around, too, looking back at me. And she give me a great big smile.

I didn't know too much in them days, but that's when I first got to thinking about how it's got to be different ways to be, from the way people be around my way. It's got to be places where it don't matter to nobody if you all dressed up on Sunday morning or you ain't. That's how come I started saving money. So, when I got enough, I could go away to some place like that.

Afterwhile I begun to see there wasn't no point in waiting around for handouts, and I started thinking of ways to earn my own money. I used to be running errands all the time—mailing letters for old Grandma Whittaker and picking up cigarettes and newspapers up the corner for everybody. After I got bigger, I started washing cars in the summer, and shoveling people sidewalk in the wintertime. Now I got me a newspaper route. Ain't never been no girl around here with no paper route, but I guess everybody got it figured out by now that I ain't gonna be like nobody else.

The reason I got me my Peugeot was so I could start to explore. I figured I better start looking around right now, so when I'm grown, I'll know exactly where I wanna go. So I ride around every chance I get.

Last summer, I used to ride with the boys a lot. Sometimes eight or ten of us'd just go cruising around the streets together. All of a sudden my mama decide she don't want me to do that no more. She say I'm too old to be spending so much time with boys. (That's what they tell you half the time, and the other half the time they worried cause you ain't interested in spending more time with boys. Don't make much sense.) She want me to have some girl friends, but I never seem to fit in with none of the things the girls doing. I used to think I fit in more with the boys.

But I seen how Mama might be right, for once. I didn't like the way the boys was starting to talk about girls sometimes. Talking about what some girl be like from the neck on down, and talking all up underneath somebody clothes and all. Even though I wasn't really friends with none of the girls, I still didn't like it. So now I mostly just ride around by myself. And Mama don't like that neither—you just can't please her.

This boy that live around the corner on North Street, Kenny Henderson, started asking me one time if I don't ever be lonely, cause he always see me by myself. He say don't I ever think I'd like to have me somebody special to go places with and stuff. Like I'd pick him if I did! Made me wanna laugh in his face. I do be lonely, a lotta times, but I don't tell nobody. And I ain't met nobody yet that I'd really rather be with than be by myself. But I will someday. When I find that special place where everybody different, I'm gonna find somebody there I can be friends with. And it ain't gonna be no dumb boy.

I found me one place already, that I like to go to a whole lot. It ain't even really that far away—by bike—but it's on the other side of the Avenue. So I don't tell Mama and them I go there, cause they like to think I'm right around the neighborhood someplace. But this neighborhood too dull for me. All the houses look just the same— no porches, no yards, no trees—not even no parks around here.

Every block look so much like every other block it hurt your eyes to look at, afterwhile. So I ride across Summit Avenue and go down that big steep hill there, and then make a sharp right at the bottom and cross the bridge over the train tracks. Then I head on out the boulevard—that's the nicest part, with all them big trees making a tunnel over the top, and lightning bugs shining in the bushes. At the end of the boulevard you get to this place call the Plaza.

It's something like a little park—the sidewalks is all bricks and they got flowers planted all over the place. The same kind my mama grow in that painted-up tire she got out from masquerading like a garden decoration—only seem like they smell sweeter here. It's a big high fountain right in the middle, and all the streetlights is the real old-fashion kind. That Plaza is about the prettiest place I ever been.

Sometimes something going on there. Like a orchestra playing music or some man or lady singing. One time they had a show with some girls doing some kinda foreign dances. They look like they were around my age. They all had on these fancy costumes, with different color ribbons all down they back. I wouldn't wear nothing like that, but it looked real pretty when they was dancing.

I got me a special bench in one corner where I like to sit, cause I can see just about everything, but wouldn't nobody know I was there. I like to sit still and think, and I like to watch people. A lotta people be coming there at night—to look at the shows and stuff, or just to hang out and cool off. All different kinda people.

This one night when I was sitting over in that corner where I always be at, there was this lady standing right near my bench. She mostly had her back turned to me and she didn't know I was there, but I could see her real good. She had on this shiny purple shirt and about a million silver bracelets. I kinda liked the way she look. Sorta exotic, like she maybe come from California or one of the islands. I mean she had class—standing there posing with her arms folded. She walk away a little bit. Then turn around and walk back again. Like she waiting for somebody.

Then I spotted this dude coming over. I spied him all the way cross the Plaza. Looking real fine. Got on a three piece suit. One of them little caps sitting on a angle. Look like leather. He coming straight over to this lady I'm watching and then she seen him too and she start to smile, but she don't move till he get right up next to her. And then I'm gonna look away, cause I can't stand to watch

142

nobody hugging and kissing on each other, but all of a sudden I see it ain't no dude at all. It's another lady.

Now I can't stop looking. They smiling at each other like they ain't seen one another in ten years. Then the one in the purple shirt look around real quick—but she don't look just behind her—and sorta pull the other one right back into the corner where I'm sitting at, and then they put they arms around each other and kiss—for a whole long time. Now I really know I oughtta turn away, but I can't. And I know they gonna see me when they finally open they eyes. And they do.

They both kinda gasp and back up, like I'm the monster that just rose up outta the deep. And then I guess they can see I'm only a girl, and they look at one another—and start to laugh! Then they just turn around and start to walk away like it wasn't nothing at all. But right before they gone, they both look around again, and see I still ain't got my eye muscles and my jaw muscles working right again yet. And the one lady wink at me. And the other one say, "Catch you later."

I can't stop staring at they backs, all the way across the Plaza. And then, all of a sudden, I feel like I got to be doing something, got to be moving.

I wheel on outta the Plaza and I'm just concentrating on getting up my speed. Cause I can't figure out what to think. Them two women kissing and then, when they get caught, just laughing about it. And here I'm laughing too, for no reason at all. I'm sailing down the boulevard laughing like a lunatic, and then I'm singing at the top of my lungs. And climbing that big old hill up to Summit Avenue is just as easy as being on a escalator.

nominated by Seal Press

HAPPINESS OF THE GARDEN VARIETY

fiction by MARK RICHARD

from SHENANDOAH

I FELT REALLY BAD about what we ended up having to do to Vic's horse Buster today, not that looking back all this could have been helped, all this starting when Steve Willis and I were ripping the old roof off of where we live in the shanty by the canal on Vic's acres. Vic was up to Norfolk again checking on a washing machine for his many-childed wife, Steve Willis and I left to rip off the roof and hammer in the new shingles. We were doing this in change for rent. Every month we do something in change for rent from Vic. Last month previous we strung three miles of pound net with bottom weights and cork toppers. What we change for rent usually comes to a lot more than what I'm sure the rent is for our four-room front porch shanty on the canal out back of Vic's, but Steve Willis and I like Vic and Vic lets us use his boat and truck for side business we do on new-moon nights.

Let me tell you something about what makes what we ended up doing to Vic's horse Buster all the worse. This is not to say about Vic less than Buster, me, I personally, and I know Steve Willis did too, hated Buster, Steve Willis having had to watch from far away Buster kill two of Vic's dogs. There'd be a stomp and a kick of dust and then a splash in the canal and it's a crab festival on old Tramp or Big Spot. Then there was Buster's biting and kicking of us humans, Buster having bit me on the shoulder once when I was scraping barnacles off one of Vic's skiffs in change for rent, and then he didn't even make a move back when I came at him with a sharp-sided hoe.

Steve Willis had Buster kick in the driving side of his car door after Buster had been into some weeds Vic had sprayed with the wrong powder. Buster kicked in the door so hard Steve Willis still has to crawl in from the other way. It was this eating that got Buster in the end though not reading the right label is something about Vic which made him have us around.

This is what I mean, this about Vic, and about what we did to his horse to make things all the worse: Vic could not read nor write, and this about Vic affected the way we all were with him, what I mean all, means Vic's wife and his children and Buster and his dogs and all the acres we all lived on down by the canal, and everything on all the acres, and everything on all the acres painted aquamarine blue, because one thing about Vic, and I say this to show how Steve Willis and I made this all the worse, was that Vic not reading nor writing seemed to make him not to think about things like they had names that he had to remember by way of thinking that needed spelling, but instead Vic seemed to think about things in groups, like here is a group of things that are my humans, here is a group of things that are my animals, here is a group of things I got for free, here is a group of things I got off good deal making, and here is a group of things I should keep a long time because I got them from some people who had kept them a long time, and maybe because of a couple of these reasons put together, Vic had another group of things painted aquamarine blue because he had gotten a good deal on two fifty-five gallon barrels of aquamarine paint, and everything, even Vic's humans and animals who could not help but rub against it somewhere because it was everywhere wet, everything was touched the color of aquamarine, though all of us calling it *ackerine*, because even spelling it out and sounding it out to Vic it still came out of his mouth that way, ackerine, keeping in mind here is a man who can't read nor write, and Steve Willis and I always saying ackerine like Vic said it, for fun, because it also always seemed like somehow we were always holding a brush of it somewhere putting it on something in change for rent.

So what made what we did to Buster worse were some ways in Vic's thinking which were brought on by him not reading nor writing. Just because somebody had kept Buster a long time to Vic made it seem Buster was very valuable, and even though the horse did come with some history tied to it, the real reason the people who had Buster for so long was because they were old and could not seem

145

to kill the horse by just shooting it with bird shot over and over even though they tried again and again, them just making Buster meaner and easier for Vic to buy when the two old people saw him in church and asked did he want a good deal on a historical horse. The history Buster had was he was the last of the horses they used at Wicomico Light Station to run rescue boats into the surf. To Steve Willis and I when we heard it said So what? but to Vic this was some history he could understand and appreciate being an old sailor himself and it being some facts that did not have to be gotten from a history book that he could not read from in the first place.

What I came to find out later on was the heart tug Vic felt about this old horse that had to do with when Vic grew up, Vic's father having boarded a team of surf horses in a part of the house Vic slept in when he was a boy because all the children from Vic's parents spilled out of the two-room clapboard laid low in the dunes, not a far situation from Vic's own children who as long as Steve Willis and I have been living here I don't think I have seen all of because they keep spilling out of the house barefoot all year around and maybe it's because there are so many of them that Vic can't seem to re-member all their names rather than the fact he can't place in his mind what they are called because Vic can not read nor write.

Anyway, the point I'm leading to about the heart tug is that where Vic spent his life as a child was sleeping with two other brothers in a hayloft over the team of rescue surf horses, and a hayloft mostly empty at that, not even because there was no hay to be had on an island of sand but because the team always grazed on the wild sea oats in the dunes, and this is what makes what we did the worse, this tug on Vic's heart to his younger days that Buster had, me hearing Vic tell it to Buster one day when Vic didn't know I did, the feeling Vic remembered best of laying snug warm with his brothers, all of them laid all over each other to keep warm during winter north-easters that shook the two-room clapboard and the tacked-on horse stalls where they slept, remembering them in the early mornings keeping warm while down below the horses would be stirring to go out, making droppings and the smell coming up to the warm, all over each other boys, the warm smell of wild sea oats passed through the two solid horses breathing sea fog breath.

So that was the heart tug Buster had and I don't mean to make Vic out strange owing to him liking the smell of an old horse passing gas, I think if you think about it there's really nothing there that doesn't fit with a man not thinking thoughts he has to read nor write, but fits well with a man who thinks of things as being good when they are human or animal especially if they came about by getting them free or from off a good deal.

I guess that is the main reason about Vic besides using his boat and truck on new-moon nights that Steve Willis and I stuck around, us in a couple of groups in Vic's mind mainly getting a good deal off of, us stringing nets, ripping roofs and painting everything not breathing what we called ackerine, and that is also the main reason what we ended up doing ended up all the worse.

So like I said, this all started when Steve Willis and I were ripping the old roof off our four-room front porch shanty by the canal in change for rent. Vic had gone to Norfolk because he had heard of a good deal some people from church told him about to do with some washing machines, and Vic, having stood in water barefoot while plugging his old washer in and getting thrown against a wall by the shock, naturally to his mind thought it was broken and needed replacing. Vic had left in the morning coming in to get Steve Willis and I up around dawn to finish the roof and said only one other simple thing, the real easy thing, to please keep Buster out of the garden no matter what we did. Then Vic was off through the gate in his good deal truck he had painted ackerine blue one night after supper the week before.

It was July hot, and before we started Steve Willis and I just walked around our shanty roof, just looking, because the island we live is flat with just scrub pine and wandering dunes and from a single story up you can see Wicomico Light, the inlet bridge and the big dunes where the ocean breaks beyond. It was a good morning knowing Vic's wife would come soon out bringing us some sticks of fried fish wrapped in brown paper, her knowing for breakfast we usually had a cigarette and a Dr. Pepper. For a long time Steve Willis and I had not made any new-moon runs to Stumpy Point to make us watch the one lane down to Vic's acres for cars we wouldn't like the looks of and I could look at Steve Willis and Steve Willis could look at me and we could feel good to be one of Vic's humans in a house on all of Vic's acres.

About midway through the morning after their chores about a half a dozen of Vic's kids came spilling barefoot out of Vic's ackerine blue house to ride the ackerine bicycles and tricycles and to play on the good deal ackerine swing set and jungle gym. The older Vic's kids got to play fishing boat and battleship down on the canal dock as long as one of them stayed lookout to keep a count of heads and watch for snakes.

From over my shoulder I was watching what Buster was up to. He stood looking up at me in the middle of the midday morning hot yard not seeking shade like even a common ass would but just standing in the yard near where the incline made of good deal railway ties came out of the canal and to the boat shed. Buster stood not even slapping his tail at the blackflies that were starting to work on Steve Willis and I up on the roof ripping shingles, but standing so still as if knowing not to attract one bit of attention to himself on his way to he and I knew where. I would rip a row of shingles and then look over my shoulder and Buster would be standing perfectly still not even slapping his tail at the blackflies or even showing signs of breath in and out of his big almost to the ground slouching belly. Just standing as if he was a big kid's toy some big kid was moving around in the yard when I wasn't looking, all the time moving closer by two or one feet to the garden.

So I would rip a row and look, rip a row and look, never seeing him move even by inches, and I saw Steve Willis was not even bothered by looking to keep an eye on Buster out of the garden even though Vic had told us both to do it, and the reason was a simple one for Steve Willis not to care and boiled down, this is it: the evening Vic went over to make the good deal off the old people who had Buster for so long he rode Buster home and when he showed up at the gate to Vic's acres needing one of us, me or Steve Willis to come down off the porch of our shanty to open the gate, it was me who came down to let Vic and Buster in the yard. That is the reason for Steve Willis not caring about Buster, not one thing more. Steve Willis stayed on the porch with his feet up on the railing watching Vic ride Buster by and me close the gate, and ever since, anything Vic tells us to do or about or with Buster, it is me who does it or me who listens even though Vic is telling us both, it is me and not Steve Willis, all from me getting down to open the gate that one time. That is why today Steve Willis was just ripping rows and not looking at Buster sneak, and I tell you, I like this forward thinking in Steve Willis when we make our new-moon runs but around Vic's back acres it can become tiresome and make you job-shy.

Just about lunch time, just about the time for the little Vic's children to come into their house to get cold pieces of fried fish and

Kool-Aid for lunch the big Vic's children down by the dock all shouted Snake and ran about fetching nets, poles and paddles. This was a good time for Steve Willis and I to break so Steve Willis and I broke for a cigarette to watch what would all Vic's kids be telling around the table all supper long. Vic's big kids ran up and back the dock trying to catch the snake with their poles and paddles, and the poor snake swam from side to side in the boat slip with his escape cut off by one of Vic's big kids poling around in a washtub trailing a minnow seine. One of Vic's big girl kids caught the tired-out snake on the surface and dipped him out with a canoe paddle and one of Vic's big boys snapped it like a bullwhip popping its neck so it went limp. Vic's dogs that Buster hadn't yet kicked into the canal barked and jumped up on the boys playing keepaway with the snake until the boys took it up to the outside sink where we clean fish to skin it out and dry what the dogs didn't eat in the sun.

As they all paraded up to the house I came to notice the yard seemed even emptier than it should have been with Vic's kids and dogs up at the big house, then I realized what piece was missing when between the wooden staked out rows of peabeans I saw a patch of sparrow shot ragged horsehair and a big horse behind showing out by the tomatoes. I shouted a couple of times and spun a shingle towards where Buster was at work munching cabbage and cucumbers but the shingle just skipped off his big horse behind and went into the canal.

By the time I got down from the roof leaving Steve Willis up there ripping shingles, Steve Willis not being the one to open the gate that first time Buster came to Vic's acres, Buster had eaten half the cabbage heads we had. I knew better than to come up from behind a horse who can kick a full grown collie thirty yards so I picked up the canoe paddle the big Vic's girl had used to fling up the snake on the dock with and went through the corn to cut Buster off at the cabbage.

But head to head, me shouting and making up and down wild slicing actions with the canoe paddle Buster had no focus on me. Instead he was stopped in mid chew. Then the sides of his almost to the ground slouched belly heaved out then in and then more out moving more out so much that patches of horsehair popped and dropped off and I took a half step backward fearing for an explosion. I called for Steve Willis to come down, to hurry up, but all Steve Willis said was what did I want, and I said I think Buster is sick from whatever Vic had sprayed on the cabbage probably not getting anybody to read the label to begin with, and then Buster side stepped like he was drunk through two rows of stake-strung peabeans and then he pitched forward to where I was backing up with the canoe paddle of little good, I was thinking, against an exploding horse, and then Buster, I swear before God, Buster burped and farted at the exact same time before his knees shook out from under him and he went down among the tallest tomatoes in Vic's garden wiping out the un-ate cabbage and some cucumber pickles too.

By this time Steve Willis had come down off the roof to look at the tragedy we were having in Vic's garden. It was hard to count the amount of summer supper vegetables Buster had ruint and smushed. Steve Willis called Buster a son of a bitch for wiping out the tomatoes, Steve Willis' favorite sandwich being tomato with heavy pepper and extra mayonnaise.

Steve Willis asked me did I hit him in the head or what with the canoe paddle but I promised I hadn't given him a lick at all with it, though we were both looking at how hard I was holding on to the handle. Steve Willis pushed in on Buster's big blowing up belly with his toe and air started to hiss out of Buster's mouth like a nail-stuck tire, and the fear of explosion having not completely passed, we both stepped back. You could tell the little hiss was coming out near where Buster's big black and pink tongue stuck pretty far out of his mouth laying in the dirt between where the tomatoes were smushed and the cabbage used to be.

Steve Willis said This is not good.

Usually when Steve Willis and I have a problem in our on the side new-moon business, we say we have to do some Big Thinking, and we are always seeming to be doing Big Thinking in all our business, but since this was a Buster problem and since Steve Willis didn't come down off the porch that first time to open the gate, it was coming clear to me I would have to be the Big Thinker on this one. I stepped away to think really big about the tragedy, figuring from where the garden is situated around the boat shed by our shanty on the canal you can't see it from the big house. I figured I had a fair while to figure where to go with Buster after I got him out of the garden, hoping to find a hole nearby big enough for such a big animal and do it all while Vic's little children slept out of the afternoon sun and while Vic's big children went to afternoon summer Bible study.

In the first part of thinking big I went up to the garage to get a good deal riding lawn mower to yank Buster out until I remembered it had a broken clutch, and when I came back Steve Willis was holding back a laugh to himself, and I will say about Steve Willis, he is not one to laugh right in your face. He was holding back a laugh holding the rope I'd given him to put around Buster to yank him out. Steve Willis asked me what kind of knot would I suggest he tie a dead horse to a broken riding lawn mower with.

I could see how far I could get Steve Willis to help with the Buster tragedy so I took the line out of his hand and put a timber hitch around one of Buster's hind legs saying out loud A timber hitch seems to work pretty well thanks a whole hell of a lot. I paid the line out from the garden and started to get that sinking feeling of a jam panic, a jam closing in needing Very Big Thinking, with not the July hot sun in the yard baking waves of heat making me feel any better at all. You get that sinking jam panic feeling, and I got it so bad that while I was paying out the line across the yard, and even though I knew I could not ever possibly do it, I stopped and held hard to the line and gave it a good solid pull the hardest I could to yank Buster out, straining, pulling, even when I saw when it was hopeless, and even with the jam panic worse, I had to let go of the line, and all the difference I had made was that now there was air hissing out from where black flies were moving around and settling back underneath the dirty place by Buster's big stringy tail.

This was even better than before to Steve Willis who stepped behind what tall tomatoes were left so he wouldn't have to laugh at me to my face. I picked up a shingle I'd thrown at Buster from the roof and spun it towards Steve Willis but it sliced to the right and shattered our side kitchen window and I could tell Steve Willis had to go behind the boat shed to laugh not in my face this time after you couldn't hear glass falling in the shanty anymore.

I gathered up the line bunched at my feet and trailed it over to the boat shed down to the dock. Vic's big Harker Island rig, our new-moon boat with the Chrysler inboard was gassed up with the key rusted in the ignition. I cleated the line that ran across the yard from Buster's hind leg onto the stanchion on the stern and shouted over to Steve Willis in the garden to at least help me throw the lines.

I felt for an instant better starting up the big Chrysler engine so that the floorboards buzzed my feet, feeling the feeling I get that starts to set in running the Harker Island rig over to the hidden dock on the south bay shore on new-moon nights, the feeling of the chance of sudden money and the possibility of anything, even danger and death, and feeling now in a July hot sun the feeling of Big Thinking a way out of a bad tragedy. With the engine running it was now possible in my mind that we wouldn't lose our place of life over something like letting a big horse die.

I was feeling better as Steve Willis threw off the stern line and I choked the wraps on the stanchion leading to where I could just see two big-legged hooves hung up in the tomatoes where I could snatch Buster out and decide what to do then, but the sound of the big engine turning over brought out the dogs from underneath the big house, them being used to going out with Vic in the mornings to check five miles of pound nets, and then some of the older kids not yet set off for Bible study, started to spill out of the house to see what Steve Willis and I were up to this time with their daddy's boat, and if I looked harder at the house, which I did, I could see the little Vic's children in the windows with diapers and old Vic's t-shirts on wanting to follow the big kids out, but not coming, them having to sleep in away from the July hot sun.

Vic's dogs got down to us first, and even old Lizzie's tan and gray snout, a snout she let babies pull without snapping, and a snout which would, when you were bent over fooling with getting the lawn hose turned on, come up and give you a friendly goose in your rear end, even old Lizzie's tan and gray snout snarled back to show sharp ripping wolflike teeth when she saw that old bastard of a horse Buster was down, and then she and all of Vic's other dogs were on the carcass and there was no keeping them away.

Now I had the problem of everybody in Vic's acres coming down to see what I had let happen to Buster, topped off by the dogs having their day going after Buster's body biting his hind legs and ripping away at the ears and privates. The sight of the dogs on Buster was no less than the sound they made, blood wild, and here came the rest of the kids to see all this, this even being better than chasing the watersnake around and out of the canal for a supper table story.

I had to Big Think quick so I pulled Steve Willis by his belt into the boat, starting over at that point about me and him and anything to do with Buster, forgetting that first time him not getting down to open the gate. I pushed forward on the throttle but did it cutting the bow off where I knew the sand bar was, still being in the right mind to know not to double up a dead horse tragedy with bad boatmanship. When I rounded the dock and the line leading to where the pack of wild-acting animals were in the tomatoes with the horse carcass snugged tight, our bow rose and our stern squared, and I really gave the big old lovey Chrysler the gas and, looking over my shoulder, I saw Buster slide from the garden with still the dogs around, this time giving chase to the dragging legs, because in their simple minds they were probably thinking the only way to stop something with legs is to bite its feet whether they are standing on them or not.

I knew that I was not just pulling Buster out of the garden now but that we had him sort of in tow, so that as we turned onto the canal proper and Buster skidded across the bulkhead and onto the dock that I knew wouldn't take his weight, I really had to pour the engine on, and I was right, Buster's big body humped the bulkhead over and came down splintering the dock we had just been tied to, but for an instant even over the dogs barking and the children yelling and the big Chrysler giving me any of anything making me feel better about all of this, just for an instant I heard Buster's hooves hit and scrape the good deal planking of the dock before bringing it down, and in that second of hearing horse's hooves on plank I had to turn back quick and look because it passed over me that maybe I would see Buster galloping behind us giving chase of me and Steve Willis out of Vic's garden instead of us dragging his big, dead body to sea in tow.

We still had plenty of canal to cover before we broke out into open ocean. The dogs raced along beside as far as they could but it was a game to them now, their wolf-like leaps mellowed out into tongue-flapping lopes. A couple of neighbors on down the canal came out to watch and the wake and spray from Buster cutting along ass backwards threw water into their yards. One of Vic's cousins Malcolm was working in a boat and seeing us coming he held up a pair of waterskis pointing to Buster laughing as we passed, but I could see open ocean so I throttled down and leaned hard forward to balance against the rising bow. I was glad I had enough forward thinking of my own to pull Steve Willis into the boat starting us over about Buster because I could look at him in the stern watching the big horse carcass we had in tow by a stiffed up leg like it was a weird submarine we were pulling by its periscope, and looking at Steve Willis I could see it was sinking in that when Vic came home from

Norfolk and threw me out of the back acres by the canal it would be Steve Willis himself being thrown out too.

I burned up about three hours of fuel looking for the right place in the ocean to cut Buster loose. One problem we had was one time we stopped to idle the engine and pull up a floorboard so I could check the oil and while we sat to drifting Steve Willis noticed that Buster floated. You could tell how the body was like a barrel just below the surface that it was the air or the gas or whatever was in Buster's big belly keeping him afloat. When I got up from checking the oil I threw to where Steve Willis was standing in the stern a marlin spike and he looked down at the marlin spike and then he looked up to me like he was saying Oh no I won't punch a hole, and I looked back to him wiping the oil off my hands, looking back like Oh yes you will too punch a hole, and when it came time for me to cut Buster loose out near the number nine sea buoy and it came time for Steve Willis to punch a hole, I did and he did and it was done.

So here we are really feeling bad about what we finally ended up doing to Vic's horse Buster, us drinking about it in the First Flight Lounge after we called Vic's wife at home and she said Un huh and Nunt uh to the sideways questions we asked her about Vic being home yet, trying to feel out how bad was the tragedy, and her hanging up not saying goodbye, and us wondering did she always do that and then us realizing we'd never talked to her on the telephone before.

After we tied up Vic's rig in the ditch behind the First Flight Lounge we started to wonder if shouldn't we have let Vic had his say about what to do with his finally dead horse, so therein started us having the lack of forward thinking and of Big Thinking, and instead we were left to second guessing and after we had left the rig with its better feeling hum and came in to drink, with the drink buzzes coming on ourselves, we started to feel naked in our thinking especially when a neighbor of Vic's came in and shook his head when he saw us and then walked back out.

So what Steve Willis and I have done is to get down off the wall the tide chart and figure out where the most likely place for Buster to wash in is. We'll head out over there when the tide turns and wait for Buster to come in on the surf and then drag him up to take him home in a truck we'll somehow Big Think our way to fetch by morning. The tide tonight turns at about two thirty, just about when the lounge closes too, so that is when we think we will make our move to the beach by the Holiday Inn, which is where we expect Buster back.

So Steve Willis and I sit in the First Flight Lounge not having the energy to begin to think about where we are to live after having to get ready to be kicked out of Vic's acres, much less having the energy to Big Think about pulling a sea-bloated horse out of the surf at two-thirty in the morning. Here we are sitting not having the energy to Big Think about all of this when Vic walks in barefooted and says Gintermen, gintermen, another one of the ways he says things because he can't read nor write and doesn't know how things are spelled to speak them correct.

There is a nervous way people who don't drink, say a preacher, act in bars but that is not Vic. Vic sits at our table open armed and stares at all the faces in the place, square in the eye, including our own we turn down. He sits at the table that is for drinking like it could be a table for anything else. Vic says he saw his rig in the ditch behind the lounge on his way home from Norfolk, would we want a ride home and come get it in the morning.

Steve Willis and I settle up and stand to go out with Vic who says he's excited about the good deal he's come back with. Looking at Steve Willis I still see it's to me to start telling Vic about us having to wait for his favorite animal in his animal group to wash up down the beach, all at our hands.

Out in the back of Vic's truck Vic runs his hands over six coin washing machines, something he does to all his new good deal things to make them really his. Vic says he got them from a business that was closing down, won't his wife be happy. Vic says our next change for rent will be to rewire the machines so they can run without putting in the quarters, what did we think. I start to tell Vic about Buster and the tragedy in the garden. I can't see Vic in the dark when they turn off the front lights to the First Flight Lounge but I can hear him say un huh, un huh as I talk.

When I finish the part with Steve Willis and I waiting for the tide to turn Vic says Come on boys, we ought to get on home oughten we. All three of us sit up front of the truck riding across the causeway bridges home. All Vic says for a while is well, my horse, my old horse, not finishing the rest, if there is anything to finish, and I get the feeling Vic is rearranging groups in his mind like his animal group things and his human group things and his good deal off people things, and maybe making a new group of really awful people things with just me and Steve Willis in it. But then Vic starts talking about how in change for rent Steve Willis and I are also going to build a laundry platform with a cement foundation and a pine rafter shedding, and Vic starts to talk like even after taking a rearrangement of all his things in all his groups everything still comes up okay. Vic says oughten we lay the foundation around near the downside of the shanty where Steve Willis and I live so the soap water can drain into the canal, and after we figure how to put the sidings and braces up oughten we put a couple of coats of paint on it to keep the weather out, maybe in change for some rent, and what color would us boys say would look good, and Steve Willis and I both sit up and yell Ackerine! at the same time, us all laughing, and me feeling crossing the last causeway bridge home I'm happy heading there as a human in Vic's acres again.

nominated by Gordon Lish and Shenandoah

LEARNING FROM CHEKHOV

by FRANCINE PROSE

from WESTERN HUMANITIES REVIEW

THIS PAST YEAR I taught at a college two and a half hours from my home. I commuted down once a week, stayed overnight, came back. Through most of the winter I took the bus. The worst part was waiting to go home in the New Rochelle Greyhound Station. The bus was unreliable, as was the twenty-minute taxi ride I took to get there, so I wound up being in the station, on the average, forty minutes a week.

One thing you notice if you spend any time there is that although the bus station is a glassed-in corner storefront, none of the windows open, so the only time air moves is when someone opens the door. There is a ticket counter, a wall of dirty magazines, a phone, a rack of dusty candy. It's never very crowded, which is hardly a comfort when half the people who *are* there look like they'd happily blow your brains out on the chance of finding a couple of Valiums in your purse.

Usually I bought a soda and a greasy sugar cookie to cheer myself up and read *People* magazine because I was scared to lose touch with reality for any longer than it took to read a *People* magazine article. Behind the counter worked a man about sixty and a woman about fifty, and in all the time I was there I never heard them exchange one personal word. Behind them was a TV, on constantly, and it will give you an idea of what kind of winter I had when I say that the first ten times I saw the Challenger blow up were on the bus station TV. I was having a difficult time in my life, and every minute that kept me from getting home to my husband and kids was painful. Many of you who have commuted will probably know what I mean.

Finally the bus came, the two drivers who alternated—the nasty younger one who seemed to slip into some kind of trance between Newburgh and New Paltz and went slower and slower up the thruway, and the older one who looked like a Victorian masher and had a fondness for some aerosol spray which smelled like a cross between cherry Lifesavers and Raid. The bus made Westchester stops for half an hour before it even got to the highway.

As soon as I was settled and had finished the soda and cookie and magazine from the bus station, I began reading the short stories of Anton Chekhov. It was my ritual, and my reward. I began where I'd left off the week before, through volume after volume of the Garnett translations. And I never had to read more than a page or two before I began to think that maybe things weren't so bad. The stories were not only—it seemed to me—profound and beautiful, but also involving, so that I would finish one and find myself, miraculously, a half hour closer to home. And yet there was more than the distraction, the time so painlessly and pleasantly spent. A great sense of comfort came over me, as if in those thirty minutes I myself had been taken up in a spaceship and shown the whole world, a world full of sorrows, both different and very much like my own, and also a world full of promise, an intelligence large enough to embrace bus drivers and bus station junkies, a vision so piercing it would have kept seeing those astronauts long after that fiery plume disappeared from the screen. I began to think that maybe nothing was wasted, that someday I could do something with what was happening to me, to use even the New Rochelle bus station in some way, in my work.

Reading Chekhov, I felt not happy, exactly, but as close to happiness as I knew I was likely to come. And it occurred to me that this was the pleasure and mystery of reading, as well as the answer to those who say that books will disappear. For now, books are still the best way of taking great art and its consolations along with us on the bus.

In the spring, at the final meeting of the course I was commuting to teach, my students asked me this: if I had one last thing to tell them about writing, what would it be? They were half joking, partly because by then they knew me well enough to know that whenever I said anything about writing, I could usually be counted on to come up—often when we'd gone on to some other subject completely— with qualifications and even counterexamples proving that the opposite could just as well be true. And yet they were also half serious. We had come far in that class. From time to time, it had felt as if, at nine each Wednesday morning, we were shipwrecked together on an island. Now they wanted a souvenir, a fragment of seashell to take home.

Still it seemed nearly impossible to come up with that one last bit of advice. Often, I have wanted to somehow get in touch with former students and say: remember such and such a thing I told you? Well, I take it back, I was wrong! Given the difficulty of making any single true statement, I decided that I might just as well say the first thing that came to mind—which, as it happened, was this: the most important things, I told them, were observation and consciousness. Keep your eyes open, see clearly, think about what you see, ask yourself what it means. *and read Chekhov!*

After that came the qualifications and counterexamples: I wasn't suggesting that art necessarily be descriptive, literal, autobiographical or confessional. Nor should the imagination be overlooked as an investigational tool. Italo Calvino's story, "The Distance of the Moon," about a mythical time when the moon could be reached by climbing a ladder from the earth, has always seemed to me to be a work of profound observation and accuracy. If clearsightedness— meant literally—were the criterion for genius, what should we do about Milton? But still, in most cases the fact remains: The wider and deeper your observational range, the better, the more interestingly and truthfully you will write.

My students looked at me and yawned. It was nine in the morning, and they'd heard it before. And perhaps I would not have repeated it, or repeated it with such conviction, had I not spent the year reading and rereading all that Chekhov, all those stories filled and illuminated with the deepest and broadest—at once compassionate and dispassionate—observation of life that I know.

I have already told you what reading the Chekhov stories did for me, something of what they rescued me from and what they brought me to. But what I have to add now is that after a while I started noticing a funny thing. Let's say, for example, that I had just come from telling a student that one reason the class may have had trouble telling his two main characters apart is that they were named Mikey and Macky. I wasn't saying that the two best friends in his story couldn't have similar names. But, given the absence of other distinguishing characteristics, it might be better—in the interests of clarity—to call one Frank, or Bill. The student seemed pleased with this simple solution to a difficult problem, I was happy to have helped. And then, as my bus pulled out of New Rochelle, I began Chekhov's "The Two Volodyas."

In that story, a young woman named Sofya deceives herself into thinking she is in love with her elderly husband Volodya, then deceives herself into thinking she is in love with a childhood friend, also named Volodya; in the end, we see her being comforted by an adoptive sister who has become a nun, and who tells her "that all this is of no consequence, that it would all pass and God would forgive her." What I want to make clear is that the two men's having the same name is not the point of the story; here, as in all of Chekhov's work, there is never exactly "a point." Rather, we feel that are seeing into this woman's heart, into what she perceives as her "unbearable misery." That she should be in love—or not in love—with two men named Volodya is simply a fact of her life.

The next week, I suggested to another student that what made her story confusing was the multiple shifts in point of view. It's only a five-page story, I said. Not *Rashomon*. And that afternoon I read "Gusev," one of the most beautiful of Chekhov's stories about a sailor who dies at sea. The story begins with the sailor's point-of-view, shifts into long stretches of dialogue between him and another dying man. When Gusev dies—another "rule" I was glad I hadn't told my students was that, for "obvious" reasons, you can't write a story in which the narrator or point-of-view character dies—the point of view shifts to that of the sailors burying him at sea and then on to that of the pilot fish who see his body fall, to the shark who comes to investigate, until finally—as a student of mine once wrote—we feel we are seeing through the eyes of God. What I have found—what I've just proved—is that it's nearly impossible to *describe* the end of this story with any accuracy at all. So I will quote the last few marvelous paragraphs. What I want to point out—what needs no pointing out—is how much would have been lost had Chekhov followed the rules.

He went rapidly towards the bottom. Did he reach it? It was said to be three miles to the bottom. After sinking sixty or seventy feet, he began moving more and more slowly, swaying rhythmically, as though he were hesitating, and, carried along by the current, moved more rapidly sideways than downwards.

Then he was met by a shoal of the fish called harbor pilots. Seeing the dark body the fish stopped as though petrified, and suddenly turned round and disappeared. In less than a minute they flew back swift as an arrow to Gusev, and began zigzagging round him in the water.

After that another dark body appeared. It was a shark. It swarmed under Gusev with dignity and no show of interest, as though it did not notice him, and sank down upon its back, then it turned belly upwards, basking in the warm transparent water, and languidly opened its jaws with two rows of teeth. The harbor pilots are delighted, they stop to see what will come next. After playing a little with the body the shark nonchalantly puts its jaws under it, cautiously touches it with its teeth, and the sailcloth is rent its full length from head to foot; one of the weights falls out and frightens the harbor pilots, and, striking the shark on the ribs, goes rapidly to the bottom.

Overhead at this time the clouds are massed together on the side where the sun is setting; one cloud like a triumphal arch, another like a lion, a third like a pair of scissors. . . . From behind the clouds a broad green shaft of light pierces through and stretches to the middle of the sky; a little later another, violet-colored, lies beside it; next to that, one of gold, then one rose-colored. . . . The sky turns a soft lilac. Looking at this gorgeous enchanted sky, at first the ocean scowls, but soon it too takes tender, joyous, passionate colors for which it is hard to find a name in human speech.

Around this same time, I seem to remember myself telling my class that we should, ideally, have some notion of whom or what a story is about—in other words, whose story is it? To offer the reader that simple knowledge, I said—I must have been in one of my ironic moods—wasn't really giving much. A little clarity of focus cost the writer almost nothing and paid off, for the reader, a hundredfold. And it was about this same time that I first read "In the Ravine," perhaps the most heartbreaking and most powerful Chekhov story I know, in which we don't realize that the peasant girl Lipa is our heroine until almost halfway through. Moreover, the story turns on the death of a baby—just the sort of incident I advise students to stay away from because it is so difficult to write well and without sentimentality. Here—I have no pedagogical excuse to quote this, but am only including it because I so admire it—is the extraordinarily lovely scene in which Lipa plays with her baby.

> Lipa spent her time playing with the baby which had been born to her before Lent. It was a tiny, thin, pitiful little baby, and it was strange that it should cry and gaze about and be considered a human being, and even be called Nikifor. He lay in his cradle, and Lipa would walk away towards the door and say, bowing to him: "Good day, Nikifor Anisimitch!"
>
> And she would rush at him and kiss him. Then she would walk away to the door, bow again, and say: "Good day, Nikifor Anisimitch!" And he kicked up his little red legs and his crying was mixed with laughter like the carpenter Elizarov's.

By now I had learned my lesson. I began telling my class to read Chekhov instead of listening to me. I invoked Chekhov's name so often that a disgruntled student accused me of trying to make her write like Chekhov. She went on to tell me that she was sick of Chekhov, that plenty of writers were better than Chekhov, and when I asked her who, she said: Thomas Pynchon. I said I thought both writers were very good, suppressing a wild desire to run out in the hall and poll the entire faculty on who was better—Chekhov or Pynchon—only stopping myself because— or so I'd like to think —the experience of reading Chekhov was proving not merely enlightening, but also humbling.

Still there were some things I thought I knew. A short time later I suggested to yet another student that he might want to think twice about having his character—in the very last paragraph of his story— pick up a gun and blow his head off for no reason. I wasn't saying that this couldn't happen, it was just that it seemed so unexpected, so melodramatic. Perhaps if he prepared the reader, ever so slightly, hinted that his character was, if not considering, then at least capable of this. A few hours later I got on the bus and read the ending of "Volodya":

> Volodya put the muzzle of the revolver to his mouth, felt something like a trigger or a spring, and pressed it with his finger. Then he felt something else projecting, and once more pressed it. Taking the muzzle out of his mouth, he wiped it with the lapel of his coat, looked at the lock. He had never in his life taken a weapon in his hand.
>
> "I believe one ought to raise this," he reflected. "Yes, it seems so."
>
> Volodya put the muzzle in his mouth again, pressed it with his teeth, and pressed something with his fingers. There was the sound of a shot. Something hit Volodya in the back of his head with terrible violence and he fell on the table with his face downwards among the bottles of glasses. Then he saw his father as in Mentone, in a top hat with a wide black band on it, wearing mourning for some lady, suddenly seize him by both hands, and they fell headlong into a very deep dark pit. Then everything was blurred and vanished.

Until that moment we'd had no indication that Volodya was troubled by anything more than the prospect of school exams and an ordinary teenage crush on a flirtatious older woman. Nor had we heard much about his father, except that Volodya blames his frivolous mother for having wasted his money.

What seemed at issue here was far more serious than a question of similar names and divergent points of view. For as anyone who has ever attended a writing class knows: the bottom line of the fiction workshop is motivation. We complain, we criticize, we say that we don't understand why this or that character says or does something. Like parody method actors, we ask: What is the motivation? Of course, all this is based on the comforting supposition that things, in fiction as in life, are done for a reason. But here was

Chekhov telling us that—hadn't we ever noticed?—quite often people do things—terrible, irrevocable things—for no good reason at all. No sooner had I assimilated this critical bit of information than I happened to read "A Dull Story," which convinced me that I had not only been overestimating, but also oversimplifying the depths and complexities of motivation. How could I have demanded to know clearly how a certain character felt about another character when—as the narrator of "A Dull Story" reveals on every page—our feelings for each other are so often elusive, changing, contradictory, hidden in the most clever disguises even from ourselves?

Clearly Chekhov was teaching me how to teach, and yet I remained a slow learner. The mistakes—and the revelations—continued. I had always assumed and probably even said that being insane was not an especially happy state, that the phrase "happy idiot" was generally an inaccurate one and that, given the choice, most hallucinating schizophrenics would opt for sanity. And maybe this is mostly true, but as Chekhov is always reminding us, "most" is not "all." For Kovrin, the hero of "The Black Monk," the visits from an imaginary monk are the sweetest and most welcome moments in his otherwise unsatisfactory life. And what of the assumption that, in life and in fiction, a crazy character should "act" crazy, should early on clue us into his craziness? Not Kovrin, who, aside from these hallucinatory attacks and a youthful case of "upset nerves," is a university professor, a husband, a functioning member, as they say, of society, a man whose consciousness of his own "mediocrity" is relieved only by his conversations with the phantasmagorical monk, who assures him that he is a genius.

Reading another story, "The Husband," I remembered asking: What is the point of writing a story in which everything's rotten and all the characters are terrible and nothing much happens and nothing changes? In "The Husband," Shalikov, the tax collector, watches his wife enjoying a brief moment of pleasure as she dances at a party, has a jealous fit and blackmails her into leaving the dance and returning to the prison of their shared lives. The story ends:

> Anna Pavlovna would scarcely walk. She was still under
> the influence of the dancing, the music, the talk, the
> lights, and the noise; she asked herself as she walked
> along why God had thus afflicted her. She felt miserable,
> insulted, and choking with hate as she listened to her

husband's heavy footsteps. She was silent, trying to think of the most offensive, biting and venomous word she could hurl at her husband, and at the same time she was fully aware that no word could penetrate her tax collector's hide. What did he care for words? Her bitterest enemy could not have contrived for her a more helpless position. And meanwhile the band was playing, and the darkness was full of the most rousing, intoxicating dance tunes.

The "point"—and, again, there is no conventional "point"—is that in just a few pages, the curtain concealing these lives has been drawn back, revealing them in all their helplessness and rage and rancor. The point is that lives go on without change, so why should fiction insist that major reverses should always—conveniently—occur?

And finally, this revelation. In some kind of fit of irritation, I told my class that it was just a fact that the sufferings of the poor are more compelling, more worthy of our attention than the vague discontents of the rich. So it was with some chagrin that I read "A Woman's Kingdom," a delicate and astonishingly moving story about a rich, lonely woman—a factory owner, no less—who finds herself attracted to her foreman . . . until a casual remark by a member of her own class awakens her to the impossibility of her situation. By the time I had finished the story, I felt that I had been challenged, not only in my more flippant statements about fiction but in my most basic assumptions about life. In this case, truth had nothing to do with social justice, or with morality, with right and wrong. The truth was what Chekhov had seen and I—with all my fancy talk of observation—had somehow overlooked: cut a rich woman and she will bleed just like a poor one. Which isn't to say that Chekhov didn't know and know well: the world being what it is, the poor do get cut somewhat more often and more deeply.

And now, since we are speaking of life, a brief digression, about Chekhov's. By the time Chekhov died of tuberculosis at the age of forty-four, he had written—in addition to his plays—588 short stories. He was also a medical doctor. He supervised the construction of clinics and schools, he was active in the Moscow Art Theater, he married the famous actress, Olga Knipper, he visited the infamous prison on Sakhalin Island and wrote a book about that. Once when someone asked him about his method of composition, Chekhov picked up an ashtray. "This is my method of composition," he said. "Tomorrow I will write a story called 'The ashtray.' " Along the way, he was generous with advice to young writers. And now, to paraphrase what I said to my class, listen to Chekhov instead of me. Here are two quotations from Chekhov's letters, both on the subject of literary style:

> In my opinion a true description of Nature should be very brief and have the character of relevance. Commonplaces such as "the setting sun bathing in the waves of the darkening sea, poured its purple gold, etc."—"the swallows flying over the surface of the water twittered merrily"—such commonplaces one ought to abandon. In descriptions of Nature one ought to seize upon the little particulars, grouping them in such a way that, in reading when you shut your eyes, you get the picture.
>
> For instance you will get the full effect of a moonlit night if you write that on the milldam, a little glowing star point flashed from the neck of a broken bottle, and the round black shadow of a dog or a wolf emerged and ran, etc. . . .
>
> In the sphere of psychology, details are also the thing. God preserve us from commonplaces. Best of all is it to avoid depicting the hero's state of mind; you ought to try to make it clear from the hero's actions. It is not necessary to portray many characters. The center of gravity should be in two people: he and she.

> You understand it at once when I say "The man sat on the grass." You understand it because it is clear and makes no demands on the attention. On the other hand it is not easily understood if I write, "A tall, narrow-chested, middle-sized man, with a red beard, sat on the green grass, already trampled by pedestrians, sat silently, shyly, and timidly looked about him." That is not immediately grasped by the mind, whereas good writing should be grasped at once—in a second.

Another quotation, on the subject of closure:

My instinct tells me that at the end of a story or a novel I must artfully concentrate for the reader an impression of the entire work, and therefore must casually mention something about those whom I have already presented. Perhaps I am in error.

And here are a number of quotations on a theme which comes up again and again in his letters—the writer's need for objectivity, the importance of seeing clearly, without judgment, certainly without prejudgment, the need for the writer to be, in Chekhov's words, "an unbiased observer."

That the world "swarms with male and female scum" is perfectly true. Human nature is imperfect. . . . But to think that the task of literature is to gather the pure grain from the muck heap is to reject literature itself. Artistic literature is called so because it depicts life as it really is. Its aim is truth—unconditional and honest. . . . A writer is not a confectioner, not a dealer in cosmetics, not an entertainer; he is a man bound under compulsion, by the realization of his duty and by his conscience. . . . To a chemist, nothing on earth is unclean. A writer must be as objective as a chemist.

It seems to me that the writer should not try to solve such questions as those of God, pessimism, etc. His business is but to describe those who have been speaking or thinking about God and pessimism, how and under what circumstances. The artist should be not the judge of his characters and their conversations, but only an unbiased observer. *that is why I cannot/do not write. I'm genetically judgmental.*

You are right in demanding that an artist should take an intelligent attitude to his work, but you confuse two things: solving a problem and stating a problem correctly. It is only the second that is obligatory for the artist.

You abuse me for objectivity, calling it indifference to good and evil, lack of ideas and ideals, and so on. You would have me, when I describe horse thieves, say: "Stealing horses is an evil." But that has been known for ages without my saying so. Let the jury judge them; it's my job simply to show what sort of people they are. I write: you are dealing with horse thieves, so let me tell you that they are not beggars but well fed people, that they are people of a special cult, and that horse stealing is not simply theft but a passion. Of course it would be pleasant to combine art with a sermon, but for me personally it is impossible owing to the conditions of technique. You see, to depict horse thieves in 700 lines I must all the time speak and think in their tone and feel in their spirit, otherwise . . . the story will not be as compact as all short stories ought to be. When I write, I reckon entirely upon the reader to add for himself the subjective elements that are lacking in the story.

And now, one final quotation, which given my track record for making statements and having to retract them a week later, struck me with particular force:

> It is time for writers to admit that nothing in this world makes sense. Only fools and charlatans think they know and understand everything. The stupider they are, the wider they conceive their horizons to be. And if an artist decides to declare that he understands nothing of what he sees—this in itself constitutes a considerable clarity in the realm of thought, and a great step forward.

Every great writer is a mystery, if only in that some aspect of his or her talent remains forever ineffable, inexplicable and astonishing. The sheer population of Dickens' imagination, the fantastic architecture Proust constructs out of minutely examined moments, etc., etc. We ask ourselves: How could anyone do that? And of course, different qualities of the work will mystify different people. For me, Chekhov's mystery is first of all one of knowledge: how does he know so much? He knows everything we pride ourselves on having learned, and of course much more. "The Name Day Party," a story about a pregnant woman, is full of observations about pregnancy which I had thought were secrets.

The second mystery is how, without ever being direct, he communicates the fact that he is not describing The World or how people should see The World or how he, Anton Chekhov, sees The World, but only one or another character's world for a certain span of time. When the characters are less than attractive, we never feel the author hiding behind them, peeking out from around their edges to say, "This isn't me, this isn't me!" We never feel that the Gurov, the "hero" of "The Lady with the Pet Dog" is Chekhov, though, for all we know, he could be. Rather we feel we are seeing his life—and his life transformed. Chekhov is always, as he says in his letters, working from the particular to the general.

The greatest mystery for me—and it's what, I think, makes Chekhov so different from any other writer I know—is this matter he keeps alluding to in his letters: the necessity of writing without judgment. Not saying, Stealing horses is an evil. To be not the judge of one's characters and their conversations but rather the unbiased observer. What should, I imagine, be clear, is that Chekhov didn't live without judgment. I don't know if anyone does, or if it is even possible except for psychotics and Zen monks who've trained themselves to suspend all reflection, moral and otherwise. My sense is that living without judgment is probably a terrible idea. Nor, again, is any of this prescriptive. Balzac judged everyone and found nearly all of them wanting; their smallness and the ferocity of his outrage is part of the greatness of his work. But what Chekhov believed and acted on more than any writer I can think of is that judgment and especially prejudgment was incommensurate with a certain kind of literary art. It is, I believe, what—together with his range of vision—makes him wholly unique among writers. And why, for reasons I still can't quite explain, his work comforted me in ways Balzac just simply could not.

Before I finish, I'd like to quote Vladimir Nabokov's summation of his lecture on Chekhov's story, "The Lady with the Pet Dog":

> All the traditional rules of storytelling have been broken in this wonderful story of twenty pages or so. There is no problem, no regular climax, no point at the end. And it is one of the greatest stories ever written.
>
> We will now repeat the different features that are typical for this and other Chekhov tales.

First: The story is told in the most natural way possible, not beside the after-dinner fireplace as with Turgenev or Maupassant, but in the way one person relates to another the most important things in his life, slowly and yet without a break, in a slightly subdued voice.

Second: Exact and rich characterization is attained by a careful selection and careful distribution of minute but striking features, with perfect contempt for the sustained description, repetition, and strong emphasis of ordinary authors. In this or that description one detail is chosen to illume the whole setting.

Third: There is no special moral to be drawn and no special message to be received.

Fourth: The story is based on a system of waves, on the shades of this or that mood. . . . In Chekhov, we get a world of waves instead of particles of matter. . . .

Sixth: The story does not really end, for as long as people are alive, there is no possible and definite conclusion to their troubles or hopes or dreams.

Seventh: The storyteller seems to keep going out of his way to allude to trifles, every one of which in another type of story would mean a signpost denoting a turn of the action . . . but just because these trifles are meaningless, they are all-important in giving the real atmosphere of this particular story.

Let me repeat one sentence which seems to me particularly significant. "We feel that for Chekhov the lofty and the base are not different, that the slice of watermelon and the violet sea and the hands of the town governor are essential points of the beauty plus pity of the world." And what I might add to this is: the more Chekhov we read, the more strongly we feel this. I have often thought that Chekhov's stories should not be read singly but as separate parts of a whole. For like life, they present contradictory views, opposing visions. Reading them, we think: How broad life is! How many ways there are to live! In this world, where anything can happen, how much is possible! Our whole lives can change in a moment. Or: Nothing will ever change—especially the fact that the world and the human heart will always be wider and deeper than anything we can fathom.

And this is what I've come to think about what I learned and what I taught and what I should have taught. Wait! I should have said to that class: Come back! I've made a mistake. Forget about observation, consciousness, clearsightedness. Forget about life. Read Chekhov, read the stories straight through. Admit that you understand nothing of life, nothing of what you see. Then go out and look at the world.

nominated by Joyce Carol Oates and C. E. Poverman

THE GUEST ELLEN AT THE SUPPER FOR STREET PEOPLE

by DAVID FERRY

from RARITAN A QUARTERLY REVIEW

The unclean spirits cry out in the body
Or mind of the guest Ellen in a loud voice,
Torment me not, and in the fury of her unclean
Hands beating the air in some kind of unending torment—
Nobody witnessing could possibly know the event
That cast upon her the spell of this enchantment.

Almost all the guests are under some kind of enchantment:
Of being poor day after day in the same body;
Of being witness still to some obscene event;
Of listening all the time to somebody's voice
Whispering in the ear things divine or unclean,
In the quotidian of unending torment.

One has to keep thinking there was some source of torment,
Something that happened someplace else, unclean.
One has to keep talking in a reasonable voice
About things done, say, by a father's body
To or upon the body of Ellen, in enchantment
Helpless, still by the old forgotten event

Enchanted, still in the unforgotten event
A prisoner of love, filthy Ellen in her torment,
Guest Ellen in the dining hall in her body,
Hands beating the air in her enchantment,
Sitting alone, gabbling in her garbled voice
The narrative of the spirits of the unclean.

She is wholly the possessed one of the unclean.
Maybe the spirits came from the river. The enchantment
Entered her, maybe, in the Northeast Kingdom. The torment,
A thing of the waters, gratuitous event,
Came up out of the waters and entered her body
And lived in her in torment and cried out in her voice.

It speaks itself over and over again in her voice,
Cursing maybe or not a familiar obscene event
Or only the pure event of original enchantment
From the birth of the river waters, the pure unclean
Rising from the source of things, in a figure of torment
Seeking out Ellen, finding its home in her poor body.

Her body witness is, so also is her voice,
Of torment coming from unknown event;
Unclean is the nature and name of the enchantment.

nominated by Lloyd Schwartz and Tom Sleigh

TALKING TO GOD

by VICTORIA HALLERMAN

from NORTH DAKOTA QUARTERLY

You were in all domes,
you were in the Union Terminal, arching
your palm above us, who but you
could have made a sky in there and filled it up
with giants? constellations of the WPA.
Meanwhile every night I praised you,
squeezing my eyes shut so hard I made
meteor showers in the red and black
dome inside my head.

You lived in the Maxfield Parrish print behind
Aunt Lottie's piano,
a castle with a winged child, swinging
on a swing like mine, a child
who every night went in to heaven.
You were an old man at first, with trailing beard,
then you were Blake's inventor-god with compass,
but men were fallible, like my father,
bringing his things home from work in a cardboard box,
starting a business of his own and failing
then starting again.

You were drink to my mother in the end
who measured freely her own death
from the green glass cup
she kept above the kitchen sink,

the vermouth left standing when she died,
cases and cases in the basement,
erect as missiles.
By then you had become
the purple spot inside my head when my eyes
close, the stars
with their nothing, beyond nothing

nominated by Dan Masterson

TENDERNESS

by STEPHEN DUNN

from POETRY

Back then when so much was clear
   and I hadn't learned
young men learn from women

what it feels like to feel just right,
   I was twenty-three,
she thirty-four, two children, a husband

in prison for breaking someone's head.
   Yelled at, slapped
around, all she knew of tenderness

was how much she wanted it, and all
   I knew
were back seats and a night or two

in a sleeping bag in the furtive dark.
   We worked
in the same office, banter and loneliness

leading to the shared secret
   that to help
National Biscuit sell biscuits

was wildly comic, which led to my body
   existing with hers
like rain water that's found its way

underground to water it naturally joins.
   I can't remember
ever saying the exact word, tenderness,

though she did. It's a word I see now
   you must be older to use,
you must have experienced the absence of it

often enough to know what silk and deep balm
   it is
when at last it comes. I think it was terror

at first that drove me to touch her
   so softly,
then selfishness, the clear benefit

of doing something that would come back
   to me twofold,
and finally, sometime later, it became

reflexive and motiveless in the high
   ignorance of love.
Oh abstractions are just abstract

until they have an ache in them. I met
   a woman never touched
gently, and when it ended between us,

I had new hands and new sorrow,
   everything it meant
to be a man changed, unheroic, floating.

nominated by Kathy Callaway, Henry Carlile, Stanley Lindberg and Jim Simmerman

EAGLE POEM

by JOY HARJO

from STREETFARE JOURNAL

To pray you open your whole self
To sky, to earth, to sun, to moon
To one whole voice that is you
And know there is more
That you can't see, can't hear
Can't know except in moments
Steadily growing, and in languages
That aren't always sound but other
Circles of motion.
Like eagle that Sunday morning
Over Salt River. Circled in blue sky
In wind, swept our hearts clean
With sacred wings.
We see you, see ourselves and know
That we must take the utmost care
And kindness in all things.
Breathe in, knowing we are made of
All this, and breathe, knowing
We are truly blessed because we
Were born, and die soon within a
True circle of motion,
Like eagle rounding out the morning
Inside us.
We pray that it will be done
In beauty.
In beauty.

nominated by Eugene Redmond, William Pitt Root and Christina Zawadiwsky

WHAT IS IT THEN BETWEEN US?

fiction by EHUD HAVAZELET

from THE ONTARIO REVIEW

LIKE THIS.

I breeze through town and she takes me in. Call from Chinatown, Port Authority, Yankee Stadium. Can I see you now. Tonight. Arrive with flowers, a quart of Jack, Glenn Gould playing Bach. The energy of the city square between my shoulders, I seek the light of occasion in her eyes.

She has a man, now. She gets him out of the way. She makes the bed and looks around the room, struck that its casualness is just right—empty coffee mugs, poetry books tumbled in a corner. She turns to me and says—all we need is cool sheets, a bottle of wine, and Cary Grant on the late show. We could go on forever. We will, I answer her. We already have.

Then six blocks to the university. In the campus bar, they still have jazz, but not for us, the dark, the precision. We drink furiously and I make her laugh the way no one can, bringing that sheen to the surface. I'm back now, I tell her. I've got plans for us. I lean forward and smile. I tease myself with her breasts but there is no need to touch her; we are beyond urgency. It is a glorious return—back in the city, annealed, a beautiful woman to take me home, and only the vaguest memories of another night, fear drying the words on my

179

tongue. Our earlier life plays about our table as formless and whimsical as smoke.

The doorman doesn't recognize me. An old man, he regards me with dim suspicion, says my name means nothing to him. He dials her on the house phone, keeping his eyes on me, brown eyes sifted through with grey, watchful.

A man down here, Miss. Says he knows you.

He hands the phone to me and I dredge for the night I had planned—poetry and jazz, memorable times—but I find nothing. I hold the phone to my mouth, his old man smell lifting off the plastic. I say hello into the receiver. I'm downstairs, I say. I just got in.

I listen to the swaying of phone sounds, a distant keening on the wire. The doorman reaches out. Just as he is about to take the phone, she says, four months. Where have you been four months?

North, I say. Around. I've been planning to call.

Four months. And before I can answer, she says, come up, then. I wouldn't want to keep you waiting.

I watch her sleep. In the blue before dawn with the curtains thick against the street, I am nothing more than the tip of a cigarette, its arc to my lips, its smolder and weave. I have swallowed just one more little beauty, because sleep was out of the question, because she didn't want me in her bed. I am calm, now. I can sit as long as I must. She moves in her sleep, an arm across empty sheets. The room is a high-ceilinged box, a chamber, a place to be sealed away. Everything is here, everything we would need. I sit at the other edge and it is cold in her room. But she is there, under the blankets, mounding naked and silken in her dozing heat, ample, gathering strength. She does not want me in her bed but she will not make me leave. The curtains are thick and they hold off the light. I bring cigarettes to my lips and away again. They make sounds like small kisses in the dark.

I was born in this city. They don't hand out passports here. I conquered it, assaulting it from all sides, laying siege from the boroughs, plotting my approach. I climbed the Empire State, the Chrysler, the Riverside Church, and I saw it from the skies. I crossed the Williamsburg and the Willis Avenue, and looked down at the roiling gray water. I stood on the Palisades in another state

taking in the island whole with one flex of my neck. I rode the
subway to the end of the line, the end of all the lines— South Ferry,
Coney Island, Pelham Park, 179th Street in Bayside, Queens. I
knew the tubular caverns and freight elevators of the uptown IRT,
and the endless underground miles of Grand Central. I knew the
tunnels where the winos slept, the bag ladies, and the hole in the
Flushing Line wall where you could see rats streaming like cells in
the blood. I could recite the skyline, eyes closed, knew a fountain
in Central Park deserted and completely overgrown, and I understood how Times Square beat back the night almost to extinction. I
rode this city like Triton rides the waves and I never should have
left. My one question for you. Why would I ever want to leave?

In the Ansonia, Harry and I count out beauties over bottles of
beer. Roland Kirk is on the stereo, as always, and there are speakers
all over the room—by the windows, concealed in closets, on stray
chairs and overturned boxes—so the sound does not emanate, does
not travel, simply is, everywhere, at once. Roland Kirk was a hero,
a master of circular breathing, which means he had evolved to a state
where he was breathing 100% of the time, alive that way every
moment, until his body gave out from joy and exhaustion, you would
have to believe. Roland Kirk could play an alto and a tenor at the
same time and in harmonies much stiffer than simple thirds. We
saw this, at the Bottom line, the loft on Second Avenue. He could
then put a penny whistle in each nostril and blow there too, he
could play out of his ears, legend had it, but the union clamped
down on this, and then his manager who wanted to harness a good
thing, and then his doctors, in simple honest fear. When Roland
Kirk died at forty-one, after a stroke and heart trouble, his body
closing down in pieces, there were spontaneous processions all over
the island, people needing to walk, to get outdoors, to look around
for themselves. Radios played in every window, out of cars and
restaurants, and for a day, an afternoon, perhaps, all of Manhattan
spoke the same new language.

Harry slits the skin of a beauty with a thumb nail and pours the
bitter powder on his tongue. His smile is horrible as the crystals
work around his mouth.

Have you seen her, he says.

Sure, I say. First thing.

What did you tell her?

That I'm back. I'm okay. We're all gonna be okay, I told her.

Harry looks at me. He palms beauties into a paper sack. He punches numbers into a calculator. Around us, Roland Kirk soars, unceasing, and I have to work for a part of Harry's attention.

I remember when you moved in this place, I tell him. Stokes' wedding cake, you called it, Harry. Babe Ruth had lived in this very apartment, you said, Caruso across the hall. You told me Heifetz was on the thirteenth floor, blind and nobody knowing it, and that Isadora Duncan used to come Tuesday afternoons to see a Rumanian who never left his apartment. You told me these things, Harry, I say. Would you deny that now?

Harry punches in more numbers, writes on a yellow pad. Roland Kirk has abandoned the melody, and his accompanists are left behind to tap out rhythms. Roland Kirk hears notes he has never heard before.

There's more you told me, I say to Harry. You told me Apartment 14-B has been sealed off by the police until the year 2000. You told me the walls are three feet thick and neighbors could only guess what went on at Maria Callas's nights the mayor was seen waiting outside her door, the governor, the ambassador from Mexico City. Don't tell me now you didn't say these things, I tell Harry. I remember.

Harry has finished his calculating. He sweeps crystal off the table top and smears a thumb across his gums. He pushes the bag over and points out what I owe. I am standing, trying to get above the sound, but Roland Kirk finds me there, too.

Harry says, you remember a lot.

Everything, I say. All of it.

Me, I remember just a thing or two, he says, and the look on his face is not of a friend. I am pulling bills out of my pocket, grabbing the paper bag, searching for the door. I remember a phone call, almost morning, Harry says, a certain girlfriend of yours. Did I know where you were. Did anybody know where you were. I remember a taxi ride uptown, Harry says, and he has followed me into the hallway, halfway to the bank of elevators. I remember we went to your place, he calls out, she was afraid what she would find so I went along. I remember the place was empty, Harry shouts, his voice ringing through me in the deep stairwell. The lights were out and you were gone. That's what I remember.

The Ansonia Hotel was built in 1903 by William Earl Dodge Stokes, an eccentric with money to burn. Originally planned for twenty stories, construction was halted at sixteen, when Stokes decided that was the height at which he preferred to live. To evade the city fire insurers, Stokes instructed the builders to make the terra cotta walls thirty-six inches thick, to lace the edifice with dozens of intricate connecting balconies, to install extra plumbing and water supply. The Ansonia immediately became a favorite among artists, musicians and celebrities, people who, for one reason or another, required insulation from the world outside. On the roof, Stokes raised chickens and goats, selling the eggs to his tenants at a discount, keeping the goat milk for a diet he had adopted while travelling once in the Orient. To run the two fully-stocked restaurants, he lured Chef Gurnsey Webb away from the Plaza Hotel. Many older celebrities still keep apartments in the building, and though its fortunes have declined somewhat—the restaurants have given way to a Shoe Repair and a Chinese laundry, and the lobby is home to many whose business there is uncertain—its distinctive finials and cupolas, the delicate latticework of its balconies, the matching towers and the astounding detail of its facade, still rise above the subway lines on 72nd Street and draw the eye of the curious and those given to infatuation.

In the lobby, I stand in shadow and collect my thoughts. I clench my hand around the bag in my pocket, try to formulate plans. A man has been sleeping against the far wall and he opens his eyes to watch me. I take a step toward the door. The lobby has only weak bulbs high in the ceiling and their light is dim, aqueous. The marble walls are so thickly veined they seem to pulse and for a moment I think I feel the massive old building shift and settle above me in respiration. The door at the end of the lobby is a bright rectangular plane. Outside, taxis careen and truck drivers open their mouths to shout. The man gets up from the floor and walks over. He reaches a hand out to me and I put a shoulder into him, hard, and head for the exit, but again I stop, just a step or two short. I watch the glass doorframe where fast shapes and men's voices contend in the violent light.

In other days, Central Park was grassland and the animals roved wild. There were gaslights on the avenues and a garden in Madison

Square. There was a reservoir on 42nd Street like a vanquished pyramid, and on a Spanish tower, Diana raised her bow at the heavens. I tell her these things. Listen, I say. Please, I say. I know a woman on Park Avenue who keeps geraniums in bloom through the winter, moss roses, peonies, lily-of-the valley. In Washington Square, I tell her, Minetta Brook bubbles an arm's length from the surface. I know a man who spins the water through a tube in his basement. He would show you. Please.

We are in her room with the curtains wide, the sun blasting up against the windows. I waited hours on her doorfront, away from the old man, and when she saw me, she made a slight hesitation, as if she might turn the corner again, head crosstown or to the park. But I called out. I ran to her and she let me follow her upstairs.

While I talk, she dresses, making ready to leave. I talk quickly, holding her there until the right words form, pausing only a moment, discreetly, to slip a beauty under my tongue, precise consolation. She looks at me once in a while. She changes her shirt right there, puts a skirted leg on a chair to buff a shoe, but there is no seduction in these movements. She would do the same if she were alone. When she is done, she stands in front of the chair where I sit.

Is that what you came to tell me? she says. Stories? A history lesson?

No, I say. More. Much more.

Drop in after months to discuss the city that never was, is that it?

No, I say. Wait. Listen.

You wait, she tells me, and walks closer until the blue weave of her skirt presses hard against my knees. You listen. I don't live in that world. I never heard of that city. I'm not acquainted with sports heros, potentates, figures out of legend. In my world, it's a good day if the buses run on time, you come out of the subway without some stranger's fingerprints all over your body. In my world, drunks swerve across the median doing ninety, terrorists from a country you've never heard of carry machine guns into the restaurant where you're trying to have a quiet meal. In my world, morning follows night, she says, and people are accountable. You want to hear about my world? She takes my face in her hands, brings it up sharply. You ran, she says. It was your party, your friends. Influential people, a town house in Riverdale. Open your mind, you said, grow, you said, and it was fine as long as they left me alone. But not later. He got me in a corner, I was frightened, and what do you say? Be nice, it's his place. I said I wanted to leave. I looked right at you and said I wanted to go. But you weren't watching me. I was begging you. What's going to happen here, I said, but you weren't looking at me, you were looking at him, this dealer, this important person, this sleazy old man with his hand up your lover's thighs. And you didn't go for some air, or for a final blow with the boys around the pool. You ran. You left me there and ran out of town, out of my life. You're nothing, she says to me, and lets my face drop from her hands. You're not even here.

In the first New York Blackout, Kevin Simmons was a small boy in Queens, angry at his mother. He took his Tom Tresh Louisville Slugger and gave every streetlight on his block a solid whack. They rang like church bells. When he whaled into the last one, all the lights in the city went out. He went to the police then, by himself, and told them he was surprised, but he couldn't say he was sorry.

When the banks foreclosed on Eugene's grandfather, between the wars, the old man closed up shop in the middle of the day. He brought the truck around back and loaded it full as could be. He drove to City Hall, where he covered the steps and half the lawn with bread and sausages, pasta, pickled foods in great yellow jars, canned goods, eighty-dozen eggs. It made the papers. When La-Guardia arranged a postponement for Eugene's grandfather, he told his reporters, "What else was I going to do?"

Steve Brodie was the first to survive leaping off the Brooklyn Bridge. They made a Broadway play based on his life. Though it was soon revealed he had never actually gone through with the jump, it was a hero's world then, and he was a famous and happy man to the end of his days.

One summer, before the gas wars, Lucky Linda disappeared into Harlem. Get me another one of these, she told me. I'll be right back. Okay, I said, what are they. It doesn't matter; she was in the doorway by then, and in the half-light, she was already losing form. It doesn't matter. Something cool in a tall glass.

My moment is brief, diminutive by these standards. I leave her for the second time, the final time, and I wander. I stockpile little beauties, I collect on some old debts, establish a few new ones. I think of going to the Cloisters or Battery Park on sunny days, and I assume I will, I assume I will. It is night on Fulton Street when my moment arrives. I have been eating only beauties for days, too many perhaps, until everything threatens to fuse into long skeins of silver and black, loops of orange and aquamarine. They illuminate the sky at night now, the Empire State, green and red for Christmas, blue and white for the World Series. The Chrysler is an elaborate spear to snag careless angels. The city exults in light.

I hear it as if I have heard it countless times. How long has she been calling, "Stop that man, Somebody do something." He flashes by me, quick. The knife gleams. The knife actually gleams. I run before I can question myself. He looks over a shoulder and I swear, he laughs. He lopes, without effort, but I am in his wake, I am considering leaving my feet altogether.

We turn down alleyways, into streets where the moon reaches only rooftops and upper-story windows. I am gaining no ground but I am holding firm, attached to him and he knows it. He can go nowhere without me. I empty into my eyes, my legs, my lungs, like a star exploding. He turns onto the FDR exit ramp; I follow, mesmerized, adoring. Over his shoulder again, I see the knife. We run onto the highway. Ahead of us, car lights, endless, are rows of teeth in Leviathan's jaw. He skips into the center lane and heads uptown, against traffic, daring me to follow. I follow. We run toward the lights, toward midtown and the Bronx, Hudson Bay and the Arctic, until our hearts stop, until we are swallowed clean, entire.

nominated by John Daniel and D. R. MacDonald

AFTER YITZL

by ALBERT GOLDBARTH

from THE GEORGIA REVIEW

> *It is not for nothing that a Soviet historian once remarked that the most difficult of a historian's tasks is to predict the past.*
>
> —*Bernard Lewis*, History

I

THIS story begins in bed, in one of those sleepy troughs between the crests of sex. I stroke the crests of you. The night is a gray permissive color.

"Who do you think you were—do you think you were anyone, in an earlier life?"

In an earlier life, I think, though chance and bombs and the saltgrain teeth in ocean air have destroyed all documents, I farmed black bent-backed turnips in the hardpan of a *shtetl* compound of equally black-garbed bent-backed grandmama and rabbinic Jews.

My best friend there shoed horses. He had ribs like barrel staves, his sweat was miniature glass pears. (I'm enjoying this now.) On Saturday nights, when the Sabbath was folded back with its pristine linens into drawers for another week, this Yitzl played accordion at the *schnapps*-house. He was in love with a woman, a counter girl, there. She kept to herself. She folded paper roses in between serving; she never looked up. But Yitzl could tell: she tapped her foot. One day the cousin from Milano, who sent the accordion, sent new

Author's Note: In the writing of this essay/poem/story I drew on many rich sources of information and inspiration, two of which deserve special mention: Douglas Curran's *In Advance of the Landing: Folk Concepts of Outer Space* (1986) and Alex Shoumatoff's *The Mountain of Names: An Informal History of Kinship* (1985).

music to play—a little sheaf with American writing on it. *Hot* polka. Yitzl took a break with me in the corner—I was sipping sweet wine as dark as my turnips and trying to write a poem—and when he returned to his little grocer's crate of a stand, there was an open paper rose on his accordion. So he knew, then.

In this story-*in*-my-story they say "I love you," and now I say it in the external story, too: I stroke you slightly rougher as I say it, as if underlining the words, or reaffirming you're here, and I'm here, since the gray in the air is darker, and sight insufficient. You murmur it back. We say it like anyone else—in part because our death is bonded into us meiotically, from before there was marrow or myelin, and we know it, even as infants our scream is for more than the teat. We understand the wood-smoke in a tree is aching to rise from the tree in its shape, its green and nutritive damps are readying always for joining the ether around it—any affirming clench of the roots in soil, physical and deeper, is preventive for its partial inch of a while.

So: genealogy. The family tree. Its roots. Its urgent suckings among the cemeterial layers. The backsweep of teat under teat. The way, once known, it orders the Present. A chief on the island of Nios, off Sumatra, could stand in the kerosene light of his plank hut and (this is on tape) recite—in a chant, the names sung out between his betel-reddened teeth like ghosts still shackled by hazy responsibility to the living—his ancestral linkup, seventy generations deep; it took over an hour. The genealogical record banks of the Mormon Church contain the names and relationship data of 1½ to 2 billion of the planet's dead, "in a climate-controlled and nuclear-bomb-proof repository" called Granite Mountain Vault, and these have been processed through the Church's IBM computer system, the Genealogical Information and Names Tabulation, acronymed GIANT.

Where we come from. How we need to know.

If necessary, we'll steal it—those dinosaur tracks two men removed from the bed of Cub Creek in Hays County, using a masonry saw, a jackhammer, and a truck disguised as an ice-cream vendor's.

If necessary, (two years after Yitzl died, I married his *schnapps*-house sweetie: it was mourning him that initially drew us together; and later, the intimacy of hiding from the Secret Police in the burlap-draped back corner of a fishmonger's van. The guts were heaped to our ankles and our first true sex in there, as we rattled like bagged bones over the countryside, was lubricated—for fear kept

her dry—with fishes' slime: and, after . . . but that's another story)
we'll make it up.

II

Which is what we did with love, you and I: invented it. We needed
it, it wasn't here, and out of nothing in common we hammered a
treehouse into the vee of a family tree, from zero, bogus planks, the
bright but invisible nailheads of pure will. Some nights a passer-by
might spy us, while I was lazily flicking your nipple awake with my
tongue, or you were fondling me into alertness, pleased in what we
called bed, by the hue of an apricot moon, in what we called our life,
by TV's dry blue arctic light, two black silhouettes communing: and
we were suspended in air. If the passer-by yelled, we'd plummet.

Because each midnight the shears on the clock snip off another
twenty-four hours. We're frightened, and rightfully so. Because
glass is, we now know, a "slow liquid"; and we're slow dust. I've
heard the universe howling—a conch from the beach is proof, but
there are Ears Above for which the spiral nebulae must twist the
same harrowing sound. Because pain, in even one cell, is an ant: it
will bear a whole organ away. And a day is so huge—a Goliath; the
tiny stones our eyes pick up in sleeping aren't enough to confront it.
The marrow gives up. We have a spine, like a book's, and are also
on loan with a due date. And the night is even more huge; what we
call a day is only one struck match in an infinite darkness. This is
knowledge we're born with, this is in the first cry. I've seen each
friend I have, at one time or another, shake at thinking how susceptible and brief a person is: and whatever touching we do, whatever
small narrative starring ourselves can bridge that unit of emptiness,
is a triumph. "Tell me another story," you say with a yawn, "of life
back then, with—what was her name?" "With Misheleh?" "Yes, with
Misheleh." As if I can marry us backwards in time that way. As if it
makes our own invented love more durable.

The Mormons marry backwards. "Sealing," they call it. In the
sanctum of the Temple, with permission called a "temple recommend," a Mormon of pious state may bind somebody long dead
(perhaps an ancestor of his own, perhaps a name provided by chance
from a list of cleared names in the computer)—bind that person to
the Mormon faith, and to the flow of Mormon generations, in a
retroactive conversion good "for time and all eternity." (Though the

dead, they add, have "free agency" up in Heaven to accept this or not.) A husband and wife might be "celestially married" this way, from out of their graves, and into the spun-sugar clouds of a Mormon Foreverness . . . from out of the Old World sod . . . from sand, from swampwater . . . Where does ancestry *stop*?

To pattern the present we'll fabricate the past from before there *was* fabric. Piltdown Man. On display in the British Museum. From sixty-five million years back—and later shown to be some forgery of human and orangutan lockings, the jawbone stained and abraded. Or, more openly and jubilant, the Civilization of Llhuros "from the recent excavations of Vanibo, Houndee, Draikum, and other sites" —in Ithaca, New York, Norman Daly, professor of art at Cornell and current "Director of Llhurosian Studies" has birthed an entire culture: its creatures (the Pruii bird, described in the article "Miticides of Coastal Llhuros"), its rites (". . . the Tokens of Holmeek are lowered into the Sacred Fires, and burned with the month-cloths of the Holy Whores"), its plaques and weapons and votive figurines, its myths and water clocks, its poems and urns and a "nasal flute." An elephant mask. An "early icon of Tal-Hax." Wall paintings. "Oxen bells." Maps. The catalogue I have is 48 pages—135 entries. Some of the Llhuros artifacts are paintings or sculpture. Some are current garbage, given ancient life. Properly anachronismed, a five-and-dime on-sale orange juicer becomes a *trallib*, an "Oil container . . . Middle Period, found at Draikum." A clothes iron: "Late Archaic . . . that it may be a votive of the anchorite Ur Ur cannot be disregarded." Famous athletes. Textiles. "Fornicating gods."

Just open the mind, and the past it requires will surface. "Psychic archaeologists" have tranced themselves to the living worlds of the pyramids or the caves—one chipped flint scraper can be connection enough. When Edgar Cayce closed his eyes he opened them (inside his head, which had its eyes closed) in the undiluted afternoon light of dynastic Egypt: wind was playing a chafing song in the leaves of the palm and the persea, fishers were casting their nets. "His findings and methods tend to be dismissed by the orthodox scientific community," but Jeffrey Goodman meditates, and something —an invisible terraform diving bell of sorts—descends with his eyes to fully twenty feet below the sands of Flagstaff, Arizona: 100,000 B.C., his vision brailling happily as a mole's nose through the bones set in the darkness there like accent marks and commas.

Going back . . . The darkness . . . Closing your lids . . .

A wheel shocked into a pothole. Misheleh waking up, wild-eyed. Torches.

"We needed certain papers, proof that we were Jews, to be admitted to America. To pass the inspectors there. And yet if our van was stopped by the Secret Police and we were discovered in back, those papers would be our death warrant. Such a goat's dessert!— that's the expression we used then."

"And . . . ?"

"It comes from when two goats will fight for the same sweet morsel—each pulls a different direction."

"No, I mean that night, the escape—what *happened*?"

"The Secret Police stopped the van."

III

Earlier, I said "in a trough between crests"—sea imagery. I mean in part that dark, as it grows deeper, takes the world away, and a sleepless body will float all night in horrible separation from what it knows and where it's nurtured. Freedom is sweet; but nobody wants to be flotsam.

Ruth Norman, the eighty-two-year-old widow of Ernest L. Norman, is Uriel, an Archangel, to her fellow Unarian members and is, in fact, the "Cosmic Generator," and Head of all Unarius activities on Earth (which is an applicant for the "Intergalactic Confederation" of thirty-two other planets—but we need to pass a global test of "consciousness vibration"). In past lives, Uriel has been Socrates, Confucius, Henry VIII, and Benjamin Franklin—and has adventured on Vidus, Janus, Vulna, and other planets. All Unarians know their former lives. Vaughn Spaegel has been Charlemagne. And Ernest L. himself has been Jesus (as proved by a pamphlet, *The Little Red Box*), and currently is Alta; from his ankh-shaped chair on Mars he communicates psychically and through a bank of jeweled buttons with all the Confederation. Everyone works toward the day Earth can join. The 1981 Conclave of Light, at the Town and Country Convention Center in El Cajon, California, attracted over 400 Unarians, some from as far as New York and Toronto. Neosha Mandragos, formerly a nun for twenty-seven years, was there; and George, the shoe-store clerk, and Dan, assistant manager of an ice-cream parlor.

Uriel makes her long-awaited entrance following the *Bolero*-backed procession of two girls dressed as peacocks, led by golden chains, then two nymphs scattering petals from cornucopias, someone wearing a feathered bird's head, and various sages. Four "Nubian slaves . . . wearing skin bronzer, headdresses, loincloths and gilded beach thongs" carry a palanquin adorned with enormous white swans, atop which . . . Uriel! In a black velvet gown falling eight feet wide at the hem, with a wired-up universe of painted rubber balls representing the thirty-two worlds, that dangles out to her skirt's edge. According to Douglas Curran, "the gown, the painted golden 'vortex' headdress, and the translucent elbow-length gloves with rapier nails have tiny light bulbs snaked through the fabric. The bulbs explode into volleys of winking. Waves of light roll from bodice to fingertips, Infinite Mind to planets." People weep. Their rich remembered lives are a sudden brilliance over their nerves, like ambulance flashers on chicken wire, like . . . like fire approaching divinity. Nobody's worrying here over last week's sales of butter-pecan parfait.

We'll sham it. We need it. It's not that we lie. It's that we *make* the truth. The Japanese have a word especially for it: *nisekeizu*, false genealogies. Ruling-class Japan was obsessed with lineage and descent, and these connived links to the Sewangezi line of the Fujiwaras qualified one—were indeed the only qualification of the time —for holding office. "High birth." "Pedigree." It's no less likely in Europe. In the seventeenth century, Countess Alexandrine von Taxis "hired genealogists to fabricate a descent from the Torriani, a clan of warriors who ruled Lombardy until 1311."

European Jews, who by late in the 1700's needed to take on surnames in order to cross a national border, often invented family names that spoke of lush green woods and open fields—this from a people traipsing from one cramped dingy urban ghetto to another. Greenblatt. Tannenbaum. Now a child born choking on soot could be heir to a name saying miles of mild air across meadows. Flowers. Mossy knolls.

Misheleh's name was Rosenblum. I never asked but always imagined this explained the trail of paper roses she'd left through Yitzl's life. My name then was Schvartzeit, reference to my many-thousand-year heritage of black beets. The name on our papers, though, was Kaufman—"merchant." This is what you had to do, to survive.

I remember: they were rough with us, also with the driver of the van. But we pretended being offended, like any good citizens. It could have gone worse. This was luckily early in the times of the atrocities, and these officers—they were hounds set out to kill, but they went by the book. A hound is honest in his pursuit. The rat and the slippery eel—later on, more officers were like that.

They might have dragged us away just for being in back of the van at all. But we said we were workers. In this, the driver backed us up. And the papers that shouted out *Jews*? My Misheleh stuffed them up a salmon. Later, after the Secret Police were gone, and we clumped across the border, we were on our knees with a child's doll's knife slicing the bellies of maybe a hundred fish until we found it! Covered in pearly offal and roe. We had it framed when we came to America. Pretty. A little cherrywood frame with cherubim puffing a trump in each corner. We were happy, then. A very lovely frame around an ugliness.

"And you loved each other."

Every day, in our hearts. Some nights, in our bodies. I'll tell you this about sex: it's like genealogy. Yes. It takes you back, to the source. That's one small bit of why some people relish wallowing there. A burrowing, completely and beastly, back to where we came from. It tastes and smells "fishy" in every language I know. It takes us down to when the blood was the ocean, down the rivers of the live flesh to the ocean, to the original beating fecundity. It's as close as we'll ever get.

And this I'll tell you, about the smell of fish. For our earliest years, when I was starting the dry goods store and worrying every bolt of gabardine or every bucket of nails was eating another poem out of my soul—which I think is true—we lived over a fish store. Kipper, flounder, herring, the odors reached up like great gray leaves through our floorboards. And every night we lived there, Misheleh cried for a while. After the van, you see? She could never be around raw fish again, without panic.

But on the whole we were happy. There was security of a kind, and friends—even a social club in a patchy back room near the train tracks, that we decorated once a month with red and yellow crepe festoons and paper lanterns pouring out a buttery light.

Once every year she and I, we visited the cemetery. A private ritual: we pretended Yitzl was buried there. Because he'd brought us together, and we wanted him with us yet. For the hour it took, we always hired a street accordionist—it wasn't an uncommon instrument then. Like guitar now. Play a polka, we told him—*hot*. It drove the other cemetery visitors crazy! And always, Misheleh left a paper rose at the cemetery gates.

We heard that accordion music and a whole world came back, already better and worse than it was in its own time. Harsher. Gentler. Coarser. Little things—our *shtetl* dogs. Or big things too, the way we floated our sins away on toy-sized cork rafts once each spring, and everybody walking home singing . . . All of that world was keeping its shape but growing more and more transparent for us. Like the glass slipper in the fairy tale. The past was becoming a fairy tale. In it, the slipper predicates a certain foot and so a certain future.

At night I'd walk in my store. The moon like a dew on the barrel heaped with bolts, and the milky bodies of lamps, and the pen nibs, and shovels . . . Kaufman. Merchant.

IV

Within a year after death we have what Jewish tradition calls "the unveiling"—the gravestone dedication ceremony. September 14, 1986: I arrived in Chicago, joining my mother, sister, two aunts, and perhaps thirty others, including the rabbi, at the grave of my father Irving Goldbarth, his stone wrapped in a foolish square of cheesecloth. A stingy fringe of grass around the fresh mound. The burial had taken place in bitter city winter, the earth (in my memory) opening with the crack of axed oak. Now it was warmer, blurrier, everything soft. My mother's tears.

The rabbi spoke, his voice soft: to the Jews a cemetery is "a house of graves" . . . but also a "house of eternal life." The same in other faiths, I thought. There are as many dead now as alive. A kind of balance along the ground's two sides. That permeable membrane. Always new dead in the making, and always the long dead reappearing over our shoulders and in our dreams. Sometimes a face, like a coin rubbed nearly smooth, in a photo. We're supposed to be afraid of ghosts but every culture has them, conjures them, won't let go. Our smoky ropes of attachment to the past. Our anti-umbilici . . . My mind wandering. Then, the eldest and only son,

I'm reciting the *kaddish*. "Yisgadahl v'yisgadosh sh'may rahbbo . . . " In back, my father's father's grave, the man I'm named for. Staring hard and lost at the chiseling, ALBERT GOLDBARTH. My name. His dates.

In 1893 "Albert Goldbarth An Alien personally appeared in open Court and prayed to be admitted to become a Citizen of the United States . . . "—I have that paper, that and a sad, saved handful of others: September 15, 1904 he "attained the third degree" in the "Treue Bruder Lodge of the Independent Order of Odd Fellows." Five days after, J. B. Johnson, General Sales Agent of the Southern Cotton Oil Company, wrote a letter recommending "Mr. Goldbarth to whomsoever he may apply, as an honest and hardworking Salesman, leaving us of his own accord." That was 24 Broad Street, New York. In two years, in Cleveland, Ohio, John H. Silliman, Secretary, was signing a notice certifying Mr. Albert Goldbarth as an agent of The American Accident Insurance Company. And, from 1924: "$55 Dollars, in hand paid," purchasing Lot Number 703—this, from the envelope he labeled in pencil "Paid Deed from Semetery Lot from Hibrew Progresif Benefit Sociaty." I'm standing there now. I'm reading this stone that's the absolute last of his documents.

There aren't many stories. Just two photographs. And he was dead before I was born. A hundred times, I've tried inventing the calluses, small betrayals, tasseled mantel lamps, day-shaping waves of anger, flicked switches, impossible givings of love in the face of no love, dirty jokes, shirked burdens, flowerpots, loyalties, gold-shot silk pagemarkers for the family Bible, violin strings, sweet bodystinks from the creases, knick-knacks, lees of tea, and morning-alchemized trolley tracks declaring themselves as bright script in the sooted-over paving bricks—everything that makes a life, which is his life, and buried.

And why am I busy repeating that fantastical list . . . ? We're "mountain gorillas" (this is from Alex Shoumatoff's wonderful study of kinship, *The Mountain of Names*) who "drag around moribund members of their troop and try to get them to stand, and after they have died" (above my grandfather's grave, imagining bouts of passion with imaginary Misheleh over my grandfather's grave now) "masturbate on them and try to get some reaction from them." An offering, maybe. A trying to read life backwards into that text of dead tongues. Give us any fabric scrap, we'll dream the prayer shawl it came from. Give us any worthless handful of excavated soil, we'll dream the scrap. The prayer. The loom the shawl took fragile shape on, in the setting *shtetl* hill-light. The immigrant ships they arrived in, the port, the year. We'll give that year whatever version of semen is appropriate, in homage and resuscitory ritual. We'll breathe into, rub, and luster that year.

1641: On a journey in Ecuador, a Portuguese Jew, Antonio de Montezinos, discovered—after a week-long, brush-clogged hell trek through the hinterlands—a hidden Jewish colony, and heard them wailing holy writ in Hebrew. Yes, there in the wild domain of anaconda and peccary—or so he told the Jewish scholar and eminent friend of Rembrandt, Menasseh ben Israel. Or so Menasseh claimed, who had his own damn savvy purposes; and based on his claim that the Ten Lost Tribes of Israel were now found in the New World, and their global equidispersion near complete—as the Bible foretells will usher in an Age of Salvation—Britain's Puritan leaders readmitted their country's exiled Jews, the better to speed the whole world on its prophesied way to Redemption. (Maybe Rembrandt was an earlier body of Ernest L. Norman? Maybe the massed Confederation planets were holding their astrocollective breath even then, as destiny wound like spoolthread on the windmills. And maybe, in the same Dutch-sunset oranges and mauves he let collect like puddled honey in his painted-dusk skies, Rembrandt helped Menasseh finagle this plot on behalf of a troubled people, tipped a flagon of burgundy in a room of laundered varnish rags, and plotted as the radiotelescope Monitor Maids of planet Vidus lounged about in their gold lamé uniforms, listening . . .)

Maybe. Always a maybe. Always someone forcing the scattered timbers of history into a sensible bridge. The Lost Tribes: China. The Lost Tribes: Egypt. The Lost Tribes: Africa. India. Japan. They formed a kingdom near "a terrible river of crashing stones" that roared six days a week "but on the Jewish Sabbath did cease." Lord Kingsborough emptied the family fortune, won three stays in debtor's prison, "in order to publish a series of sumptuously illustrated volumes proving the Mexican Indians . . . " Ethiopians. Eskimos. The Mormons have them reaching America's shores as early as "Tower of Babylon times" and later again, about 600 B.C., becoming tipi-dwellers, hunters of lynx and buffalo, children of Fire and Water Spirits . . . Maybe. But today I think these caskets in Chicago soil are voyage enough. The moon's not that far.

We visit the other family graves: Auntie Regina (brain cancer) . . . Uncle Jake (drank; slipped me butterscotch candies) . . . Miles square and unguessably old, this cemetery's a city, districted, netted by streets and their side roads, overpopulated, undercared. Dead Jews dead Jews dead Jews. *Ruth Dale Noparstak * Age 2 Weeks * 1944*—death about the size of a cigar box.

My mother says to Aunt Sally (a stage whisper): "You'll see, Albert's going to write a poem about this." Later, trying to help that endeavor: "Albert, you see these stones on the graves? Jews leave stones on the graves to show they've visited." Not flowers? Why not flowers? . . . *I think I farmed black bent-backed turnips in the hardpan of a shtetl compound of equally black-garbed bent-backed grandmama and rabbinic Jews.*

My mother's parents are here in the Moghileff section, "Organized 1901." "You see the people here? They came from a town called Moghileff, in Russia—or it was a village. Sally, was Moghileff a town or a village? —you know, a little place where all the Jews lived. And those who came to Chicago, when they died, they were all buried here. Right next to your Grandma and Grandpa's graves, you see?— Dave and Natalie?—they were Grandma and Grandpa's neighbors in Moghileff, and they promised each other that they'd stay neighbors forever, here."

"Your Grandma Rosie belonged to the Moghileff Sisterhood. She was Chairlady of Relief. That meant, when somebody had a stillbirth, or was out of a job, or was beat in an alley, she'd go around to the members with an empty can and collect five dollars." Sobbing now. "Five dollars."

On our way out there's a lavish mausoleum lording it over this ghetto of small gray tenanted stones. My Uncle Lou says, still in his Yiddish-flecked English: "And *dis* one?" Pauses. "Gotta be a gengster."

V

The Mormons marry backwards. "Sealing," they call it.

"Is that the end of your story of Misheleh and you?"

The story of marrying backwards never ends.

In Singapore not long ago, the parents of a Miss Cheeh, who had been stillborn twenty-seven years before, were troubled by ghosts

197

in their dreams, and consulted a spirit medium. Independently, the parents of a Mr. Poon consulted her too—their son had been still-born thirty-six years earlier and, recently, ghosts were waking them out of slumber. "And the medium, diagnosing the two ghosts' problem as loneliness, acted as their marriage broker." The Poons and the Cheehs were introduced, a traditional bride price paid, and dolls representing the couple were fashioned out of paper, along with a miniature one-story house with man-servant, car and chauffeur, a table with teacups and pots, and a bed with bolster and pillows. Presumably, on some plane of invisible, viable, ectoplasmic endeavor, connubial bliss was enabled. Who knows?—one day soon, they may wake in their version of that paper bed (his arm around her sex-dampened nape, a knock at the door . . .) and be given the chance to be Mormon, to have always been Mormon, and everlastingly Mormon. They'll laugh, but graciously. She'll rise and start the tea . . .

These ghosts. Our smoky ropes of attachment. And our reeling them in.

Eventually Misheleh and I prospered. The store did well, then there were two stores. We grew fat on pickled herring in cream, and love. I suppose we looked jolly. Though you could see in the eyes, up close, there was a sadness: where our families died in the Camps, where I was never able to find time for the poetry—those things. Even so, the days and nights were good. The children never lacked a sweet after meals (but only if they cleaned their plates), or a little sailor suit, or kewpie blouse, or whatever silliness was in fashion. Before bed, I'd tell them a story. *Once, your mother and I, we lived in another country. A friend introduced us. He was a famous musician. Your mother danced to his songs and a thousand people applauded. I wrote poems about her, everyone read them. Gentlemen flung her roses . . .*

I died. It happens. I died and I entered the kingdom of Worm and of God, and what happens then isn't part of this story, there aren't any words for it. And what I became on Earth—here, in the memory of the living . . . ?—isn't over yet, it never ends, and now I'm me and I love you.

Because the ash is in this paper on which I'm writing (and in the page you're reading) and has been from the start. Because the blood is almost the chemical composition of the ocean, the heart is a swimmer, a very sturdy swimmer, but shore is never in sight. Because of entropy. Because of the nightly news. Because the stars care even less for us than we do for the stars. Because the only feeling a bone can send us is pain. Because the more years that we have, the less we have—the schools don't teach this Tragic Math but we know it; twiddling the fingers is how we count it off. Because because because. And so somebody wakes from an ether sleep: the surgeons have made him Elvis, he can play third-rate Las Vegas bars. And so someone revises the raven on top of the clan pole to a salmon-bearing eagle: now his people have a totem-progenitor giving them certain territorial privileges that the spirits ordained on the First Day of Creation. So. Because.

In *He Done Her Wrong*, the "Great American Novel—in pictures—and not a word in it" that the brilliant cartoonist Milt Gross published in 1930, the stalwart square-jawed backwards hero and his valiant corn-blonde sweetheart are torn from each other's arms by a dastardly mustachioed villain of oily glance and scowling brow, then seemingly endless deprivations begin: fist fights, impoverishment, unbearable loneliness, the crazed ride down a sawmill tied to one of its logs . . . And when they're reunited, as if that weren't enough, what cinches it as a happy ending is uncinched buckskin pants: the hero suddenly has a strawberry birthmark beaming from his tush, and is known for the billionaire sawmill owner's rightful heir . . .

Because it will save us.

The story-in-my-story is over: Misheleh and the children walk home from the cemetery. She's left a stone and a paper rose. We never would have understood it fifty years earlier, sweated with sex, but this is also love.

The story is over, too: the "I" is done talking, the "you" is nearly asleep, they lazily doodle each other's skin. We met them, it seems a long while ago, in what I called "a trough between crests." Let their bed be a raft, and let the currents of sleep be calm ones.

Outside of the story, I'm writing this sentence, and whether someone is a model for the "you" and waiting to see me put my pen down and toe to the bedroom—or even if I'm just lonely, between one "you" and the next—is none of your business. The "outside" is never the proper business between a writer and a reader, but this I'll tell you: tonight the rains strafed in, then quit, and the small symphonic saws of the crickets are swelling the night. This writing is almost over.

But nothing is ever over—or, if it is, then the impulse is wanting to *make* it over: "over" not as in "done," but "again." "Redo." Re-synapse. Re-nova.

I need to say "I love you" to someone and feel it flow down the root of her, through the raw minerals, over the lip of the falls, and back, without limit, into the pulse of the all-recombinant waters.

I meet Carolyn for lunch. She's with Edward, her old friend, who's been living in the heart of Mexico all of these years:

> Our maid, Rosalita, she must be over 70. She had "female troubles" she said. She needed surgery. But, listen: she's from the hills, some small collection of huts that doesn't even bear a name, so she hasn't any papers at all—absolutely no identification. There isn't a single professional clinic that can accept you that way. There isn't any means for obtaining insurance or public aid.
>
> So we went to a Records Division. I slipped the agent *dinero*. He knew what I was doing. It's everywhere. It's the way Mexico works. And when we left, Rosalita was somebody else. She had somebody else's birth certificate, working papers—everything.
>
> She had somebody else's life from the beginning, and she could go on with her own.

nominated by Barry Goldensohn

REDNECK SECRETS

by WILLIAM KITTREDGE

from OWNING IT ALL (Graywolf Press)

Back in my more scattered days there was a time when I decided the solution to all life's miseries would begin with marrying a nurse. Cool hands and commiseration. She would be a second-generation Swedish girl who left the family farm in North Dakota to live a new life in Denver, her hair would be long and silvery blonde, and she would smile every time she saw me and always be after me to get out of the house and go have a glass of beer with my buckaroo cronies.

Our faithfulness to one another would be legendary. We would live near Lolo, Montana, on the banks of the Bitterroot River where Lewis and Clark camped to rest on their way West, "Traveler's Rest," land which floods a little in the spring of the year, a small price to pay for such connection with mythology. Our garden would be intricately perfect on the sunny uphill side of our 16 acres, with little wooden flume boxes to turn the irrigation water down one ditch or another.

We would own three horses, one a blue roan Appaloosa, and haul them around in our trailer to jackpot roping events on summer weekends. I wouldn't be much good on horseback, never was, but nobody would care. The saddle shed would be tacked to the side of our doublewide expando New Moon mobile home, and there would be a neat little lawn with a white picket fence about as high as your knee, and a boxer dog called Aces and Eights, with a great studded collar. There would be a .357 magnum pistol in the drawer of the bedside table, and on Friday night we would dance to the music of old-time fiddlers at some country tavern and in the fall we would go into the mountains for firewood and kill two or three elk for the freezer. There would be wild asparagus along the irrigation ditches and morels down under the cottonwoods by the river, and we would always be good.

And I would keep a journal, like Lewis and Clark, and spell bad, because in my heart I would want to be a mountain man—"We luved aft the movee in the bak seet agin tonite."

WE MUST NOT gainsay such Western dreams. They are not automatically idiot. There are, after all, good Rednecks and bad Rednecks. Those are categories.

So many people in the American West are hurt, and hurting. Bad Rednecks originate out of hurt and a sense of having been discarded and ignored by the Great World, which these days exists mostly on television, distant and most times dizzily out of focus out here in Redneck country.

Bad Rednecks lose faith and ride away into foolishness, striking back. The spastic utility of violence. The other night in a barroom, I saw one man turn to another, who had been pestering him with drunken nonsense. "Son," he said, "you better calm yourself, because if you don't, things are going to get real Western here for a minute."

REAL WESTERN. Back in the late '40's when I was getting close to graduating from high school, they used to stage Saturday night prizefights down in the Veterans Auditorium. Not boxing matches but prizefights, a name which rings in the ear something like *cockfight*. One night the two main-event fighters, always heavyweights, were some hulking Indian and a white farmer from a little dairy-farm community.

The Indian, I recall, had the word "Mother" carved on his hairless chest. Not tattooed, but carved in the flesh with a blade, so the scar tissue spelled out the word in livid welts. The white farmer looked soft and his body was alabaster, pure white, except for his wrists and neck, which were dark, burned-in-the-fields red, burnished red. While they hammered at each other we hooted from the stands like gibbons, rooting for our favorites on strictly territorial and racial grounds, and in the end were all disappointed. The white farmer went down like thunder about three times, blood snorting from his nose in a delicate spray and decorating his whiteness like in, say, the movies. The Indian simply retreated to his corner and refused to go on. It didn't make any sense.

We screeched and stomped, but the Indian just stood there looking at the bleeding white man, and the white man cleared his head and looked at the Indian, and then they both shook their heads at one another, as if acknowledging some private news they had just then learned to share. They both climbed out of the ring and together made their way up the aisle. Walked away.

Real Western. Of course, in that short-lived partnership of the downtrodden, the Indian was probably doomed to a lifetime on the lower end of the seesaw. No dairy farms in a pastoral valley, nor morning milking and school boards for him. But that is not the essential point in this equation. There is a real spiritual equivalency between Redmen and Rednecks. How sad and ironic that they tend to hit at each other for lack of a real target, acting out some tired old scenario. Both, with some justice, feel used and cheated and disenfranchised. Both want to strike back, which may be just walking away, or the bad answer, bloody noses.

NOBODY IS CLAIMING certain Rednecks are gorgeous about their ways of resolving the pain of their frustrations. Some of them will indeed get drunk in honky-tonks and raise hell and harass young men with long hair and golden earrings. These are the bad Rednecks.

Why bad? Because they are betraying themselves. Out-of-power groups keep fighting each other instead of what they really resent: power itself. A redneck pounding a hippie in a dark barroom is embarrassing because we see the cowardice. What he wants to hit is a banker in broad daylight.

But things are looking up. Rednecks take drugs; hippies take jobs. And the hippie carpenters and the 250-pound, pigtailed lumberjacks preserve their essence. They are still isolated, outrageous, lonely, proud and mean. Any one of them might yearn for a nurse, a doublewide, a blue roan Appaloosa, and a sense of place in a country that left him behind.

LIKE THE INDIAN and the buffalo on the old nickel, there are two sides to American faith. But in terms of Redneck currency, they conflict. On the one side there is individualism, which in its most radical mountain-man form becomes isolation and loneliness: the standard country-and-western lament. It will lead to dying alone in your motel room: whether gored, boozed or smacked makes little difference. On the other side there are family and community, that pastoral society of good people inhabiting the good place on earth that William Bradford and Thomas Jefferson so loved to think about.

Last winter after the snowmobile races in Seeley Lake, I had come home to stand alongside my favorite bar rail and listen to my favorite skinny Redneck barmaid turn down propositions. Did I say *home?* Anyway, standing there and feeling at home, I realized that good Redneck bars are like good hippy bars: they are community centers, like churches and pubs in the old days, and drastically unlike our singles bars where every person is so radically on his or her own.

My skinny barmaid friend looked up at one lumberjack fellow, who was clomping around in his White logger boots and smiling his most winsome. She said, "You're just one of those boys with a sink full of dishes. You ain't looking for nothing but someone dumb enough to come and wash your dishes. You go home and play your radio."

A sink full of dirty dishes. And laundry. There are aspects of living alone that can be defined as going out to the J. C. Penney store and buying $33 worth of new shorts and socks and t-shirts because everything you own is stacked up raunchy and stinking on the far side of the bed. And going out and buying paper plates at K-mart because you're tired of eating your meals crouched over the kitchen sink. You finally learn about dirty dishes. They stay dirty. And those girls, like my skinny friend, have learned a thing or two. There are genuine offers of solace and companionship, and there are dirty dishes and nursing. And then a trailer house, and three babies in three years, diapers, and he's gone to Alaska for the money. So back to barmaiding, this time with kids to support, babysitters.

Go home and play your radio.

THERE IS, of course, another Montana. Consider these remarks from the journals of James and Granville Stewart, 1862:

JANUARY 1, 1862. Snowed in the forenoon. Very cold in the afternoon. Raw east wind. Everybody went to grand ball given by John Grant at Grantsville and a severe blizzard blew up and raged all night. We danced all night, no outside storm could dampen the festivities.

JANUARY 2. Still blowing a gale this morning. Forty below zero and the air is filled with driving, drifting snow. After breakfast we laid down on the floor of the several rooms, on buffalo robes that Johnny furnished, all dressed as we were and slept until about two-o'clock in the afternoon, when we arose, ate a fine dinner, then resumed dancing which we kept up with unabated pleasure . . . danced until sunrise.

JANUARY 3. The blizzard ceased about daylight, but it was very cold with about fourteen inches of snow badly drifted in places and the ground bare in spots. We estimated the cold at about thirty-five below, but fortunately there was but little wind. After breakfast all of the visitors left for home, men, women, and children, all on horseback. Everyone got home without frost bites.

Sounds pretty good. But Granville Stewart got his. In the great and deadly winter of 1886–1887, before they learned the need of stacking hay for winter, when more than one million head of cattle ran the Montana ranges, he lost two-thirds of his cow herd. Carcasses piled in the coulees and fence corners come springtime, flowers growing up between the ribs of dead longhorn cattle, and the mild breezes reeking with decay. A one-time partner of Stewart's, Conrad Kohrs, salvaged 3,000 head out of 35,000. Reports vary, but you get the sense of it.

Over across the Continental Divide to where the plains begin on the east side of the Crazy Mountains, in the Two Dot country, on bright mornings you can gaze across the enormous swale of the Musselshell, north and east to the Snowy Mountains, 50 miles distant and distinct and clear in the air as the one mountain bluebell you picked when you came out from breakfast.

But we are not talking spring, we are talking winter and haystacks. A man we know, let's call him Davis Patten, is feeding cattle. It's February, and the snow is drifting three feet deep along the fence lines, and the wind is carrying the chill factor down to about 30 below. Davis Patten is pulling his feed sled with a team of yellow

Belgian geldings. For this job, it's either horses or a track-layer, like a Caterpillar D-6. The Belgians are cheaper and easier to start.

Davis kicks the last remnant of meadow hay, still greenish and smelling of dry summer, off the sled to the trailing cattle. It's three o'clock in the afternoon and already the day is settling toward dark. Sled runners creak on the frozen snow. The gray light is murky in the wind, as though inhabited, but no birds are flying anywhere. Davis Patten is sweating under his insulated coveralls, but his beard is frozen around his mouth. He heads the team toward the barns, over under the cottonwood by the creek. Light from the kitchen windows shows through the bare limbs. After he has fed the team a bait of oats, then Davis and his wife Loretta will drink coffee laced with bourbon.

Later they watch television, people laughing and joking in bright Sony color. In his bones Davis recognizes, as most of us do, that the principal supporting business of television is lies, truths that are twisted about a quarter turn. Truths that were never truths. Davis drifts off to sleep in his Barca-Lounger. He will wake to the white noise from a gray screen.

It is important to have a sense of all this. There are many other lives, this is just one, but none are the lives we imagine when we think of running away to Territory.

Tomorrow Davis Patten will begin his day chopping ice along the creek with a splitting maul. Stock water, a daily chore. Another day with ice in his beard, sustained by memories of making slow love to Loretta under down comforters in their cold bedroom. Love, and then quickfooting it to the bathroom on the cold floors, a steaming shower. Memories of a bed that reeks a little of child making.

The rewards of the life, it is said, are spiritual, and often they are. Just standing on land you own, where you can dig any sort of hole you like, can be considered a spiritual reward, a reason for not selling out and hitting the Bahamas. But on his winter afternoons Davis Patten remembers another life. For ten years, after he broke away from Montana to the Marines, Davis hung out at the dragster tracks in the San Joaquin Valley, rebuilding engines for great, roaring, ass-busting machines. These days he sees their stripped red-and-white dragchutes flowering only on Sunday afternoons. The "Wide World of Sports." Lost horizons. The intricate precision of cam shaft adjustments.

In the meantime, another load of hay.

UP IN TOWNS along the highline, Browning and Harlem and Malta, people are continually dying from another kind of possibility. Another shot of Beam on the rocks and Annie Greensprings out back after the bars are closed. In Montana they used to erect little crosses along the highways wherever a fatality occurred. A while back, outside Browning, they got a dandy. Eleven deaths in a single car accident. *Guinness Book of World Records*. Verities. The highway department has given up the practice of erecting crosses: too many of them are dedicated to the disenfranchised.

Out south of Billings the great coal fields are being strip-mined. Possibilities. The history of Montana and the West, from the fur trade to tomorrow, is a history of colonialism, both material and cultural. Is it any wonder we are so deeply xenophobic, and regard anything east of us as suspect? The money and the power always came from the east, took what it wanted, and left us, white or Indian, with our traditions dismantled and our territory filled with holes in the ground. Ever been to Butte? About half the old town was sucked into a vast open-pit mine.

Verities. The lasting thing we have learned here, if we ever learn, is to resist the beguilements of power and money. Hang on to your land. There won't be any more. Be superstitious as a Borneo tribesman. Do not let them photograph our shy, bare-breasted beauties as they wash clothes along the stream bank. Do not let them steal your soul away in pictures, because they will if they get a chance, just as Beadle's Nickel-Dime Library westerns and Gene Autry B-movies gnawed at the soul of this country where we live. Verities have to be earned, and they take time in the earning—time spent gazing out over your personal wind-glazed fields of snow. Once earned, they inhabit you in complex ways you cannot name, and they cannot be given away. They can only be transmogrified—transformed into something surreal or fantastic, unreal. And ours have been, and always for the same reason: primarily the titillation of those who used to be Easterners, who are everywhere now.

These are common sentiments here in the mountain West. In 1923 Charlie Russell agreed to speak before the Great Falls Booster Club. After listening to six or seven booster speeches, he tore up his own talk and spoke. This is what he said:

> "In my book a pioneer is a man who turned all the
> grass upside down, strung bob-wire over the dust that

was left, poisoned the water and cut down the trees, killed the Indian who owned the land, and called it progress. If I had my way, the land here would be like God made it, and none of you sons of bitches would be here at all."

So what are we left with? There was a great dream about a just and stable society, which was to be America. And there was another great dream about wilderness individuals, mountain men we have called them, who would be the natural defenders of that society. But our society is hugely corrupt, rich and impossibly complex, and our great simple individuals can define nothing to defend, nothing to reap but the isolation implicit in their stance, nothing to gain for their strength but loneliness. The vast, sad, recurrent story which is so centrally American. Western Rednecks cherish secret remnants of those dreams, and still try to live within them. No doubt a foolish enterprise.

But that's why, full of anger and a kind of releasing joy, they plunge their Snowcats around frozen lakes at 90 miles an hour, coming in for a whiskey stop with eyes glittering and icicles bright in their whiskers, and why on any summer day you can look into the sky over Missoula and see the hang-gliding daredevils circling higher than the mountains. That's why you see grown men climbing frozen waterfalls with pretty colored ropes.

And then there seems to be a shooting a week in the doublewide village. Spastic violence. You know, the husband wakes up from his drunk, lying on the kitchen floor with the light still burning, gets himself an Alka-Seltzer, stumbles into the living room, and there is Mother on the couch with half her side blown away. The 12-gauge is carefully placed back where it belongs on the rack over the breakfront. Can't tell what happened. Must have been an intruder.

Yeah, the crazy man inside us. Our friends wear Caterpillar D-9 caps when they've never pulled a friction in their lives, and Buck knives in little leather holsters on their belts, as if they might be called upon to pelt out a beaver at any moment. Or maybe just stab an empty beer can. Ah, wilderness, and suicidal nostalgia.

Which gets us to another kind of pioneer we see these days, people who come to the country with what seems to be an idea that connection with simplicities will save their lives. Which simplicities are those? The condescension implicit in the program is staggering.

If you want to feel you are being taken lightly, try sitting around while someone tells you how he envies the simplicity of your life. What about Davis Patten? He says he is staying in Montana, and calling it home. So am I.

Despite the old Huckleberry Finn-mountain man notion of striking out for the territory, I am going to hang on here, best I can, and nourish my own self. I know a lovely woman who lives up the road in a log house, on what is left of a hard-earned farmstead. I'm going to call and see if she's home. Maybe she'll smile and come have a glass of beer with me and my cronies.

nominated by Patricia Henley and C. E. Poverman

MY SON AND I GO SEE HORSES

by MARIANNE BORUCH

from THE AMERICAN POETRY REVIEW

Always shade in the cool dry barns
and flies in little hanging patches like glistening fruitcake.
One sad huge horse
follows us with her eye. She shakes
her great head, picks up one leg and puts it down
as if she suddenly dismissed the journey.

My son is in heaven, and these
the gods he wants to father
so they will save him. He demands I
lift him up. He strokes the old filly's long face
and sings something that goes like butter
rounding the hard skillet, like some doctor
who loves his patients more
than science. He believes the horse

will love him, not eventually,
right now. He peers into the enormous eye
and says solemnly, I know you. And the horse
will not startle nor look away,
this horse the color of thick velvet drapes
years and years of them behind the opera,
backdrop to ruin and treachery, all
innocence and its slow
doomed unwinding of rapture.

nominated by Patricia Henley, Laura Jensen and Wesley McNair

BIRD-WATCHING

by DENNIS SCHMITZ

from FIELD

Across the channel, Mare Island welders cut
bulkheads & winch up
riveted slabs of the WW II

mine-tender. I can see
the torches flash against visualized rust;
I can see so far
back that the war cruelties are camouflaged

as feats of scruple.
The binoculars sweat rings around my eyes,
& when my arms tire, it's the sky that comes down

fuzzy through the Zeiss
26x10 lens into debris—the shoe, paper news
& condoms, the "beauty

from brevity derived" I can't catalog.
I'm on the flyway for marbled
godwits, scooters & loons,
but taxidermy might have devised what I think

is only a dead heron peppered with grit,
marshgrass poking
out the bird's buggy eyeholes.

I want to get down,
include myself in the focus: the war,

all epithets, between memory & present things
memory can't yet reach.
Though the marsh is a constant

madras-bleed between old soda bottles
that slash grids in the earthbound
walker's boots & the heuristic dieback

of the grass, I'm on one knee
to this Bird-in-the-volleys-of-lesser-birds,
praising glut but lifting
binoculars once more to distance myself

from it. Idolatry begins in one's fear
of being the only thing, saying
to detritus, *let it linger, let even just the feathers*

of it stay—that is why I pick
up my glasses with the little men still in them.
They are so intent on forgetting;

they are so self-contained & innocent,
lit both by the small
circles of sky & by the torches they stroke
against the steel that arches over them.

nominated by Sandra McPherson

SEND PICTURES,
YOU SAID

by LAURIE DUESING

from FIVE FINGERS PRESS

On the subject of nude bodies, my father asked,
"What's the big deal? Everybody has one!"
commentary I always agreed with until you told me
to send some nude photographs while you were away
on the job in Georgia. I rummaged through
those old black and whites I took of myself 8 years ago
for an assignment in my photography class.
Beautiful and discreet, they were almost glacial
in their "I am nude" perfect, predictable poses,
their attitude of I-have-no-clothes-on but it's O.K.
because I am being artistic. I knew you didn't want
art: you wanted the body
which accounts for the snapshots I took of myself in the mirror.
It was the end of the roll and I figured so what.
Now I am looking at these 4 x 6 inch prints, shocked
by the way every fleshy part of me lifts and leans
toward the mirror, toward an idea of love.
I didn't know my lower lip was that full, my nipples
that large, my body so at ease with itself, so sure
of its desire. I did not know what a woman looks like
when she is inviting a man inside her. Besides,
it was your passion which impressed me,
a feeling so large I thought you generated it yourself,

that it drove you to me and into me.
Now, as I look at these pictures,
I see the body of a woman that pulled you into it.
You had no choice. I remember that first night
when you took off your clothes and sat on the edge
of the bed, waiting. So stunned by your beauty,
I turned my back so I could concentrate
on taking my clothes off. When I turned around,
I walked to you and rested my hands on your shoulders,
thinking, "If this is all I ever have of him, it's enough."
You dropped to your knees, wrapped your arms around
my legs, rested your head on my belly. I felt
your warm tears on my skin. All I knew
was that I was beginning something that would never end.
If I had paid more attention to those tears,
these photographs would have told me nothing.
But then I had no idea, I had no idea.

nominated by Dorianne Laux

WONDERLAND

fiction by C. S. GODSHALK

from THE IOWA REVIEW

W HEN THE ROOM WAS LIKE THIS, in the dark, with only the window letting in moonlight and the white blanket looming up pale and square, anything could be in it. Anyone. Merle could be curled up on the day bed grinding his teeth, his small knees jammed into his chest. He was. She could be rolling over on the big fold-out couch, snoring lightly, or just there. She wasn't. But in the night Paulie was never completely sure. He let this uncertainty fold over him, the dreamy possibility of his mother's presence in the room would roll up under his chin, and he would sleep.

In the morning it was just himself and Merle, but it was all right because in the morning he was energetic and there were things to do fast. Juice and cereal and Bugs Bunny vitamins and hot milk heated in the little pot on the good burner and the pot run full of water right away so he could clean it out easily when they got back. Then rinsing and stacking the dishes in the sink and smoothing out the beds. He got Merle's jacket and hat and gave him the fifty cents. He had made her fill out the form saying they needed lunch for fifty cents and not a dollar like the other kids only a lot of the other kids had the same form.

Sometimes, when he first woke up but didn't open his eyes, knowing she'd be nowhere in the room, he would panic. He'd decide then to tell them, he'd yell to them all off the backstairs of the apartment and down the halls of Our Lady of the Snows, that she had left. "What kind of a mother is she!" they would cry. "A Whore! A Drunk!" and he would rush into their arms, into all their arms. But it would be Peg holding him, smiling with her cigarette

215

and that stretched pink and silver sweater, looking nothing like anybody's mother, and a tremendous ache would fill his chest. That's when he dropped an arm off the bed and groped for his sneakers. He knew if they were there, exactly as he left them, side by side with the toes perfectly even, it would be all right and he could get up.

He poured the milk out of the pot over two bowls of Cap'n Crunch while Merle's headless form stumbled out of the bathroom. Paulie reached out with his free hand and yanked at the little boy's shirt until the large grey eyes appeared, the shirt still hitched on the nose, the face of a baby robber.

"Did you go to the bathroom? Did you DO anything?" The small boy looked up gravely, his red cheeks almost comical under Paulie's long pale chin. Despite their differences, the children shared a wide mouth and straight almost broomlike reddish hair. "That bed damn well better be dry!" Paulie said.

After the dishes, Paulie took the plastic watering can from under the sink and watered all the plants. Then he shoved Merle's arms into a leather jacket and zipped up both their jackets, checked for the key in his breast pocket, and slammed the door. That part of the day was finished right. Outside, down the rickety backstairs, they stepped carefully over the brilliant bits of ice, beneath Nudorf's underwear lifting flat and frozen in the sunlight, mid-high to the peeling bottle of Meyer's Rum shooting its tremendous cap and stars off the billboard into the bright blue sky.

The house itself listed. It looked like all the other broken down three deckers in East Boston, except it was tilted slightly forward so that, they had discovered, a marble rolled on their bathroom floor on the second floor would continue out across the linoleum, slowly increasing speed, making a little leap over the TV wire, over the kitchen door jamb and out the back door, dropping in little crystal slaps down the twenty-seven steps, staying in the depression in the middle of each, before it fell backward off the twenty-seventh step and clanked on the trash cans.

They had told Peg about the marble. Paulie told her exactly how it would go but she just shoved him away, holding her cigarette inside the cup of her hand the way she did when she touched them. Later she came out on the back porch with her fake fur jacket over her robe and grabbed Paulie's neck and steered him back inside to the bathroom and smacked a marble in his hand. She shuffled back out to the porch and yelled "Go!" and he squatted and let the marble go, he didn't push it, he just let it roll away, and it passed her dirty pink slippers and started to bounce and she leaned over the wooden rail and watched it hop down below her until the final chink on the can and she said "Holy shit!" with that smile. She wasn't drunk then and she wasn't sober. She was in between and she was nice.

That was the week before she left. He got back from school with Merle and there was a box of cream-filled cupcakes on the dinette. On top of the box was a long envelope with magic marker writing. The magic marker was still there with its top off. She never put the tops back on and they always got dry. "Paulie" it said on the envelope "I'm going away for awhile" and he closed his eyes. "I'm going on a trip. You're almost twelve. That's no baby! Make sure Merle eats and don't take any crap. If you need me, *a real emergency,* go up to Nudorf and use this number." It was the number of the new guy from Texas. Mitch. "Uncle" Mitch. Inside the envelope were eight twenty dollar bills and a piece of yellow paper. "Use this slow" it said on the paper. "I'll be back before it's gone, or I'll send your father." A bright set of her lips was pressed into the paper.

"Fuck her" he said in a high, choked voice. He ripped open the cupcakes and shoved them at Merle. Merle pushed a cupcake into his mouth and backed away.

"Fuck her!" Paulie said again and the little boy started to cry. Chocolate squeezed out of the sides of his mouth and onto his shirt. "Fuck her!" Paulie screamed, and Merle moaned, a slow bright circle of water surrounding his darkened pants as if the tears were too much for the eyes alone to discharge.

"You pig!" Paulie said, "You little pig!" Merle began to wail and Paulie shoved him into a chair and stared at him savagely until he was quiet. Then he went over and dumped out the twenty-dollar bills. He took one and folded it up and shoved it deep in his breast pocket and he stuffed the rest in a jar and put it way in back of the freezer part of the refrigerator. He took the envelope and tore it into bits and dropped them in the trash. "We're not calling her" he said, pulling off the small boy's shoes and socks and pants and wrapping him around with a dishtowel. "Ever."

He decided the first thing to do, despite the cash in the jar, was to get a job. He went to Foodland the next afternoon and applied for a job bagging. He was younger than the other bag boys, but he was tall and acted polite and they didn't hassle him. At first it was only for Saturday, but by the next week they told him he could come everyday after school. Between Foodland and Peg's cash, he figured they could last for quite awhile.

Except for the nights, which Merle screwed up, it was better than it had been. They got to school on time. The place looked good. They ate right. "If anybody asks" Paulie said to Merle repeatedly "Old man Nudorf, Sister Cecilia, *anybody*, Peg's outa town. Say we got our aunt to cook and do stuff. Say Peg sends us postcards."

"Where?" Merle suddenly brightened.

"Where what?"

"Where are the postcards?" the child's eyes shone even more. "I want to see 'em!"

"There ARE no postcards, you little shit. Pay attention!" Merle looked at him blankly. He started to rock, as if a light breeze had entered the room. "Now" Paulie said again. "What are you going to say if someone asks—like Sister Cecilia?"

"What?"

"What are YOU going to say?" Paulie's fingers dug into the small arm. "YOU say—'my aunt is staying with us and cooks and stuff. My mother will be BACK SOON!' "

"She will?" Merle cried in pain.

Paulie let go of his arm and sunk into the yellow chair. "Yeah" he said blackly. They had gone eleven days, though, and nobody asked. When Nudorf finally squared them off on the stairs, putting down his bag of soda bottles and drilling into them with small, colorless eyes, they both wet their lips. "Where's your mother?" the old man said, and before Paulie could jerk back he grabbed a pinch of white cheek. "Jesus, you two look nice!" Nudorf's eyebrows raised like little hats. "She must have run outa booze in there and had nothing to do but polish you up!" He bent over and heaved the bottles against his chest and pushed past. They watched his galoshes push up under the dirty coat, disappearing and reappearing like pedals, until the old man vanished around the bend of stair and sky.

Our Lady of the Snows elementary school was a huge yellow building set between the church on one side and the convent and rectory on the other. Our Lady herself stood in yellow stucco in front of the church, balancing her bare feet on a little globe. Merle waited here for Paulie each day because the second grade always got out before the seventh. He stood in front of Our Lady while the buses pulled up and hundreds of kids rushed out and around him and then he held onto the gate so as not to be pushed out of place. Eventually he'd see Paulie's purple ski hat bouncing through the crowd.

Paulie would push up his collar and they'd walk together to Foodland. Sometimes Angel Ruiz would join them. Ruiz was smaller and older than Paulie. He looked like a monkey with dark, skinny arms and a wide mouth. He was always happy looking. He'd shuffle up fast in his stupid little jacket, the small shoulders twitching back and forth, his sneakers bouncing.

Ruiz was the only one Paulie told about Peg. "No shit!" he said smiling, "Wow, if my old lady took off I'd grow some fucking wings or something!" He reversed to a moonwalk. Ruiz could moonwalk for blocks. "But why Foodland? I mean FOODLAND!" he slapped his forehead and rocked back drunkenly. "My old lady puts you on a roof, two hours you make fifty bucks. Just have to 'look'! Just tell 'em who's going down the street. FOODLAND!" Ruiz stumbled backwards again, laughing.

"Your old lady" Paulie said, shoving Merle forward. "How long is she going to do that thing with the string? A guy whistles in the alley—down comes Rosita's string with the stuff. I mean EVERY-BODY sees it. What does she need a guy on the roof for?" Paulie had sat on the roof with Ruiz once or twice. The last time it was freezing, and they sat there watching the street and fooling with the steam coming out of their mouths. Suddenly Ruiz jumped up and began a little break routine on the ledge, jiving fast, before Paulie yanked him back down on the tar. "Ruiz is crazy" he said to Merle later. "Don't hang around with him unless I'm there."

Usually Ruiz left them at Dean Street, but this time he went all the way to Foodland. He hung around inside for awhile, then he slipped some gum into his jeans and did a fancy move on the electric eye mat and waved good-bye without turning back.

The day after Paulie told him about Peg, Ruiz came to the apartment. He had a big bag, full of Fritos and Sprite and Spanish stuff in cans. He said he could get more if Paulie needed it. At home, Paulie knew, Ruiz ate strangely. There'd be nothing for days and then Rosita would have fifty people over and there would be meat and bananas, big cooked bananas, beans and beer and guys in beautiful tight shirts. Only now Rosita's parties were small. Ruiz suddenly had real money because of these parties. He did his first trick with two guys she had up there over Christmas. "You gotta get out of there" Paulie said when he told him. "Yeah" Ruiz smiled softly. "Next week I'm going to Miami."

After Ruiz left Foodland, Paulie put on the yellow jacket and took Merle to the receiving area in back of produce. He sat him on a box between other boxes and gave him some old comics and told him not to move. Most of the time he wouldn't. He sat there turning the pages, rubbing his feet together. The first day Paulie told the assistant manager that he had to watch Merle sometimes after school and the guy said "No way," but when he passed the small boy sitting with the comic books a few days later, he shrugged and walked away. Merle ate stuff in back of Foodland, but he was careful. Paulie told him not to take anything out of the store that wasn't in his stomach and he didn't.

Going home, they wouldn't talk for blocks. They'd walk through the alley behind the store, down and over the MTA tracks and up the small embankment toward the fading light in the west. Sometimes Paulie would pretend she was there waiting for them in the gold armchair, and the pale yellow light became part of the vast chair, her reddish hair spread out above, her wide lips smiling over the bank of clouds like something floating on a movie screen. Once the light spread out in a dappled band and he saw her suddenly in her leopard kerchief the way she was that one time she came to school. She came for the Christmas play and she stood in the hallway with her fur jacket and her hair high and puffy under the leopard kerchief. She was the only adult there and she looked somehow saved when she saw him. "Paulie! Where do I go?" He was walking in a line of boys and he just kept in line as they passed her. "Home" he spat.

"What? Whatdya mean?" she cried. "You said ten o'clock!" but he kept going. "I'm EARLY!" she screamed, rushing after him and yanking him around so that the kids in back bunched up and then walked around them, staring. "Ten o'clock yesterday" he said with venom, then pushed past. At the end of the hallway he glanced back and she was still standing there in that stupid kerchief, her hands dangling dead out of the jacket. He flung the image from his mind and twisted round to look for Merle. The small, pinched face pushed all sorrow from his heart.

By the time they turned onto their street the sun had usually disappeared, but Nudorf's laundry still caught the high lemon color, waving to them like bright cardboard cutouts of himself. The top of the huge billboard bottle glinted too in the yellow air, and they knew they were home.

One time, starting up the stairs, Paulie stopped. "What's that?" he asked, and Merle slipped a small brown ball into his pocket.

"A kiwi."

"I told you NOT to take stuff out of the store!"

"I didn't take it. I was LOOKING at them and Lifson gave me one.

"They're green inside" Merle said more quietly "like green jelly."

"Open it."

"No."

"Why not, for Christ's sake! I want to see. It'll get rotten like that other crap you stashed away."

"So what."

The boys climbed the stairs silently, the higher windows blinding them in the last iridescence. "You're saving it for her!" Paulie said suddenly. "You dumb jerk! That's what you're doing! All that stuff! The dried up Fritos, those cupcakes! You're saving them for her!" Merle pressed his baby lips together and looked away.

"Christ" Paulie said.

Inside he hung the two jackets on doorknobs and looked around. It still surprised him to get in and find everything so quiet and neat. The lousy smell was gone, the cigarette butts pushed into food were gone, her makeup all over the place was gone. She always wore make-up and she never put any of it away. He liked her best in the morning when her eyes were plain and they didn't jump out of her face like they did later. She'd start with a tube of light brown stuff and then build on it. A few times she put this stuff on Merle after she hit him. Once on his arm where Kenny had pressed it. She was nice after times like that, sometimes for days. She tried to put the brown stuff on him one time, over a split cheek, but he shoved her off.

At night the two of them usually had cereal and then watched TV in their pajamas which Paulie already took twice to the laundromat with their other stuff. Sometimes they had tuna because for some reason Peg had four years supply of tuna in the kitchen, or like this night, Paulie fried up pork chops with Wonderbread on the side, which was their favorite. He set the pink formica table with two folded pieces of toilet paper and put the small snake plant in the middle of it and two forks and two knives. The snake plant looked good in the middle of the table, it's sharp thick spikes pointing upward, dark green with no brown like when she took care of it. All the plants looked good. The big one with the ribbon and the pink foil looked great. Uncle Mitch brought it. Uncles were always bringing stuff. Crap. One day before Christmas she told him Uncle Phil was bringing them both Big Wheels and he told her she could shove Uncle Phil and all the other uncles up her ass, but that's what she did anyway, and that's when she opened his cheek with her hair dryer.

Paulie liked the plants. He got a small box of Vitagrow from Foodland and used it carefully after reading the directions several times. "You don't use too much of this stuff or you burn the roots" he said to Merle. And he watered them regularly, but not too much. "She drowned half of 'em and dried up the rest" he said.

He checked the mail each day before he dropped it in a big shopping bag. There was one tremendous, oversized post card that came from her the second week. It was a big monkey waving from the side of a skyscraper and it was all bent around the edges. "Hi guys!" it said. "Say hi to Kenny. Be good!" It was surrounded by a frame of xs and another pair of Peg's lips in the center. Kenny, she told Paulie a few years back, was his father. He might have been too, because she didn't call him Uncle Kenny and she didn't seem to like him very much. He was a pale guy who always looked like he wanted to be somewhere else. Kenny didn't seem to see Paulie when he was around. Merle's father was another guy. His name was Merle and Peg named Merle after him, but it didn't do much good because it turned out the guy hated the name. Somehow Peg must have asked Kenny to keep an eye on them. This made Paulie laugh.

On Fridays Paulie dumped out the shopping bag and sorted the mail. He did this when Peg was there too, because she wasn't too good with mail. He separated what was junk, what was important— like Boston Edison, what bills could be forgotten forever practically, and what could be forgotten for a long time. Rent could wait because Peg paid that more or less on time so Nudorf wouldn't hassle him for probably a month. The phone was no problem because it was gone. Peg flung it at the guy who came from New England Telephone to take it out. She switched her cigarette to her mouth and actually ripped it off the kitchen wall and flung it at this guy's chest, and she was a small lady. She'd do terrific stuff like that sometimes. Paulie asked Merle in bed one night if he remembered the phone guy, but Merle was asleep.

By the third week in February, there was one twenty left in the jar. Paulie walked around with the Edison bill in his jacket because he felt somehow if he had it on him, they couldn't use it. He knew this was ridiculous, but he still did it. At night he would wake up and see the long envelope, the one he had torn up, he would see it in front of his eyes, but he couldn't see the phone number written on it. That postcard came from New York anyway, not Texas, so who knew where the hell she was. There were other times when he came home and he was positive she had called. She had called Nudorf upstairs. Once he got back from the deli and Merle was in front of the TV which was on very loud the way he liked it when Paulie left him alone, and Paulie asked him.

"Did she call?"

"Who?" Merle's eyes stayed glued on the tube.

"Wonder Woman."

"Yeah."

"She DID! Christ! She DID!"

"What?"

"Did Mr. Nudorf come down?"

"No—I think—no."

"Merle!" Paulie pulled him up from the floor brutally and his head hit the side of the TV and he began to scream. In the night, on the rare occasions when Nudorf's phone rang upstairs, Paulie listened breathlessly to the old man's weight creaking over the floor. He'd wait for him to cross over to the door and start down the stairs. "Paulie!" Nudorf would shout outside their door. "Your mother is on the phone! Hey!" But he didn't.

Merle was the real problem. He wet the bed all the time now, and not just wet. The apartment smelled. Paulie kept him home from school a lot and stayed home too. He bought some postcards and wrote on them and gave them to Merle. "She sent them" he said. "She's coming back soon."

"You sent them" Merle said in a queer voice.

One night, when he made a particularly disgusting mess of his bed, Paulie hit him. He hit him hard, and Merle was quiet for a long time. He seemed all right, there was no mark, but he just wouldn't talk or anything, so Paulie finally picked him up and put him in his own bed and got in with him. He wrapped his legs around him and they slept like that and Merle was all right and didn't do anything. But when they got up the next morning, he made a mess on the floor. Paulie didn't clean it up. He got a ball point and a piece of paper from his looseleaf and he sat down and began to write. He wrote to CHATTERS at the Boston Globe. He read CHATTERS sometimes when Peg got the paper. He read it usually after Garfield and the ads for the topless bars. People wrote to CHATTERS with their problems, and other people—regular people, wrote the answers.

"Dear Chatters" he wrote "I have a small boy who wets the bed all the time and now it's more than just wetting. What do you recommend? I don't want to hit him or anything like that. Is there another mother out there with the same problem who has stopped her child from doing this? If you are the one, please answer." He signed it "Big Boy." People always signed their CHATTERS letters with funny or weird names. He mailed it right away and then he waited two days and checked a Globe at Soviero's deli, but "Big Boy" wasn't in yet. "Double Virgo" asked how to clean smudges off burnished copper. "Crazed Mom" asked how to stop spanking her four year old daughter. "Lamp Lady" asked if someone had the directions for a doll lamp. No "Big Boy."

He thought of asking Ruiz about Merle because, as crazy as Ruiz was, he sometimes gave strangely good advice. He checked for the narrow back with the black and yellow jacket in social studies, but the seat was empty. This was not unusual, half the time Ruiz never showed up. Just before recess, Sister Bonaventure, the principal, came into the classroom and put her hands together so that the big white sleeves fell back like wings and she waited until everyone was quiet. "I'm sorry, boys and girls" she said, and her big ugly face looked sorry. "We've learned that Angel Ruiz has had a terrible accident. Last night he fell off the roof of his home. He died this morning at Children's Hospital." One or two children giggled softly. "We must pray for his family, for his poor parents." Paulie saw Ruiz pass before him smiling, rotating like a wheel in the darkness, and he could not find air anywhere in the room.

"Where is he now?" Merle asked that night. "In a box" Paulie said tonelessly. "Tomorrow they'll cover the box with flowers. They'll put it in the ground and fifty people will come and eat."

The entire class went to the funeral Mass. Rosita was there with a black hat resting like an elbow over her eyes. She was swaying sideways on a smaller darker man. "At least you didn't get him"

Paulie thought savagely, and at that moment Rosita looked up and he had never seen such a sad face in all his life.

In the night Paulie balled up Ruiz and Merle, Peg and the Edison bill and Rosita, he balled up all of it and he punched it until it was hard like a rock and he flung it to the back of his skull. He decided, wildly, to clean the apartment. On Saturday he shoved Merle into his jacket and hat and gloves and put him in front of the TV and then opened all the windows and the cold air rushed in. He worked hard, scrubbing and cleaning, and when he was finished he closed all the windows and took Merle's stuff off and looked around. The place looked and smelled much better, but there was still something. The stuff on the doorknobs looked the worst. At Our Lady of the Snows they had hooks, a long line of brass hooks for coats which Paulie admired, and also rough plastic mats at the side doors where you could scrape your shoes before going inside.

The hooks were easy. He just slipped them inside his jacket at DeVito's hardware and glided toward the door so they didn't chink together. At the door he picked up a bright green rectangle of sharp plastic grass and walked out. He walked fast, waiting for a heavy weight on his shoulder to spin him around. He was ready for it, his chest filled with air, ready to tell them everything, but nobody stopped him.

Back home he made Merle hold the hooks one by one as he pounded a nail through the hole in each one. Merle winced each time, but his small hand remained steady. After three hooks were up, the door flew open and Nudorf stood with his hands clenched, bouncing over his slippers. "You wanna bring the whole god damn place down!" he cried. "I got two pictures off the wall already! Cut it out! Where's your mother?"

Merle stared at him, his mouth open wetly. Paulie riveted his eyes on the nail and went on hammering furiously and when he was done he flipped the hammer on the yellow chair.

"Get them coats!" he ordered Merle. He turned his eyes on the old man. "Did you wipe your feet?" he asked contemptuously. "That's what the green mat's for! I shouldn't have to tell you that!"

Nudorf found himself scraping his slippers, and then turned round vacantly and went out the doorway. "Close the door!" Paulie commanded, but he was already shuffling up the stairs in confusion.

Paulie worried after he left. The old guy would go upstairs and think about it, he knew, think about just the two of them being there in the apartment. He decided to go up right away and tell him about the aunt.

Upstairs Nudorf opened the door and put out his hand and pulled Paulie in by his shirt. This had never happened before and Paulie was afraid. Inside, the old man let go of him and sank into a chair. Except for the light over a table and the chair, the room was dark. It was cramped with huge furniture and the air smelled like Nudorf, only stronger.

"Paulie" the watery eyes blinked up. "She's gone, ain't she?"

"I've got to go" Paulie said. "My aunt's coming. She doesn't like me to leave Merle alone."

"How long have you been doing this?" the watery eyes swelled open. "HOW have you been doing this?" Paulie slipped back out of the light, and Nudorf was silent. For a moment the old man seemed to forget him. He picked up a spoon that had been buried in some mush and then slowly let it go. Paulie walked around touching things lightly. In the little kitchen there were a lot of large soda bottles lined up behind the sink. Lemon soda.

"What do you do with all the lemon soda?"

Nudorf jerked up, shifting toward the voice. "It goes down easy. I got problems here" he pointed to his stomach. Paulie lifted the dank curtain over the sink and look out. The bottle of rum looked different from up here. You could see the four spotlights that went on at night and the huge dry flakes peeling off the top. He dropped the curtain and continued walking around, running his hand over the heavy furniture, keeping out of Nudorf's range.

"It's okay" Nudorf said suddenly. "I was a man at twelve! I was an old man at seventeen! Now, " he pushed away the mush, "I'm a baby. You'll be all right. Better off in fact!"

Paulie fingered things while Nudorf talked. Nothing in the whole place was worth two cents. He pulled out a drawer and Nudorf stopped talking, his eyes bright with panic. "What's that! What've you got!" Paulie withdrew his hand silently. Inside the drawer he could see loose toothpicks and a photo. It was of a tan boy about his own age in a too small jacket with his arms stiffly at his sides.

"This your kid?"

"Yes. No. It's me, I think." Nudorf started to get up and Paulie slipped out the door. The air in the rancid hallway was like a breath of spring.

"You and your brother" Nudorf cried, sticking his head out the door. "I saw you crossing the tracks. Don't do that! In the snow you can't hear so good. Snow does something funny to the sound!" but Paulie had slipped down the stairs.

Inside Merle was asleep on the floor in front of the TV. Paulie took his blanket off the bed and tucked it around him and sat down and looked at the tube. A lady and two kids were smiling at a very shiny floor. It was extremely shiny, like a mirror. He looked down at the pitted linoleum between his sneakers and rolled away into the couch. He curved his arms and legs around one of the stiff pillows, kicking off his sneakers, and clung softly to what he knew was a spinning ball, with the water not falling off, with fishes hanging in it, bright sunlight on the other side, revolving fast, nothing falling off ever, he clung with his curled toes, clung to the vast cheek, the red hair lifted behind, the cigarette cupped away somewhere out in the universe.

In the morning it was abnormally quiet. It was Sunday, but that wasn't it. The room was filled with a soft luminescence. Paulie got up and shut off the TV and the lamp, but the soft brightness remained. Merle was still asleep on the floor, soaking in the sweet smell of urine. Paulie covered him with the damp blanket and got his own sneakers on quietly and then his jacket and opened the back door. The dazzling whiteness made him wince. He stood there blind in the fiery dazzle, cracking his eyes now and then until the backstairs materialized in a sparkling spiral. He made a first step, plucking his foot back out and inspecting the perfect blue imprint. Below the cars extended in softly glistening humps all the way to the end of the street. It made him suddenly happy. He threw a snowball at her once, she was standing where he was now, looking down, and he threw a fistful of snow and her eyelashes were suddenly full of snow. "Wonderland!" she said, laughing.

At the bottom of the stairs he began to walk slowly through the quiet brilliance. It was too early for traffic on the side streets. Nothing moved. In a short time he reached the overpass where the sidewalk ducked into a tunnel and the world turned abruptly black. Cars reverberated overhead and when he emerged in front of Soviero's deli, the snow was already grey and used.

The Sunday Globe was big and he couldn't thumb through it fast enough to check CHATTERS without Soviero bitching at him, so he bought it. Outside he cradled the heavy Globe and a box of doughnut holes in both arms and the change stuck inside his glove. There was a dollar thirty-four left. "In a dollar thirty-four" he thought with a strange twist to his lips "she would be back. Or a dollar thirty-three. She said before it was gone." He jerked the glove off with his teeth and flung the money away. After walking a few yards he stopped, his eyes burning, and went back. He sunk to his knees and began poking through the small, circular tunnels made by the change, then kicked the slush violently from side to side.

There was traffic on their street when he turned the corner, several black rectangles appeared where cars had been removed, and something else. His eyes narrowed, scanning back and forth over the street for what he had seen, over the buildings and the line of parked cars, and there it was, the fender of the deep red Camaro. It sat in front of the snow filled vacant lot. Mitch's car. He walked up and put his hand tentatively on the windshield, tracing the scream-ing eagle decal beneath the glass. On the bumper it said "Cowboys make better lovers." Inside there were several packs of cigarettes on the front seat, her cigarettes. He shifted the Globe and the dough-nut holes and looked up at the house and the blank second story porch, still like the others, but not like the others because behind it she was kissing and rocking Merle, and Mitch had his filthy head in the fridge searching for a beer. He sat down on the stoop by the car and leaned back. The blueness beyond the roofs seemed to fall away from his eyes, as if gravity reversed and he could fall up, up, as soon as he let go. He ached to see her, to collapse against her. He knew, in a moment, he would. He would get up and walk the hundred yards and climb the stairs and throw open the door and that would be that. But he just sat there.

A green truck idled a few doors down, the driver leaning on his horn for a car sliding sideways out of a parking space and the sound reverberating cruelly in the wet air. Across the street a boy in a big parka was playing with a little girl of about three. It looked like they were playing hide and seek in front of the stoop. Paulie watched the boy hold both the little girl's hands and spin around. Her eyes were closed and then she would continue to spin around alone, smiling with her arms out, and the boy would dart fast behind a car or the stoop and the little girl would look round and round and not see him and call him and then begin to cry. He would wait until she looked afraid and started to cry desperately, and then he would pop out and she would stop crying and look happy almost immediately and they would start to play again. After awhile he would sneak quickly behind another car and she'd call him and start to cry again. Paulie watched as both were repeated again and again, the little girl's joy, desolation, joy, as she continued to play, having too short a memory for despair, or too long for joy. He continued to watch, amazed.

nominated by The Iowa Review

HECTOR COMPOSES A CIRCULAR LETTER TO HIS FRIENDS TO ANNOUNCE HIS SURVIVAL OF AN EARTHQUAKE, 7.8 ON THE RICHTER SCALE

fiction by DAVID ZANE MAIROWITZ

from THE MISSOURI REVIEW

Mexico City. 23 September, 1985

Dear David,

Knowing that a letter from me has slightly more chance of reaching you across the world than one sent to me here (my local post office is a heap of stone), I'm preempting your questions and (I trust) your concern by making the following announcement: I AM ALIVE. THE CITY IS NOT DESTROYED. I thought at first to write to each of my friends separately but I've decided now to photocopy this brief note and send it out as a circular. (At the same time I would ask you to make copies and pass them on to any mutual friends you might think of.) I can't tell when I'll have a moment to write at length, but I'm sure you'll understand it might not be for some time. The most urgent thing is that you don't worry about me and above all not try to phone. The central communications office went down in the first quake. For the moment, just take my word for it: I'M ALIVE and not lying under the rubble of my apartment block as you may imagine.

Muchos abrazos,

                              Hector

P. S. SOME OF YOU MAY HAVE EXPECTED news of Beatrice. The fact is I can't provide any. That is to say, she is not dead, or so it would seem. I have been on her trail since the first moment the fat gourmet worms I was eating disappeared from my plate, since the cinema across from the restaurant where I was to see the reissue of *Singin' in the Rain* an hour later budged a meter to the left then one to the right before severing itself in two from the marquee, down the center aisle, exposing Gene Kelly and Debbie Reynolds to those of us sitting, too sick to be astonished, in the restaurant. What I am saying is that not only was the left side of the street spared while the right collapsed in on itself, but also that the stone edifice of the cinema appeared to have cracked while the plasterboard projection box and the flyweight movie screen stood functioning, albeit robbed of sound. And we—those of us who had been sitting along the plate glass restaurant window, which bowed but stood like the rest of our side of the street, scarcely believing yet in the tremor— watched the film.

It was in what-must-have-been-a-scarce-second that Beatrice appeared to me, as I had last seen her years before, backing out of our cemetery rendezvous, machete in hand to make sure I did not follow her, leaving for me on a gravestone the court injunction preventing me from entering her premises in future. I imagined, with Gene Kelly now swooning and ripped along the perfect axis of his dancer's body in this tiny aftershock some perhaps fifty seconds later, that everything in our lives was cleft open to miraculous spontaneity now, that catastrophe would make bitter sisters charitable, calm the distraught and reunite fractious enemies as the bombing raids of popular wars were cracked up to have done.

And so I went for her, not altogether from fear of finding her dead, but rather to see if she lay perhaps prostrate under brick and if, the choice being between suffocation and my pulling her free, she would proffer a helpless hand or retreat forever into the dark stone. In any case, in that moment of divided earth nothing could be taken for absolute, not even her hatred for me, that perfect dynamo which could in its heyday set forest fires at long distance and turn windmills on the airless caverns of the moon.

I staggered out into the street. The riot squads were already overreacting, bayonetting bystanders away from the central area, but it was gratuitous. We were becalmed in the murderous city, docile as never before, because I'm sure that we somehow always expected this, knew at every moment of our life and dreams that it would come to us haphazard and equally deserved. And in the first blindings of tear gas I made my way to the Century Hotel where I knew I could at least count on the offer of a tearful bourbon, if not a room for the night.

Whether or not he recognized me, his eyes scattering aimlessly in shock from the spectators to the first corpses being dragged out and deposited on the street, I did nothing to gain the attention of the hotel manager. Surely my designs had called for reinforced steel girders on the Japanese model to resist shocks like today's, and if these were not approved or passed under the table because of the cost it was not my fault. Still, I could not discount that the hotel-keeper, in his rage, might blame me for the smoldering rubble of his building, the only one to suffer damage on this street. Only the neon "Hotel Century" sign, hanging like a tooth from its root, still flashed amidst the shattered concrete fast turning to powder. In what must have been the seventh or eighth floor, now bluntly pinned to what might have been the third or fourth, a couple lay caressed in the clamping hotel walls. The ceiling seemed to have snapped to "his" back as he pressed "her" beneath him; three of their arms hung through the bedstead which now perched free of its support-ing wall precariously out into the summer night. The executive suite where Beatrice insisted we spend our first night simply be-cause I had built it (and where I had to use my influence with the manager to eject the honeymooners next door to provide adjoining accommodation for her police shadow) with its lackluster interior decor now sat across the street on top of another building. The mock-colonial archway of the roof terrace and the adjoining ceramic swimming pool were swept out into the eucalyptus-lined square behind the hotel from which we first heard the machine-gun fire, incessant, as I tried to push into her for the first time only to find her slipping free, creating her own space and corner into which she would receive me only when she herself had determined the angle and counterpressure of skin, and peered through the blinds, to see the rioting students being massacred under cover of night.

With all hope of transport gone, I would have to walk north across the devastation, a journey of perhaps two or three hours which would get me there in the middle of the night, an arrival which, assuming Beatrice was not sandwiched between floor and roof-beam, was to play chess with scorpions for pawns. For whatever else might have danced in a spirit like hers—the far nights of rum and mescaline-soaked Gauloises—her body also deigned, through some involuntary self-hypnosis, to accept, from time to time, sleep. That owls did not hoot or cocks dare crow during such times was not a miracle of nature, but a sure decree of her totalitarian hand.

My office was on the route. I could doze there the several hours before daylight and then choose afresh whether to go forward or not. The building was intact, save for a fissure across its face and, with all my private files and city-financed plans for demolishing the shanty towns and building new slums in their place locked inside, I was suddenly relieved I had not built it myself. The lights worked. Despite the blackouts this section of the city had been spared. I sat down at my video display terminal and thought to write my survival letter, to send it off somehow swiftly (perhaps amongst the airline hostesses I had known and pressed between arrivals and departures in neon-glaring airport hotels, who could post the thing in London, Amsterdam, or Copenhagen). Yet, as I threw the switch to illuminate the screen, I knew the earthquake had struck here too in the seclusion of my workplace. The machine was no longer silent, but somehow distantly coughing. I typed my message, exactly as you find it above, and called for a print-out, but the machine simply fused, choked, switched itself off, and, scarcely audibly, "wept."

There was nothing for it but to press into service my old portable Remington which stood on my desk next to the blueprints for some death-trap high-rise flats which would now surely (or perhaps not so) never be built. In the typewriter was a paper which read:

PLANETARY POTENTIALS:

In 1985, the big planetary lineup already began which goes until the year 2000: the planets are coming into a smaller segment of the sky. The magnetism in that area (say some prophecies) could pull the earth off her axis—earthquakes could be one of the more gentle results. . . .

Without hesitation I checked the three locks on the office door. Children had often tampered here in hopes of stealing my ball-point pens, and each time I had replaced the outmoded model with the most sophisticated in American anticrime devices. I knew that now the night patrols were already out in force, gangs of thugs dressed as Red Cross workers pushing through roadblocks in stolen ambulances to lighten jewelers' windows and banks in the city center knowing that, for once, the police were not lurking in the area, springing illegal road traps for born-yesterday motorists who would in turn be forced to paper upturned palms, but striking useful paths through gaping mobs so that anonymous corpses could be flung into make-shift mortuary wagons. Yet I was sure these had not struck here. Nothing out of place, no lock sprung. The window had not been smashed open, nor its iron bars sawn off. No, this section of town was unharmed, at least this building. Nothing could have indicated that Beatrice had been here, perhaps just steps before me, and left her mark. There was no mistaking her on the paper, not merely the threat ("earthquakes could be one of the more gentle results"), assuming, as she would, personal responsibility for natural catastrophe, but also the typewriting which, by its sure pressure to cut holes in high-quality paper, provided evidence solemn as a signature.

Allowing myself forty-five seconds of despair, I considered my immediate itinerary: write my circular letter, find the airline hostesses who would surely be grounded now and waiting for escape flights, find and strangle Beatrice, look for something to drink which could not cloud my clarity nor give me malaria nor involve archaeological exploration, lock my office door and place tiny upright matches against it to see if they were still standing the next time I returned to base.

You, all of you there on safe ground, you just can't know what it was like for us on the night of the first quake. We didn't act out of self-concern or even instinct for survival, didn't think of loved ones, nor even about the totally obvious chance of a second tremor, avoiding at all costs the inside of buildings, for most of the city went back to sleep that night in their death-traps; no, we thought on that first night of all the projects we never finished, as if we now had suddenly only a strategically limited time to do so, say, eighteen hours or less.

On the southern corner of the northern zone, on the street where I had played crucifixion football, where I hid out for days after stealing my first Mercedes hubcaps and where, behind the street's only tree, I tested the stretch-tights of a babyfat teenager from Ohio, half the roofs were blown off. I was moving further and further (as I now know) from the epicenter of the quake and you might simply turn a corner to find nothing dislodged, yet here the houses stood while the roofs caved in, whether from hasty construction or from a peculiar tilt to the fault line no one could be sure. Many had been replaced with plastic but not my mother's, which had come down like a children's slide to the pavement, blocking access to the front door. The only way in was up and over, and it was not the modest climb which checked my immediate entry but the hard-edged piano battering the night from within. For years my mother had sat out her infirmity in front of that upright, slaughtering the only piece of sheet music she owned, *Selections from* "Showboat," and that she could now, in this hour of mass death, muster a riff of honky-tonk, set me to pondering whether this newest affront of Beatrice's did not peppermint-brush the hangman's smiling teeth.

Look, I said, climbing you while my aging mother sleeps in the next partition of these paper-thin wall fills me with dread.

"I'm your mother now."

Still, Beatrice, I won't terrify that woman next wall by letting you reach the pitch of your ecstasy, knowing how you rage and bang, how you shout things that would scare her for the rest of her few years when you sit on me.

"I'll play the piano instead."

Not now, Beatrice, it's the middle of the night, but you shackled her only at your peril, why did we have to come here anyway just to satisfy her whim of running all the stops in my biography, and now the first strains of a Chopin mazurka, heavy with footwork and ferociously chorded, won the day, or rather, night, so that my wheelchaired mother, who had never known me to bring home a lover, much less a celebrity urban terrorist in semi-hiding, in wondering if this was a selection from "Showboat" left out of her sheet music, was surely suppressing a natural rage only in the staggering aura of this Afro-wigged beauty at the clavier. No, Mamacita, no this is Beatrice banging up new walls in our house, it's *the* Beatrice, bank-robbing daughter of the President of the Bank of Mexico whose glamour photo you can recognize in any post office, whom the police have official orders to shoot on sight but don't dare because she is her father's favorite and her father regularly entertains Henry Kissinger and his concubines, the very same Beatrice who has decided she will hang out with us for a time, will-us, nil-us, and that means we'll be famous on the street what with the Federales, those you see in the Chevrolet out there wearing Chicago White Sox baseball caps, watching the house and drowning out the Chopin with their breakdance transistors.

I climbed up the slope of the fallen-in roof and peered into the black hole of the house. I must have been somewhere above the tiny alcove-kitchen for I could smell the pork fat and cornmeal of recent ritual. Here I didn't dare light a match, my mother being in the habit of leaving the gas open, although, with the roof gone, the fumes would have risen up to heaven, if any.

Sliding down the inner wall I found my feet and made for the central room from which the piano assault beckoned. The room was artificially dark, but the hesitant tracks of moonlight picked out the silver paint shining in the hair of the plaster Virgin of Guadaloupe in her adobe wall-niche, the flickering ready razor of the male figure crouched by the piano, the glass cases housing actual photographs of several saints, my drunken dead father, Susan Hayward, and, by some mistake, D. D. Eisenhower. What do you want here anyway?

"I'm looting the place."

A hasty match showed a man, more a boy, scared, hanging on the piano but surely not playing it.

"There are other houses to loot, Señor. I found this one first."

"This is my mother's house, creep."

"You are going to rob your mother?"

This delightful chat might have carried us to daylight, might have taken a turn for tequila, my mother always had a cold breakfast in case someone ever turned up who of course never did, but for the piano which persisted without mercy in playing itself, starved of all and any human consort.

"What are you stealing?"

"The piano. But as soon as I touched it, it started to shake and play."

I knew my mother could not have installed a piano-roll, knew equally only one person in the entire Federal District of Mexico whose piano playing could continue long after the thunder-caress of her fingers had passed over the instrument like the Angel of Death. In any case, you could not get the piano out the front door which is barricaded. You'd have to lift it up over the walls.

"You going to help me?"

"No. Not my mother's piano. Steal something else."

236

"You got an idea?"

There is in some cupboard a silver spoon from babyhood, a collection of Gringo baseball cards is worth a peso or two, don't touch her bed linen, she'd never survive that, I've always hated that fucking Virgin of Guadaloupe but who'd buy that except a fucking Gringo. I bought her a transistor radio some years ago she never listens to.

Exploding bottles of propane lit my way across the night, showing me I was on course toward the dreadful slums of the north, on whose outskirts we have lived in relative splendor because Beatrice needed to rise from her comfort each day and witness the world as it is in its bitter holes. Never giving a penny of her father's millions to begging slum Indians (except the Mayans, for whom she had a weakness), she would nonetheless buy their cheapest rags in the open markets and dress down amongst them to do her shopping, pretending to be poor until once she failed to efface her silver nail varnish and had to run her knuckles through a potato scraper weeks after.

This was all in the era she had organized the kidnapping of her father to finance the urban guerrilla five-week plan of her ex-lover (into whose bold indentation on our marriage bed I slumped more than once), another Zapata look-alike spoiled middle-class brat who robbed drive-in banks behind the wheels of a Porsche and distributed the profits to the local Friends of Heroin Society. (But some of you surely know that story, for she would have asked for translations of the literary ransom note for the foreign press.) In any case it all came to nothing (as you no doubt know) because, on the eve of the attempt, she discovered, for the first time, that nature, whom she had kicked and bullied for years, who served (along with me) as fawning handmaiden, had deceived her. Never one to accept into herself any device or medicament which might make a clockwork of her body or control the fatal delivery of egg and blood, she had connived, after her own fashion and in the teeth of life's sadistic grinning bookmakers, to outwit the call of the species. This was at first a categorical denial of all penetration which, soon enough, did not provide any proper degree of risk for her spirit and gave way to a thousand quick-breath withdrawals orchestrated and impeccably timed by her inner clock. And then, after she had swallowed her pride to share quarters with me (as opposed to hit-and-run contractions in the back of her car, in back alleys, in the sea), she recorded her waking temperature every morning to catch her hours of fertility for a brief abstinence, and even at the front of absolute certainty she had exercised to develop a means of clamping fast the walls of her woman's self at the ultimate, damming and forcing the invading flood back down the canal of regret.

Yet despite the angry swoon she played out at the sudden hardening of her breasts and the first nasty rush of sickness, I knew (without daring to say) that such misfortune could never have taken Beatrice unaware, no, not Beatrice who must have felt the earthquake some minutes before the rest of us, as wild deer do; thus, contrary to the public face she put on the outrage against her body, she must have, from some deep reserve of peculiar normality, wanted it.

And I recall this now, walking through the crowded shanty towns in flames, hysterical fire-fighters seeking water-sources which lay buried under mortar and corpse, because in my sudden quest for Beatrice I would have to face the gloom of seeing my children for the first time in years.

Outside the district of burning shacks where the wealthy villas suddenly opened out along the eucalyptus-lined boulevards the corpses were no longer thrown in heaps but evenly spread and covered with cloth to keep off the flies, often with the name of the dead written in pink chalk on the pavement between his or her legs. And as the second killer tremor delivered itself in the first light, a 7.3 Richter this time, I heard again the words of my master builder: earthquakes don't kill people; buildings which fall on them do. For as I watched the wounded being carried into the hospital complex I'd built on the edge of the barrios to serve the rich and poor alike in my (or rather in Beatrice's) idealism, the entire works went down. Buildings that half hung in space after the first crack went to pieces now in the aftershock. But the only new catastrophe in the area seemed my hospital, the powdery bones of which stared out at me across the gates with hundreds, perhaps thousands, trapped inside. Sirens ripped the slow waking line of morning, and panic, which had not surfaced the night before, now forced the dawn to march double-time, swallowing the flat horizon against its slow nature. A hospital orderly grabbed my shoulders while rushing by, and shouted for me to join the digging team, every hand was needed.

And, to be sure, this was my rubble and death-house to scrape free bare-knuckled. But I had come a far progress from the gourmet worms to these outskirts of Beatrice, sleep was calling, the expression on my face and my mood turning murderous.

"The comrades in the Pancho Villa Faction are teaching me how to make remote-control explosives."

What for this now?

"To blast down all the ugly cheap buildings you put up."

On her street it was not merely Beatrice's Volkswagen Beetle which had survived the second quake. Other cars were overturned, their chassis severed, cherished Oldsmobiles from the American '50s had smashed their tail-fins through brick walls, some smoldered, and, in others, the tremor had set engines running only to sputter dead forever. But all the district's Volkswagens stood unharmed in place or, around the corner where another water-main had burst and made a river of the dusty street, several Beetles floated by, sooner or later coming to rest on the dry shores of other neighborhoods.

It was of course not possible for Beatrice to have gone anywhere without her car, not even down the street to retrieve the children's football from a neighbor's garden. These were not just wheels, but the wings of her absolute mobility; she had even trained as a mechanic so she could repair it herself at a moment's notice, and she might be seen under it any time of day or year, her child-full belly protruding through the designer overalls, her high-heels perched up on the pavement.

But she was not there. I had an old key, but she had changed the lock a dozen times to bar an entry I'd never intended. Anyway, the door was open to the touch. Inside, breakfast was finished, the filthy plates remained in place as always, the stereo, the television, the cassette recorder were all playing to the full, as was Beatrice's way whether *a casa* or no. In my daughter's room there was a bra thrown hastily on the unmade bed. Ah. I'd been that long away, and suddenly, in my lower back, I felt a twinge of discordant muscle to remind me of days and nights bent over my architect's blueprints which had done me permanent injury. Picking up the bra (still in pain) I could not resist examining the size on the label, at which I dropped into a (still painful) longing I could not dare allow continue for more than a scattering of seconds before noticing, to my crusty relief and the triumph of my chromosomes in her, that it was Mick Jagger on my daughter's wall, not Michael Jackson.

The little dresses in the boy's room were surely Beatrice's smart-work. An American softball was all I could find to distinguish him, no handguns, of course, no weapons for children to fit the ideology of his pistol-packin' mama, o.k., I agree, somebody has to disarm in these bullet-riddled times and why not the young boys to give example to the old boys, but were the dresses and pastel scarves his idea or Beatrice's? And did he play baseball in these frills with the t-shirted half-naked boys of the barrio and, if so, and he was assigned to pitch, how shall he raise his knee to follow through on the down foot in throwing the perfect curveball if he must avoid tangling his leg in undersilk? Yes, I know, there was to be no compulsion to perpetuate the lies of the social race; we were, after all, not the inheritors of dead-weight but pioneers of the unthinkable, cha-cha-cha, I know all that, Beatrice, but will he, this boy-thing, one day twist from his caressing do-anything chains and hate his mother for punishing him with freedom?

I'm too weary to think of an answer, and besides, I have made my way to Beatrice's bedroom where, as always on coming home (it doesn't matter how many years have passed), I rush to examine the tracks left by her latest lover. This room seemed the only part of the house affected by the earthquake, ashtrays with still-smoldering tip-ends, sheets ripped at the lower end by indiscreet toenails, the half-filled glass of Southern Comfort now comforting drowning horse-flies, underwear hanging from the slats of venetian blinds, the evidence of two head-imprints on the pillows, strands of red hair (hers) and blond (not), two coffee cups, one on either side, both lipstick marked (I see. So.), and I could think only of poor Socorro the first time I engaged her, and Beatrice walking in on her, kneeling on the wooden parquet waxing in between the cracks, asking what's this, this is Socorro, Beatrice, I've hired her to clean and cook and look after the children—do you think I will stand for having a cleaning-slave in my house?—, no, Beatrice, I knew in advance you would not tolerate it, knew you had lived the disgrace of it in your father's mansions, had your boots freshly shined and ready miraculously outside your door every morning before school, knew it would be the ultimate humiliation for your just-discovered notion that poor people should not be exploited and that you'd rather live in your filth than give this honest old woman a good-paying job which she desperately needs, look at her going pale there on the floor knowing you are going to fire her we'd better speak English, but we have no time to learn each other, Beatrice, the children steal our hours, the housework our souls, all this must sound terribly mundane for a part-time urban terrorist, I know, but we must be free, both of us, to be ourselves.

"Nobody buys or sells my freedom!"

No, this is true. Or even gives it to you gift-like. You get it in dreams or in armed hold-ups, in any case, Beatrice, you are the snatcher of it, but your snatching-wrists are lately burdened with these two small beings . . .

"Three."

Yes, in any case, three, how will you manage your Tantra Yoga classes, your commissioned statue of Zapata for the district square (which, I don't dare tell you, they will never accept in the nude), the dishwashing, get the children to school, without this gift of Socorro I'm making you, all the while trying not to hear the word "three," can you really have said that?

In the house I found no trace of this third child. Through intermediaries I discovered it was a girl, and I'm sure some of you know more about it than I do, although, as we all know, Beatrice never writes or answers letters, at best sends a costly telegram. Perhaps you know where she sleeps, where her clothes are, her chamber pot, she must drop somewhere in this asylum-inspired design of Beatrice's housekeeping.

Only the plaster reproduction of Chalchiuhtlicue, water goddess of Teotihuacan, which Beatrice had carved herself, now standing on its flat head in the middle of her sitting room, kept me from turning back and starting south for the city, Beatrice-less, my journey at an end. I have to tell you that Beatrice was in the habit of turning statues and objets d'art upside down in order to create instant ashtrays when she had misplaced, or could not be bothered to empty, her own. Still, there was no trace of dust on this unfortunate upturned queen's base; what's more, you didn't need a measure to see that she had been placed deliberately symmetrically dead center in the room.

Quickly I turned on her taps; water. This was no invocation to repair burst pipes. No, the tough precision of the thing spoke of less transitory fear. I could imagine Beatrice one day explaining that the statue had dislodged from its pedestal, rolled to the midpoint of the room, and stood on its head to announce its divine displeasure. But I knew that this indelicate position of the goddess was the fruit of black rumor, and I was already reading Beatrice's mind in this (as I was then and ever expected to do).

When it finally came to me it was on the frontier of a sleep I had avoided for more than a day's passing. It "woke" me ruthlessly, and I knew I had to get to her somehow, where she had fled into the eye of the rumor, those many kilometers away, with the city at a standstill.

Were it not for our years of falling in each other's turns of mood, the thousand daily guessings of meaning, backs turned in the conjugal bed, even before the words could form on the other's lips, I would never have found her car keys. But I knew where they were surely to be found, that is to say, somewhere buried under something, flung down in a return from the previous night's excesses, kicked or tripped over and perhaps lodged in soiled laundry, who knows. I might now have walked back to my blueprints, begun rebuilding the city for inflated fees, and been well shot (to choose a phrase) of Beatrice. But my foot went immediately to its rough work, kicking aside first the undergarments, the empty milk containers, the Patti Smith LP's free of their sleeves as usual, the *I Ching* bent face open to the following judgment:

The powerful prince will be honored with horses in great quantity. During one day he shall be three times welcomed.

Then, at last with reluctant fingers in the cactus plants, the stack of unopened letters from the year gone by, the bowl of rotting mangoes. In the pockets of her jeans on the laundry mountain were cigarette butts squashed out by fingers, a five-hundred dollar (US) bill, a spent tube of lipstick, and equally, in her handbag—amidst the collapsed Mars bars, expired passports, the pornographic snapshots of herself, a can of self-protection tear gas—but no keys. Only when I bent to wash my failing face in the sink did I notice them hanging from her toothbrush.

As I pulled away from the house the Volkswagen choked and sputtered, refusing to receive the placement of its gears, the accelerator pressing back at my foot. As most of you who visited us know, no one but Beatrice was ever allowed to occupy the driver's seat and, after all these years, the car simply could not accept the touch of alien limbs in control. Yet sensing what it wanted, I slammed the gears nastily into one another, drove with one foot on the gas, the other on the brake, blaring the horn even with no other vehicles passing, the radio switched on to overkill, headlamps alight in the glare of day, sunroof rolled open, so it could imagine itself powered by its proper mistress and carry me out of the panic-stricken city. It was equally a matter of smashing all speed limits, even without other motorists to rush up just behind and overtake, driving on the pavement if necessary or into oncoming traffic to maintain my (that is, her) pace. I expected any moment to be stopped, since all private cars were prohibited, but mine had become, in a sense, an emergency vehicle, carrying my ruins out of the devastation to this last rendezvous, and to make certain of it I held a white handkerchief out of the window as I left the city unprevented. In the glove compartment was, as always, her Colt. 45.

And a cassette tape which, when pressed into service, gave out what was clearly Beatrice's self-recorded breathing exercises and full-bellied screams in the penultimate "transition" phrase of the birth of our third child. These wails and the midwives' coo along the length of the Mexico-Laredo Highway filled me with terror, not of what was to come, but of the imperfect past.

The Pyramids of Teotihuacan were still standing. The two earthquakes had surely struck here, opening up roadside caverns for us to fall into, but the ancient sites, built not only to defy nature but to swaddle it, laughed at my own pretension to map out dynamic space and fill it with arbitrary ugliness. Running along the Avenue of the Dead I cast an eye at each of the temples but knew in advance that Beatrice, having assured herself after panic that "her" pyramids had survived, would not choose ground level for a rendezvous which must take place, knowing I would surely follow her here.

I know that most of you have seen the film she was allowed to make (over the dead bodies of the official anthropologists who were no match for Papa's influence in the government and who, anyway, were either paid to shut up or farmed out to curate minor ruins in the provinces) of herself dancing naked on the Pyramid of the Moon (and for which Papa used the Kissinger hot-line to bribe an Academy Award nomination), because you need to remember the film to set up the frame and shot (not again!) of what was to come next. Try to recall the scene in which the ancient priests (a Mariachi band hired to play the ancient flutes and ritual tambourines), flanked by the National Guard reserves (whose demanded price for protecting Beatrice and film-crew from being stoned by outraged archaeology students was to appear in the film as well as gross 1% of the box office, if any), climb the long steps of the Pyramid of the Sun behind the Sun-God, arriving at last, after an endless unedited sequence, at the summit only to discover that the Moon-Goddess has tricked them and dances instead across the street (if you like) on the Pyramid of the Moon. Now fires are lit and smoke signals sent to and fro across the impossible black ether-void which separates sun and moon. At the moment of its zenith, with the sun setting exactly symmetrically in front of its pyramid (as the ancient architects had planned it), just as both God and Goddess are about to hurl themselves into their respective sacred fires and re-emerge as the sun and moon of the solar system proper—the moon less brilliant because the other male-dominated gods have thrown a rabbit in her face (don't ask me)—there is suddenly and inexplicably a long close-up of Beatrice's belly. That she was already swelling with our third child would be evident to anyone who knew her, but why she had chosen this method to announce it to her friends and fans the world over I cannot tell.

Yes I can.

Look, Beatrice, look at us, builders of the future city on the pyramidal model (me), sculptors of the new clay gods in our own image (you, naturally), robbed of our dreams by these howling sleepless brat-nights, tortured titans who bought an ironing board and took out insurance policies. So that when she let the camera focus on her belly it was her way of telling the world and me, wherever I by that time was (in fact sitting in mortified disguise in my local cinema where the distributor had been greased a small fortune to show it as a short subject to a captive audience waiting— and howling—for the Clint Eastwood feature), that she intended to have this baby (and any number of others) despite my insistence that she take her father's private jet and fly to London to put a full stop to the first paragraph of this new biography running short in her woman's insides.

And as I climbed the long steps to the top of the Sun I began composing my circular letter in my head, to show I'd survived the earthquake along the Cocos tectonic plate, 7.8 on the Richter scale, its shock waves coming at 40 km per second, knowing you would expect this news of me, furious with myself for having nothing to write with and thinking to ask Beatrice, at the top, if she could find it in her heart to lend me her glow-in-the-dark felt-tip pen which writes simultaneously in rainbow colors and which, when fondled, gives off the scent of raspberries.

This German tourist quietly eating his lunch at the top of the pyramid was surely not Beatrice and, sitting down to get my breath, I knew I could not. I rolled myself into a tight knot, choking from the altitude and my weariness, thinking of the last Tarot Beatrice insisted on reading for me even as she meticulously cleaned and loaded the six chambers of her pistol. The Death card never even bothered to turn up. No, in the center line was the Empress— on the axis of past-future and reality-dream, flanked everywhere by numbered swords, with the Fool and the Tower-Struck-By-Lightning in the dark row of things to come. It's clear from the cards (had she fixed them?) that I have to kill you, she said, apologizing, I have to do it, if not now, then later on.

"Every time I throw my shadow up on a wall, I find you standing in it."

If so, Beatrice, it's because, from the first, I've always wanted to be just behind you so as to put whatever you might need swiftly in your hand, but I know that, just as you expected this of me long ago when we were agents of each other's desire, now I've become watch-man of your tower and I know, this being the end of us, surely, I know that what you need is to run all the red lights on the Paseo without me pressing my heels on the windscreen in panic of my tiny life, know that even now as you load your gun and I am re-minding you that there is school tomorrow and a gunshot will surely wake the children, even now my instinct to survive (as opposed to yours, to live, die if need be, and come back for a second or third joyride) is suggesting to you that you put your contact lenses in, you could not live with the indignity of missing your target and, as you fumble in your impossible handbag—stuffed with your collection of the shoelaces of ex-lovers—I'm gone.

Here on the Pyramid of the Sun this shot should at long last have found me. For there, across the Plaza of the Moon, on the other Pyramid, knelt what seemed to me (I could not be sure because the afternoon sun was caught between us) a sniper, a woman, taking aim at me. If this was or was not the shadow-work of the afternoon on the face of the Moon, I advised the sunbathing German to descend out of sight, then made my own slow path down the long steps and into the desperate valley, heading for the smaller Pyramid, not merely to ask Beatrice to take me back, but to rendezvous at last—the shadows changing and snarling again now high above me—with the gold-inlaid bullet of her dark chamber.

nominated by John Allman

BIRDS-OF-PARADISE:
A MEMOIR

by EDWARD HIRSCH

from MSS

MY MOTHER-IN-LAW is half asleep. It is six o'clock in the morning and we are in her bedroom, lying on two beds pushed unevenly together, holding hands. She is wearing an elegant pink nightgown with a ruffled white collar; I'm in faded blue pajamas. The first brown light is just starting to break through the window over our heads and the effect is large and bracing. A new day. It feels good to be awake. It feels oddly right to be lying here in my mother-in-law's suburban bedroom, lazily holding hands, watching the light as it curves along the wall, warming the paintings, starting out the morning. I like the slight angle that it shaves across the tops of the narrow leather-bound books. I like the way that it barely touches the mirror and slowly seeps into the forehead of the high, mahogany dresser. My mother-in-law has been drifting in that vague country somewhere between being awake and being asleep, and so I'm surprised when she gives my hand a little squeeze and says dreamily, "I don't think I've ever felt so happy." The words send an immediate chill shivering down my arm. When I finally turn my head towards her, though, she has already floated away, fully asleep. She is not exactly smiling, but her lips are slightly parted and she looks pleased, as if someone had given her flowers about an hour ago.

My mother-in-law has cancer—a word that no one mentions in her presence—and this is our daily routine, painstakingly worked out. The night nurse wakes Gertrude every morning at precisely five o'clock. She walks her slowly to the bathroom, gives her a warm sponge bath, helps her to change nightgowns. Here a decision is involved. There are two matching nightgowns and robes that Gertrude especially likes to wear for company: one is pink nylon and the other is a brightly colored cotton print. "Who's coming to visit today?" Gertrude will ask. The nurse checks the calendar for the day and then—by some mysterious inner logic which I have never quite been able to fathom—Gertrude decides which nightgown and robe to wear. We call it "holding court." We tease her by saying that she doesn't really get dressed in the morning; instead, she prepares herself for her daily rounds at court.

After Gertrude is dressed for the day, the nurse prepares breakfast: a soft-boiled egg, a piece of lightly-buttered toast, a cup of weak tea. The nurse puts a clean white sheet and a sheepskin pad on the rented hospital bed while Gertrude sits up in a chair and makes an effort at her breakfast; these days she sips bravely at the tea through a flexible Peter Pan straw, but the egg and the toast cause excruciating stomach pains. They must also carry on a conversation while this is going on because Gertrude can tell me about each of the nurse's personal lives: Sherry's boyfriend (he won't marry her), Bernadine's two daughters (one honor student, one cheerleader), Angela's commitment to the true church of God (a little zealous). After breakfast the nurse helps Gertrude back into bed and then—on the condition that she asks for it—the nurse gives Gertrude "a shot for the pain." (No one mentions the poignant, addictive strength of the drug, a morphine derivative.) By now Gertrude's scrawny upper legs and thin buttocks have actually turned black and blue from the needles, but nonetheless she always asks for the shot. There is no question that she needs it. When I come sleepily up the stairs at exactly five forty-five to relieve the nurse, Gertrude is in her best mood of the day. She smells slightly of perfume. She feels optimistic and vaguely euphoric.

"I slept wonderfully," Gertrude calls out when she sees me in the doorway. "I sat up in a chair for twenty minutes this morning. I drank an entire cup of tea and ate half an egg. I even read some of the paper. Isn't that nice?"

"That's good news," I tell her morning after morning. "That's a good sign."

She smiles, as if I have just said something intelligent, proving her point. I cross the carpet and lean over the hospital bed to kiss

248

her good morning. She kisses me lightly on the lips. "It feels good to sleep so well," she says agreeably. "It makes me feel lucky."

The problem is that Gertrude is every bit as sick as she looks. She has been home from the hospital for seven weeks now, and every day we can actually see her getting smaller, thinner, bonier, a little more worn and skeletal, a little closer to death itself. She appears to be all sharp angles, shadows and lines. What is happening to her is obvious to everyone, including Gertrude herself, who no longer speaks about getting well. She has a deep fear and curiosity about the literal moment of dying, but no fear at all about being dead. Nor is she a believer. "Wouldn't it be nice if there were a place where I could see Don again?" Gertrude asks wistfully, but with no real faith in the idea. What has happened to her can make the rest of us livid with anger, but Gertrude accepts it gracefully, thoughtfully, finally. How is it possible? She is sixty-three years old. At our wedding two years ago she was healthy and purposeful, radiant. The ceremony took place in her backyard and as she moved from guest to guest anyone could see that Gertrude was a woman at home in her own world, a woman at home with herself.

(When I first met Gertrude, I thought of her—half rightly, half wrongly—as the sort of upper middle-class Jewish woman that can be found in the suburbs of Washington D.C., married to an economist: stylish but not beautiful, not wealthy but certainly not poor (though with a clear, deep seated memory of poverty), generously devoted to her family, somewhat unfulfilled, somewhat insecure, but also definite, loyal, unpretentious, brave. She is passionate about classical music, a gourmet cook, a volunteer at an art museum. The sort of person who sends Chanukah presents to all of her nieces and nephews, who remembers your favorite kind of birthday cake. The sort of woman seemingly unprepared for what has befallen her.)

But now Gertrude is a widow who has had cancer for almost two years. She has had her ovaries removed, her uterus taken out, her colon re-sectioned. She has suffered through eighteen months of chemotherapy treatment, a massive radiation treatment that she thought would kill her, three difficult stays in a university hospital. She has watched her hair fall out in thick clumps. Day after day she has felt a huge tumor growing inside her body, painfully blocking her intestines, slowly killing her. She has heard herself choking in the middle of the night and seen herself spitting black bile into a restaurant sink. And she has heard her oncologist announcing that she couldn't possibly survive more than two or three more months. That was nine months ago. Gertrude has lasted longer than any of her doctors expected, but it chills me whenever she says that she is lucky.

Janet and I have been living in Gertrude's house these past nine months. Last October Gertrude's doctor told us that if we wanted to see Gertrude still walking around then we should come home within two weeks. We were living in England at the time and after the doctor called we dumped most of our stuff on an American friend and took the first flight we could get. On the plane Janet worried incessantly about how her mother would handle the news of our return, the unstated but unavoidable fact that we were coming home so abruptly because Gertrude was about to die. But Janet and I underestimated how delighted and relieved Gertrude was to see us. All that mattered to her was that we had returned. She told her friends that we couldn't stand the English climate and she ignored, or pretended to ignore, the actual reason that we had come back so hastily. "I had a feeling that you would decide to come home," she told us on the way back from the airport. "It's so damp and cold in England in the wintertime. I just knew that you wouldn't like it over there."

We had only been gone for a few months, but in the intervening time Gertrude had begun to take on that slightly grayish pallor which people sometimes get who have been sick for a long time. She wore a gray wig now—an expensive finely woven approximation of her hair, but an approximation nonetheless—and looked drawn, worn out, as if the color had been sucked out of her cheeks. She could eat hardly anything at all. But then Gertrude's tumor shifted slightly and she started to feel stronger. She could eat small meals without getting sick and sleep entire nights without pain. She was pleased not to be living alone, happiest planning family events. And she was delighted to have both of her daughters—and their husbands— living in town at the same time. Susan and Peter owned a small house less than a mile away and, at Gertrude's instigation, they came over almost nightly for dinner. They also dropped by on weekends and we seemed to see them constantly.

Gertrude's larger family also rallied around her, anxious to show their devotion. Her sister, Sophie, took most of her vacation time and visited for ten days. Once or twice a month her favorite niece,

Judy, drove her four young sons down from Baltimore for the day. Her nephew, Joel, took the train from New York City in order to introduce Gertrude to his fiancée. My own sister came for a long weekend. Even my mother, well-meaning, openly sympathetic, but also a trifle nettled by the fact that we were living in my mother-in-law's house, flew out for a few days in January. Gertrude was also capable of seizing any excuse for a small family party— not that many were needed—and she seemed always to be taking Janet and Susan (with their husbands in tow) for celebratory dinners at new restaurants. It was her indefatigable maternal plan to bring her family together as often as possible.

On a daily basis Gertrude also tried to keep up a semblance of routine. Two mornings a week she went to painting class. She had lunches with Norma, with Velma and Trixie, with Francis and Pearl. She shopped at an elegant boutique in Georgetown, attended special exhibitions at the Corcoran and the National Gallery. But every Tuesday she also went for chemotherapy treatment and came home looking drained and unhappy, forlorn, too weary to stir for the rest of the day. She was weak enough to need blood transfusions and spent whole days lying on the couch in the living room, half dozing, half listening to classical music, depressed by her fatigue and yet too exhausted to rouse herself. But invariably Gertrude would gather together enough strength to go out for the evening. Somehow she managed to keep a busy social schedule. Everyone that she knew seemed to invite her over and often she would end up going out three or four nights a week. She attended plays at the Arena Stage, recitals at the Jewish Community Center; and she regularly took Janet to concerts at the Smithsonian, the Kennedy Center, and the Library of Congress. Gertrude always dressed with elegant flair and I found it oddly moving to see her with a bright red scarf thrown across the shoulder of her coat and a fashionable hat poised at a slight angle on her head. She looked jaunty and brave.

I have a fear of gliding over the truth, of making it seem neater and cozier than it really is, nicer. I don't want to simplify feelings, to pretend that I have always enjoyed living in my mother-in-law's basement, sleeping in my wife's old room surrounded by aging dolls and children's books, engulfed by memories of preadolescence, her childhood. Often I have resented living in a suburb of Washington D.C. as a kind of appendage, a consoling presence, husband to a woman who is primarily acting as a daughter. I have complained

251

about our lack of privacy, the continuous intrusions of family, our flagging love life. And I have spent a substantial portion of the past year brooding in the rec. room: writing on the ping pong table with my books stacked up in huge boxes around me, reading on my grandmother's ugly but comfortable electric-green sofa which is buried behind our bedroom furniture and pushed up against a pair of sliding glass doors. It is an unsettling experience to live with an apartment's worth of your own furniture crammed into someone else's basement.

But what I have resented most over the past year is seeing my sister-in-law and brother-in-law so often for dinner, continually having to make conversation, as my fifth-grade teacher used to say "showing an interest." Susan and Peter began coming over for dinner so often because Gertrude especially believes in the ritual of meals, the communal figure of a family sitting down to eat together. It is as if the idea itself triggers some primitive social instinct within her. During our first few months in Washington, Gertrude and Janet often cooked our dinners together. (For the first time since I had known her, Janet and I regularly ate well-balanced meals. We may have been adults, but we were staying in her mother's house.) We even got into the habit of having drinks and hor d'oeuvres before supper. I got so accustomed to seeing Janet and Gertrude together that I forgot about the essential similarities between them, but once when I came into the kitchen and found them both leaning over a cookbook I was startled by how much they actually resemble each other. For a moment they looked like sisters. It is strangely disconcerting to see your wife's face doubled and drawn, thinned by illness, sketched out thirty-five years in advance, to see her features harshened, her skin sallow and yellowing, her eyes cavernous. Sometimes when I think about Gertrude's illness—its stark, relentless brutality—I realize how fortunate my father-in-law was to have died of a heart attack two years ago.

As the year progressed, it became increasingly difficult for Gertrude to participate in our meals. Often she would sit down to dinner with us, but food would make her dizzy and faint, and she would have to excuse herself from the table. We could hear her getting sick in the bathroom. After a while everything she ate caused excruciating stomach cramps and meals became another kind of ritual, a trial, almost a test. Eventually she spent most of them lying down on the couch with her eyes closed, tensed and slightly doubled up, lost inside her pain. The pain followed her through every meal, a shadow that left her weak and exhausted. Soon she started to go to bed earlier in the evening, to sleep later in the morning. Once, on the way home from the doctor's office, she vomited in a friend's car—an experience that mortified her—and after that she began to give her concert tickets away and seldom went to other people's houses. Gertrude asked Sophie and Ben to visit for Passover, but spent most of the time lying down on the couch in the den. She spent hour after hour on the couch trying to forget her cramps. The pain must have been unbearable because after seven months Gertrude couldn't stand to be around food anymore; even the smell or the sight of it could make her sick. Increasingly debilitated, she started going out less and less; slowly, almost imperceptibly, she became housebound. And then nine weeks ago Gertrude's digestion failed entirely; the cancer completely blocked her intestine. She couldn't eat a single thing without vomiting. She couldn't even keep down water and started to vomit up her own stomach fluids. There was no other choice. We were forced to obey the doctor and take her to the hospital.

Gertrude took the news without flinching, as a death sentence. She was terrified of the hospital, certain that she could die there. She never said anything directly, but it was clear from the way she packed a single nightgown in a small leather suitcase, in how thoroughly she moved through the rooms of the house ritually checking things, trailing her hand across the backs of chairs, reluctantly turning off lights. She didn't miss even one room. "Don and I planned this house from the ground up," Gertrude had said to me once. "We designed every single part of it." Now she was going from room to room touching things, memorizing even the smallest details, maybe remembering the past a little. She didn't say a word. When we were finally ready to leave, Gertrude sat stiffly in the front seat of the car looking straight ahead. As we pulled away from the house, everything outdoors seemed like an affront, a blow: the narrowness of the driveway, the healthy size of the trees, the very greenness of the lawn. Janet was as distraught as Gertrude and the three of us drove to the hospital in complete silence.

Gertrude's first day in the hospital was deceptively calm, as blank and airless as the corridor outside her room. She spent most of it filling out forms, reading the newspaper, lying on top of the bed with her clothes on, occasionally dozing but stubbornly refusing to get undressed, to show complicity. Nurses passed often in the hall-way, and orderlies, but no doctors appeared and Gertrude felt ig-nored, as if no one quite realized why she was there. It might have seemed unreal, an accident, a strange mistake, if it weren't for the pain, the huge tumor pressing against her abdomen. Gertrude didn't eat anything all day, but the pain persisted—sudden, stab-bing, spasmodic; that pain was all too real. It left her doubled and hunched, almost motionless, fully drained. Eventually an antiseptic young woman in a starched white uniform did come by to take Gertrude's temperature and blood pressure, and we convinced her to telephone Gertrude's doctor. She came back with a pain killer. She also persuaded Gertrude to change into a hospital gown and then propped her up in bed, surrounded by pillows. It was relief for her to capitulate. In the evening, Gertrude tried to sip a cup of broth, but she vomited it up immediately. After that, she was too tired to struggle anymore and drifted off into a by-now-familiar state of half sleep, a constant dreaminess, endless twilight. When we finally kissed her goodnight and tiptoed out of the room, she looked completely worn out, as if she had just lost an enormous fight. Even in sleep, she looked slightly bewildered, confused, pale and small against the hospital pillows.

By the time we arrived at the hospital the next morning, things had already changed dramatically. Gertrude was now being fed in-travenously and there was a thick rubber tube running into her nose. The tube had a thin weight attached to its front end— they had to force it into her body through one of her nostrils—and the idea was that the weight would slowly wriggle and snake its way through her throat, through her chest, and into her belly. At the same time the tube sucked bile and body fluids into a clear plastic bag that was taped to the side of her bed. I know it was an up-to-date and even conservative way of trying to break the tumor's stranglehold on Gertrude's intestine, but to me it looked like a vaguely medieval form of torture.

"Can you believe it?" Gertrude asked weakly when we came into the room. She tried to shake her head. "Can you believe what they are doing to me now?"

I had never seen Gertrude so miserable. She hated having that long rubber cord in her nose. She could hardly move because of it and felt wired up, controlled, bound. The damned thing had already rubbed the inside of her nose raw and created a dull soreness in her throat, an irritating ache at the top of her chest. She found it impossible to ignore or forget. Even more than the discomfort, though, Gertrude hated the indignity of it and she saw the treatment as an odd kind of humiliation, something else that her body had done to betray her, one more thing that she had to submit to and endure, an unrelieved nightmare. "I want to go home," she kept saying to the oldest and apparently most sympathetic of the nurses. It was a type of refrain. "I want to be back in my own house."

The nurse was professionally cheerful. "Of course you want to go home. But don't you want to get better, dear?" she would ask. "First you'll get well and then you can go home. Now isn't that a good idea?"

The question reduced Gertrude to a tight-lipped silence. She didn't have a response. It was as if for a moment she could actually see the possibility floating before her—fleeting, improbable—that she could get well again. Her hopes soared. But then, just as suddenly, the possibility disappeared—a plummeting kite, a sinking feeling in the pit of her stomach—and there was no hope left. Gertrude knew exactly what was happening to her. I don't think she ever fooled herself for long, or truly believed that she could recover. But nonetheless she found it hard to contradict the nurse's unrelenting cheerfulness.

At first Gertrude refused to allow any friends to visit her in the hospital. She claimed that she was too weak for company, but later admitted the truth. "I don't want anyone to see me like this," she told us once, gesturing slightly toward the tube in her nose. "It's too humiliating."

"Your friends want to see you," Janet would argue. "They don't care how you look."

"But *I* care," Gertrude would say, firmly closing the subject. "I'll see my friends later. After the doctor removes this awful tube."

The problem with Gertude's attitude was that her days in the hospital, unbroken by visitors, were unbearably long. She was starting to get shots of morphine as often as every four hours and spent most of the time in a kind of dull haze, a dazed and cloudy half sleep. Janet and her mother spent entire days alone together in Gertrude's hospital room. Often I would leave the two of them in midmorning and when I returned in the late afternoon, they would be sitting in essentially the same positions, as if they hadn't moved for hours, in a gloomy, deadening silence. Sometimes the television had been turned on—though usually without the sound—and yet neither of them would be paying the slightest attention to it. Even the air in the room, however bland and sterile, seemed thick with depression and unhappiness. I'd do my best to cheer them up by talking about this and that, my work, something ordinary that had happened which momentarily seemed funny, an acquaintance that I had accidentally met in the corridor, someone famous that I had seen crossing the street. It helped a little. It helped, too, whenever Susan arrived for a visit. Recently though, Susan had to put in more time at the architecture firm where she worked and found it difficult to get loose until the evening. And so for about a week Janet and Gertrude spent their afternoons in a blank, paralyzing stasis. "It's this cord," Gertrude would say weakly, fidgeting with the plastic bracelet on her wrist, explaining her dour mood. "As soon as this lousy weight starts to work, I'll feel better. I know it."

Gertrude was so unhappy that some nights Janet and I took turns sitting by her bedside, holding her hand while she slept, occasionally wiping her forehead with a wet cloth. Sometimes, out of a sound sleep, Gertrude would suddenly begin to speak. "I don't know how Don could do this to me," she said once. She enunciated it softly, distinctly, but also with her eyes closed, so that I couldn't tell if she was awake or asleep. Then: "I don't know how he could have abandoned me like this." It could still make her angry—with a genuine unreasonable anger that surprised her by its intensity—to remember that Don had left her alone by dying first. I started to reply, but Gertrude turned her head and was truly asleep. Somewhere else.

Later she jolted awake. "I dreamt that Don was having a heart attack," she said. "I came into the bedroom and he was kneeling on the floor, completely out of breath. I've never seen anyone so pale and colorless. He looked stricken. It was terrifying. I wanted to shout for help but for some reason I couldn't open my mouth. I couldn't even run to him. I was paralyzed. It was awful to see him like that; it was terrible to be so helpless." Gertrude fell back against her pillow, completely worn out, but still tense and upset. After her nightmares about Don, she invariably had trouble relaxing enough to go back to sleep.

Gertrude hated having a rubber tube in her nose so much that one night she dreamt that she was finally pulling it out. The pulling went on for a long time, for what seemed like hours, until her arms started to tire from the exertion. It took a long time, but eventually she could feel the weight coming back out through her nose. The pain woke her up and she discovered her fingers spotted with blood and a small weight in the palm of her hand. There were coils of rubber cord lying in a huge heap at the side of her bed, like a giant, strangely colored snake. The dream amazed her, and even cheered her up a little, but the next morning the doctors immediately began the treatment again and forced the weight back into her nose. They had to start over again from scratch. It was dispiriting. The following morning Gertrude relented about having visitors.

Gertrude's mood improved a good deal when her friends started to visit: those visits gave her something to look forward to. However, she still wanted desperately to come home and mentioned it to nearly everyone who entered her room. ("You're a woman," I heard her tell one of the late afternoon nurses. "You can understand what I'm feeling.") For all of her determination to be released from the hospital, Gertrude was oddly reticent about her feelings around her doctors. They intimidated her and she found it difficult to let them know how miserable she actually felt. It didn't help matters that her doctors—important men who made their rounds in the very early morning—generally woke her out of a sound sleep and seldom lingered at her bedside. Gertrude would complain about the tube in her nose, but not tell them how determined she was to go home. Or she'd get flustered and forget to ask the questions which she'd thought of the day before. Whenever Janet and I managed to confront a doctor about Gertrude's treatment, he would equivocate. ("It may be working . . . " "We can't tell yet if the weight has reached the tumor . . . " "We're not magicians . . . " Etc.) It was apparent from their general demeanor that, at the very least, the treatment could go on for a long while. Even worse, there was no real evidence that it was working.

Every day Gertrude was perceptibly weaker, thinner, that much more sunken and, ultimately, disheartened, that much closer to dying. It was beginning to seem as if she would be forced to die in the hospital. Late one night I came into our bedroom and found Janet sitting up with her back pressed against the wall. "I can't stand it anymore," she confided to me. "My mother looks terrible. She looks as if she's been in a concentration camp. It's too horrible." Then she wrapped her arms around her knees and started to cry, but silently, as if she were trying to keep Gertrude from hearing her. Sometimes she could sob like that for ten minutes at a time, in almost total silence. I put my arm around her shoulders to calm her and tried to think of something useful to say. Eventually I went to get some kleenex. In the bathroom I discovered my own face wet with tears. When I came back Janet was staring helplessly at the dolls on the bookcase, the faded blue wallpaper of her childhood room. "It's awful," she whispered fiercely. "It's too awful. We've got to do something about it."

The next morning Janet and I finally confronted Gertrude's oncologist, Dr. Cohn, in the hallway outside of her room. Cohn was a reserved, fairly uptight, professionally friendly, middle-aged doctor who wore rimless spectacles and spoke with a vestigial New Jersey accent. But he had a fondness for the truth and we were determined to have a frank conversation with him. That's when, however cautiously, he at last let us understand that Gertrude was far too frail for an operation—the only treatment that could ever seriously work —and that the rubber cord was a kind of last resort, at best a temporary measure, temporary hope. There was no sign that it was succeeding. Even more important, there was no real hope of stopping a cancer that had spread throughout Gertrude's system. He refused to predict when—he had already made that mistake once— but Gertrude was evidently going to die in the very near future. "Maybe we can forestall things a little," he told us. "We can certainly make her more comfortable." I could feel Janet flinch when he said the word "comfortable." The news was devastating.

Gertrude's treatment could at best work temporarily—if at all. Ultimately, there was no hope of saving her. And that's when we began to lobby seriously for Gertrude's release. Gertrude was insistent about coming home and we were determined to help her. We would do our best to take care of her. The question was whether or not we could convince the doctors to let her go.

It wasn't easy. Not many people besides us thought that a dying woman should be released from the hospital. One of the doctors called Janet "misguided." A brash young intern called us "hopelessly mistaken," and actually recommended surgery. So, too, the chief resident said that I was "stubborn and intractable," and decided that Gertrude couldn't survive a week without being fed intravenously. "She'll die in three days," he announced to both of us one afternoon. "You'll be fully responsible."

But Gertrude abhorred the hospital. "I can manage without being fed intravenously," she would argue. "I'll eat as much as I can." Then she'd say: "I want to sit on my own furniture. I want to wear my own nightgown. A woman would understand why I want to be in my own home."

Eventually Gertrude's doctors relented, agreeing to let her go. One morning, Dr. Yovine, Gertrude's personal favorite, went into the room and had a long conversation with her. We never did find out precisely what they said to each other, but Gertrude never mentioned chemotherapy again; she stopped talking about recovery. "You can take her home," Dr. Yovine told us when he came into the hallway afterwards. "But you have to agree to bring my friend Gertrude back if you can't take care of her."

We arranged to have a party for Gertrude on the day she was released from the hospital and when we got home the living room was filled with people. Gertrude was thrilled to be home, delighted by all the attention. Even the hospital bed, which we had rented from a medical agency and pushed up against her own bed, didn't seem to faze her. "I promise to rest tomorrow," she kept saying to us. "I'm not tired at all." Later I heard her blurt out suddenly, "The house looks marvelous. It's such a gorgeous house!" She was spilling over with happiness.

Gertrude's mood was contagious. It wasn't until everyone left a few hours later that Janet and I started to get queasy, to feel the full weight of what we had done. We weren't prepared to take care of a dying woman. We weren't capable of handling an emergency. Because of us Gertrude would probably die overnight. All at once we were terrified. Gertrude, on the other hand, was sitting comfortably on the couch, looking rejuvenated. She was still ecstatic about the party. "I haven't felt so good in months," she announced to no one in particular. "I think I'll go to my painting class tomorrow." She looked at us shyly. "Wouldn't that be nice? Maybe I really could go to my painting class?" It was a kind of musing question that we weren't really expected to answer. Instead, Gertrude decided that she was going to sleep. "I can make it myself," she said, waving away our help, slowly crossing the room. I had never seen her so happy in quite such an independent and singular way. She went to bed feeling radiant and tired.

But the next morning Gertrude felt sick again and the next afternoon she was too weak to even get out of bed. Her illness reas serted itself with a vengeance and she never mentioned going to painting class again. During her second day at home, she must have vomited at least five or six times. One of us would bring her a little plastic pan and she would spit up into that, pushing it away when she was done. She'd take a sip of cool water and fall back onto her pillow, exhausted. She spent much of the day wearily dozing. Every now and then she would wake up with a sudden start and call for us, at the same time reaching for the plastic pan. By the end of the day her voice was so weak that we had trouble hearing her. That evening she was too tired to get out of bed when she absolutely needed to, and so we started bringing her a bedpan. We also bought a little brass bell which she could ring whenever she wanted us.

At first we hired a nurse to stay with Gertrude overnight. She'd give Gertrude her pain shots and take care of her during the long, slow hours of the night. But Gertrude needed enough care and attention that soon we hired a second nurse to work in the afternoons. Thus, for most of the time that Gertrude has been back home, we have had a nurse in the house for two shifts a day. One nurse (usually a crisp, taciturn young woman named Jeanette, Tamara, or Mary Beth) works from two in the afternoon until ten in the evening; the other (Sherry, Bernadine, or Angela, all of whom are for some reason softer and sweeter, slightly older, calmer) comes over at about ten p.m. and usually stays until six in the morning. It is awkward to have a stranger in the house for so many hours a day —someone else to talk to and consult, some other authority to deal with—but Gertrude likes and perhaps even requires the constant personal care. Having a nurse in the house so much of the time has also lessened our dread about being able to care for Gertrude.

When Gertrude first came home from the hospital, she was so sick that we really did think she would die immediately. But then— in the mysterious inner rhythm of her illness—her tumor must have once more shifted, however infinitesimally, because Gertrude began to feel a little better and could once more sip small amounts of liquid without immediately getting sick. Beyond every prediction, beyond even the wildest of expectations, her life continued.

After Gertrude's first troubled and uneven days at home, our daily lives began to settle into a pattern, often a surprising and even unnervingly pleasant pattern, at times almost comfortable, unexpectedly enjoyable. It has evolved like this: every morning Gertrude talks to her sister in Chicago on the telephone; every afternoon Janet plays the piano for her; every evening Susan and Peter come to visit. Gertrude especially likes company and her friends have come often to visit; indeed, so many people have wanted to come over that Gertrude has trouble limiting herself to one visit in the morning and one in the afternoon. These visits leave her depleted but happy. She spends much of the rest of the time sleeping—a heavy, profound, lumbering sleep—as if she were practicing for something more permanent.

Every third day I drive over to a nearby pharmacy and pick up a bottle of Gertrude's medicine. She has begun to take "a pain cocktail" every three and a half hours now, and never misses or even delays a shot. The one thing that truly terrifies her is the pain—which she says is like a horse kicking her in the stomach—and after about three hours, without fail, Gertrude always asks for her shot. Her medicine is so strong and addictive that the pharmacist will only dispense it in small doses, hence my routine trip to the shopping center.

There is also a floral shop next door to the pharmacy and every now and then I stop in to buy Gertrude flowers. At first I brought flushed purple lilacs, or deep crimson-colored roses, but lately I have come home with a pair of Gertrude's favorite flowers, two long-stemmed, oddly shaped birds-of-paradise. I tend to think of the large-blossomed blue and orange flowers as preening, stylish, exotic, almost foreign to our soil, so unlike other ordinary garden flowers. But Gertrude adores them. She is especially pleased by the gift and keeps her two flowers in a glass bowl on the dresser where she can see them clearly. "Aren't they gorgeous?" Gertrude asks one morning when she notices me staring at them. "They have such a streaked, fragile beauty, almost like rare birds. I can't get over them. Don't they make you just want to cry?"

The question is rhetorical, but nonetheless I try to keep my thoughts to myself: intense, brooding, unhappy. Gertrude seldom lets herself really cry anymore. Delighted to be back in her own home, determined to obliterate the awful memory of the hospital, she no longer complains about her illness. "I'm just happy to be here," she says simply. Or: "I'm trying to enjoy each day as much as I can."

At times over the past few weeks there has been a strange, disquieting gap between Gertrude's mood and her appearance. She is resolutely optimistic and yet we have watched her getting more and more frail, skinnier than I have ever seen another human being, so that by now she is truly skeletal, almost wasted away. In a way, her features look as if they have actually grown, so that her eyes and her nose seem larger, harsher; her cheekbones are high and pronounced, purplish, almost brittle. As a result, her face seems unusually stark, crow-like. She no longer wears a wig and her thick white hair is now sparse and stringy, cropped close to her head. It can be an unsettling sight and lately Janet and I find ourselves cushioning friends and relatives who haven't seen her for a while. "Get ready," we warn them. "Be prepared." I myself am careful not to seem in any way startled when I come into Gertrude's bedroom in the morning. Sometimes I find myself hesitating outside her door, bracing myself for how she will look. As a result, I am surprised at just how genuinely pleased I am to see her.

"Good morning," Gertrude will cry out when she sees me standing in the doorway. "I slept beautifully. It's a perfect day."

It is the mornings that have come to matter most to me. Every day I come upstairs before the night nurse departs and spend the first few hours of the morning with Gertrude. The idea is to give Janet a chance to sleep later, though Gertrude and I also have begun to take a secret illicit pleasure in the sweet laziness of our mornings together. Often we lie on adjoining beds, while Gertrude tells me about her dreams, which these days are nearly always happy. Her favorite dream is about the family. "I dreamt that Don was still alive," she confided to me one morning. "The girls were small. They were wearing those white organdy dresses with appliqued strawberries that I made them for Passover. They looked adorable. I was putting on my hat and gloves when I heard the car door slamming in the garage. I can't believe how clear the sound was. Janet and Susan were getting over the chickenpox and so it must have been our first year in the new house. We still didn't have a front lawn. We were going to Mrs. Kaye's for dinner. We always took the girls to Mrs. Kaye's for Mother's Day."

Gertrude and I usually listen to records during our mornings together. The two of us have developed a particular fondness for listening to Bach before anything else, and so I put on a record of Szeryng playing the unaccompanied sonatas and partitas. For a change we listen to Menuhin playing the violin concertos. The records sound a bit worn and scratchy, but the violin is charged and radiant. Sometimes, while we are listening, Gertrude wordlessly reaches over and places my hand on her stomach so that I can feel its extraordinary tautness, the enormous tumor swelling and pushing out against her skin, like a football. She wants me to feel how large and heavy the tumor has become, how audacious. Despite her painful sticklike thinness, her stomach itself has become increasingly wider and thicker, fuller; for months the tumor has been taking over the entire middle of her body. I don't know what to say and shake my head in silent amazement. For one long fluttering moment my hand feels frozen to her stomach, but then slowly, tentatively, I try to take it back. "Listen to me," the violin seems to be crying from the next room. "Listen to me."

It is at such moments when I realize, I mean truly realize, that my mother-in-law—a woman I have come to love in a complicated, irrevocable way—is about to die. She can't possibly last much longer. But if time could stop, I think that this is where I would stop it: in this place, at this unlikely time. It is as we are in the morning that I am going to remember us, lying together on adjoining beds, shadowed by first light, drifting near two paradisial flowers, slowly getting drowsy. My father-in-law is dead, my wife still asleep, and the two of us are momentarily alone together, here, in this bedroom. Nothing changes or moves; nothing interrupts us. And so in my mind's eye Gertrude and I are forever falling asleep in the early morning, the record player still going, our faces tilted towards each other, our breath rising, our fingers intertwined.

nominated by Richard Jackson, Robert Pinsky and MSS

JUSTICE WITHOUT PASSION

by JANE HIRSHFIELD

from ZYZZYVA

My neighbor's son, learning piano,
moves his fingers through the passages
a single note at a time, each lasting an equal interval,
each of them loud, distinct,
deliberate as a camel's walk through sand.
For him now, all is dispassion, a simple putting in place;
and so, giving equal weight to each mark in his folded-back book,
bending his head towards the difficult task,
he is like a soldier or a saint: blank-faced, and given wholly
to an obedience he does not need to understand.
He is even-handed, I think to myself,
and so, just. But in what we think of as music
there is no justice, nor in the evasive beauty of this boy,
glimpsed through his window across the lawn,
nor in what he will become, years from now,
whatever he will become.
For now though, it is the same to him:
right note or wrong, he plays only for playing's sake
through the late afternoon, through stumbling and error,
through children's songs, Brahms,
long-rehearsed, steady progressions,
as he learns the ancient laws—that human action is judgment,
each note struggling with the rest.
That justice lacking passion fails, betrays.

nominated by Zyzzyva, Stephen Corey, and Michael Ryan

BETWEEN FLIGHTS

by MARK JARMAN

from POETRY NORTHWEST

You won't need to make a story up about us.
If you have overheard us, then you know
The one we're telling each other will do.
It's about an everyday catastrophe
That makes us wonder if our childhood
Was all we thought it was, a place
We have left but that remains intact.
I have a layover and my sister has brought
Her baby with her to chat for my two hours.
She drove out through the flat, tangled miles
Of lunchtime traffic. Luckily, the baby
Is happy and sang to her, screeching his joy
And throwing his body in its fits of pleasure
Against the carseat straps. He's freer now
To lunge out of his high chair at our coffee.
We can't change our lives to bring them closer.
The plate glass window by our table
Turns a kind of photographic gray
When the clouds baffle the sun, then blue again.
I can't keep from noticing, below us,
The space outdoors filled with patterned traffic
Coming and going in the terminal
Over and under causeways, and above us, the sky,
What's visible, with the same geometry.
She's worried that her baby's eczema
Will stay with him for life, but already,
Using a different diet and way of washing him,
She's erased the itchy-looking scales
Around his neck—there's just a ring of dryness

Circling his mouth. Joy works him like
A spring, popping him up, and people's heads turn.
That's how we've gotten attention. But our talk
Is only an old story, one you know.
We live so far apart, we're now the ages
Our parents were, etc. Except, last year,
It ended—their life together stopped.
The worst part is now we talk about them
As if they both were dead and not going on
Separately. Our conversation stops
The moment the baby sweeps my plate
To the floor. But that makes us smile
Ruefully, pick up the pieces, try
To calm him with a muffin he can gnaw on,
And let him scatter crumbs instead.
Consider this, listeners around us.
We protect within ourselves a secrecy
That is the code to our happiness, the black box
Recorded with the last message of childhood.
My sister and I could play it back for you
But it would make no sense. I even wonder
If it would sound like gibberish to us.
Doesn't it describe another country,
And in that country a coastal town,
And in that town, set in a gray row
With others like it, an oblong garden
Where summer hangs like a pane of glass
Slanting toward its fall? A hailstone
Or meteor, so high it seems to drift,
Aims at it, then rushes suddenly, and
Suddenly, it's gone. A tiny missile,
No bigger than a key that scalds the hand,
Shatters summer, garden, childhood.
How commonplace, that we cannot explain
Ourselves, that all we can give you is
Our brisk completion now it's time to leave,
Our kisses, our regards, and our goodbyes.

*nominated by Christopher Buckley, Edward Hirsch, Andrew Hudgins,
William Matthews, and Vern Rutsala*

MOTHER TERESA

by DAVE KELLY

from RACCOON

Again, morning finds us, a little chilly,
sitting alone in the room and thinking of ways
to use the name, Savonarola, without guilt.
Looking back past the storage shed, past the
outhouse and the notice on the outhouse door,
we learn that 1976 was probably the last good year
for self-realization and that '73 was an excellent
one for the Beaujolais grape, not too much sun,
enough rain and a Pope who understood baseball
like a native, not to mention those films of
our childhood, the foreshadowed gesture, the
whisper of death across an aunt's face, the slow
drive home from the funeral, vacation over . . .
it was time at last to learn why the wealthy smile
whenever they talk about work or buy us a drink,
time to find out why the poor look down, into
their hands each morning the Bishop drives by, why
the grocer lies at night, a vacuum cleaner hose
in his right hand, across the backseat of his
Oldsmobile, and why the girl on the right in
the group picture is dead in her father's house
or a right hook to your face, more or less,
can change a smile for the rest of its life.
So, not wanting to be an embarassment to my
family, my friends, I move far away and take up
the lives of estrangement, of silence and disguise.

Living in the forest, I tell myself, I could
give up strangling, I could make sandwiches
for the poor, as unaware of the breakfast for
the hangover as that woman we know will ascend,
undead, to the right hand of the Father, that hand
held by the Bengali dying that never has time
for magazines or magazine recipes while so many
rob the fish of their unborn young and stretch a gallon
into a mile or a quart into a single dinner, self-
fullfillment oozing out the pores as the sun
creeps back to the world, as we die each morning
into a sump of insulted fathers and wives, of sorrows
the dying don't feel, night or day, across
their canyon of stomach, of body, of undivorced mind.

nominated by Gary Gildner

STAR, TREE, HAND

fiction by LYNNE MCFALL

from NEW ENGLAND REVIEW/BREAD LOAF QUARTERLY

"WE ARE CONSIDERING no trivial question," I say to the mechanic at the All-Night Exxon when he quotes me fifty dollars for the inch-square piece of black plastic necessary to fix the light switch on my car.

"Nobody's twistin' your arm, lady. You want the part, you pay the price." A string of spit talks when he talks. His thumbs hang like guns from empty belt loops.

"How much could it cost, do you think, to create this little piece of black plastic. A dollar? Two? How much did it cost you?"

Grease-covered silence. He stares up into the guts of an old blue Chevy. "Fifty dollars," he repeats. "Take it or leave it."

"But why do you think it's all *right* to charge fifty dollars for what cost you five?" Spoken in the philosophical voice of an insolent child, shrill and rising.

"I *can*," he says, and his black fuck-you eyes back him up.

I look down at the rusted license plate like a cue card on the front bumper of my car. LIVE FREE OR DIE.

Our eyes lock in an embrace.

I do a little dance, a step my father taught me as a girl—the Teaberry Shuffle, I believe he called it—get in, slam the door, gun the engine, pop the clutch, leaving rubber like a gift.

We are considering no trivial question, but how a person should live.

The room was so white.

She said, "My life is quiet now, well-ordered and filled with light. What my mother would call a good life. It was not always like this, and sometimes when I hear a harmonica played in a certain key, or sudden reckless laughter, I am forced to recall a time I would say I regret.

"I am a sensible woman, unprone to extravagant emotions, the mess most people call a life. But in those I have loved most, there is a streak of perversity that bears no relation to malice, a deep respect for the unwise impulse, a belief in their own necessities. Mostly they come to grief, but in this soft, shutdown day, their grief seems to me more sacred than anyone's happiness.

"Morris Brink has all three. He was not a rebel because rebels know what they're against. He was himself alone, a beating head without a wall, less a man than a force, which is why I never told anyone when I married him. I knew he could not be kept.

"When we met he was planning his next intricate assault on the possible world. I am writing a book, he said, that will destroy all the books in print. *The Seven Deadly Virtues*, it was to be called. I asked him what they were and he said idle curiosity was not one of them.

"He could steal a tape deck from a locked car in seventeen seconds. I don't know what significance this has, but it's the outstanding fact by which my friends remember him. I have my own memories.

"The first time we made love I sobbed and could not stop trembling for hours—as if someone had plugged a human body into a light socket and flipped the switch. Cartoon passion. I am a woman most people would call tough. Wary, not easily touched. But the fierceness with which he held me—I thought my bones would crack, could feel his teeth pressed hard against my teeth—ripped something essential from me, something I would not willingly give because I hold self-possession too highly.

"People will smile and say love like that can't last. Better gentle, everyday affection, something steady and real. But they're wrong and it can. For a year and a half when he touched my breast my heart stopped under his hand. I am a tall, largeboned woman, ungiven to such displays, but he would pick me up, whirl me around, hold me close. My pulse beat in my stomach and I'd forget to breathe. Honey, he'd whisper, and I wondered what I did before I touched him, what electricity I ran on, how lonely my skin must've been. Seven years later, I saw him, see him now—in the San Fran-

270

cisco airport when I went home for my father's funeral. I cried out at the sudden assault of terror and joy, my hands ached for days, the minister's words lost, my father's last face.

"My God, the stories we tell.

"Twice he beat me, not out of anger—though I have a mouth to make a meek man murder—but from some terrible need to work his will on the world. That is what I believe. I know the words that women of a certain sort will say, how their tongues will cluck and a warrant will be sworn out for the bad name I have given my race. *People think they know what happiness is when they are really sick*. I have said such things myself. He beat me and still I stayed.

"I am no masochist, no weak and whimpering woman afraid of the dark. For years I led a solitary life, made my way in a world of conventionally acceptable sadists—the ones who try to put you in the place they think you fit, who smile and smile and then trip you. I have eyes of my own and I have said, repeatedly, I know who you are and I saw what you did. I do not concede.

"Why then?

"Except for the violence he was the most deeply gentle man I have known. It sounds a paradox or a lie. A black eye is not a caress, I admit."

She waits.

"It's not that I couldn't help myself. I could. I chose not to. Because the world would stop dead as a thousand fireflies in a forgotten jar if I'd left him. Some things cannot be explained to the deaf."

She takes a sip of water from the sweating glass, places it back on the bedside table.

"When he walked out the door I was relieved. You can't live with your heart in your mouth that long and survive. What I know wouldn't fill a shot glass but I know that."

She looks down at her swaddled wrists. "Another time, another place. Another person.

"My husband is a good man—decent, kind, dear to me. I am not an easy woman to put up with. There is a talent for daily living and I do not have it. I get stomach aches and bad dreams if there are not long, slow days with no one in the room. I don't know if others are like this, what missing piece made me unfit to live with. But with him the fault is less noticeable. Sometimes he goes off for days, a traveling husband, leaving me alone in the empty house, the bed a place I stretch instead of hunch in, the books my own. I can breathe

271

then, careless. And when he comes home, he doesn't hate me for it. I am grateful. No, grateful is not harsh enough. I am amazed. Kurnberger says that whatever a man knows, whatever is not mere rumbling and roaring that he has heard, can be said in three words. *I love him.*"

She breathes with the effort of thought. The room is so white the overhead bulb seems a joke.

"But today the boy next door, a beautiful and wayward child of sixteen, was playing his harmonica out back at that stopped hour between twilight and dark, and something carefully assembled came undone. I bit the knuckles of my fist, bit hard, but still I grieved—and later wondered whether I and every lesser thing is just this: a story we tell ourselves to make it from hell to breakfast."

"The last thing I remember is, when I looked up a Mack truck was coming at me."

"Life is just one whiplash after another," she says, assaulting the pillow while I lean slightly forward in the bed. Her face is cracked into perpetual sorrow above the happy face button with her name on it. Rosemary. "Three days," Rosemary says. "You were out for *three days*. We were beginning to worry." She sounds like my mother used to sound when I didn't come home on Saturday night. Only I wasn't anywhere else.

She gives the pillow a last punch, then soothes it. "There now. Better?" She surveys the room, looks pleased with herself, then walks out, her white shoes squishing like water-logged boots.

Is there anyone who has not awakened some midnight, smooth with sweat, not from dreaming but from the absence of dreams, and seen the world from outside, as if from a great height, as one not human might see, not a person, but an eye, devoid of memory or desire—and, looking down from that height, beheld the arbitrary order beneath, as if a child has connected random dots—star, hand, tree—and made a picture of nothing; even the body in the bed, known to be one's own in one's sleeping life, seems ludicrous, small, with its ratlike round of habits and hates, loves and losses, the work it does to keep itself, of trivial importance, like a pigfarmer who grows the corn to fatten the pigs to buy more land to grow more corn . . . ; and every human endeavor—history, science, art—is the body in the bed, the child, the pigfarmer blown large?

272

Sleep is not possible in such a state, until the dawn gives back the color and substance of ordinary objects, remakes the bed in its human form of comfort, warmth, dismisses the midnight beliefs as phantoms of a cracked brain.

After three days in the dark, the waking is like that of the dreamless sleeper, only the dawn gives nothing back.

"How do I look?" the woman in the bed beside me asks, pulling the sleeves of a yellow cardigan down over her tender wrists. She shifts her gaze from the bandages to the small compact mirror, squints.

Her name is Evelyn and she is going home today to her husband. She has combed her hair and put on lipstick, a pale shade of pink. Against the crisp white sheets, her life looks possible.

"Lovely," I tell her.

With the proper shift and squint, I could go back, to what memory makes of a life—consider the usual codes of human conduct a reasonable request; the common beliefs, well-founded; the lover loved and left for uncommon virtues, uncommon faults—ordinary doubts.

"Not bad for an old woman," she says and laughs, taking a last look in the compact mirror, snapping it shut.

Picture this: a woman in a hospital gown, bare ass to the wind, tanglehaired, barefoot, thumb out, at the edge of Interstate 80 at four a.m.

Within the last five minutes two cars have come so close that the hem of her hospital gown whips her legs, but they do not stop. She thinks of a story she heard at the Red Dog Saloon in Juneau, Alaska. A man lost his brakes doing sixty on the only road to town from Auke Bay. The car rolled over twice, caught fire, then fell into the water. The man was thrown free. Though his shoulder was dislocated and a leg or two broken, he counted his blessings.

Make that singular.

Some time later, a pickup truck driven by a drunk teenager was coming back from town. The driver didn't see the lucky man and ran him over.

A fourwheeler whips by making a parachute of the hospital gown as her fingers and toes start to go numb. She hears, as from a distance, sudden laughter, wild and deep. This is what she thinks: Star. Tree. Hand.

"Get in," the man says, then reaches across my lap to pull the door of the pickup truck shut; locks it. "What is a nice girl like you doing standing by the side of the road in the dead of winter in nothing but a—what—slip?"

I shiver in pleasure at the sudden warmth of the truck.

"Old man throw you out?" he asks, pulling back onto the highway.

He waits for me to answer. "The strong silent type," he says. "I like that in a woman."

I smile then, but only slightly.

"Lucky Redbord," he says, putting his hand out.

I take it. Rough, gentle, warm.

"Is that a nickname?"

"No ma'am. My mother really named me that." He takes his wallet out of his back pocket, causing the truck to swerve a little; opens it with one hand, lifts a cracked yellow piece of paper out.

"Certificate of Live Birth," I read. "Lucky Redbord. Born: September 23, 1952. Havre, Montana. Mother: Lucille Ellen Redbord. Father: Unknown."

"My father was a song my mother sang just once," he says, folding the ratty piece of paper and putting it back in his wallet. "She wanted an abortion but the local butcher was the only person in that one-bar town she could get to even consider it, and he expected more than money for payment. To him, women were just so much *meat*."

I study his face in the pale green light of the instrument panel to see if this is a joke. Dark eyebrows drawn into a silent discourse on human folly, firm and forgiving mouth. No ma'am.

"She told me this in first grade—when I found out that most kids had a father, which I guess I knew, but did not take to be an absolute necessity before anyone brought it up. Little bastard, they said. Then I did. So I asked her about it and she told me."

I try to imagine him that little and helpless but can't. Six foot two, maybe; black boots, Levis, Pendleton shirt; the hands of a man who has had his way, without asking.

"Told me it was a simple point of integrity, both in the matter of the butcher and of my father. Said she'd never slept with a man she didn't want and wouldn't marry a man she didn't love. On account of this strict adherence to a life of principle, I had no live-in father, but also was not aborted. She named me Lucky, she said, because I *was* lucky. Lucky to be alive."

"Nice laugh," he says, nodding his head slowly, as if adding something up. "The next year my mother left me in Waxahachie, Texas, with an aunt and uncle I'd never met—pinched lips, dead eyes, you know the type, *du*tiful—and went off in search of the true love she thought she deserved but had not found yet."

"Did she find it?"

"No. She's on husband number four now, I think. Some phony cowboy she picked up in a saloon in Jackson Hole, Wyoming. You know the type—big hat, no cows."

"I know. I met him in Tucson, Tucumcari, Corpus Christi . . . "

He laughs. "Where now?"

"I don't know . . . "

"Well there's one good thing about that," he says.

"What?"

"You can afford to take your time getting there." He reaches across the seat, touches my knee.

I think of a woman I saw on the news in the late sixties—tangled black hair to her waist, a slash of sunburn beneath blue eyes, sandals, halter top, cut-off Levis—being interviewed by a three-piece suit with a microphone attached to the necktie at an on-ramp of the Santa Monica Freeway. "Why," he asked, "do you continue, knowing the danger?" There had been, in the previous week, three rape-killings of hitchhikers, the high school pictures of three girls in Peter Pan collars and the same face flashed over and over on the screen.

She said, "I do it cuz I dig it."

It seemed a good enough reason then. Now I wonder: Was it the danger she craved, or the peace that followed it? Or the hope of a better place?

"Where am I?" I ask, trying to get my eyes to focus, pulling the hem of the hospital gown down over my knees, feeling the cold naugahyde seatcover beneath. Who is this? How did I get here?

"Howard Johnson's. It could be anywhere."

"I feel like a rat slept in my mouth."

"Here. This might help." He hands me a white styrofoam cup of coffee.

"Thanks." I take a sip, shiver, feel the hairs rise on my arms.

"You might find something to put on in that duffel bag behind the seat. It won't be satin but it'll keep you from freezing your ass off."

275

I hand him the coffee, get the bag out, choose a gray flannel shirt, faded Levis, black socks; put them on while he watches. What is propriety to the freezing?

"Matches your eyes," he says, giving me the coffee. His hand trembles and I take back something I'd thought.

"The shirt or the socks?"

He doesn't smile: starts up the truck, turns on the heater, wipes off the rearview mirror with the back of his wrist. I want to touch his large graceful hand but I don't dare. Strangers do not touch each other except in strange beds, and then only for sexual purposes.

"Maybe it's none of my business," he says carefully. "But did your old man do that?"

"No. I lost the right of way to a Mack truck."

He doesn't talk then, for a long time. I want to ask him a question but he is no one that I know.

I watch the mile posts and the green rectangular signs, as if they carried a clue. Nothing else to look at but endless expanses of flat, snow-covered land, an exit now and then—to Elyria, South Bend, Chicago.

It begins to snow, and he turns the windshield wipers on. There's no one on the road, and it gives you the sense of being caught in one of those paper-weight worlds you wanted as a child.

"Dubuque, 27 miles," he reads. "We're almost home."

Home.

I imagine that this is the man I married at nineteen. Charlie Tate. We are driving back from Indianapolis, his hand on my knee, drinking pink champagne out of a thermos lid, happy because of the trophy on the floor beside our feet.

He tells me again. "The secret to winning is in not lifting. You have to be able to keep your foot to the floor when your car is in flames and the wall is coming at you." He leans over and rubs his beard against my cheek. "Lifting is to winning as choking on a chicken bone is to breathing. Fatal."

After winning the Stockton 500 that year, he drove his silver blue hardtop off Highway 17 in the Santa Cruz mountains—no skid marks, no fog—a highway he'd driven a hundred times with his eyes closed, one-handed, straightening the curves out, as he called it.

I look at him, squint, but the likeness won't hold. Still, maybe he would know. Did the woman on the six o'clock news ever find out why anyone did what she did?

276

Across the dark seat, he smiles. "Almost home," he says again. Should one say that, even at the last, Charlie Tate didn't lift?

Suppose you woke slowly from a deep sleep. By the clock it is midnight. A quarter moon cuts your thigh, misses your face. Where are you? What? Only this slow waking, no clue to who you've forgotten you are except the snow on the sill of the window, your own eyes.

This bed you don't recognize—white sheets turned back to a deep blue comforter—or the way the shadows play what must be trees along one wall. Your room, you guess, like some psychotic detective investigating the mystery of her own disappearance. But how can you tell? There is no evidence of struggle, no stranger by your side, only your strange self. Who are you? What is the nature of your crime?

Perhaps you are a simple waitress, late for the midnight shift. Even now, your fellow workers frown and wonder where you are. (Is it like you to be late?) The customers, impatient, stare at the door, their plates of pancakes and scrambled eggs growing cold beneath the heat lamps.

No. It's too unlikely.

How do you know? There are some general truths you remember; imagine still hold—that snow suggests a winter and guilt implies a crime. But general truths are useless in this case. Syllogisms will not save you.

You try to place yourself in time. What midnight is it? Winter, but what month? The moon isn't talking. A calendar would help, but you'd have to know where to look in the dark room. And even so, the calendar won't tell which month it is, only a page; a number for each day but not the day.

The mirror! Perhaps the mirror will give you back your life.

Who are you? What do you want? you ask, as if a stranger at your own door. Without the memory of pleasure and pain, you don't know. Not a bad face—the gray eyes with their dark corneas of grief, the lines that sketch a history of scepticism, arrogant bones in hollow cheeks—but whose? Somehow the crack that makes a spiderweb in a corner of the bright glass seems more familiar. You smile. You smile to see what it looks like but there's nobody in it. An animal's consciousness, fear and no history. It smiles and hands you back your eyes, empty.

277

Perhaps you should hire a detective—the famous sleuth, what was his name? Ha! You don't even remember your own. How can you look up a word in the dictionary when you don't know how to spell it? A childish question, of high seriousness, you see that now.

Maybe the man who fits the clothes in the closet has gone out for ice cream. How sweet! (Which flavor would you like—chocolate? Vanilla? Pralines 'n' Cream?) At any moment he will come home, through some door you cannot yet imagine, and tell you your name. What do you think? What are the chances of it?

Small. Nearly none. You who scorn weakness (now there's a simple fact to grasp at!) whimper quietly beneath the cool sheets.

What do you do now? You decide to wait. You decide to wait because there is no other choice. (How clever you must've been when you were . . . someone.)

Then it comes to you—the thought that assembles the dark: When there is no story one can tell, no story at all, here there is certainty.

Deserted by everything that matters, you sleep.

———————————

I woke to the smell of bacon frying, saw the hospital gown on the arm of the bentwood rocker, remembered the accident, the hospital, the knight in the white pickup truck.

"Ah have *al*ways. Depended. On the kindness of strangers," I say, in my best fake Southern accent.

He is standing at the stove, cooking eggs. "You're up early."

"What about you?"

"I always get up early. It's the best time of the day. When it's quiet . . . and there are shadows still on the edges of things."

"What do you do out here all alone?"

"Grow a little corn. Raise a few pigs."

"A *pig*farmer," I say, snuffling behind my hand.

"If I'd known you felt that way, I'd've left you on the road."

"I never met a pigfarmer is all. I thought it was something people did in economics texts."

"City girl."

"No. My father killed chickens and cows."

"What does he do now?"

I snap my fingers. "He got killed in an automobile accident. Some crazy fool going the wrong way down a one-way street. Him." I shake my head.

278

"Sounds like a story to me."

I consider the possibilities—from simple indignation to outrage, grief. "Actually he sailed off into the sunset when I was ten. No note. Nothing."

He looks at me sceptically, but lets it pass. "You ready to eat?" he asks, putting the plate in front of me. Bacon, eggs, toasted English muffin. Coffee.

"I never eat breakfast."

"Well then, I hope you don't mind watching me." He gets himself a cup of coffee, moves the plate to the other side of the table, sits down.

I watch for a few minutes in silence. The loveliest hands.

"How can you stand eating that stuff after looking them in the eyes every day?"

"Pigs are smart," he says, picking up another piece of bacon, studying it, then taking a bite. "But they have no loyalty."

He doesn't talk then, just eats—slowly, thoughtfully, as if eating were something sacred.

When he's finished, he gets up, takes his plate over to the sink, washes the dish and the pan, dries them, puts them away.

"You'd make somebody a good wife. Ever been married?"

"Once. You?"

"He left me with the dirty dishes."

"Spoken like a bitter woman."

"No. After the divorce I broke them. A sort of ceremony of my own. I took every plate out of the cupboard. The dinner plates in one stack, the platters in another. Then I got the kitchen stool, climbed up on it, lifted the plates high above my head. *Crash*. Then came the glasses, assorted cups and saucers. I set them carefully on the table, then, with the length of one arm, *swept* them against the wall. Louder this time. *Crash!*"

"What then?"

"Paper plates."

He laughs. "More coffee?"

I nod.

He brings the pot over to the table, pours the coffee with a neat flourish of the wrist, as if attention to small gestures could save us.

"You haven't told me your name."

"Jesse." I put my hand out; he takes it, holds it a moment too long. Any minute, I think, he will ask for his clothes back.

279

"Which way to town?"

"North. Seven miles."

"If you give me your address, I'll see that these are returned," I say, bowing to his clothes.

"No need to do that," he says, staring at the large front pockets of his gray flannel shirt.

Here it comes, I think, then shrug. From the point of view of eternity, what's one man more or less?

"Consider it an early Christmas present," he says.

"Thanks."

I walk to the front door, turn around. "And for the coffee. And the bed."

He doesn't move, just nods.

When I get to the end of the driveway, my socks already soaking wet, I look back. He is standing in the doorway, a toothpick in his mouth, the fingers of one hand in the front pocket of his pants. The early morning light catches his eyes. "You won't get very far in this snow dressed like that."

"I'll take my chances."

"You're pretty independent," he says, "for somebody with un-combed hair, no coat, and unless you're hiding it somewhere I don't know about, no money."

"No shoes. You forgot, no shoes."

"The way I figure it, there's two things I could do."

"I know one."

"I could take you back to the highway. Or . . . "

Here it comes.

" . . . give you a job."

"What's the job?"

"You good with your hands?"

"Some people seem to think so. What did you have in mind?"

"There's a loft out there needs fixing," he says, nodding toward the barn. "I'd do it myself, but I have a bad back."

"What's the pay?"

"Free room and board, a few bucks."

"And I get to screw the boss."

He looks at me as if imagining some act you could only ask a stranger for. I consider how far I would get if I started to run.

"No fringe benefits," he says.

280

Pigs are among the homeliest of animals, second only to aardvarks and armadillos—the sly smiling slit of a mouth that's buried beneath the rude snout, two black holes not quite deep enough for fingers; watery eyes, ashamed at the thick crude skull that thickens to the swollen body without relief, except for the large stupid ears; no graceful line of distinction in this embodiment of filth, even the simple twist of the tail is the punchline of a dirty joke.

Having fallen off of the ladder I had carefully positioned beneath the loft, I picked myself up out of the wallow, wondering if pigs attack humans. I remembered reading somewhere once that they eat their young. Perhaps it's this that limits my sympathy, or maybe it's the eyes, too human in the hulking head and obscene body, as if a sculptor had set out to depict a failed human life, each feature the mark of a specific loss, and left only the eyes to bear witness.

"How's it going?" he asks, standing in the double doorway of the barn, looking up at me. The late afternoon light makes a halo for the dark hair.

"Bad."

I am once more balanced on my back on top of the ladder, stockinged feet tucked behind one rung, trying to pound a nail into the two-by-four meant to support the platform of the loft. Beneath me the pigs snort in their own muck, trying to get warm.

"The first nail was too short. The second one was long enough but too thick—it split the two-by-four halfway down. Then I fell off the ladder. Into *that*," I say, pointing to the half-frozen mud or worse.

"If it was easy they'd let girls do it."

I give him a drop-dead look. "When I want your opinion I'll beat it out of you," I say, pounding the nail in perfectly.

He laughs. "Here," he says, "I brought you some boots and a jacket." He holds them out to me. "If the boots are too big you can always wear another pair of my socks."

"Who was your charity case this time last year?" I ask, immediately wishing I'd kept the nails in my mouth.

He looks as if somebody had slapped him, sets the boots slowly down, lays the jacket on top, then turns and walks toward the house. I watch him go, upside down, an odd perspective. He moves as if he were proud of having a human body.

When I come into the house an hour later, I'm wearing the boots and the jacket; my way of saying I'm sorry, but he isn't listening.

"Job's done," I say cheerfully, blowing on my hands. "You got a towel I can use to take a shower?"

"In the closet at the end of the hall," he says, not looking up from the newspaper he's reading at the kitchen table.

In this manner a tenuous living arrangement was made. I did the jobs he requested. After the loft I patched all the holes in the barn to keep the snow out. Then I put a new shingle roof on the shed, where I found boxes of old mildewed books, which I'd read or not read at night in the half-moon light of the tall brass lamp, sitting in the square oak chair by the fireplace, when he'd go into town. *Things of This World. The Far Field.* Poetry mostly. Some history. No philosophy.

He never asked me to cook. Or do dishes.

"Take what you need," he said, putting money in the drawer by the kitchen sink. I counted it twice the first week: $200 in twenties and tens; then, on Friday, $325—but I left it in the drawer. I figured I'd stay until New Year's—ten days away—then take a couple of hundred and buy a bus ticket to wherever I'd decided by then I was going. Dubuque was not a place I'd ever wanted to visit, much less to live. Much less with a touchy pigfarmer. I knew the type: tall, dark, and lonesome. But he'd kept his word—no fringe benefits. And in this respect he was like no man I had ever met.

A silver box lay on the nightstand beside the bed.

He must've come into the room while I slept. He must have watched me sleep. I feel violated, unclean; have always hated the idea of someone looking at me when I can't look back. It's one of the reasons I want to be cremated. Scatter the ashes. Let them look at that.

I sit up in bed, light a cigarette, look again at the silver box, the small white card. *Merry Christmas.*

I have always hated Christmas, even before Santa Claus was dead—the attempt to bully goodness by appealing to greed; strange aunts who smothered you in powdered breasts and brought divinity cut in large sickening squares, required eating; the excruciating wait that ended with pretty paper in the fire, the best present; the day my father left, went out for breakfast and never came back.

Isn't it just, I thought, staring out at the snowcovered trees—isn't it just like a grade-B movie?

Then, too, a present had lain by the bed.

Give the gift of hindsight. But where were the clues? His books and clothes were gone from the house before New Year's, his face burned out of all the pictures in the photograph album in the cedar chest. How many cigarettes had it taken, I wondered, to make of this man a walking wound? I'd touched the places where his face had been, the ash coming off on my hands. Gone, gone, as if I had fathered myself and invented a likely past.

I tried to reconstruct it—every Christmas, going over the features like a blind person—the fine dark hair that fell over his forehead in a shock, black on pale, blue eyes with flecks of gold in the irises, the straight thin nose that gave his face its insolence, its pride, full lips like a woman's, then the cleft in the chin that had seemed to deepen as the day went.

I was the only one in the family who hadn't gotten it—that deep cleft. "Touched by God," my mother always said. I was not touched by God. "We ran out when we got to you." That was my father's line, making the loss less a matter of grace, more of chance. He didn't believe in God; believed only in human stupidity, taking every instance of it as a personal assault, as if a better possible world actually existed, this one made intolerable by comparison. "Crazy fool," he would mutter, "crazy fool," shaking his head, and for years I had thought it one word: craziful.

"There are some folks bound to regard the world with a dark eye," my mother would say. "Your father gets the prize." She the optimist, or the pessimist, depending on your view, what you expected. "Too good," she would say with sweet disdain. "He thinks he's too good for this world." A sneer of her own. "Quit every decent job he ever had. And me with three little ones."

When our father had gone, she would lecture us kids—my sister Ellen, my brother David, and me. "Don't kill yourself trying to get your elbow in your ear, it won't fit. There's no more light than what light there is."

I see her now, a small failed woman with a look of intense concentration, focused somewhere in the past. What did she think, when she knew for certain that he was not coming back? Good morning, good-bye. What story do you tell yourself about that?

"Maybe he didn't like the way I fixed his eggs," she said once, laughing, standing there in front of the heavy black skillet, her hair going gray under a tight bandanna, one hand on her hip, fingers back, staring into the yolks of the eggs, watching them harden then burn, the smoke rising high in the yellow kitchen.

Maybe. The word's a thumbscrew.

There's a knock at the door. "You going to sleep all day?" Lucky asks.

"Be out in a minute," I say, standing up, stretching, wondering what's in the box, the silver box no longer there on the nightstand, gone, I must've imagined it.

"Lazybones," he says, when I come into the kitchen, sit down at the round oak table, cross my arms, put my chin on my wrists.

"New snow," he says, looking out the window over the kitchen sink. "Isn't it beautiful?"

Cheerful son of a bitch.

"You change your mind about breakfast? There's plenty here for both of us. A person should eat a good breakfast. At least on Christmas morning."

I decide to let the irony pass. "No. Thank you."

"You're getting skinny," he says. "Downright scrawny. You better eat."

"It's the clothes," I say, looking down at the Levis rolled up three times at the cuffs, cinched in at the waist with one of his belts; the plaid wool shirt several sizes too large.

"There's something for you in there under the tree. Open it while you watch me eat."

I go into the livingroom, get the box—wrapped in red foil, not silver—bring it back to the kitchen table.

"Open it," he says, making his eyes wide, like a little kid.

I open the present slowly, pulling the tape off with care, not wanting to tear the paper. A red longsleeved cableknit pullover, black pants, lacy black underwear. I hold them up, raise an eyebrow.

"Don't worry," he says. "Kathleen picked them out. Do you like it?"

"Why are you so good to me?"

"You're cheap labor," he says. "And besides, I'm getting used to having you around."

"Who's Kathleen?"

"Kathleen Evans. You'll meet her this evening. I've invited a couple of people over for Christmas dinner."

284

The lover, I think. "Does she know about me?"

"Sure."

"What did you tell her?"

"The truth. That you're my hired hand. What else?"

I feel something flare inside, go out; tell myself it's just curiosity: What sort of person would pick out black underwear for the woman who's living with her lover?

"What a spread." The counter is laid with turkey, dressing, cranberry sauce, mashed potatoes, gravy, baked ham, sweet potatoes with marshmallows on top, green beans with bits of bacon, hot rolls, fruit salad, green salad, and two kinds of pie.

"Ham lamb chicken ram turkey hog dog frog, everything but rabbit squirrel and black-eyed peas, y'all," he says, doing a little tap dance.

I laugh, take the glass of egg nog laced with rum that he holds out to me.

"Don't you look fine in your new duds," he says, raising his glass. "Merry Christmas."

The doorbell rings and he goes to answer it. I follow him out.

"Kathleen, I'd like you to meet Jesse . . . "

"Walker. Hi."

"Pleased to meet you," Kathleen says, and looks genuinely pleased.

A short bald man with close-set eyes comes up the walk, stamps his boots on the front steps, then falls through the door.

"That's Earl down there," Lucky says, picking him up, setting him inside the door. "Been hitting it already, huh, Earl?"

"I simply lost my footing." Earl says.

"Earl Sweet, Jesse Walker."

Earl wipes off his hand, wet with snow, and holds it out. "Hello."

"Let me hang those up for you," Lucky says, taking their coats and throwing them in a chair. "Now. What can I get you? Kathleen?"

"A little white wine, honey. If you've got it."

"Whiskey," Earl says.

"The man wants whis-key," Lucky says, whistling the word.

"*Well*," Kathleen says, turning to me when Lucky has left the room. "How are you *do*ing? Lucky said you'd been in some kind of *a*ccident." Her eyes pop like Olive Oyl's.

"I'm fine now. Can't say the same for the car," I say, wondering if she always talked in italics.

"Well even *so*, I never could see how anyone could *hitch*hike. It must take a lot of, well, *cour*age, I guess. I mean, you never know *who's* going to pick you up, *what* they might take it into their heads to . . ."

"There's a difference between courage and stupidity," Earl says.

"That's what my mother always said."

"What's that?" Lucky asks, bringing the drinks in.

"We were just discussing the difference between courage and stupidity," Earl says.

"Here," Lucky says. "This'll give you a little of both."

"It's courage if you succeed, stupidity if you don't. That's my considered judgement," Earl says, raising his glass. "To success."

"That's what I told myself when I bought this pig farm," Lucky says. "And it didn't make me feel any better knowing it."

"What did you do before that?" I ask, realizing for the first time that he didn't come into existence that morning on the highway.

"New York, nine to five, pinstripe suit, working for some half-assed publisher who specialized in dead cat books."

"A learned man. We have here a learned man," Earl says. Then he turns his beady eyes on me. "What do you do?"

"Didn't he tell you? I'm his hired hand."

"Before this, I mean. What was your line of work before this?"

"Oh. I don't know. Traveled around a lot."

"A woman of mystery," Earl says.

"No. I just could never keep a job. What about you?"

"Earl tends bar down at the Crazy Horse. Builds the best Long Island Tea you ever tasted."

"They call it Texas Tea where I come from," I say.

"Where's *that?*" Kathleen asks.

Earl looks at her like she's too dumb to live. "Texas," he says.

"I knew that. I *knew* that. I was only kidding. To anyone else, that would have been perfectly *ob*vious."

"Kathleen tears tickets down at the Bijou," Earl says. "In case you were wondering how she exercises her formidable intelligence."

"I'm not so dumb I don't know an *in*sult when I hear one," Kathleen says, drawing herself up to an unimpressive height. "I hope you've got a nice warm place to *sleep* tonight, Earl."

So it's Kathleen and Earl, I thought.

"It's Christmas," Lucky says. "Peace on earth, good will, and all that."

"I'm sorry," Earl says. "Truly. Forgive me, Katie?"

Kathleen rolls her green eyes, puts a manicured fingernail to her check, and appears to be considering the possibility. "All right," she says finally. "*I* guess. *All* right. In the spirit of Christmas."

"Well we've got the names and occupations straight," Lucky says. "Let's eat."

When we are all seated at the kitchen table, our plates filled, Lucky bows his head. "Somebody say grace."

"Grace," I say, and he smiles like this is the right answer to every question he'd ever asked.

"Let's play strip poker," Kathleen says, when the table is cleared.

"An old Christmas tradition," Earl says, jerking a thumb at Kathleen.

"Have you got any *bet*ter ideas?"

"Yes. We could just sit here quietly watching the snow fall, remembering old times."

"Like the time all you got in your Christmas stocking was an *or*ange? No thanks. I'd rather see Lucky naked."

"I thought we'd listen to a little music," Lucky says, and puts on Willie Nelson singing *Pretty Paper*.

"Cryin' and dyin' music," I say. "Just right for Christmas."

"That was the year I was seven," Earl says. "Or was it eight? Anyway, it was a bad year for farmers because of the drought and Daddy said I'd be lucky if I got an empty box with a bowribbon on it. It builds a person's character to go without now and then, Mama said."

"That depends on what sort of character you're *aim*ing at," Kathleen says, running a hand over her breast.

Earl ignores it. "May I continue?"

Kathleen slumps on the couch, closes her eyes, and pretends to sleep.

Lucky looks at me above their heads, winks.

"Well anyway, as I was saying when I was so rudely interrupted, I was seven or eight at the time. It was a bad year for farmers. . . ."

It was midnight when Kathleen and Earl left.

"They really go at each other, don't they?"

"It's not serious."

"He treats her like she's a moron."

"People have their own ways of getting along. Better not to make it too political. Kathleen likes playing the dumb broad."

Like you like playing the dumb pigfarmer, I think. "I don't like to hear women called *dumb broads*."

"What would you call her?"

I consider this a moment. "Not too bright."

"Oh that's much more polite. I'll tell her the next time I see her. Kathleen, you're not too bright, but you are not, by any means, a dumb broad." He snuffles into the top of his beer bottle.

"I was beginning to like you."

"And now that we disagree, you don't."

"You're not as easygoing as you act."

"No. And you're not as tough as you pretend."

"Well I'll be leaving soon," I say, getting up, "and then you won't have to put up with it."

He gives me a one-beer salute and says, "Don't let the door hit you in the ass on the way out."

I have a talent for leaving. I'm not especially fond of those traveling-man songs that make a breastbeating virtue of it—*Baby, Baby, don't get hooked on me. Look out your window, I'll be.* . . . Always a man going and some goddam weeping woman hanging at his knees—but I have been one acquainted with the temptation to move on. If you've ever left somewhere in the middle of a night too cold to put a foot on the floor without whimpering, come home one twilight from a soulselling job and called the landlady to say she could keep the deposit and the furniture, found yourself heading west on Interstate 80 when the only direction you had in mind was *long gone*, then you know what I mean.

I'm not saying it's easy. Running away, maybe; but not moving on. There are rules for running away. A motive and a point of departure. Moving on requires an act of pure imagination. It's a card game without cards, sleight of hand in an empty theatre; no way to count your losses, no applause. Except spatially, running away bears no relation to moving on.

I know when to leave—the precise point beyond which a person is not a person and becomes a dancing dog. Did you hear about that slave-wage DJ down in Austin who locked herself in the sound room and played *Take This Job and Shove It* for three and a half hours until the big boss came with the key and the police? That's only the most dramatic exit. I've quit so many jobs my resume is a study in geography. But the real test of talent for leaving is leaving a man. Love is litmus; in the metaphysics of farewell, the final exam.

The only thing I took when I left my last husband was a vow of promiscuity. I thought I knew all about traveling light. My favorite line from a movie was, "I don't stop for nothin', honey, but I slowed down for you." It is better to have loved and lost. Speak softly and carry a passport. When you're leaving you're already gone. . . .

I knew by the way my hand lingered on the objects in the borrowed room that I wouldn't go. New Year's Day came and went. We shared a hangover. I said a hangover is not the proper point of view for beginning a journey. I said it was because I couldn't take his money but it wasn't that.

The body remembers every extraordinary kindness, makes its own allies.

It was one of those nights—walking through my life as if it were a train station, my mind an empty suitcase. No, more like this. Driving along in the car once, my ghetto blaster beside me, I slipped in a Judy Collins tape, turned it on; only I pushed *Record* by mistake, and the first half of *The Moon Is a Harsh Mistress* was erased. Playing it back, there was nothing but the machine recording its own noise, a senseless roaring sound.

I had gone to take a shower, hoping something would come to me—in the pattern of the tile, the texture of the thick blue towel, a memory of water. I let the hot water beat on my skin for a long time, then got out, wiped the steam from the full-length mirror on the back of the door, stood staring at the portrait of the stranger in glass.

He walked in on me like that.

"I'm sorry," he said, backing up. "I didn't know . . . "

"It doesn't matter. It's only a body."

He closed the door, came toward me, put his hands on my shoulders, looked down. I didn't move. Then I saw, in the mirror, him kneeling, his mouth on my breast, while I leaned slightly forward, my knees on his knees, felt his hands grip the backs of my thighs. He lay down, and I watched the woman in the mirror unbutton his shirt, undo his belt with one hand, unzip his pants, pull them lower;

watched, as her mouth found its way down his chest, her wet hair on his belly, down. He cried out and I quieted him, "Shh, shh," wondering who the woman, why this man, why here on the dark blue linoleum still damp.

He picked me up and carried me into the bedroom, laid me down on the bed. My body was still wet from the shower and it tingled where the cool air moved over it. He touched my breasts where the cool air had been, the insides of my arms, my palms. "Pretty pretty," he said. I tried to touch him but he moved my hand away. "This one's on me," he said, getting up from the bed, looking down at me. He smiled, took off his shirt and his socks—all that was left—and his cock rose stiff in the air, as if some strange and lovely bird. He lay beside me, watched my face, as his fingers touched one nipple then the other. There was a heaviness, a pulsebeat between my legs, and I tried to move his hand lower but he wouldn't be hurried. "Not yet," he said, taking a nipple between his teeth, biting gently, flicking it with his tongue, now the other, as if time were all he had, as if this were not prologue but a long meditation on pleasure. A quarter moon cut my thigh, lay on the dark blue cover, and he touched me, where the light entered. Slowly, gently, as if something of great importance depended on this slow and steady pleading of hands. "Is this what you want? Is this it?" he asked, and when I didn't answer he stopped. The absence of pleasure seemed an assault. "Yes." He began again, his mouth then, his fingers filling me up while his tongue moved over the small hard bead of skin, the pleasure coming from too many sources for the body to understand. He straddled me then, his mouth taking turns with my breasts, holding them high and taut, the nipples like hard candy. He let his cock dangle between my legs, and I lifted my hips, rubbed against him, but he raised up, away, went on with my breasts, holding my arms above my head, against the pillow. I raised my hips as high as I could, to the ceiling it seemed, but only the tip was in, only the tip. "I want . . . " "What do you want?" "I *want* . . . " "What? Say it." "I want you inside me." Already at the edge, one simple thrust put me over but he didn't stop. He moved my hands down to my sides, held the wrists tightly, watching my face, every outward movement a loss. Another wave hit and I felt my body heave and tremble, my thighs grab and heave, then he put my legs around his neck to bring him deeper, so deep I thought I would drown. I was crying then, surprising sobs. "Am I hurting you? I

290

don't want to hurt you." "No," I said, wiping the sweat from his face, suddenly dear, but he took my legs from his shoulders and turned me gently over. I raised up on my knees, felt his thighs tight against me, his hand on his cock, guiding it in. He began again, the slow and steady movements that made me think pleasure had an exact and single rhythm. "I've wanted to do this since the first day," he said. "Before then." I lay my wet face on the pillow, gripped the pillow with both hands, pressed against him, and we came together with such force that my bones ached and I wondered at the difference between pleasure and pain—then he let go, a sound like grief ripped from him. We trembled together, fell still, the substantial weight of him against my back, his open mouth on my neck; stayed wrapped like that for what seemed a night, then he took himself gently away, lay by my side, held my face in his hands, and kissed me. "Oh Sweetie," he said. "Oh Sweetie." As if the woman were a child wakened from a bad dream, and only this rocking could soothe her. "Never," I whispered, meaning what? Never again? Never like this? "I'm gone," he said. "I'm a goner." Then he laughed, and I remembered that this was a particular man, with a history of his own, and a face I must see in the morning. "I don't love you," I told him, so there would be no mistake.

But the body has reasons that reason itself knows nothing of. And in the morning this world will seem certain, necessary as if a long line of argument had led to this place, with the inevitability of deduction.

He will look at me with sympathy or regret, quiet as usual but deeper drawn, his eyes avoiding my eyes, like a child caught staring, conscious of his hands.

"Only a night," I will say, "only a night, it doesn't matter."

"It matters," he will say, getting up, taking my face in his hands. Then he will make me breakfast, and I will eat it, the last breakfast, only hand and mouth away from saying it: yes, it matters, yes. Because one cannot live *sub specie aeternitatis*.

Nominated by New England Review and Bread Loaf Quarterly

THE BLUE BABY

fiction by LEON ROOKE

from TRIQUARTERLY

T HERE WAS A TIME down in North Carolina when nothing ever happened.

There was the time up north in the Yukon when a man I knew locked up another man I knew inside a freezer and the man froze.

There were those times and there were other times.

I don't know which times to tell you about.

There was the time when I was twelve and riding a bicycle around and around a small shrub in the backyard and the front tire hit a brick and the bicycle crumpled beneath me and I broke a tooth and she did not care.

I am convinced she did not care.

So there was that time too.

There were the times she would bounce me on her knees and ask, Who do you love most, him or me? You didn't remember him or anything about him, but there were those times she asked that. He was like your nickel which rolled between the floorboards into the utter, unreachable darkness of the world. He was like that. Who do you love most, him or me? And though you knew the answer you never said a word, not one. You would only hang your head and wait for the knee-ride to begin again. She would stop the ride to take your face in her hands and ask that. And though you knew the answer, knew it to the innermost ache of your heart, you never said a word, not one.

You couldn't say, Ride me, Mama. You could only squint at the thin darkness between the floorboards and wonder what else over the long years had fallen between those cracks.

Him or me?

For years and years she asked this and you always knew but never answered, and now you are here by her bedside and still you can't.

So there were those times. Some of the times were good times, but they do not belong here. I don't know where they belong.

Here is another one. Sometimes on a dark night you could stand under a tree in front of your house and see two naked fat people in the upstairs room in the house across the street.

I thought, if only they knew how ugly they are.

I thought, Why do they do that?

I thought, Why don't they turn off that light?

The fat man up there lived in another place, lived across the river, and I thought he should stay in the place he came from.

My friends on that street would gather under that tree and they would say, Oh baby, look at them go, and you never could get your friends away from that tree. Shut up, they would say, what's eating you?

My mother was a friend of this woman. She was to be seen in this woman's company, in this fat woman's company, she was to be seen with them. I wondered whether my mother knew what went on up there with this fat couple, and why, when she went out on double dates, she had to go out with people like this.

He had a car, that's why.

On Saturday nights they went to dances together in a place called Edgewater, Virginia.

I stand corrected on this one small matter. I said "car" but it was not a car. His was a stingy little truck, dusty and black, with narrow, balding tires and corncobs and empty fertilizer sacks in the rear. When they went out to these dances the fat woman would sit up under the fat man's arms and my mother would sit in the cab on her date's lap, her head folded up against the ceiling, and all four would be hooting with laughter.

That was one time.

There was that time I broke a tooth falling against a brick while riding my bicycle around and around this little shrub and my mother said, Now no girl will ever marry you, but I knew she didn't care. She hardly even looked, scarcely even glanced at me, because I wasn't bleeding.

I got hit in the jaw once with a baseball, there was that time.

I pulled long worms out of my behind, there were those times, and I didn't tell her.

There was the time a dentist, my first dentist, took out an aching tooth, the wrong tooth, with a pair of garage pliers and charged two dollars.

You could see those worms up in white circles on my cheeks and across my shoulders and people would look at you, they'd say, Look at that boy, he has worms.

You took a folded note to the store one time which you were not supposed to read, but you read it and it said, Give him head lice powder, I will pay you later.

You stole a nickel from her purse one time and it rolled between the floorboards and you have not yet confessed that.

You were such a nice little boy, so sweet and good.

You had to sit on a board when you got a haircut. You'd see the barber pick up the board and sling it up over the arms of the chair and you wanted to hit him.

You put a penny in the weight machine in front of the drugstore and got your fortune told. You would put in the penny or one of your friends would, and then that friend would step up on the scale with you or you would step up beside him, step up carefully, not to jiggle or the red cover would slam down over the numbers, and then one of you would step off, step carefully off, not to jiggle, and the numbers would roll back to reveal your own true weight, although both of you had the same fortune.

For two years I never weighed more or less than eighty-seven pounds. There was that time.

Women—young girls, ladies—would come to the door and they would ask, Is So-and-So here? Where is So-and-So? But you weren't supposed to tell them, even if you knew, because So-and-So had washed his hands of these women, was done with them, yet they wouldn't leave him alone.

Policemen knocked on the door, too, they too wanted to know where So-and-So was.

So-and-So was in trouble with women, with the law, with the family and with everyone else, and what you heard was he was no good, he was mean, he cared about no one, he would as soon hit you as look at you, but he was my mother's brother and she was ever defending him and hiding him and if anyone didn't like it they could go climb a pole.

You had to go to the store to buy your mother's Kotex, because no one else would or no one else was around, and that was terrible. The storekeeper would say, Speak up, boy, and you would again grumble the word. He would put the Kotex up on the counter and everyone would stare at it, would say this or that, they'd look at me, look me over closely, then the storekeeper would wrap the box in brown paper like a slab of meat and take your money and go away rubbing it between his fingers.

Sometimes a strange dog would come up and follow you for a bit, follow you home even, even stand scratching at the door, but you never knew whose dog it was or what name you could call it except Dog or what means you could devise to make it stay.

Mrs. Whitfield next door refused to return any hit ball which landed in her yard.

The one pecan tree in this place I am talking about was surrounded by a high fence and you could not reach the limbs even with poles and no matter how hard or long you tried.

At night you threw rocks at the light hanging from a cable supported by poles at either side of the gravel street and when you hit it you ran, because Mrs. Whitfield would be calling the law.

The policemen patrolled these streets like beings from another side of the world.

A boy my age jumped or fell from the water tower at the edge of town, there was that time.

There was the time a car was parked in the same alley that ran behind our house, with a hose hooked up from the exhaust to a window, but only the woman died. The man with her had awakened in the night, had changed his mind and fled. She was some other man's wife and her blouse was open and below the waist she had nothing on except her green shoes. My mother said to us all, she said, What kind of scum would leave her like that?

The town smelled. It smelled because of the paper mills and sometimes a black haze would cover the sky and you would have to hold your nose.

Those fat, naked people in the room upstairs, you would see them drink from a bottle sometimes. You would see them with their arms around each other and then a hand would reach down to the windowsill and pick up the bottle.

You would see the light bulb hanging from their ceiling and a fly strip dangling to catch the flies.

A body was discovered one summer in a stream called the Dye Ditch, the stream you had to cross to reach grammar school, but you went down to look at that place in the ditch where the body was discovered but no one was there, no corpse was there, and after a while you didn't hear anyone speak of it and you never knew who it was had been stabbed in that ditch. The ditch was deep, with steep clay walls, the walls always wet, wet and smooth and perfect, but clay was not a thing you knew to do anything with. You found a shoe in the woods just up from the bank, a shoe with the tongue missing, and you said, This was the stabbed man's shoe and you asked yourself why So-and-So had done it, because of some woman, most likely.

Some days the ditch water was one color, some days another color, vile colors, and at other times it was a mix of many.

You couldn't dam up that stream although you spent endless days trying, and you put your bare foot in the stabbed man's shoes but you still didn't know why or how it had happened.

You were such a nice little boy. You were so nice. You tried making biscuits once, as a surprise for your mother when she came in from work, but you forgot to mix lard in, and the salt and baking powder, and the biscuits didn't rise, and when she came in you'd forgotten to wipe up the flour from the table and floor.

She would sit you on her knees and hold your shoulders as she bounced you up and down and she would say, Which do you love best, him or me?

You were swinging on a tree-rope by the Dye Ditch, swinging high, into the limbs, and you let go and flew and when you landed a rusty nail came up all the way through your foot and as you hobbled the half-mile home you were amazed that it hurt so little and bled so little, and when you got home your brother pulled out the nail with pliers and your mother rubbed burning iodine over the wound and said, Be sure you wear clean socks for the next little while.

Three streets were paved, all others were gravel, and all of the streets were named after U. S. presidents. There was an uptown called Rosemary and a downtown called Downtown, and uptown was bigger, while Downtown was dying, was dead, but was the place you had to go through if you wanted for whatever reason to cross the river.

Across the river was nothing, it was death across the river. The fat man had come from across the river, so had my mother when she was fourteen and fleeing death, which was exactly how she spoke of it. Oh, honey, it was death on that farm.

He was down between the cracks, my father was, that's where he was.

There was another time, an early time, when I walked with my grandfather across the fields and when he stopped to pick up soil and crumble it and let it sift between his fingers I would pick up soil and do the same.

Your grandfather let you walk down the rows with him, he let you hold the plow, and he said, Just let the mule do the work, but you couldn't hold the plow handles and the reins at the same time and the plow blade kept riding up out of the ground. When you came to the end of a row the mule would stop and your grandfather would look at both of you, look and flap his hat against his leg, and say, Now let's see which of you have the better sense. You stood behind your grandfather's chair in the evenings and combed his balding head, but your grandmother said, I've got enough plates to get to the table, why should I get theirs? Why can't she come and take away these that are hers and leave me with those that are mine?

No one asked her to marry that drinker.

Didn't we tell her sixteen was too young?

She made her own bed. There ain't one on their daddy's side ever had pot to pee in or knew what pot was for.

So there was the time she came and packed your goods, your brother and sister's goods, in a paper sack, and took you to town for the first time. The town was only seven miles away, but it was the first time and it was quite a town. It had a downtown called Downtown and an uptown called Rosemary, and she had two upstairs rooms downtown on Monroe Street, and you had to be very quiet up there because the woman who lived below lived alone and she was so stupid she thought every sound meant a thief was coming to steal her money.

She had a blue baby, this baby with an enormous blue head, and all of the light bulbs in her rooms were blue so that you wouldn't know she had a blue baby.

Every day for five days in the week, sometimes six, your mother left for work before daylight, you would hear the car out on the street honk for her, you would hear the car door slam, hear the engine, the roll of tires, and she would be gone. You would hear her moving softly about you, you would feel her tucking you in, then she would be gone. You went to school that first week and for five days stood in the woods watching the children at play outside, then the bell would ring and they would go inside, and when the yard had cleared you would tramp through the woods back home, you would dawdle at the Dye Ditch and check where you could and could not jump it and be amazed at all the vile colors, you would sit on the bank and grieve and tell yourself that tomorrow you would go inside with them. Then you would sneak up the stairs and never make a sound all day, just you and the blue baby and the baby's mother in that silent house. You would sit at the table drawing rings of water on the yellow top. At the end of the day your mother would come in with a bag of groceries, come in with a sweater looped over one arm, come in with cotton fuzz in her hair, and she would say, How do you like your new school, is it a nice school? How do you like your new friends?

She would sit you on her knees and bounce you and say, How is my handsome man today?

You were such a good little boy.

On Fridays you got up early to deliver the local paper and the people would not pay, they would say, It is not worth my nickel, and you kept returning but they rarely would pay, although they did not tell you to stop delivering their paper and if you did stop they would call the editor, they would say, Where's my paper?

There was the time I knocked on one door and my Uncle So-and-So answered without his clothes on and he said, You haven't seen me, you don't know where I am, and he gave me a dollar.

The blue baby died and went to heaven, but the woman downstairs did not change her light bulbs.

On Mondays you would take your mother's white blouse and black skirt to the cleaners and on Saturdays you would see her wearing these. You would see her in heels, her legs in nice stockings, her mouth red, and she would say, How do I look?

She would say, Say Hello to Monty, but you wouldn't

She would say, He's so cute when he's pouting, and that would make you grin.

She would say, I'll be home early, but you stayed up late with your head pressed against the window and she never came, no, she never.

There was the time she said, You smell like four dead cats in a trunk, why don't you wash? And she flung your clothes off and scraped at your knees, elbows and heels, she twisted a cloth up in your ears, she said, This crust will never come off, and when she had your skin pink and burning she said, Your father is coming, you want to look nice for him, don't you?

But he didn't come, and I put back on my dirty clothes and hid under the house until past bedtime, until past the time she'd stopped walking the street and calling my name, and then I went in and would talk to no one.

There was the time she said, I want the three of you out of this house, I want you out this minute, if I don't get a minute's peace I will stab myself with these scissors. So she dressed you and your brother in identical *Little Boy Blue* short-pant suits with straps that came over the shoulder, and she washed your faces and necks and ears and slicked your hair down with water. She gave your sister thirty-six cents from her red purse and she said, Take them to see the moving picture show at the Peoples Theater and don't you dare come back until the picture is over. My sister said, Mama, how will we know when the picture is over? and my mother said, When the rest of the audience gets up to leave that's when you leave, and not a second before. So we trouped down to the movie, hurrying to get there because we couldn't imagine what it might be like to see a moving picture show. We entered in the dark and sat in seats at the very rear, while up on the screen you saw the back of a man's head and a woman with her head thrown back and they were kissing. We sat on the edge of our seats, holding hands, my sister in the middle and telling us not to kick our legs, as the man got into a jeep and drove off, not returning the wave of the woman who was running after him, and he got smaller and smaller in his jeep as the music got louder, and then we saw tears slide down the woman's face and she collapsed to her knees in the muddy road and in the next second the theater lights were rising and everyone was getting up. They were getting up, they were all leaving.

On the way home the three of us bawled and my sister said it wasn't worth thirty six cents, it wasn't worth nothing and Mama must be crazy.

So that was that time and that is why I have hated movies to this day.

You weighed eighty-seven pounds for so many of those years.

You wore socks so stiff with filth you could barely work your feet into them in the morning. Your nose ran, always ran, and you wiped the snot on your sleeves until they turned stiff also, from cuff to elbow.

You would feel this tickling movement, this wriggling motion, while you sat on the toilet, and you'd stand up and wrench yourself over and there would be this long worm coming out of your behind. You couldn't believe it that first time, but here it was, proof that worms were living inside you, and it made you ache with the shame that if worms did, lived inside you, then what else could?

You will tell no one. You would be walking down the street and you'd feel it, feel the worm, and you'd reach a hand inside your britches and pull the worm all the way out and you'd think it never was going to stop coming.

Who do you love best, him or me?

There was the time all this ended, but you never knew when it was that time was, so it was as though that time never ended, which is one reason to think about it. I think about it because it ended, but never really ended, that is why I think about it.

They were always washing your ears.

They were always saying, Tie your shoelaces.

You were always being shoved one way or another by one person or another and you never gained an ounce through so many years.

We got home from the moving picture show fifteen minutes after we left and our mother was sitting in her slip in the kitchen chair, with her eyes closed and both wrists up white in her lap and her feet in a pan of water.

Cotton fluff was in her hair.

One year you asked your mother whatever happened to that fat old guy with the truck who went with that woman across the street, and she didn't know who you meant. Some days later, while washing her hair over a white bowl, she suddenly clapped her hands and said, Oh him, they are not going together any longer, it was never serious anyhow. It's just that he treated her decently and he wasn't a tightwad, and he liked good fun. Why are you asking about something like that?

300

Why are you? Sometimes I find myself thinking you are a strange little boy.

You're odd. That's how you strike me sometimes.

I think about it now because now she lies in this bed with tubes up her nose and tubes attached to her shaved head and she's holding my hand, or rather her hand is limp in mine and you can't hear her breathe. You can't see her chest rise and her lids never move. Her fingers are silent in mine.

You think of the man you knew who was locked up in the freezer in the Yukon and how he froze.

You think of the freezer and of opening the door, but when the door is opened after all of these years all you see is the freezer empty and the frosty tumble of air.

You think of these things and of those times.

She has been this way for an hour or more, not moving, and so have I, the two of us here, neither of us moving and nothing happening, her hand cold in mine and the night darkening and I still haven't answered.

Nominated by M. E. Elevitch and Gordon Lish

HENRY JAMES AND
HESTER STREET

by CARL DENNIS

from SALMAGUNDI

Two or three characters talking in a lamplit parlor
Beside a fire, the curtains closed—
So the novel begins, and James is happy.
What a relief to reach this quiet shelter,
Back from America, far from the castles of Fifth Avenue,
From their fresh, unweathered vulgarity,
Far from change run wild, the past trundled away,
His father's dependable neighborhood
Forced to give ground to "glazed perpendiculars"
That compel the passers-by to feel equal, equally small.

In the curtained parlor, where tea is being served,
The banker protagonist fills the cups so graciously
I'm convinced he's gathered his treasure with spotless hands,
His flaws as fine as the hairline cracks
In the landscapes from the Renaissance that adorn the walls.
Why shouldn't James protect his characters from the world
If that's what he thinks they need to be free?
Soon they'll have problems enough of their own
Without being made to feel what their maker felt
Touring Manhattan slums, shoved to the curb
By hordes of "ubiquitous aliens." Imagine those crowds
Hawking and bargaining on Hester Street,

Their clanging pushcarts and swarming children,
Immigrants like the couple in the photograph in my hall,
My mother's father and mother fresh off the boat.
Had I stood where James stood back then
They'd have made me uneasy too,
Though now I assume they felt even more alien
Than James felt when he left for good.

As the banker, setting his cup down,
Peers at a landscape to inspect some travelers
Sheltered under a plane tree in a storm,
I inspect the faces in the photograph
As they stare out, eager and sober,
Brave though confused. Their faith in a life
Whose outlines even now are still concealed
Inspires me, just as James's fidelity to his muse
Must have inspired the younger writers who visited.
Pulling their coats on, they stepped out into the chill
And grimy fog they planned to describe in plainer,
Ruder detail, but in a light more revealing
Than the murky light of history, the day more meaningful
Than any November Tuesday in 1913.

Nominated by Robert Pinsky and Gerald Stern

THE DOGWOOD TREE

by JENNIFER ATKINSON

from POETRY

Mown once at midsummer, the field
has taken months to recover
its half-wild hodge-podge of color—
the shades now of early fall.
From the window, she can guess at
what grows there. The purple must
be joe-pye weed, the yellow tufts
would be goldenrod. That red
bush is a blueberry, that blue
spire a cedar. She hasn't
been moved to walk down there all year—
among the briars and broken
stalks—to find the small lives distance
obscures. But in the center
of the field there's a dogwood tree,
as straight and perfectly round
as a child would draw it. The leaves
have gone red, and the berries,
past ripe, are now wine. She can tell
by the birds. A whole flock of
something black—grackles or starlings—
has descended to feast on
the fruit. It happens every year.
And every year the birds fall,
drunken from the hidden branches,
easy—almost willing prey.

This year she would like to touch one,
open its vulnerable
wings in her hands, feel its talons,
its fear, the glare of its black,
yellow-rimmed eye. And she would like
to return the bird unharmed
to the ground where it fell, reeling,
close to what she might call joy.

Nominated by John Drury

DIM MAN, DIM CHILD

by MICHAEL BURKARD

from IRONWOOD

Why do the boats error?
The boats error because the overcoats error:
they each seek a plural master.

When the horizon begs upon its final twilight:
then the leaves simmer,
branches remain some mindless color
of togetherness,

then summer, lame summer, finds its
plural master in the summer nights.
I saw a child climb

the night as if it was a ladder.
It was a ladder. I saw the plural master

begging all the boats ashore:
morning was dim,
dim blue. Man and child

in thick overcoats, man and child
looking for the sign
of the morning star. Streets,

branches of togetherness
against the dim blue boats, against
the man and child

just before lame light began
riding across the sky

somewhere far away in that place
referred to as on the horizon.

Oh togetherness,
oh horizon in your overcoat of errors,
oh man and child
begging each boat ashore.

In another life I must have been a boat.
And there is a very long story I will tell someday,
about this life as a boat, about the precarious places
the other life paid voyage to, how my being,
being the body,

slept for years and years: precariously, in error.
Precariously.

Nominated by Laura Jensen

THE ERA OF GREAT
NUMBERS

fiction by LEE K. ABBOTT

from EPOCH

HEAD COACH Woody Knapp stood in the center of his office, a manorial layout that put him in mantic frame of mind. He had parquet floors, coromandel screens, a cream brocade sectional sofa, a mile of Marie Antionette moldings. Through a window which opened onto the players' locker room, he saw backfield coach Nate Creer methodically beating a sophomore, second-string scatback named Krebs. Coach Knapp had one thought, possibly warmhearted, about the relationship of discipline to pedagogy; and another, this about what it meant to play football in the 21st century.

Near his desk, his publicist, Lefty Mantillo was on the phone, answering questions from a reporter for a special issue of *Jane's Fighting Ships*.

"They wonder if you'll use the Umayyad," Lefty said, "and how gravitons might compliment the game plan."

Coach Knapp watched Nate Creer pummeling the bench-warmer. Groans were heard, as were thumps and bone-noise. He was reminded of the Turner painting of Piazza San Marco, "Juliet and her Nurse."

"Tell them I agree with Einstein," Coach Knapp said. "Football, like nature, is simple and beautiful."

Lefty had come to the team from the night-world of rock'n'roll. He had made famous "The Unfinished Business of Childhood," a band which took turmoil as a theme to speak for the beleaguered.

"They're interested in the pre-game meal," Lefty said.

Coach adjusted his tie. It was silk, crafted by the adjunct faculty in the Division of Careless Movements.

"Mango sorbet," Coach began. "A milk concoction."

"They like that," Lefty told him.

Coach read the rest: West Beach Cafe taquito, beignets, grillades, Mardi Gras King Cake, hearts-of-palm salad, Cat Chateau Petrus, lobster medallions, and rosettes of chestnut puree.

"One more question," Lefty said.

Lefty had the bald, thickly-veined egghead of a B-movie Martian. He was said to have had in the old days an affiliation with the Monternero guerrillos of Argentina, a single-minded group with an explicit interest in hemispheric chaos.

"They want to know the pre-game talk," Lefty was saying. "Chapter and verse, your perspective."

The pre-game talk, Coach announced, would be the usual—about grief, how it is total and deep. "As I see it," he concluded, "we have three choices: move, ascend or vanish."

Nate Creer was finished with his player. Coach Knapp saw a puddle on the floor—necessary private fluids, perhaps—and he heard the sound of something pulpy, but in cleats, scraping toward the showers.

"Remember," Coach said, "truth is indifferent and men with guns are everywhere."

When Creer entered the room, Lefty exited in a flourish. Creer had been with Coach Knapp from the beginning, the intramural squads in the Louisiana playing field of the Organization of American States. His virtues were a scientist's attention to detail, plus the wry imagination of a sneak-thief. He was thought to have a wife somewhere—in the First Republic of Albuquerque?—whose face had the texture of igneous rock.

"What was that beating all about?" Coach asked.

"Sloth," Creer said. "I spoke about digging deep within the self. I used the words *ontology* and *entelechy*. I appealed to the old conventions of manhood, of self-worth. I respected our differences within the mutality of shared purpose. I aimed to address the issues of sacrifice, which leads to the loftimost, and puerilism, which does not. Then I pounded the stuffings out of him."

Coach Knapp picked up his briefcase, his silver whistle. "You mentioned Aquinas, I trust. And Vasco De Gama."

Nate Creer nodded. "Lordy," he said, "I love it when they smart-mouth."

Woody Knapp walked through the locker room slowly. The air was stale, yellow, heavy. Several odors reached him: unguents, ointments, salves. His people, his players, were monodonists, ligubriates, inspired by Saracens. They spoke Igorot, Kimbundu, fluent New Orleans. Missing eyes, ears, toes, one or two limbs, they believed in firmaments, unified fields, what infants yearn for. In one locker, he noticed a two-page discussion of spasm-dose ratios, nuclear throw-weights; in another, a beaded reticule. He could see skull caps, jellabas, a garter belt, a life-size china snow leopard. They wore shawls, prophylacteries, vinyl jump suits. Coach Knapp heard a tape-player somewhere, a tune called "More Facts About Life." It mentioned the pineal gland, what to do with floccose. Like snowfall in July, its effect was eerie. One wall—this of Pentellic marble—was covered with graffiti unique to the intimate acts of man: birth, death, sport. The gods here were Cytrons and Maronites, metal constructions from the firms of Mattel and Fisher-Price in the old ages; and the atmosphere seemed basinesque, Carribean, having to do with body-whomping and sly ways of using sweat. It brought to mind flickering torches, low but constant fevers, what can be accomplished by heedlessness.

At the entrance to the tunnel which led under the stands to the stadium, Coach Knapp met Eppley Franks, the editor of the alumni quarterly, *The Vulgate*. He was the ghost-writer for Coach's autobiography, *The Era of Great Numbers*.

"I got the galleys back yesterday," Franks was saying. His eyes were full of flecks and various luminous colors. In addition to talk linking him to specific jungle-spawned narcotics, he was said to like all things thalloid and most spore-bearing creatures.

"They want to delete the chain-mail," he was saying. "They're in conference now about the anga coats and Mrs. K's silk turban. Textiles upset them."

"What do they want to substitute?"

Eppley Franks pawed through a folder of documents at his feet. His was the handwriting of an Ostrogoth, but he had the virtue of a prose style direct enough to cause excruciating pain.

"There's talk of Huns, Hittites. I heard the name Ramses II once. There's concern with the subtext. 'Despotic' is a word that gets mentioned a lot."

"Where do we stand on this?" Coach wondered.

Eppley Franks glanced at his notes. At one time he'd apparently written on ox hide.

"Statute supports us on this one. We have Bishop De Quadra, Lord Robert. Prothalamion's our big gun. They, of course, control the paper and ink."

Coach Knapp was watching the cheerleaders practicing in the near end zone. They seemed to have come from the only cities in the world: Islamabad and Trenton, New Jersey. Lithe and sufficiently buxom, they had a cheer artful and acrobatic enough to serve increase and weal.

"Touch my hand," Coach said. "What do you hear?"

"I hear compromise," Franks said. "Expediency."

Coach was watching the smokes in the southern distances—pink and yellow and green. Fires were said to be still smoldering in El Paso. There were rumors of fierce, eccentric hot winds and the habits of displaced housewives. One heard stories—set in other regions of the baked, white deserts—of hungry dogs and the howling flood fleeing them.

"One more thing, Coach."

The cheerleaders were chanting about gore.

"Speak to me, Eppley. I'm in a hurry."

"No more philosophizing, okay? I'm getting grief from just about everybody. Stick to the basics, they say. Carnage, things you've won, why everybody loves you."

In his observation tower near the fifty yard line, Coach Knapp was approached by his defensive line coordinator, Teak Warden. His was the face of a monast—bony, hollow-eyed, mean. At his belt flopped a walkie-talkie.

"I am lonely," Teak said. In his manner was the suggestion of loud voices, hanging meat. "I like to toy with my food. I'm starting to hear songs. I'm beginning to assign gender to inanimate objects, concepts. A phrase keeps popping up: 'the curves of time.' I can't sleep, I fear my bedclothes."

On a scrimmage field beyond the open end of the stadium stood the marching band practicing a brassy, optimistic composition, basic oom-pah-pah with a fair amount of human shrieking in it. They had instruments of hair, vinework, dried fibers—flutes, bouzoukis, shells, bells. They liked to prance on the field at halftime, all five

311

hundred of them, to form words or symbols. At the TCU game in Ft. Worth, they spelled out a single declarative sentence: *Being is not different from nothingness*. They had names for man's slangy parts and knew where angst came from.

"I'm working on a purer vision," Teak was saying. "I keep seeing a place like this—vast, silent, full of rubble."

The walkie-talkie came to life: "Victor-Zulu-King, this is Almighty, do you copy?"

In the distance, the clouds were beasts, serpents, civil ruin.

"I had a dream the other night," Teak said.

"Why are you telling me this?"

"It was profound. Religious. There was horror involved."

Down below Coach's players were yammering in Pali, Tamil, Oriya. Moving in slow-motion, the linebackers raised their fists, grunting. In helmets and pads, they brought to mind vaulted cisterns, limestone caves, the lamps the holy worship by.

"We're a serious people," coach Knapp said.

Teak Warden nodded. "Ain't that the truth?"

"It's a lyric mode we seek, something to satisfy the animal in us. Wist extends, diminishes our purpose. There is danger of ambiguity, of winding down."

The walkie-talkie crackled again: "Almighty, Almighty, this is Victor-Zulu-King, we have contact. Repeat: we have contact, do you copy?"

"These are sad times, Teak Warden," Coach said.

"The saddest."

A hot wind had come up, like jet exhaust.

"We're in a strange business."

"Affirmative," Teak Warden said.

"There is the laying on of hands," Coach said, "and the hurling of bodies. Information is exchanged. We objectify, polarize. Screams are heard. There is hooting and other meaningful tumult."

"There are chains of being," Teak Warden said. "We are prescience. I'm thinking matrix. I'm thinking the moral life, a negotiation of the same."

Coach was watching the grandstands opposite him, tier upon tier of seats and gleaming metal benches. Plastered to the upper walls were banners from the Pep club: Refute Belief, Visual Messages Are Not Discursive, Self-Expression Requires No Artistic Form. There

312

were impressive drawings from *Tractatus Logico-Philosophicus* and *The Ape and the Child*. Conference flags were whipping back and forth: Griffins, Knave-life, The Hidden Imman.

"Teak," Coach said, "who is that?"

He indicated a figure squatting beside a meager fire high up in the stands.

It was a man, certainly, who seemed wrapped in a half-century of north-country outerwear.

The walkie-talkie hissed to life again. Someone was calling for help.

"Accept no higher being," a voice said. "Let's go out there and thwart somebody."

"Don't know," Teak Warden said. "Student possibly."

"Whose?"

Teak Warden waved and yonder, out of the clothes, shot an arm. It snapped up and down several times, then disappeared. Something about it suggested delirium.

"Ours," Teak said, "definitely ours."

On the field, defensive line coach Archie Weeks, carrying a brushed aluminum briefcase, had assembled his players in a semi-circle. A dozen pens stuck out of his breast pocket. His view of sport was admirably cerebral. He was now referring to a chalkboard dense with numbers and letters, arrows and stars. He was very nimble for someone who sweated and twitched.

"I want penetration," he was saying. "Give me an emotion, lower organs. I want a rising up and a putting asunder."

His players—Cud, Onan, Redman, Univac, The Prince of Darkness—were serious, attentive. They had majors from every page in the catalogue: disquiet, vigor, happenstance. They were beef with heads that swiveled a little.

"I take failure personally," Archie Weeks was saying. "I want luridness out there tomorrow. Verve approaching madness."

Coach Knapp remained to one side. There would be several more lectures by his assistants, then he would have to say something. He was watching the mountains in the east. They were called the Organs and seemed associated with conditions best explained in poetry: rue, torment, befuddlement. Between them and him—indeed, all around, from horizon to horizon—lay the desert full of stunted trees, scrub, spines, thorns, savage hooks. People were believed to be out there—tribes of very unpleasant, dark-minded citizens. They had sores and mangy pelts, and every now and then they roared out of the spectacular wastes to watch football.

"I'm talking about conspiracies," Archie Weeks was saying. "Insinuations, betrayals. I'm talking about piling on, about getting one's licks in."

Next was Gene Jenks, offensive line coach. He looked like circus property. He had the need to lean into people's faces and yowl.

Gene Jenkins spoke of the ideal sportsman. A half winged creature, it could be any of the human colors, but it knew everything: how wish works, what to say when the glands call. It was a machine. Something with many fine parts. A quiet, high-speed operation with uncommonly expressive shoulderwork. It had a chemical description and delightful physical properties. It had girth and heft, and slammed about in the current hub-bub being heroic.

"Things could be worse," Gene Jenkins said. "Things could be much worse."

Vigorous applause greeted Coach Knapp when he stepped to the center of his players. He had visited each of their homes—their tents, cabins, lean-to's, caves. He had seen what they'd eaten, how they'd prepared themselves, and they had confessed to him their joys, their nightmares. Mesomorphs, hairy, porcine, thick as tree stumps—they were all the ilks folks come in. They read Erasmus, Cato, referred to themselves as loin or chop. Many of them slept upright and appeared better for it. They had thick parts and amusing ways of getting from hither to yon. They did not mumble. Nor did they lose direction, wander off. One would address them and, at the signal, they would go. Footwear was vital to them, as were rigor and singlemindedness. What did one say to such beings? He had met their parents, their distant relations. He'd met their mates—names came to him: Lulu, Jo Ann, Dottie. These women were life principles and part of winning itself. Coach's players believed in ritual and magic. They carried lucky thread, well-thumbed coins, medals which promised protection against smite itself. They had special words: *miasma, columbine, Umgang*. They were held together—apart from the claim of the larger world—by tape and plastic, by miracle fabrics and bolts. One used an elaborate rhetoric of colors and numbers, a code of doing and being done to. "Blue, forty-six, slant left," one would say and an instant later there would be a pile of very satisfied sportsmen. All over the fallen world such exchanges were being made: language became action and the human measure of it. Unusually large men were speaking to almost round things and beating each other for the sake of them. This was not war. It was earth and wind, fire and water. It was biology and the shedding of unnecessary parts. One said, "Red, dish-right, on eight," and immediately there was a collision and the crawling away from it.

"Sleep, eat, wash," Coach Knapp said, at last. "This is what we do. When we work, life is easy. We get to go places and hear ourselves talked about. This is what I like. Don't disappoint me."

In the locker room Coach Knapp came upon one of his people reading a book. The player was a free safety—a former wood-chopper named Herkie Walls, Coach believed—and he wore a T-shirt with a picture of the new universe. There were curlicues, as well as runes, objects made important by desire. The kind of collapsed, special ruin hope had once lived in.

"I have questions," the kid said. "I have doubts, grow depressed. My vocabulary's shrinking."

A wind had risen, steady and full of far-away dirts.

Coach Knapp gestured to the book: "What're you reading?"

Herkie Walls held the thing aloft, his playbook. It was open to the pages relevant to humbug and derring-do.

"I could have been a thousand things," the kid said. His eyes suggested fear. "For one birthday I received a field jacket. It was khaki, its hem bordered with formal Kufio lettering. I preferred to wear it with polychrome sateen. I had the need to stand out and be incorrigible."

Tension was involved here, a wariness. Worry was one parameter of Coach's profession; faith, the other. Eleven, sometimes twelve times a year he ushered his people onto one turf or another. He gave instructions, rules, rubrics. He urged them toward the manifest in themselves, put before them images of fleece and wax. He reminded his people what their opponents were: creatures without spawn, vermiculate matter that ambled on two legs. Coach Knapp created stories, narratives featuring a random selection of humans who find themselves in a remote, austere venue. In every version, the endings were identical: this collection—this cadre of gristle and girth—discovers unfamiliar and surprising things and returns to the world changed in some way.

"Where are you from, free safety?"

Almost black with blood, a hand appeared, pointed. "The Province of Florida, I think. You recruited me."

A light went on in Coach Knapp's memory. He saw—anew and in a way quite compelling—a thatched hut, a puny fire, a mewling thing. The common elements.

"I said you were a state of mind, I believe. I said if you ran very swiftly and were acceptably violent, you would be admired."

A smile came to the free safety, Herkie Walls. He had been bamboozled, the floor of himself given away, and now he was not.

"Thinking is a performing art, Coach. That's what you said."

Like father and son, they consulted the playbook. Its pages, light and precious as human skin, were garish with hexagons, exotic birds, palmette stars. Its language ran from border to border and defined the seat the self sits in. The product of a dozen minds, it avoided terms like "capitulation" and "surrender." Unlike the playbooks of the older, icier ages—the times of Sooners and Razorbacks and Nittany Lions—this volume trafficked in parables, allegories, fables. It was to be read in a wild silent pace; it made the muscles tight and strong, set the organs tingling. Among other things, it spoke of love, which was the things that happened and what we said about them. Though it mentioned sulfur and brimstone, what speeds the stupid travel at, its effect was hortatory; its purpose, to heal and to promote fellowship.

"So what do we know now?" Coach asked.

In the kid's open locker was fabric which recalled mirth and what swine are for.

"We know one meaning of life," the kid said "We've learned to discriminate, not to be deflected or deferred."

"We have learned not to read between the lines," Coach said. "To speak clearly and to hoist heavy things."

"Fucking-A," the kid said.

Coach Knapp made his way across campus in his customary manner, in a straight line, his step springy as modernity itself. The sky had turned greenish yellow, what blasphemy was said to look like once upon a time. Everywhere was evidence of scholarship: scrolls, cudgels, sacks to tote. In front of the music building, a dozen students dressed in shimmer stood in a precise file. They had fierce, determined faces, what Kamikazes were thought to look like, and muttered into their fists. Admissions reported that there were thousands of students now—the craven and the mighty, fans of one science or another. They resembled hounds or crawling quadrapeds. Some had affiliated themselves with social clubs, drawn near one another by a shared interest in bombast or rowdiness. They were cowboys, memphitites, Janissaries. To class, they brought jackstays, epodes, sporules. They dedicated themselves to epigraphy, to sponsion, to what inflammation means. In keeping with tradition, Coach Knapp had attended their parties. They celebrated complexity, nuance. They were the gummata, the kinematic. At the School of Applied Practice, they traveled in groups. One heard them in the early morning, theirs a sing-song that had to do with kindredness. In other hours, one heard screech and riot given syntax. They painted their residences to resemble objects of desire and people they'd once loved.

"What is it we subscribe to?" one group was saying now. Their leader was a senior named Don, and around him in a ragged circle sat the females he hunkered with. They believed in tigers burning bright and gnarled trees of mystery.

"Where are you going?" Don hollered.

"Up," was the answer.

Don had a worried man's face, a creased thing suffused with darkness. Soon he would graduate and toil in the outlands.

"When are we going?"

"Now," they said.

On the steps nearby, uncommonly rigid and sharp-eyed, had gathered the matriculants of the Department of Poesy. Each affected the face of his favorite versifier: Rah, the sylphides, Lex Luthor. These were to be the next generation of literateurs, Coach knew. They would produce books, tracts, documents that refuted the accepted wisdom. In the end, another generation would come along. Tricks would be played, points of view offered, positions debated. Scholars would hear of afflatus, disquisitions, stuff in dreadful tongues. In its way, writing was like football itself: there was contact and joy at the end of it.

Outside the President's door sat a secretary using the phone. Several things about her—her whichaway hair, her upcast eyeballs, one hand sawing in the air—said motherhood, a concern for others.

"Are you listening?" she was saying as Coach Knapp stepped by her. "First, it appears with green eyes, copper skin, a mouth tender as a child's. It has horns, fangs, forked appendages. It sprouts, blossoms, shrivels, has tendrils, converts easily to liquid. It serenades, wheedles, cajoles, barks. Its body is indescribable—features of goat, canine, scale of a fish. It's made of dross, it's made of sputum. It causes a bloody flux."

The President was waiting. He was part Arab, part something else. Oklahoman maybe. Nobody knew. One of seven cousins who owned the college, he had discovered something in the Wadi, in the Heights, in the Gulf. It was a process, a refinement, a radical personal philosophy. Soon there was capital, assets, plunder, booty. Things were organized and produced. Titles were conferred. The cousins owned goods, services, personalities. Their logo—and the team's own name—was an arrangement of tiny but essential bones that had to do with longevity.

"I've been thinking about reality," the President said. "Particularly its specifications, the hardware vital to it. It's a big subject."

The President had a seal's thick black hair, as well as the hands and precious feet of a jazz dancer. He liked to host parties which involved glee and out-of-body travel.

"Let's stand by the window," the man said. "We can watch."

Coach Knapp could still hear the secretary in the other room. "It's under the N's," she was saying. "Nosology, nostic, nostril—in there somewhere. It ravishes, torments, has gall. What a marvel it is."

In the distance, half in the shadow of the stadium itself, Coach Knapp saw his players moving like an army. They carried torches, pen lights, smoky kerosene lamps, and they were headed for their dormitory, an exclusive facility that towered over its neighbors. Once inside, they'd prepare themselves. They would review, recapitulate, speculate. Out would go furniture, accoutrements, luxuries; in would come victuals and liquids, what the creature in them cried for. They were men who yearned for that agreement which could only be found in another man's bulky arms.

"I adore these moments," the President remarked.

"As do I," Coach Knapp said.

"Pads, headgear, scurrying in one direction—I am enamoured of the whole thing."

"It is a spirit," Coach said. "Relationships, various coordinations. I'm humbled by the purity of it."

The men stood shoulder to shoulder. Below, on a stubbed, litter-strewn acre known as The Square of Past Mistakes, a pep rally was beginning.

"Still," the President said, "there are issues to guard against."

"One hopes to have a positive effect," Coach Knapp said. "Yet it is seldom the kids say anything to you. There's a barrier, I create it. My people don't call me Woody. My father's people used to call him Moe, and often I think it would be nice to be called Woody, to be friends. But that's not my job. My job is to treat them brutally; theirs, to love it."

From the other room came that voice again, the secretary. "Geniculation," she was saying, "the state of being geniculate."

Down below, the coach for the other team was being burned in effigy. His people were the Dukes, their mascot the dainty por-ringer of Count Yugo Malatesta. They were big, it was rumoured. Like storybook farm life. And strong. They had one play, Wild Pinch Ollie, which did not involve the ball but which called upon an underclassman named Ham to lift his arms and pray in an annoy-ing voice.

"I have the need to reveal myself to you," the President said. "I can trust you, I feel. I have confessions. At times, I am quite bad. I am headstrong, for example. I don't know any Greek. I give money away. Other times, I am surprised by my own goodness. I am generous to my wives. I like to breed. Ideas come to me, I scribble them down, attempt to bring them to fruition. I can make a scarf joint."

"You would have been an excellent weakside linebacker."

"Yes," the President said, "when one dashes off the field, there shouldn't be anything left."

"It's unfortunate you're not a coach," Woody Knapp said. "We could study film together, confide in each other. At halftime, you could stand up and make one hundred youngsters feel very inadequate."

"I could have been responsible for recruiting, say. Or the defen-sive backfield."

"You could show them what the world looks like and why there is so much screaming."

The fire below was beautiful. In the past fans had charred the likenesses of Gator and Bruin. This season they would incinerate the Schismata, the Tartars. This year the Gentoo, the hymenopterous insects, the Galbanum—all the disagreeable, seductive notions they stood for—would go up in flames. The same songs would be heard, "Tell Me What You Know" and "All Hail The Power." Insights would be advanced, meanings detailed. Months from now one would have numbers to measure achievement.

"One more thing, Coach."

"Yes."

"Explain, please, the Strong G Wham."

Woody Knapp's hands fluttered like birds. He described movements, a frame of reference, what work the heart did. He discussed action in terms of phyla, genre, a specific ligament. He offered metaphor. Deep structure. Deconstruction. Tool and man.

"Check Magoo," he said. "Stem to cover Three. Willie Sam Flop One. The Cat's gotta get into the middle. Up blasts the Monster. Think turnover. Rover has deep responsibility, Red Ryder the underbody. We defoliate and make a Sweep. Then there's the Nether Parts."

"And Little Piggy?"

"Little Piggy stays home."

Outside, in the twilight, Coach Knapp moved quickly but deliberately. It was one of his precepts. "Pick a place and go to it," he would say. "Conceive and act." All around him, by contrast, wandered the distracted and the aimless. Sport—especially sport which required constant pain and doctoring—would have made everyone more saintly. There were things which could only be understood at the bottom of a mound of flesh. Coming toward him, accelerating like a steam train, charged Lefty Mantillo, the publicist. He was wearing a new outfit now, one of bangles and chrome hasps, his evening dress.

"I'm glad I found you," he said. "I got an inspiration."

Coach Knapp could see a line of lights on the mesa above the valley. Fans, he thought. Like players, they moved in bunches now. They wore red, or black, and had the look of humans who scrambled dawn to dusk. They could not gambol. Neither could they cavort.

"We do a movie," Lefty was saying, "a feature. Super Eight, three-quarter tape, noise reduction—the works. We change your mother's name. Serena, Philomel—something with lilt. We allude to Catamites. You moralize, hector. I have ideas for vistas, soft focus, stop-action, you in the misty twilight, leaves on the ground, billowy cloudwork. A narrator. Flow and irony. We loop in the bullshit in post-production."

Coach Knapp was saddened by the image of himself. There was so much to learn nowadays—where beautiful women came from, what to make of metaphysics, the subtleties of the shuddery arts.

"The first reel's all special effects," Lefty continued. "Birth, youth, rites of passage. The second, I don't know yet. Hoopla, maybe. Hurly-burly. Bad things happen. You emerge. Football enters the current times."

"I like it," Coach said.

"I hums, sahib. It says tie-in, promotion, Scratch-n-Sniff. It's killer material, that's what it is. Contemplative but with the rough stuff left in."

"I have to go, Lefty."

Mantillo's eyes went out of focus, came back. He hugged himself as if something—a crucial tissue, a fluid—were about to spill out.

"Ten-four, Coach. I gotta get back to work. I'm excited, I tell you. It's like getting aroused. I love this art business."

Coach Knapp ducked around one corner. And another. Direction signs stood up all over, from the folks in Orientation: ESCHEW GLUTTONY; THE TIMES ARE NEVER SO BAD; GO BACK, THIS IS NOT FOR YOU. A few people in that department were former players who held convocations to propose answers to impossible questions. They quoted Karl Barth, the Wallendas, seers from the dark atomic years. "Suck it in," they ordered. "Stand up tall. Don't be a drag-ass."

Now Coach Knapp was aware of someone following him. There was shambling, a trepidation. Nerve was being summoned. Soon there would be a clearing of the throat. Then speech.

"Who are you?" Coach asked.

Out of the gloom shuffled a figure, something wrought. It was the person in the stands earlier in the afternoon, the one who'd waved.

"I know you," Coach said. "Your name is Griggs. Emile, possibly. You were called the Snake, I believe. This was ages ago. The Lizard. A member of the reptile family."

The man came closer, smiling.

"Height, six-two. Weight, one ninety-six. I never forget these statistics. Your favorite dinner, what you dreamed. You attended school in Cupertino, I remember. Had trouble with world geography."

"Culver," the man said. "It's not there anymore."

Griggs looked like the poorly fitted parts of many other men. His posture said, "Assemble with care." It said, "Close cover before striking."

"What do you want, Mr. Griggs?"

"Football," he answered. "I want to wear what everyone else does. I want to take directions from somebody named Lance or Butch. I want knowledge alien to the outside world."

A fiber had let go in Coach Knapp, a link to memory. Here was ash, here was dust.

"Are you still fast?"

Griggs raced away, darted back. "I'm fast."

"Are you strong, mean?"

"I could apply myself," Griggs said. "Things could be applied to me."

"What about age?" Coach said. "You must be middle, late thirties."

"I have wisdom," Griggs insisted. "I know things. The fornix, for example. How to foregather, where to look for ground water. I have enthusiasm."

"I could've used you ten years ago."

Grigg's edged forward, his posture an underling's.

"You could use me now," he said. "I could be a conduit, a transitor, your voice in the muddle. I could be a moral value. Truth, say. Something vaunted, an idealization. I'd be a whirlwind."

A noise composed of yowling and shouting had risen in the west. Coach Knapp believed it the cries those in history were famous for. Ideas, in the form of people, were colliding. Bad, or weak, ideas would be seen in the morning like trash on a beach.

"You are staying nearby?" Coach asked.

Griggs nodded. He had a residence. Four stakes in the dirt, a rag to crawl under in the dark.

"Go there," Coach said.

"You'll call for me?"

Coach thought he might.

"I could offer myself elsewhere," Griggs said. "I have a list— opponents, those without scruple. I can't take much more wandering. I thirst, I hunger."

Griggs was moving off, bent and sly, the animal half of him alert and watchful. In the distance, the shrieking had become speech, then prattle again. A concord was being reached, disunion overlooked.

"Griggs?" Coach called. "What's your greatest thrill?"

The man had a smile like daylight.

"To break the plane of the goal line," he yelled back. "I want to vault forward and dance by myself in front of eighty thousand people."

Outside his office, Coach Knapp found Nate Creer interrogating a player. The kid was strapped to a chair, a gooseneck lamp over his head, its light a noontime glare. Around them, on the floor, were scattered groundnuts, alkaloids, an overnight bag. "We've been here a while," Creer explained. The kid was in shock, eyes bulging, sweating.

Nate was name-calling. "Hydroid dipstick, muck-faced fartbreath," he was screaming. "Colewort mother humper. Salmon slime!"

"What's the problem here?" Coach asked.

"He says he's hurt."

The kid's face went three or four directions.

"I'm hurt,"the kid said. "I'm hurt."

"He denies he's a dickweed."

"I deny," the kid blubbered. "I deny."

"He swears on his mother, his father."

The kid's jaw dropped. He swore, he swore.

"What's his story?"

"The usual," Nate began. "Parturition, a time of running about unsupervised, body hair. Hormones, friendships—the years all run together. A succession of pets, an allowance. A world view develops, life becomes complicated. An attitude is adopted. Vocabulary expands, paperwork accumulates. Courtship, a tearful reunion, admissions of guilt. There is commingling, disappointment."

"Then what?"

Nate Creer pounded his fist in exasperation.

"Then this squirrel-faced, rat-eyed squamoid yellow-belly fractures his wrist."

Up went the kid's arm. Knobby and blue, it looked like a peculiarly cunning but soft club.

"I figure an hour more, then I let him go," Nate Creer said "I got things to say here, a position to defend."

"This is a bad sign, Nate."

The man shrugged. "Bad signs are everywhere, Coach. I tend to ignore them."

In his office, Coach Woody Knapp kept the lights off. The dark had its comforts. It encouraged reflection, maximun self-awareness. It allowed for a summing up, a casting forward. He would be home in an hour. There would be food, badinage. Mrs. Knapp, Helen, would tend to him. All had been done that could be. There would be sleep, morning. Time would shrink, disappear. Then he would be back here again, his people ready, his advice delivered. There would be football then. And nothing else.

nominated by Stephen Corey

ANDANTINO

fiction by EVE SHELNUTT

from WESTERN HUMANITIES REVIEW

ROSELLE WAS TIRED of the piano.

Tired of planks of notes which began each score. She was left, then, to build whole edifices. When she was through practicing for the day, she'd look at her hands, expecting them to be raw. She felt orphaned, tossed into the cold, although it was never cold where they lived.

Sitting in the wing-back chair with his newspaper and hearing Roselle sigh, Frank said, "Well, Honey, why not just quit, now that I've got the third dealership open?" This, since the small amount of money Roselle made was not the question, was Frank's way of saying he loved her either way, with music or without.

He'd found her in Escanaba, Michigan during her rest cure, after her mother's death. He'd said upon looking into her eyes and at the pouches of gray beneath them, "Well! It's obvious you've got to give up the big stuff"—meaning Tanglewood, Wolf Trap, her long and flowing dresses, about which Roselle had talked so tentatively.

Then Frank's face had ignited with an idea. "Play where the *kids* can hear you, someplace like this."

Eddie's Lounge: where Roselle had been sipping coffee when Frank came upon her. Hamburgers 59 cents, a consideration to Roselle when she'd spent so little money without her mother's presence. And in Eddie's, a blanket of smoke when she'd needed it, grief a spotlight.

"Me," Frank had announced at the end of his two-week vacation in Escanaba where the fishing was good. "You probably need me."

Frank, from Ft. Lauderdale.

Was she sad then *and* now? Now it was summer, 1959.

Roselle was at age 35 prettier than she'd ever been or would be again, although no one was keeping track. Frank saw her from his chair as if she perched in a tableau of angles made by the baby grand's lifted lid, or as an outline against the dark in which they sometimes made love.

In Ft. Lauderdale's off-season month, you could cut the lights in the showroom *and* the lots, leave the cars gleaming in light cast off from elsewhere, drive the quiet streets with your own lights off, and slip onto bed as if the whole process were one of Roselle's rest notes.

What Frank didn't register of Roselle's habits, Roselle's mother, now that she was dead, kept with her there—wherever. For instance, how Roselle in sleep cupped her hands under her chin. *She* had watched Roselle, had given her Rachmaninoff for safe-keeping. "So misunderstood," Roselle's mother had said, pained to the quick.

The time after dinner, when Frank returned to work, Roselle thought of as her own, distinct from the daylight hours when, though he never had, Frank might come rushing in looking for papers in the secretary or in the cardboard file boxes in the laundry. In her mind, the papers related to the black limousine for funerals or a governor's entourage or for the local campus should Borges or Auden come to read, the traveling companion behind the driver, view obstructed by the black cap.

Anything, Roselle thought, could happen in daylight, in glare, wind, the taste of salt in the air. Trees so low they were a ceiling holding up the limitless sky. Under it, as if capped, she was participating in love, like anybody, was she not?

And when the season began and college kids tore into town, it grew so hot the piano keys sometimes stuck, even Roselle's fingers sticking to the keys. Then a bird of panic would flutter in her throat.

In a month they would come again—the kids—and her second year with Frank would have passed. Frank would take an extra shirt to work, he showed so many cars then. And rent for the duration a vacant lot on a side street, filling it with cars brought down from Orlando, junkers, he called them, should the kids get stranded, wire home for money and, what the heck, blow it on a car. It was his season.

On Saturday nights at the lounge where Roselle played, Arthur, the owner, would tell Roselle to liven it up a bit, Roselle having wondered during the past season if *this* were the time for Rachmaninoff, whose music she'd never liked. Then thinking not.

Once Frank had called her on the bar phone, Roselle walking through the crowd with her heart pounding as if she had a child who might have turned sick in her absence. She pictured for a second the child's hair matted in fever. "Holding up?" Frank had shouted into the receiver.

Once, on what Roselle had thought of as an ordinary day, Frank had brought home a box from the Quality Bakery, set it on the table, flipped open the lid, lit candles, and called her to get up from the piano. "What is it?" Roselle had called, afraid to move closer.

"Well *look*, Honey."

And when Roselle had looked, one hand at her throat, had seen the numerals and the one word—1.5 YEARS, overlooking the speck of pink frosting which separated the 1 from the 5—she had believed for an instant that Frank *had* known her all that time, had been in the background just off stage, had seen her climb onto the bench beside her mother, who worked the pedals years before anyone like Frank could have been interested.

Frank had touched a knife to the pink dot, lifted it up, saying, "That'll be us someday, Sweets, and we'll have grown old together." Roselle had felt her breath lower in her body, a fish's bubble in reserve.

From her sickbed, Roselle's mother had advised, "If you ever get stuck in your career, do volunteer work," which Roselle knew meant offering a master class at the local college. But, having taken to wearing her mother's faded voiles against the heat, Roselle could not imagine having boys in Bermuda shorts and tennis shoes look at her. Or girls with mustard seeds at their necks. No matter what they imagined they wanted to know of music, Roselle was sure she could not talk loudly enough between passages for them to hear.

Instead, in the kind of restlessness which makes the brain flare, Roselle began sitting in a lawn chair on what Frank called their patio, in front of the clapboard garage where he'd dug up concrete and laid rows of sod, putting a white picket fence as separation from the sidewalk.

Roselle would wear a wide-brimmed hat, one of Frank's long-sleeved work shirts, and, across her legs because she thought she ought not tan, a blue cotton sheet. She would shut her eyes and, with her left hand, reach down beside her to turn on the portable radio Frank used when one of the boys at work took him fishing.

In the garage were her boxes of sheet music and records, even of herself playing four-handed compositions with her mother, when Roselle was fifteen and her mother was trying to give her a leg-up, she said, on the concert stage.

When Roselle dozed and would waken suddenly because a car or children on bikes rode by, in her mind would be a picture of Frank's house, containing nothing, Roselle imagined, but Frank's chair, the piano with its lid down, and the table in the alcove where they ate. No chairs, no hanging chandelier.

If she were reading when Frank drove up for supper, she heard first the honk of his Buick horn, and then he called over the fence, "Hey, Rosie," and tossed her his *Wall Street Journal*. Under the blue cotton sheet, her legs would be stuck together.

Or if he found her sleeping, Frank would tiptoe to her chair and whisper, "What's for supper?" to which Roselle would have to say, "I don't know, tuna?" But Frank would drive to the Chinese restaurant and bring little boxes of food, whistling as he spooned her portions out, as if nothing Roselle could do or neglect to do would disturb him ever.

Sometimes Roselle felt as if she hadn't awakened altogether, that, as they ate, it was another couple she watched—a movie, distant, on a large screen though she had never been to a drive-in.

If she asked him as they ate if he'd sold a car, Frank laughed, saying, "How do you think it happens? You don't sell a car every day!"

And truly, Roselle didn't understand how it happened, Frank saying she needn't worry about it a bit.

I wasn't worrying, Roselle said to herself.

Outside, in the sun, she didn't actually listen to the radio—it was a hum, mostly of voices—the timpani section, practicing, she imagined, without the violins or oboes—louder when the commercials came on, Frank's among them, recorded by Frank. She hadn't heard it—his revving up for the season.

Mostly she slept, as if waiting or as if sleep were the only natural state.

"That's him," she thought she heard a child say one day. But when Roselle looked up, struggling to awaken, like surfacing through water, all she saw was a pair of girls on bicycles at the end of the road where the trees seemed to meet. A dream, she thought, of when I met Rudolf Serkin and Momma's hands shook.

If Roselle *were* waiting to be gotten, there were no relatives in America to come for her, the Hungarian ones not even making it over when her mother died. "An upheaval's coming," they had written, "and we're sorry." Then it had come.

"You don't know it, but that's him," a girl was saying, Roselle lifting the brim of her hat to see her standing by the fence. Beside her sat a bag from the A & P and, in the distance, another girl, walking, turned to yell, "You're going to *get* it."

"Who are you?" Roselle asked, keeping one hand at the brim of her hat.

"Annie." She wore white knee socks, ribbons dangling from her braids.

"And 'him'?"

The girl twirled one braid with the fingers of her left hand, the right hand resting on the fence. "My daddy. That's him." She tossed her head. "And *she* thinks this is half-way, but this ain't no half-way."

Half-way to where? Roselle wondered silently. She heard the girl sigh and lift the bag; she had actually watched the girl but it was the sound Roselle felt.

"I gotta go or they'll kill me. And he wouldn't like that. So bye."

Her white socks slipped down as she walked. Roselle watched her lean to pull them up, then walk on, the sun in her hair, Roselle noticed, making it appear almost white. I had socks like that, Roselle said to herself.

On the radio, a man was reading softly. Just before she slipped into sleep, Roselle imagined that the girl stopped to turn every few feet to see if she were listening.

Roselle tried to find the same voice on the radio when she woke. Then she began to wait for the girl, who did not come the next day, of which Roselle was sure because she hadn't even dozed. Then, on a Wednesday, when Roselle had almost forgotten the girl, was almost asleep, she heard the voice: "Turn it up, would you?"

"But he's not on," said Roselle. "I've been listening and I don't think he's on." Roselle had taken off her hat; the sun burned her scalp where she put one hand as if to rub the sun in. This time the girl wore a dress with sashes dangling to the sidewalk.

"Thirteen-point-nine-on-your-radio-dial," said the girl. "I bet you don't have it on thirteen-point-nine. He don't work all over the dial!"

"Oh." So Roselle turned the knob, past gospel music and what sounded like Frank shouting inside a tunnel, and past news of more heat. When she found the station, she turned to the girl, saying over the noise of drums, "See?"

"Well, he can't be on *all* the time! He's *coming* on," and the girl looked up at the sun. "He'll *be* on. He'll be on for thirty minutes and that's it. Mondays, Wednesdays, Fridays. And I always gotta be *out* of the house if I wanna hear him 'cause Momma and her"—she nodded toward the road as if the other girl were there on her bike— "won't *let* me."

"Your sister," said Roselle, a statement, as if she knew all about sisters.

"Yeah, her and all."

"Ah," said Roselle.

The girl sat cross-legged on the grass between Frank's fence and the sidewalk. Roselle looked at her through the slats. "Wouldn't you like to come in?"

"Ain't no way."

"*Isn't.*"

"Isn't. And if I climbed over and tore my dress, Momma'd like to kill me."

Roselle almost added, " 'And he wouldn't like that,' " but would the girl smile? Each sentence, Roselle noticed, was a burst of sound, as if the girl's mouth clamped shut to build more steam between each sentence. And Roselle realized for the first time that Frank hadn't put in a gate.

The girl sat with her head resting against the slats of the fence— Roselle could imagine the indentations forming beneath the girl's wisps of hair. "Well," she said, "you could. . . . "

"Hush up, here he comes." And so Roselle clamped her own mouth shut and reached down to turn up the volume. The girl smiled and closed her eyes.

When it was over: "This is Jim with 'A Time for Us' "—and the sun was slipping behind the trees, the girl opened her eyes and looked around as if surprised to see Roselle. "He does that every other day."

Roselle leaned forward in her chair, peering through the fence-slats. "He reads *Sonnets from the Portuguese* and plays a little Peter Duchin between them every other day?" Roselle asked.

"I don't know about Peter-whoever, but see," the girl explained getting up and tying her sash as she talked, "he gets to do the whole book through three times. Then that's it. It's his speciality. Then he goes on to some other station, *if* they pay him a talent fee, and he starts all over. But I gotta go."

Roselle watched the girl named Annie hop down the street. Roselle leaned back in the chair when the girl disappeared, taking deep breaths as if she needed them.

Sometimes Annie came at 5:00 and sometimes she didn't. She never came on the off-days and so, in deference, as Roselle thought of it, she turned the radio off. On the days she listened to "A Time for Us" alone, it was as if Annie's eyes were on her the whole time. Or Jim's; he wondered, maybe, Where is Annie?

"You're getting tan," said Frank. "Don't burn yourself up," to which Roselle said, quickly, "I won't, I won't," as if Frank's very voice were a gnat flitting. The heat made her scalp tingle—what the leaping fish must feel.

How many pages did Annie think were in the book? And, she thought, Jim's voice—flat, matter-of-fact—was the anodyne to music so sweet Roselle's mouth turned as if she'd eaten a persimmon or quince. He knew it—all about contrasts, tones, some music as sugar until the voice said "no."

"Why doesn't he have an accent like you do?" asked Roselle.
"Trained himself out of it," said Annie.
"Where will you go next?" asked Roselle.
"*He* knows," said Annie.

She wouldn't come inside the fence, no matter that Roselle told her how she could walk through the piano room, into the alcove, and out the side door.

"Can't," she said. "You're a stranger. You talk more like him."
"Oh," said Roselle. "So I do."
"Where're you from?"

"Lots of places," said Roselle, suddenly able to picture them all, only her mother's place inaccessible, or Budapest after the storm of fire.

And if Roselle could come from those places to here, then Annie could sit inside Frank's fence.

"Best not." So, when Annie listened, always she leaned her forehead against the fence slats, shut her eyes, and did not move until Jim's program was over. When she rose to go, her forehead seemed flattened. Sometimes at night, lying beside Frank and waiting for sleep, Roselle knew how Annie's body felt—tilted and so still the ears were all the body knew of itself.

"He has a nice voice," said Roselle.

"Everybody knows that!" said Annie. "Even them," motioning with her head to the lots beyond the trees where Roselle imagined his fat wife sat fanning herself on the porch while the sister read comics on the sofa.

On the fourth Saturday after Roselle had begun to listen to "A Time for Us" and Frank was letting her out of the car in front of Arthur's, Roselle said, "Don't forget—you can't call. I've got to be calm when I play even when it's nothing at all."

"Be calm!" said Frank, "be calm!" smiling as he backed up, and waving.

Roselle called before he pulled away. "Sell lots of cars tonight," as if in recompense. And, all that night, she couldn't concentrate.

"I'll probably have to quit before Arthur's fills up all the way with kids," she said when Frank came for her at 1:00.

"Well, that'll be just fine," said Frank, slapping one palm on the steering wheel, settling it. At the red lights he reached over to put a hand on her left knee.

"I'll never need to wear glasses," said Roselle, out of nowhere.

One Monday Roselle heard Jim say: "I can wade grief/ Whole pools of it/ I'm used to that," and, languid in the heat, near sleep, Roselle said, "You are *not*," under her breath as if he were in a room with her. And only slowly did it come to her, not what was different in the words but in the rhythms. He's changed, she thought, and for minutes Roselle tried to calculate how. Abruptly she pulled herself from the lawn chair and went into the garage where Frank had stored all her music and books from Roselle's mother's house. Humming, Roselle searched until she found the book he read from now. "Ah ha!" she whispered.

When Annie next came, Roselle let Annie rest her head against the slats as always—*let:* how Roselle thought of it—let Annie close her eyes. "Mine," said Jim, signing off, "while the ages steal!"

Roselle let Annie sigh, shake herself back into time.

"*That,*" said Roselle, "is Emily Dickinson. He *finished,* on the day before yesterday, *Sonnets from the Portuguese* the third time through."

"*They* don't know it,"whispered Annie through the slats. "And you won't tell them, will you?"—Annie looking up at Roselle as if all her breath were gone.

"Me?" asked Roselle, thumping her hot chest with her fingers. "Me?" And then Roselle began laughing while Annie watched her, until Annie laughed too. Roselle's sunburnt head felt dizzy.

"You know what they want?" Annie asked one Monday before Jim came on. "They want him to do *weather.* And he won't do weather if they pay him the moon."

"I expect not," said Roselle, as if she knew. But she did know—in his voice and in his Ft. Lauderdale time pouring out.

"*And,*" said Annie, "they think, when every motel for miles is filled with kids and old people on their way to St. Petersburg, he can play Fats Domino. He ain't *ever* going to play Fats Domino or any of *them.* And he won't sell beer on radio time."

Roselle lifted her head to look into Annie's eyes. "Who said?"

"*Him,*" Annie shouted, flinging her head up. "Who'd you think? If he wasn't about to come on, I'd *leave.*" She put her forehead back against the fence. "He don't *drink* beer, he don't *sell* beer."

"Well, don't go," said Roselle softly.

And, as it turned out, his wife wasn't fat.

Annie had walked by on a Sunday, in a church dress. When Frank saw her leaning over the fence, he called to Roselle, "Got yourself a little friend, I see."

"Who's he?"

"Frank," said Roselle.

"Oh," said Annie, as if she'd heard of Frank. "Anyway, I got something to show you."

So Roselle waved to Frank, went walking with Annie, down through the heat, the glare, the sound of motorcycles on Main Street. "What?" asked Roselle.

"You'll see," said Annie, leading so that it was Roselle who felt like the child.

"There," said Annie, pointing to an 8 by 10 glossy photograph in the window of Hafferty's Clothing Store for Men. "That's him."

"Oh!" said Roselle.

"Well, you shoulda knowed!"

"Known what?" asked Roselle, one hand at the collar of Frank's shirt.

"That he's handsome!"

"I did," said Roselle, a discovery which left her feeling as if she had suddenly floated belly-up in the sea. "I did," Roselle said again to herself.

"People write to him all the time," said Annie.

Ladies, Roselle said to herself, correcting Annie.

"This contest—see? You vote at the drugstore," said Annie, pointing, "and whoever gets the most votes for March of Dimes, then that person gets a suit. But *even* when he gets it, even *if* it's silk, he's not staying."

At the drugstore, they voted, Annie's five dimes and Roselle's three dollar bills changed into dimes.

Over ice cream, Roselle asked, "Is she fat?"

"Her, you mean?"—Roselle nodding. "No, Momma ain't fat. She's thin, she's so thin you can about see through her. And she ain't going when he goes. When she opens her mouth, her jaw cracks. But that ain't why she won't go."

Roselle wanted to reach over the water glasses, touch Annie's braids, ask: "Would *you* cry?"

Or ask: "Her? I might run into *her* at any time from now out?"

Then Jim signed off for the last time. "Stay close," he said into the microphone. "Keep one hand on your heart," and he paused. "For me."

Roselle heard Annie sigh, watched her rise from the grass. "Well . . ." Annie said.

"Will you come back?"

"Maybe," said Annie, "but it wouldn't be no use," and she turned, began walking down the sidewalk.

Roselle watched her go, noticing the ends of her braids were wet, thinking, She always chews her braids when he's on. Roselle felt her own hair—dry, hot. Her palm seemed to burn on the dome of her head. "Wait!" Roselle called. "Wait!"

Through the yard, into the house, through the alcove, the piano room, and out the front door, running and leaping. Roselle caught Annie by the shoulders. She turned her around, lifting Annie's chin with one hand.

"What?"

Roselle looked above Annie's head, off into the sky, thinking *Oh my God* and, What now? She panted.

"You go with him," said Roselle. "No matter what."

As if passion, indefatigable, *had* a right to exist apart from judgment, ranging the world in all seasons.

nominated by Jim Barnes

THE WOMAN POET: HER DILEMMA

by EAVAN BOLAND

from THE AMERICAN POETRY REVIEW

I BELIEVE THAT the woman poet today inherits a dilemma. That she does so inevitably, no matter what cause she espouses and whatever ideology she advocates or shuns. That when she sits down to work, when she moves away from her work, when she tries to be what she is struggling to express, at all these moments the dilemma is present, waiting and inescapable.

The dilemma I speak of is inherent in a shadowy but real convergence between new experience and an established aesthetic. What this means in practical terms is that the woman poet today is caught in a field of force. Powerful, persuasive voices are in her ear as she writes. Distorting and simplifying ideas of womanhood and poetry fall as shadows between her and the courage of her own experience. If she listens to these voices, yields to these ideas, her work will be obstructed. If, however, she evades the issue, runs for cover and pretends there is no pressure, then she is likely to lose the resolution she needs to encompass the critical distance between writing poems and being a poet. A distance which for women is fraught in any case—as I hope to show—with psycho-sexual fear and doubt.

Dramatize, dramatize said Henry James. And so I will. Imagine then that a woman is going into the garden. She is youngish; her apron is on and there is flour on her hands. It is early afternoon. She

336

is going there to lift a child for the third time who is about to put laburnum pods into its mouth. This is what she does. But what I have omitted to say in this small sketch is that the woman is a poet. And once she is in the garden, once the child, hot and small and needy is in her arms, once the frills of shadow around the laburnum and the freakish gold light from it are in her eyes, then her poetic sense is awakened. She comes back through the garden door. She cleans her hands, takes off her apron, sets her child down for an afternoon sleep. Then she sits down to work.

Now it begins. The first of these powerful, distracting voices comes to her. For argument's sake, I will call it the Romantic Heresy. It comes to her as a whisper, an insinuation. What she wants to do is to write about the laburnum, the heat of the child, common human love—the mesh of these things. But where—says the voice in her ear—is the interest in all this? How are you going to write a poem out of these plain janes, these snips and threads of an ordinary day? Now—the voice continues—listen to me and I will show you how to make all this poetic. A shade here, a nuance there, a degree of distance, a lilt of complaint and all will be well. The woman hesitates. Suddenly the moment that seemed to her potent, emblematic and true appears commonplace, beyond the pale of art. She is shaken. And there I will leave her, with her doubts and fears, so as to look more closely at what it is that has come between her and the courage of that moment.

The Romantic Heresy, as I have chosen to call it, is not Romanticism proper. Although it is related to it. "Before Wordsworth," wrote Lionel Trilling, "poetry had a subject. After Wordsworth its prevalent subject was the poet's own subjectivity." This shift in perception was responsible for much that was fresh and re-vitalizing in nineteenth-century poetry. But it was also responsible for the declension of poetry into self-consciousness, self-invention.

This type of debased Romanticism is rooted in a powerful, subliminal suggestion that poets are distinctive, not so much because they write poetry but because, in order to do so, they have poetic feelings about poetic experiences. That there is a category of experience and expression which is poetic and all the rest is ordinary and therefore inadmissible. In this way a damaging division is made between the perception of what is poetic on the one hand, and, on the other, what is merely human. Out of this emerges the aesthetic which suggests that in order to convert the second into the first you must romanticize it. This idea gradually became an article of faith in nineteenth-century, post-Romantic English poetry. When Matthew Arnold said at Oxford, "the strongest part of our religion is its unconscious poetry," he was blurring a fine line. He was himself one of the initiators of a sequence of propositions by which the poetry of religion became the religion of poetry.

There are obvious pitfalls in all of this for any poet. But the dangers for a woman poet in particular must be immediately obvious. Women are a minority within the expressive poetic tradition. Much of their actual experience lacks even the most rudimentary poetic precedent. "No poet," said Eliot, "no artist of any kind has his complete meaning alone." The woman poet is more alone with her meaning than most. The ordinary routine day that many women live—must live—to take just one instance, does not figure largely in poetry. Nor the feelings that go with it. The temptations are considerable therefore for a woman poet to romanticize these routines and these feelings so as to align them with what is considered poetic.

Now let us go back to the woman at her desk. Let us suppose that she has recovered her nerve and her purpose. She remembers what is true: the heat, the fear that her child will eat the pods. She feels again the womanly force of the instant. She puts aside the distortions of Romanticism. She starts to write again and once again she is assailed. But this time by another and equally persuasive idea.

And this is feminist ideology or at least one part of it. In recent years feminism has begun to lay powerful prescriptions on writing by women. The most exacting of these comes from that part of feminist thinking which is separatist. Separatist prescriptions demand that women be true to the historical angers which underwrite the Woman's Movement; that they cast aside pre-existing literary traditions; that they evolve not only their own writing, but the criteria by which to judge it. I think I understand some of these prescriptions. I recognize that they stem from the fact that many feminists—and I partly share the view—perceive a great deal in pre-existing literary expression and tradition that is patriarchal. I certainly have no wish to be apologetic about the separatist tendency within poetry because it offends or threatens or bores—and it does all three—the prevailing male literary establishments. That does not concern me for a moment. There is still prejudice—the

Irish poetic community is among the most chauvinist—but as it happens that is not part of this equation.

What does concern me is that the gradual emphasis on the appropriate subject matter and the correct feelings has become as constricting and corrupt within Feminism as within Romanticism. In the grip of Romanticism and its distortions, women can be argued out of the truth of their feelings, can be marginalized, simplified and devalued by what is, after all, a patriarchal tendency. But does the separatist prescription offer more? I have to say—painful as it may be to dissent from one section of a Movement I cherish—that I see no redemption whatsoever in moving from one simplification to the other.

So here again is the woman at her desk. Let us say she is feminist. What is she to make of the separatist suggestion by a poet like Adrienne Rich that "to be a female human being, trying to fulfill traditional female functions in a traditional way, is in direct conflict with the subversive function of the imagination." Yet the woman knows that whether or not going into the garden and lifting her child is part of the "traditional way," it has also been an agent and instrument of subversive poetic perception. What is she to do? Should she contrive an anger, invent a disaffection? How is she to separate one obligation from the other, one truth from the next? And what is she to make of the same writer's statement that "to the eye of the feminist, the work of Western male poets now writing reveals a deep, fatalistic pessimism as to the possibilities of change . . . and a new tide of phallocentric sadism." It is no good saying she need not read these remarks. The truth is that Adrienne Rich is a wonderful poet and her essay—"When We Dead Awaken"—from which these statements are quoted is a seminal piece. It should be read by every poet. So there is no escape. The force and power of the separatist prescription must be confronted.

Separatist ideology is a persuasive and dangerous influence on any woman poet writing today. It tempts her to disregard the whole poetic past as patriarchal betrayal. It pleads with her to discard the complexities of true feeling for the relative simplicity of anger. It promises to ease her technical problems with the solvent of polemic. It whispers to her that to be feminine in poetry is easier, quicker and more eloquent than the infinitely more difficult task of being human. Above all, it encourages her to feminize her perceptions rather than humanize her femininity.

But women have a birthright in poetry. I believe—though no separatist poet would agree—that when a woman poet begins to write she very soon becomes conscious of the silences which have preceded her, which still surround her. These silences will become an indefinable part of her purpose as a poet. Yet, as a working poet, she will also—if she is honest—recognize that these silences have been at least partly redeemed within the past expressions of other poets, most of them male. And these expressions also will become part of her purpose. But for that to happen, she must have the fullest possible dialogue with them. She needs it; she is entitled to it. And in order to have that dialogue, she must have the fullest dialogue also with her own experience, her own present as a poet. I do not believe that separatism allows for this.

Very well. Let us say that after all this inner turmoil the woman is still writing. That she has taken her courage in her hands and has resisted the prescriptions both of Romanticism and separatism. Yet for all that, something is still not right. Once again she hesitates. But why? "Outwardly," said Virginia Woolf, "what is simpler than to write books? Outwardly what obstacles are there for a woman rather than for a man? Inwardly I think the case is very different. She still has many ghosts to fight, many prejudices to overcome." Ghosts and prejudices. Maybe it is time we took a look at these.

II

I am going to move this essay once again away from the exploratory and theoretical into something more practical. Let us say, for argument's sake, that it is a wet, Novemberish day in a country town in Ireland. Now, for the sake of going a bit further, let us say that a workshop or the makings of one has gathered in an upstairs room in a school perhaps, or an Adult Education Centre. The surroundings will be—as they always are on these occasions—just a bit surreal. There will be old metal furniture, solid oak tables, the surprising gleam of a new video in the corner. And finally, let us say that among these women gathered here is a woman called Judith. I will call her that as a nod in the direction of Virginia Woolf's great essay "A Room of One's Own." And when I—for it is I who am leading the workshop—get off the train or out of the car and climb the stairs and

340

enter that room, it is Judith—her poems already in her hand—who catches my eye and holds my attention.

"History," said Butterfield, "is not the study of origins; rather it is the analysis of all the mediations by which the past has turned into our present." As I walk into that room, as Judith hands me her poems, our past becomes for a moment a single present. I may know, she may acknowledge, that she will never publish, never evolve. But equally I know we have been in the same place and have inherited the same dilemma.

She will show me her work diffidently. It will lack almost any technical finish—lineation is almost always the chief problem—but that will not concern me in the least. What will concern me, will continue to haunt me, is that she will be saying to me—not verbally, but articulately nonetheless—I write poetry but I am not a poet. And I will realize, without too much being said, that the distance between writing poetry and being a poet is one that she has found in her life and her time just too difficult, too far and too dangerous to travel. I will also feel—whether or not I am being just in the matter—that the distance will have been more impassable for her than for any male poet of her generation. Because it is a preordained distance, composed of what Butterfield might call the unmediated past. On the surface that distance seems to be made up of details: lack of money, lack of like minds and so on. But this is deceptive. In essence the distance is psycho-sexual, made so by a profound fracture between her sense of the obligations of her womanhood and the shadowy demands of her gift.

In his essay on Juana de Asbaje, Robert Graves sets out to define that fracture: "Though the burden of poetry," he writes, "is difficult enough for a man to bear, he can always humble himself before an incarnate Muse and seek instruction from her. . . . The case of a woman poet is a thousand times worse: since she is herself the Muse, a Goddess without an external power to guide or comfort her, and if she strays even a finger's breadth from the path of divine instinct, must take violent self-vengeance."

I may think there is a certain melodrama in Grave's commentary. Yet, in a subterranean way, this is exactly what many women fear. That the role of poet added to that of woman may well involve them in unacceptable conflict. The outcome of that fear is constant psycho-sexual pressure. And the result of that pressure is a final reluctance to have the courage of her own experience. All of which adds up to that distance between writing poems and being a poet, a distance which Judith—even as she hands me her work—is telling me she cannot and must not travel.

I will leave that room angered and convinced. Every poet carries within themselves their own silent constituency, made of suffering and failed expression. Judith and the 'compound ghost' that she is—for she is, of course an amalgam of many women—is mine. It is difficult, if not impossible, to explain to men who are poets— writing as they are with centuries of expression behind them—how emblematic is the unexpressed life of other women to the woman poet, how intimately it is her own. And how, in many ways, that silence is as much part of her tradition as the Troubadours are of theirs. "You who maintain that some animals sob sorrowfully, that the dead have dreams," wrote Rimbaud, "try to tell the story of my downfall and my slumber. I no longer know how to speak."

How to speak. I believe that if a woman poet survives, if she sets out on that distance and arrives at the other end, then she has an obligation to tell as much as she knows of the ghosts within her, for they make up, in essence, her story as well. And that is what I intend to do now.

III

I began writing poetry in the Dublin of the early sixties. Perhaps began is not the right word. I had been there or thereabouts for years: scribbling poems in boarding school, reading Yeats after lights out, revelling in the poetry on the course.

Then I left school and went to Trinity. Dublin was a coherent space then, a small circumference in which to be and become a poet. A single bus journey took you into College for the day. Twilights over Stephen's Green were breathable and lilac-coloured. Coffee beans turned and gritted off the blades in the windows of Roberts and Bewleys. A single cup of it, moreover, cost ninepence in old money and could be spun out for hours of conversation. The last European city. The last literary smallholding.

Or maybe not. "Until we can understand the assumptions in which we are drenched," writes Adrienne Rich, "we cannot know ourselves." I entered that city and that climate knowing neither myself nor the assumptions around me. And, into the bargain, I was priggish, callow, enchanted by the powers of the intellect.

If I had been less of any of these things I might have looked about me more. I might have taken note of my surroundings. If history is, as Napoleon said, the agreed lie, then literary traditions are surely the agreed fiction. Things are put in and left out, are pre-selected and can be manipulated. If I had looked closely I might have seen some of the omissions. Among other things, I might have noticed that there were no women poets, old or young, past or present in my immediate environment. Sylvia Plath, it is true, detonated in my consciousness, but not until years later. As it was, I accepted what I found almost without question. And soon enough, without realizing it, without enquiring into it, I had inherited more than a set of assumptions. I had inherited a poem.

This poem was a mixture really, a hybrid of the Irish lyric and the British Movement piece. It had identifiable moving parts. It usually rhymed, was almost always stanzaic, had a beginning, middle and end. The relation of music to image, of metaphor to idea, was safe, repetitive and derivative. "Ladies, I am tame, you may stroke me," said Samuel Johnson to assorted fashionable women. If this poem could have spoken it might have said something of the sort. I suppose it was no worse, if certainly no better, than the model most young poets have thrust upon them. The American workshop poem at the moment is just as pervasive and probably no more encouraging of scrutiny. Perhaps this was a bit more anodyne; the 'bien-fait' poem as it has since been called; the well-made compromise.

This then was the poem I learned to write, laboured to write. I will not say it was a damaging model because it was a patriarchal poem. As it happens it was, but that matters less than that I had derived it from my surroundings, not from my life. It was not my own. That was the main thing. "Almost any young gentleman with a sweet tooth," wrote Jane Carlyle of Keats's Isabella, "might be expected to write such things." The comment is apt.

In due course I married, moved out of the city and into the suburbs—I am telescoping several years here—and had a baby daughter. In so doing I had, without realizing it, altered my whole situation.

When a woman writer leaves the centre of a society, becomes a wife, mother and housewife, she ceases automatically to be a member of that dominant class which she belonged to when she was visible chiefly as a writer. As a student perhaps, or otherwise as an apprentice. Whatever her writing abilities, henceforth she ceases to be defined by them and becomes defined instead by subsidiary feminine roles. Jean Baker Miller, an American psychoanalyst, has written about the relegation to women of certain attitudes which a society is uneasy with. "Women," she writes, "become the carriers for society of certain aspects of the total human experience, those aspects which remain unsolved." Suddenly, in my early thirties, I found myself a 'carrier' of these unsolved areas of experience. Yet I was still a writer, still a poet. Obviously something had to give.

What gave, of course, was the aesthetic. The poem I had been writing no longer seemed necessary or true. On rainy winter afternoons, with the dusk drawn in, the fire lighted and a child asleep upstairs, I felt assailed and renewed by contradictions. I could have said with Eluard, "there is another world, but it is in this one." To a degree I felt that, yet I hesitated. "That story I cannot write," said Conrad, "weaves itself into all I see, into all I speak, into all I think." So it was with me. And yet I remained uncertain of my ground.

On the one hand poetic convention—conventions moreover which I had breathed in as a young poet—whispered to me that the daily things I did, things which seemed to me important and human, were not fit material for poetry. That is, they were not sanctioned by poetic tradition. But, the whisper went on, they could become so. If I wished to integrate these devalued areas into my poetry I had only to change them slightly. And so on. And in my other ear feminist ideology—to which I have never been immune—argued that the life I lived was fit subject for anger and the anger itself the proper subject for poetry.

Yet in my mind and in the work I was starting to do a completely different and opposed conviction was growing: That I stood at the centre of the lyric moment itself, in a mesh of colours, sensualities and emotions that were equidistant from poetic convention and political feeling alike. Technically and aesthetically I became convinced that if I could only detach the lyric mode from traditional Romantic elitism and the new feminist angers, then I would be able at last to express that moment.

The precedents for this were in painting rather than poetry. Poetry offered spiritual consolation but not technical example. In the genre painters of the French eighteenth century—in Jean-Baptiste

Chardin in particular—I saw what I was looking for. Chardin's paintings were ordinary in the accepted sense of the word. They were unglamorous, workaday, authentic. Yet in his work these objects were not merely described; they were revealed. The hare in its muslin bag, the crusty loaf, the woman fixed between menial tasks and human dreams—these stood out, a commanding text. And I was drawn to that text. Romanticism in the nineteenth century, it seemed to me, had prescribed that beauty be commended as truth. Chardin had done something different: He had taken truth and revealed its beauty.

From painting I learned something else of infinite value to me. Most young poets have bad working habits. They write their poems in fits and starts, by feast or famine. But painters follow the light. They wait for it and do their work by it. They combine artisan practicality with vision. In a house with small children, with no time to waste, I gradually reformed my working habits. I learned that if I could not write a poem I could make an image; and if I could not make an image I could take out a word, savour it and store it.

I have gone into all this because, to a certain extent, the personal witness of a woman poet is still a necessary part of the evolving criteria by which women and their poetry must be evaluated. Nor do I wish to imply that I solved my dilemma. The dilemma persists; the cross-currents continue. What I wished most ardently for myself at a certain stage of my work was that I might find my voice where I had found my vision. I still think that this is what matters most and is threatened most for the woman poet.

I am neither a separatist nor a post-feminist. I believe that the past matters, yet I do not believe we will reach the future without living through the womanly angers which shadow this present. What worries me most is that women poets may lose their touch, may shake off their opportunities because of the pressures and temptations of their present position.

It seems to me, at this particular time, that women have a destiny in the form. Not because they are women: it is not as simple as that. Our suffering, our involvement in the collective silence does not—and will never—of itself guarantee our achievement as poets. But if we set out in the light of that knowledge and that history, determined to tell the human and poetic truth, and if we avoid simplification and self-deception, then I believe we are better equipped than most to discover the deepest possibilities and subversions within poetry itself. Artistic forms are not static. Nor are they radicalized by aesthetes and intellectuals. They are changed, shifted, detonated into deeper patterns only by the sufferings and self-discoveries of those who use them. By this equation, women should break down barriers in poetry in the same way that poetry will break the silence of women. In the process it is important not to mistake the easy answer for the long haul.

nominated by Pamela Stewart

ELEGY FOR ROBERT WINNER (1930–1986)

by THOMAS LUX

from THE QUARTERLY

I dreamed my friend got up and walked;
he was taller than me
and we were young, striding
down some stairs, two at a time, headlong,
on our way to sports or girls.
What did it mean—my psyche
freeing him, freeing me? My friend
is gone; no, no metaphors: dead, who broke
his neck in 1946, six months
before I was born, and then forty years

in a wheelchair. A medical
miracle—he's in the textbooks—to live that long
with a shattered spine,
and now he's dead, whom I loved.
He was a poet and administered
a cemetery, a profession, a business
like any other. He had an office
there, and now, a grave.
We talked mostly poetry, not business.
In my dream I wish we smashed his chair.

sent its bent wheels wobbling
over a cliff; or I wish we ran
to where the boulder is—just beneath
the surface of the stream—on which
he broke his neck,
and dove in together, emerged,
dove again, and emerged . . .
I dreamed my friend got up and walked.
We were striding down some stairs
and he was tall, taller than me . . .

nominated by Michael Ryan

TU DO STREET

by YUSEF KOMUNYAKAA

from INDIANA REVIEW

Searching for love, a woman,
someone to help ease down the cocked hammer
of my nerves & senses. The music
divides the evening into black
& white—soul, country & western,
acid rock, & Frank Sinatra.
I close my eyes & can see
men drawing lines in the dust,
daring each other to step across.
America pushes through the membrane
of mist & smoke, & I'm a small boy
again in Bogalusa skirting tough talk
coming out of bars with *White Only*
signs & Hank Snow. But tonight,
here in Saigon, just for the hell of it,
I walk into a place with Hank Williams
calling from the jukebox. The bar girls
fade behind a smokescreen, fluttering
like tropical birds in a cage, not
speaking with their eyes & usual
painted smiles. I get the silent
treatment. We have played Judas
for each other out in the boonies
but only enemy machinegun fire
can bring us together again.
When I order a beer, the mama-san

behind the counter acts as if she
can't understand, while her
eyes caress a white face;
down the street the black GIs
hold to their turf also.
An off-limits sign pulls me
deeper into alleys; I look
for a softness behind these voices
wounded by their beauty & war.
Back in the bush at Dak To
& Khe Sahn, we fought
the brothers of these women
we now run to hold in our arms.
There's more than a nation divided
inside us, as black & white
soldiers touch the same lovers
minutes apart, tasting
each other's breath,
without knowing these rooms
run into each other like tunnels
leading to the underworld.

nominated by Maura Stanton and David Wojahn

MENSES

by MARIE HOWE

from AGNI REVIEW

This fullness in my breasts and belly
    will ache until it goes away
breaking down like sludge running through
    the rushing gutters, this tenderness
impossible to bear, like a love
    for everything that never was. Outside
my window, even the trees look incredulous
    as if they had just remembered
their cyclical forgetting, and all week
    apart from you, the snow falls heavily
mixed with inconstant dirty rain.

I wait, and watch a single robin step
    among the paper plates that lie
face down where the fraternity boys
    have left them, smeared with ketchup,
mustard, bits of soggy roll, and wonder
    how one seed erupts into a hungry
vine, spitting morning glories.
    This afternoon, I'll cook eggs
for lunch until they are white and solid
    and dead enough to eat.

What is permitted me is only a sure dull sorrow,
    and a sense of skittering on the very
edge of things, about to fall again,

sadly deliberate as rain.
You call from the farm to tell me three
   lambs are born, black and bleating
in their stall. The ram that will not breed
   will be sold for meat, only the ewes
will be kept and nurtured and named.
   I cry for no reason and plead with you,
name them Mercy, Patience.

nominated by Michael Ryan

THE GOLDEN ROBE

fiction by MELISSA LENTRICCHIA

from FICTION INTERNATIONAL

I AM NOT going to put on the lady's golden robe, even though it is the color of the body of my son. It is too soon. The robe is so heavy in my hands and it is also so light that I can roll it into a ball and hold it next to me under one arm. It rests against my hip. I know of no smoothness that is so smooth as the golden robe. But not one time until last night did I show to the lady how much I have wanted to touch the robe with both my hands and dream of somebody else's life.

The lady said I was to die for. She said it on the first day that I was brought to her and on many days after that. She made me speak long American sentences to the ladies who came to play cards in her living room. I do not know why she wanted to die for me.

Last night the lady said to me that the golden robe was to die for and that I knew why. But now it is resting against my hip and I am not dead.

I am remembering the first day, one year ago. The lady was so angry at the weather, which was very cold. It was even colder than it is today. Her red hands took away my coat and they took away my sweater and then they turned me in a circle so that she could see my whole self. The lady said she knew that I was different. She said that she wanted me to love my room. She said that the room had been especially designed by a designer of rooms.

My room is behind the kitchen where there are blue and red and green tiles on the floor and on the walls and on the counters. The tiles in the lady's kitchen were made in my country. The lady owns many precious objects that were made so long ago by the Mayan people of my country. Many times company has come to her house to touch these objects and to stare at her view of the ocean and to eat the food that her caterers make.

My room is next to the room where I have washed and folded the lady's large white towels and where I have ironed her heavy white sheets and where only one time did I stroke my face and my neck with her undergarments, which have no color.

I do not need a mirror to know how I will look when I put on the golden robe. But there is a mirror in my bathroom. I am the only one who is supposed to use my bathroom, but many times I have found the lady's old son with his lips loose against the seat of my toilet, sick with drunkenness, so heavy and so soft when I have tried to lift him up and send him back to his own place that is on top of the lady's garage.

He comes to this house for his meals every day. He does not speak to the lady. He has knocked on the back door and on the front door this morning, but I have not let him in. One time he came to my room and cried for so long when I refused to suckle him.

Yesterday I became forty-eight years old. I said to the lady when she came into my room last night that I would never let my son's two golden daughters die in a room like this, but the lady did not answer.

I am not afraid. I am not afraid of the red eyes of the lady's old son. I am not afraid of the black water that surrounded the boat that brought me here. I am not afraid of the lady's hands. I am not afraid of this place which they call in my own language Corona del Mar.

The walls in my room are grey. The blinds are white. The drawers are white. The carpet is black. The bedspread is black and white and grey. On the wall beside the bed is a large painting of black and blue streaks. The towels in my bathroom are dark red like the color of the blood of my son.

I am remembering when the lady had so much company she wanted her old son to stay in his place on the top of her garage. But he would not go. He stayed with me in the kitchen and drank his liquor and talked. I did not look at him too many times. He is an albino man. He told me that he wears white clothes to hide it. I told him that he looks as if he were designed by the designer of my room. He laughed. His lips were pink and wet the whole time. The lady's caterers pretended that he was not there, even though he talked very much.

354

He asked me many questions about my son. What does he look like? Once he was golden. Once? Now he looks like you. Like me? Now he looks like death. Where does he live? In a grave in the town of Concepción del Oro. He is dead? He could not swim fast enough. How old was he when he died? At the moment when the ocean filled his body he was very old. How old? Twenty-two. Was he married? He was. For how long? For three years that felt like three minutes. Children? Two. Boys? Girls. Where are they now? With the Sisters at the Church of the Angels until I return. Was he brave? His hair was thick and wet. Was he strong? His dark eyes saw California. Was he handsome? He could not run fast enough. Can I stay with you when I take you back to your village? No. Can I stay with you? You cannot stay. Can I?

The lady's old son went to sleep on my bed. I sat on the white stool in my room and went to sleep two times. The second time I woke up and I knew that I must never put my brown hands around his white white throat and hold him tight against my hip. I woke up and I knew that his sickness was a sign. The lady's old son had vomited on the beautiful tiles on the kitchen floor many times.

I have cleaned all the tiles in the kitchen two times every week. One time every week I have polished the lady's silver. I do not like to polish the silver. In order to polish it I must look at it. I cannot look away. I always see my round brown face in the lady's shining silver trays. I do not see myself clearly, but I know that it is me.

I am remembering the silver vase that is so high and so wide that I must carry it with both my hands and still it is heavy. I had to see my face stretched out long and thin in the vase while I polished. I was not myself when I saw myself in that vase. Then I saw the lady's yellow hair and her long pink face in the vase next to mine. She smiled. In the vase the lady's smiling teeth were as long as the tiger's. I did not smile into the vase. But still we looked like long sisters. One pink, one brown, both silver. I could not make my eyes go away from those faces until the lady said to me that she wanted to wash my hair. I did not let her do that.

Now I will have to open the door and speak to the lady's old son. But first I must iron the wrinkles from the golden robe. The lady never put on the robe when it was wrinkled. She would always call someone who would come to her house and take the robe away. For a whole day the robe would be gone somewhere to be cleaned and ironed by strangers. Yesterday this happened. She would not let me do it. She did not worry when they took the robe away. I am the one who has always worried that they will lose it or steal it or forget to bring it back.

Last night I was asleep when the lady opened the door to my room and came in. She said for me to wake up and then she tried in my own language to wish me many more birthdays. She was wearing the golden robe. I was so happy that the robe was back with us. That was when I showed to her in my face what I had vowed not to show her.

She sat down on the end of my bed. She leaned her yellow hair against the grey wall and began to tell me her memories of many happy birthday parties. Her big teeth bit at her dry lips and made them bleed. Her long hands were red and so dry. They were holding a crystal goblet, like that of a priest. In the goblet there was milk mixed with liquor. The lady's yellow hair snapped from the static in the air. Strands of her snapping hair grabbed onto the grey wall where she was leaning. She ran one of her dry hands over the bedspread and laughed at the sparks that her hand made.

I got out of the bed. I put on my black sweater over my nightgown. I sat on the white stool in my room while the lady talked. The golden robe covered every part of her except her head and her hands. It also covered the bed and it poured down onto the floor.

The lady drank from the goblet. She said that on her last birthday she gave herself the ruby ring that she wears on her right hand. She told me to look at the ring. She said that she might decide to give the ring to me. But I did not want to look at the ring because the lady's right hand was holding and rubbing her breasts. Her right hand with the ruby ring was moving the golden robe around and around her nipples. I did not want to look at the robe moving over and over the lady's breasts because it was my own breasts that the robe wanted most to touch.

I said that my year in her house was over. I said that her old son would take me back to my granddaughters. I said that I must go back. She could not make me stay. I said that I did not want the ruby ring. The lady pressed the golden robe between her legs.

I said that I did not know what to do.

The lady leaned toward me and I took the goblet from her. I drank some of the grey milk. She let the robe fall open. I did not want to see her soft pink body. I did not want to see her wrinkled stomach or her limp breasts that were swollen at the tips from rubbing.

The golden robe was everywhere.

The lady put some of it into her mouth. I knew that she wanted me to go into the robe with her. That is what she wanted me to do. Both of us inside the robe moving it over and over our breasts and between our legs in so smooth a circle many times. That is what she wanted us to do. She wanted us to love the robe. She took it out of her mouth and rubbed herself with the wet piece and said that I wanted it too, many times.

I told her that she must leave my room and that she must leave the golden robe with me. I do not know why I spoke to the lady as if I were the lady. I said that she will do as I say. I do not know why I said that. Then the lady stood up. Her yellow hair snapped and flew. She stood up so fast that the golden robe filled with air. The lady looked like a pink bat with golden wings that did not belong to it. The lady knew that is how she looked, but she did not care. I told her that she must leave the robe with me because it was mine and not hers and that she must not move it over and over her breasts.

The lady laughed very loud. She brought the golden wings of the robe down and around me where I stood in front of the white stool in my room. When I did not let her kiss me on the mouth, she slapped me hard, two times, with the back of her hand. And then three more times. I slapped her back. I slapped the lady with the crystal goblet that was in my hand. I slapped it hard against her dry mouth and her pink ears. The rest of the grey milk splashed into her flying hair. The lady's face was bleeding. I hit her again. Then she fell down.

The golden robe was all over her. I could not see her. I did not want the blood from her face to soil the robe, so I removed it with both my hands because it is so heavy. I tried not to look at the lady curled up on the black carpet in my room.

Then she said that she wanted to give me something for my birthday. She said that she wanted to give me the golden robe.

That was all the lady said.

At home in my broken village I will put on the golden robe. Then I will stand atop the highest hill and look out upon the brown and yellow land that surrounds us. I will stare in the direction of the black and selfish ocean that gives me no peace. For many days I will supplicate the blank white sky while I feel the golden robe so smooth against my skin. The people of my village will gather at the bottom of the hill. They will gaze upon the golden robe for many days. And the ancient eyes that have lost their color will see that when I wear the golden robe I look like an Aztec princess. And the dead eyes that have watched the heavens every day and have seen always the same empty sky will believe that I look like an Angel of God. And the dark eyes that belong to the daughters of my son and have seen everything already will think that I look like the Statue of Liberty that stands somewhere in America.

nominated by Garrett Kaoru Hongo

LITERARY TALK

by LEONARD MICHAELS

from THE THREEPENNY REVIEW

About forty years ago, in a high school English class, I learned that talking about literature, like talking about yourself, incurs little dangers of self-revelation, but literary talk is distanced by logic and standards of objectivity, and is controlled by good manners—a social activity of nice people.

My teacher's name was McLean, a thin man with a narrow head and badly scarred tissue about the mouth which was obscured by his moustache. It looked British and military. The scar tissue was plain enough, despite the moustache, like crinkled wrapping paper with a pink sheen.

Listening to him, looking at his face, I heard his voice as crushed; softly crushed by the grief around his mouth and whatever caused it. He'd been in the airforce. I supposed it happened during the war, though I couldn't imagine how.

McLean usually wore an old brown tweed suit and a dull appropriate tie, and he had a gentle, formal manner. Whenever he made some little joke, he chuckled slightly, as though embarrassed, having gone too far, exceeding the propriety of the classroom. Telling jokes, I think, calls attention to your mouth; his for sure. On some days, as if sensitive to weather or nerves, the scar tissue looked raw, hot, incompletely healed.

Long before McLean's class, I knew the strong effects of stories and poems, but, through him, I discovered you could talk about the effects as if they inhered in the stories and poems, just as his voice inhered in his face. When McLean read poetry aloud, his voice became vibrant and lyrical, and the air of the room was full of pleasure, feeling its way into me with my very breathing. Reading alone or being read to was always an anxious sort of happiness. I knew that I'd never recover from its effects, since they only deepened my need for more.

One afternoon, discussing *The Winter's Tale*, McLean came to a passage I didn't like. I worried if it might be deeply good Shakespearean stuff, beyond me to know how good. In the passage, Paulina and Dion debate whether or not King Leontes should remarry. Years have passed since Leontes practically murdered the former queen, Hermione. Paulina says to Dion, "You are one of those/ Would have him wed again." Dion then makes a complicated reply:

> "If you would not so,
> You pity not the state nor the remembrance
> Of his most sovereign name, consider little
> What dangers, by his highness fail of issue,
> May drop upon the kingdom and devour
> Incertain lookers on. What were more holy
> Than to rejoice the former queen is well?
> What holier than, for royalty's repair,
> For present comfort and for future good,
> To bless the bed of majesty again
> With a sweet fellow to't?"

McLean relished the little paradoxes. First, "his fail of issue/ May drop . . ." That is, failing to drop—or produce—a child, drops problems on Leontes' kingdom. Second, "to rejoice the former queen"—poor dead Hermione—"is well." The queen is dead, long live the queen. All in all, Dion's speech has the dead queen alive, "blessing the bed of majesty again," in another woman's body, which will make "A sweet fellow to't."

The last line, ending "to't," like bird belching rather than tweeting, struck me as disgusting, and the whole speech, conflating a real dead woman and an imagined living one, was very creepy. I raised my hand. McLean glanced at me. I said, "Necrophilia."

McLean asked me to stay after class and then went on, enraptured by the moment when Hermione steps out of the stone statue of herself and back into the living world. Leontes, much older now than the long dead Hermione—their daughter being grown up and marriageable—can look forward to going to bed with Hermione again, making love to her. The prospect seemed ghoulish to me. Old Evil eating innocence, as in a black vision of Goya. I wouldn't accept the idea of her statue showing her as aged. I wouldn't see it. I couldn't.

After class, everyone but McLean and me left the room. I went up to his desk. He fooled with his papers, as if he didn't notice me standing there, and I seemed to wait a long time. Of course he couldn't simply turn to me and say what was on his mind. Too direct. Not his style. So he collected papers, ordered them, collecting himself, I suppose.

I was scared. I was always scared, but especially now. Not being a good student, I didn't feel morally privileged to receive McLean's attention—alone; this close. It was always hard for me even to raise my hand amid the pool of heads, then speak, then survive the pressure of McLean's response, though he was gentle and careful, never making anyone feel impertinent or stupid. I'd raise my hand very rarely, and then I'd go deaf when McLean responded, and I'd sit nodding like a fool, understanding nothing, the blood so noisy in my head and my tie jumping to my heart beat. Though barely perceptible, it could be seen.

Still looking at his papers, McLean said, "Some people make a practice of burying their dead quickly and getting on with life." My people, presumably. I didn't know why he said that, but I took the distinction without resentment. There was nothing pejorative in his tone. He was merely thinking out loud, unable to talk to me otherwise, perhaps too embarrassed by what he wanted to say, or else by his inability to say it. Then he said, "I was a ball turret gunner," and—I suddenly understood—he was telling me a story.

Ball turret gunners, in the belly of a B17, the most vulnerable part, were frequently killed. McLean said he would become terrified in action, and he'd spin and spin the turret, firing constantly, even if the German fighter planes were out of range. He gazed at me now, but his eyes weren't engaging mine, perhaps seeing a vast and lethal sky, the earth whirling below in flames.

On his last mission, he said, he was ordered to replace the side gunner of another B17 who had been killed. It was the worst mission of all. The B17 was hit repeatedly and lost an engine and the landing gear was destroyed. It was going to crash land on its belly. The man in the ball turret had to get out quickly, but there was mangled steel above him. He couldn't move; he was trapped. As they went down, McLean bent over him. He looked up at McLean. "His eyes were big," said McLean. "Big."

I felt myself plummet through the dark well of my body. McLean watched me, his eyes big, big, like the man in the ball turret.

In that moment of utter horror, he whispered, "It's a great play, *The Winter's Tale*. Can you believe me?"

nominated by David Wojahn

ATLAS OF CIVILIZATION

by SEAMUS HEANEY

from PARNASSUS: POETRY IN REVIEW

At the very end of his life, Socrates' response to his recurring dream, which had instructed him to "practice the art," was to begin to put the fables of Aesop into verse. It was, of course, entirely in character for the philosopher to be attracted to fictions whose *a priori* function was to expose the true shape of things, and it was proper that even this slight brush with the art of poetry should involve an element of didacticism. But imagine what the poems of Socrates would have been like if, instead of doing adaptations, he had composed original work during those hours before he took the poison. It is unlikely that he would have broken up his lines to weep; indeed, it is likely that he would not only have obeyed Yeats's injunction on this score, but that he would have produced an oeuvre sufficient to confound the master's claim that "The intellect of man is forced to choose/ Perfection of the life or of the work."

It would be an exaggeration to say that the work of the Polish poet Zbigniew Herbert could pass as a substitute for such an ideal poetry of reality. Yet in the exactions of its logic, the temperance of its tone, and the extremity and equanimity of its recognitions, it does resemble what a twentieth-century poetic version of the examined life might be. Admittedly, in all that follows here, it is

BOOKS CONSIDERED IN THIS ESSAY:

Zbigniew Herbert. *Barbarian in the Garden*. Translated by Michael Marsh & Jaroslaw Anders. Carcanet 1986. 180 pp. $14.95

Zbigniew Herbert. *Selected Poems*. Translated by Czeslaw Milosz and Peter Dale Scott, with an Introduction by A. Alvarez. The Ecco Press 1986. 138 pp. $7.50 (paper)

Zbigniew Herbert. *Report from the Besieged City and Other Poems*. Translated, with an Introduction and Notes by John Carpenter and Bogdana Carpenter. The Ecco Press 1986. 82 pp. $12.50 $8.50 (paper)

an English translation rather than the Polish originals which is being praised or pondered, but what convinces one of the universal resource of Herbert's writing is just this ability which it possesses to lean, without toppling, well beyond the plumb of its native language.

Herbert himself, however, is deeply attracted to that which does not lean but which "trusts geometry, simple numerical rule, the wisdom of the square, balance and weight." He rejoices in the discovery that "Greek architecture originated in the sun" and that "Greek architects knew the art of measuring with shadows. The north-south axis was marked by the shortest shadow cast by the sun's zenith. The problem was to trace the perpendicular, the holy east-west direction." Hence the splendid utility of Pythagoras' theorem, and the justice of Herbert's observation that "the architects of the Doric temples were less concerned with beauty than with the chiselling of the world's order into stone."

These quotations come from the second essay in *Barbarian in the Garden*, a collection of ten meditations on art and history which masquerade as "travel writings" insofar as nine of them are occasioned by visits to specific places, including Lascaux, Sicily, Arles, Orvieto, Siena, Chartres, and the various resting places of the paintings of Piero della Francesca. A tenth one also begins and ends at a single pungent site, the scorched earth of an island in the Seine where on March 18, 1314, Jacques de Molay, Grand Master of the Order of the Templars, burned at the stake along with Geoffroi de Charney and another thirty-six brothers of their order. Yet this section of the book also travels to another domain where Herbert operates with fastidious professional skills: the domain of tyranny, with its police precision, mass arrests, tortures, self-inculpations, purges, and eradications, all those methods which already in the fourteenth century had begun to "enrich the repertoire of power."

Luckily, the poet's capacity for admiration is more than equal to his perception of the atrocious, and *Barbarian in the Garden* is an ironical title. This "barbarian" who makes his pilgrimage to the sacred places is steeped in the culture and history of classical and medieval Europe, and even though there is situated at the center of his consciousness a large burnt-out zone inscribed "what we have learned in modern times and must never forget even though we need hardly dwell upon it," this very consciousness can still muster a sustaining half-trust in man as a civilizer and keeper of civilizations. The book is full of lines which sing out in the highest registers of intellectual rapture. In Paestum, "Greek temples live under the golden sun of geometry." In Orvieto, to enter the cathedral is a surprise, "so much does the facade differ from the interior—as though the gate of life full of birds and colours led into a cold, austere eternity." In the presence of a Piero della Francesca: "He is . . . like a figurative painter who has passed through a cubist phase." In the presence of Piero's *Death of Adam* in Arezzo: "The entire scene appears Hellenic, as though the Old Testament were composed by Aeschylus."

But Herbert never gets too carried away. The ground-hugging sturdiness which he recognizes and cherishes in archaic buildings has its analogue in his own down-to-earthness. His love of "the quiet chanting of the air and the immense planes" does not extend so far as to constitute a betrayal of the human subject, in thrall to gravity and history. His imagination is slightly less skyworthy than that of his great compatriot Czeslaw Milosz, who has nevertheless recognized in the younger poet a kindred spirit and as long ago as 1968 translated, with Peter Dale Scott, the now reissued *Selected Poems*. Deliciously susceptible as he is to the *"lucidus ordo*—an eternal order of light and balance" in the work of Piero, Herbert is still greatly pleasured by the density and miscellany of what he finds in a book by Piero's contemporary, the architect and humanist Leon Battista Alberti:

> Despite its classical structure, technical subjects are mixed with anecdotes and trivia. We may read about foundations, building-sites, bricklaying, doorknobs, wheels, axes, levers, hacks, and how to 'exterminate and destroy snakes, mosquitoes, bed-bugs, fleas, mice, moths and other importunate night creatures.'

Clearly, although he quotes Berenson elsewhere, Herbert would be equally at home with a builder. He is very much the poet of a workers' republic insofar as he possesses a natural affinity with those whose eyes narrow in order to effect an operation or a calculation rather than to study a refinement. Discussing the self-portrait of Luca Signorelli which that painter entered in *The Coming of the Anti-Christ* (in the duomo at Orvieto) alongside a portrait of his master, Fra Angelico, Herbert makes a distinction between the two men. He discerns how Signorelli's eyes "are fixed upon reality . . . Beside him, Fra Angelico dressed in a cassock gazes inwards. Two glances: one visionary, the other observant." It is a distinction which suggests an equivalent division within the poet, deriving from the co-existence within his own deepest self of two conflicting strains. These were identified by A. Alvarez in his introduction to the original 1968 volume as the tender-minded and the tough-minded, and it is some such crossing of a natural readiness to consent upon an instinctive suspicion which constitutes the peculiar fiber of Herbert's mind and art.

There is candor and there is concentration. His vigilance never seems to let up and we feel sure that if he is enjoying himself in print (which is memory), then the original experience was also enjoyed in similar propitious conditions. All through *Barbarian in the Garden,* the tender-minded, desiring side of his nature is limpidly, felicitously engaged. In a church in a Tuscan village where "there is hardly room enough for a coffin," he encounters a Madonna. "She wears a simple, high-waisted dress open from breast to knees. Her left hand rests on a hip, a country bridesmaid's gesture; her right hand touches her belly but without a trace of licentiousness." In a similar fashion, as he reports his ascent of the tower of Senlis Cathedral, the writing unreels like a skein long stored in the cupboard of the senses. "Patches of lichen, grass between the stones, and bright yellow flowers"; then, high up on a gallery, an "especially beautiful Eve. Coarse-grained, big-eyed and plump. A heavy plait of hair falls on her wide, warm back."

Writing of this sort which ensures, in Neruda's words, that "the reality of the world should not be underprized," is valuable in itself, but what reinforces Herbert's contribution and takes it far beyond being just another accomplished print-out of a cultivated man's impressions is his skeptical historical sense of the world's unreliability. He is thus as appreciative of the unfinished part of Siena Cathedral and as unastonished by it as he is entranced by what is exquisitely finished: "The majestic plan remained unfulfilled, interrupted by the Black Death and errors in construction." The elegance of that particular zeugma should not blind us to its outrage; the point is that Herbert is constantly wincing in the jaws of a pincer created by the mutually indifferent intersection of art and suffering. Long habituation to this crux has bred in him a tone which is neither vindictive against art nor occluded to pain. It predisposes him to quote Cicero on the colonies of Sicily as "an ornamental band sown onto the rough cloth of barbarian lands, a golden band that was frequently stained with blood." And it enables him to strike out his own jocund, unnerving sentences, like this one about the Baglioni family of Perugia: "They were vengeful and cruel, though refined enough to slaughter their enemies on beautiful summer evenings."

Once more, this comes from his essay on Piero della Francesca, and it is in writing about this beloved painter that Herbert articulates most clearly the things we would want to say about himself as an artist: "The harmonized background and the principle of tranquillity," "the rule of the demon of perspective," the viewing of the world as "through a pane of ice," an "epic impassiveness," a quality which is "impersonal, supra-individual." All these phrases apply, at one time or another, to Herbert's poetry and adumbrate a little more the shapes of his "tough-mindedness." Yet they should not be taken to suggest any culpable detachment or abstraction. The impassiveness, the perspective, the impersonality, the tranquillity, all derive from his unblindable stare at the facts of pain, the recurrence of injustice and catastrophe; but they derive also from a deep love for the whole Western tradition of religion, literature, and art, which have remained open to him as a spiritual resource, helping him to stand his ground. Herbert is as familiar as any twentieth-century writer with the hollow men and has seen more broken columns with his eyes than most literary people have seen in their imaginations, but this does not end up in a collapse of his trust in the humanist endeavor. On the contrary, it summons back to mind the whole dimensions of that endeavor and enforces it once more upon our awareness for the great boon which it is (not *was*), something we may have thought of as vestigial before we began reading these books but which, by the time we have finished, stands before our understanding once again like "a cathedral in the wilderness."

Barbarian in the Garden was first published in Polish in 1962 and is consequently the work of a much younger man (Herbert was born in 1924) than the one who wrote the poems of *Report from the Besieged City.* But the grave, laconic, instructive prose, translated with such fine regard for cadence and concision by Michael Marsh and Jaroslaw Anders, is recognizably the work of the same writer. It would be wrong to say that in the meantime Herbert has matured, since from the beginning the look he turned upon experience was penetrating, judicial, and absolutely in earnest; but it could be said that he has grown even more secure in his self-possession and now begins to resemble an old judge who has developed the benevolent aspect of a daydreamer while retaining all the readiness and spring of a crouched lion. Where the poems of the reissued *Selected Poems* carry within themselves the battened-down energy and enforced caution of the situation from which they arose in Poland in the 1950s, the poems of the latest volume allow themselves a much greater latitude of voice. They are physically longer, less impacted, more social and genial in tone. They occur within a certain spaciousness, under a vault of winnowed comprehension. One thinks again of the *lucidus ordo*, of that "golden sun of geometry"; yet because of the body heat of the new poetry, its warm breath which keeps stirring the feather of our instinctive nature, one thinks also of Herbert's eloquent valediction to the prehistoric caves of the Dordogne:

> I returned from Lascaux by the same road I arrived. Though I had stared into the 'abyss' of history, I did not emerge from an alien world. Never before had I felt a stronger or more reassuring conviction; I am a citizen of the earth, an inheritor not only of the Greeks and Romans but of almost the whole of infinity. . . .
>
> The road opened to the Greek temples and the Gothic cathedrals. I walked towards them feeling the warm touch of the Lascaux painter on my palm.

It is no wonder, therefore, that Mr. Cogito, the poet's alibi/alias/persona/ventriloquist's doll/permissive correlative, should be so stubbornly attached to the senses of sight and touch. In the second section of "Eschatological Forebodings of Mr. Cogito," after Herbert's several musings about his ultimate fate—"probably he will sweep/ the great square of Purgatory"—he imagines him taking courses in the eradication of earthly habits. And yet, in spite of these angelic debriefing sessions, Mr. Cogito

> continues to see
> a pine on a mountain slope
> dawn's seven candlesticks
> a blue-veined stone
>
> he will yield to all tortures
> gentle persuasions

but to the end he will defend
the magnificent sensation of pain

and a few weathered images
on the bottom of the burned-out eye

3

who knows
perhaps he will manage
to convince the angels
he is incapable
of heavenly
service

and they will permit him to return
by an overgrown path
at the shore of a white sea
to the cave of the beginning

The poles of the beginning and the end are crossing and at the very moment when he strains to imagine himself at the shimmering circumference of the imaginable, Mr. Cogito finds himself collapsing back into the palpable center. Yet all this is lightened of its possible portentousness because it is happening not to "humanity" or "mankind" but to Mr. Cogito. Mr. Cogito operates sometimes like a cartoon character, a cosmic Don Quixote or matchstick Sisyphus; sometimes like a discreet convention whereby the full frontal of the autobiographical "I" is veiled. It is in this latter role that he is responsible for one of the book's most unforgettable poems, "Mr. Cogito—The Return," which, along with "The Abandoned," "Mr. Cogito's Soul," and the title poem, strikes an unusually intimate and elegiac note.

Mostly, however, Mr. Cogito figures as a stand-in for experimental, undaunted *Homo sapiens*, or, to be more exact, as a representative of the most courageous, well-disposed, and unremittingly intelligent members of the species. The poems where he fulfills this function are no less truly pitched and sure of their step than the ones I have just mentioned; in fact, they are more brilliant as intellectual reconnaissance and more deadly as political resistance; they are on the offensive, and to read them is to put oneself through the mill of Herbert's own personal selection process, to be tested for one's comprehension of the necessity of refusal, one's ultimate gumption and awareness. This poetry is far more than "dissident"; it gives no consolation to papmongers or propagandists of whatever stripe. Its whole intent is to devastate those arrangements which are offered as truth by power's window dressers everywhere. It can hear the screech of the fighter bomber behind the righteous huffing of the official spokesman, yet it is not content with just an exposé or an indictment. Herbert always wants to probe past official versions of collective experience into the final ring of the individual's perception and endurance. He does so in order to discover whether that inner citadel of human being is a selfish bolt hole or an attentive listening post. To put it another way, he would not be all that interested in discovering the black box after the crash, since he would far prefer to be able to monitor the courage and conscience of each passenger during the minutes before it. Thus, in their introduction, John and Bogdana Carpenter quote him as follows:

> You understand I had words in abundance to express my rebellion and protest. I might have written something of this sort: 'O you cursed, damned people, so and sos, you kill innocent people, wait and a just punishment will fall on you.' I didn't say this because I wanted to bestow a broader dimension on the specific, individual, experienced situation, or rather, to show its deeper, general human perspectives.

This was always his impulse, and it is a pleasure to watch his strategies for showing "deeper, general human perspectives" develop. In the *Selected Poems*, dramatic monologues and adaptations of Greek myth were among his preferred approaches. There can be no more beautiful expression of necessity simultaneously recognized and lamented than the early "Elegy of Fortinbras," just as there can be no poem more aghast at those who have power to hurt and who then do hurt than "Apollo and Marsyas." Both works deserve to be quoted in full, but here is the latter one, in the translation of Czeslaw Milosz:

> The real duel of Apollo
> with Marsyas

(absolute ear
versus immense range)
takes place in the evening
when as we already know
the judges
have awarded victory to the god

bound tight to a tree
meticulously stripped of his skin
Marsyas
howls
before the howl reaches his tall ears
he reposes in the shadow of that howl
shaken by a shudder of disgust
Apollo is cleaning his instrument

only seemingly
is the voice of Marsyas
monotonous
and composed of a single vowel
Aaa

in reality
Marsyas relates
the inexhaustible wealth
of his body

bald mountains of liver
white ravines of aliment
rustling forests of lung
sweet hillocks of muscle
joints bile blood and shudders
the wintry wind of bone
over the salt of memory
shaken by a shudder of disgust
Apollo is cleaning his instrument

now to the chorus
is joined the backbone of Marsyas
in principle the same A
only deeper with the addition of rust

this is already beyond the endurance
of the god with nerves of artificial fibre

along a gravel path
hedged with box
the victor departs
wondering
whether out of Marsyas' howling
there will not some day arise
a new kind
of art—let us say—concrete

suddenly
at his feet
falls a petrified nightingale
he looks back
and sees
that the hair of the tree to which Marsyas was fastened
is white
completely

About suffering he was never wrong, this young master. The Polish
experience of cruelty lies behind the poem, and when it first appeared it would have had the extra jangle of anti-poetry about it.
There is the affront of the subject matter, the flirtation with horror-
movie violence, and the conscious avoidance of anything "tender-
minded." Yet the triumph of the thing is that while it remains set
upon an emotional collision course, it still manages to keep faith
with "whatever shares / The eternal reciprocity of tears." Indeed,
this is just the poetry which Yeats would have needed to convince
him of the complacency of his objection to Wilfred Owen's work
(passive suffering is not a subject for poetry), although, in fact, it is
probably only Wilfred Owen (tender-minded) and Yeats (tough-
minded) who brought into poetry in English a "vision of reality" as
adequate to our times as this one.

"Apollo and Marsyas" is a poem, not a diagram. By now, the
anti-poetry element has evaporated or been inhaled so that in spite
of that devastating A note, the poem's overall music dwells in the
sorrowing registers of cello or pibroch. The petrified nightingale,
the tree with white hair, the monotonous Aaa of the new art, each
of these inventions is as terrible as it is artful, each is uttered from

the dry well of an objective voice. The demon of perspective rules while the supra-individual principle reads history through a pane of Francescan ice, tranquilly, impassively, as if the story were chiseled into stone.

The most celebrated instance of Herbert's capacity to outface what the stone ordains occurs in his poem "Pebble." Once again, this is an *ars poetica*, but the world implied by the poem would exclude any discourse that was so fancied-up as to admit a term like *ars poetica* in the first place. Yet "Pebble" is several steps ahead of satire and even one or two steps beyond the tragic gesture. It is written by a poet who grew up, as it were, under the white-haired tree but who possessed no sense either of the oddity or the election of his birthright. Insofar as it accepts the universe with a sort of disappointed relief—as though at the last minute faith were to re-nege on its boast that it could move mountains and settle back into stoicism—it demonstrates the truth of Patrick Kavanagh's contention that tragedy is half-born comedy. The poem's force certainly resides in its impersonality, yet its tone is almost ready to play itself on through into the altogether more lenient weather of personality itself.

> The pebble
> is a perfect creature
>
> equal to itself
> mindful of its limits
>
> filled exactly
> with pebbly meaning
>
> with a scent which does not remind one of anything
> does not frighten anything away does not arouse desire
>
> its ardour and coldness
> are just and full of dignity
>
> I feel a heavy remorse
> when I hold it in my hand
> and its noble body
> is permeated by false warmth

—Pebbles cannot be tamed
to the end they will look at us
with a calm and very clear eye

This has about it all the triumph and completion of the "finished
man among his enemies." You wonder where else an art that is so
contained and self-verifying can possibly go—until you open *Report
from the Besieged City.* There you discover that the perfect moral
health of the earlier poetry was like the hard pure green of the
ripening apple: now the core of the thing is less packed with tartness
and the whole oeuvre seems to mellow and sway on the bough of
some tree of unforbidden knowledge.

There remain, however, traces of the acerbic observer; this, for
example, in the poem where Damastes (also known as Procrustes)
speaks:

I invented a bed with the measurements of a perfect man
I compared the travelers I caught with this bed
it was hard to avoid—I admit—stretching limbs cutting legs
the patients died but the more there were who perished
the more I was certain my research was right
the goal was noble progress demands victims

This voice is stereophonic in that we are listening to it through two
speakers, one from the setup Damastes, the other from the privileged poet, and we always know whose side we are on. We are
meant to read the thing exactly as it is laid out for us. We stand with
Signorelli at the side of the picture, observantly. We are still, in
other words, in the late spring of impersonality. But when we come
to the poem on the Emperor Claudius, we are in the summer of
fullest personality. It is not that Herbert has grown lax or that any
phony tolerance—understanding all and therefore forgiving all—
has infected his attitude. It is more that he has eased up on his own
grimness, as if realizing that the stern brows he turns upon the
world merely contribute to the weight of the world's anxiety instead
of lightening it; therefore, he can afford to become more genial
personally without becoming one whit less impersonal in his judg-
ments and perceptions. So, in his treatment of "The Divine Clau-

dius," the blood and the executions and the infernal whimsicality
are not passed over, yet Herbert ends up speaking for his villain
with a less than usually forked tongue:

> I expanded the frontiers of the empire
> by Brittany Mauretania
> and if I recall correctly Thrace
>
> my death was caused by my wife Agrippina
> and an uncontrollable passion for boletus
> mushrooms—the essence of the forest—
> became the essence of death
>
> descendants—remember with proper respect and honor
> at least one merit of the divine Claudius
> I added new signs and sounds to our alphabet
> expanded the limits of speech that is the limits of freedom
>
> the letters I discovered—beloved daughters—
> Digamma and Antisigma
> led my shadow
> as I pursued the path with tottering steps
> to the dark land of Orkus

There is more of the inward gaze of Fra Angelico here, and
indeed, all through the new book, Herbert's mind is fixed constantly on last things. Classical and Christian visions of the afterlife
are drawn upon time and again, and in "Mr. Cogito—Notes from
the House of the Dead," we have an opportunity of hearing how the
terrible cry of Marsyas sounds in the new acoustic of the later work.
Mr. Cogito, who lies with his fellows "in the depths of the temple of
the absurd," hears there, at ten o'clock in the evening, "a voice //
masculine / slow / commanding / the rising / of the dead." The
second section of the poem proceeds:

> we called him Adam
> meaning taken from the earth
>
> at ten in the evening
> when the lights were switched off
> Adam would begin his concert

to the ears of the profane
it sounded
like the howl of a person in fetters

for us
an epiphany

he was
anointed
the sacrificial animal
author of psalms

he sang
the inconceivable desert
the call of the abyss
the noose on the heights

Adam's cry
was made
of two or three vowels
stretched out like ribs on the horizon

This new Adam has brought us as far as the old Marsyas took us, but now the older Herbert takes up the burden and, in a third section, brings the poem further still:

after a few concerts
he fell silent

the illumination of his voice
lasted a brief time

he didn't redeem
his followers

they took Adam away
or he retreated
into eternity

the source
of the rebellion
was extinguished

and perhaps
only I

                    still hear
                    the echo
                    of his voice

                    more and more slender
                    quieter
                    further and further away

                    like music of the spheres
                    the harmony of the universe

                    so perfect
                    it is inaudible.

Mr. Cogito's being depends upon such cogitations (one remembers
his defense of "the magnificent sensation of pain"), though unlike
Hamlet, in Fortinbras's elegy, who "crunched the air only to vomit,"
Mr. Cogito's digestion of the empty spaces is curiously salutary.
Reading these poems is a beneficent experience: they amplify im-
mensely Thomas Hardy's assertion that "if a way to the Better there
be, it exacts a full look at the Worst." By the end of the book, after
such undaunted poems as "the Power of Taste"—"Yes taste / in
which there are fibers of soul the cartilage of conscience"—and such
tender ones as "Lament," to the memory of his mother—"she sails
on the bottom of a boat through foamy nebulas,"—after these and
the other poems I have mentioned, and many more which I have
not, the reader feels the kind of gratitude the gods of Troy must
have felt when they saw Aeneas creep from the lurid fires, bearing
ancestry on his shoulders and the sacred objects in his hands.

   The book's true subject is survival of the valid self, of the city, of
the good and the beautiful; or rather, the subject is the responsibility
of each person to ensure that survival. So it is possible in the end to
think that a poet who writes so ethically about the *res publica* might
even be admitted by Plato as first laureate of the ideal republic;
though it is also necessary to think that through to the point where
this particular poet would be sure to decline the office as a dangerous compromise:

   now as I write these words the advocates of conciliation
   have won the upper hand over the party of inflexibles
   a normal hesitation of moods fate still hangs in the balance

cemeteries grow larger the number of the defenders is smaller
yet the defense continues it will continue to the end
and if the City falls but a single man escapes
he will carry the City within himself on the roads of exile
he will be the City

we look in the face of hunger the face of fire face of death
worst of all—the face of betrayal

and only our dreams have not been humiliated

(1982)

The title poem, to which these lines form the conclusion, is pivoted
at the moment of martial law and will always belong in the annals of
patriotic Polish verse. It witnesses new developments and makes old
connections within the native story and is only one of several poems
throughout the volume which sweeps the string of Polish national
memory. If I have been less attentive to this indigenous witnessing
function of the book than I might have been, it is not because I
undervalue that function of Herbert's poetry. On the contrary, it is
precisely because I am convinced of its obdurate worth on the home
front that I feel free to elaborate in the luxurious margin. Anyhow,
John and Bogdana Carpenter have annotated the relevant dates and
names so that the reader is kept alert to the allusions and connections which provide the book's oblique discharge of political energy.
As well as providing this editorial service, they seem to have managed the task of translating well; I had no sense of their coming
between me and the poem's first life, no sense of their having
interfered.

Zbigniew Herbert is a poet with all the strengths of an Antaeus,
yet he finally emerges more like the figure of an Atlas. Refreshed
time and again by being thrown back upon his native earth, standing his ground determinedly in the local plight, he nevertheless
shoulders the whole sky and scope of human dignity and responsibility. These various translations provide a clear view of the power
and beauty of the profile which he has established, and leave no
doubt about the essential function which his work performs, that of
keeping a trustworthy poetic canopy, if not a perfect heaven, above
our vulnerable heads.

nominated by Parnassus: Poetry In Review

TO CHARLOTTE BRONTË

by JOAN ALESHIRE

from THE AMERICAN SCHOLAR

Your teacher's letter, when it comes
at last, seems like another lesson
in conversational French: "It is necessary
that you not write so often. I have not
time to answer more than two times
a year." You run your fingers
over the fine script, over the seal,
as if the touch of ink, of wax, could
bring him closer than words placed clearly,
evenly, pointed and impenetrable as a fence.
In the bare sitting room, watching your sisters
bend their smooth heads to their work—
flies caught in webs of their own invention—
you wonder if you imagined afternoons
in a Belgian schoolroom, speaking a French
you've almost forgotten, delighting
your teacher, whose eyes became pools
that invited you to swim.
You begin a reply: "I am well aware
I burden you with words. I will try
to restrain myself." Over a hundred years
later, writing a man, I use almost
your words, my usual speech formal
with hesitation. I think of you searching
for the French "restreindre," staring,
as if you'd find it in the moors—gray

379

and undulating as the waves that keep
England from Belgium, bare as the years
you must fill alone. "Me restreindre,"
you write at last, gripping the pen
as other words—unruly, unkempt,
so like my own—shoulder their way
between the lines: "My life is nothing without you."

nominated by Maura Stanton

BOX

by CAROL MUSKE

from THE AMERICAN POETRY REVIEW

Where her right index fingernail should be—
there is a razorblade—
and the blackhaired inmate pushes
the smaller one to the wall.

I remember it happening as I came
down the hall, with my copy
of the *The Voice That is Great Within Us:*

the two figures, one hunched over
the other, the blade hand hovering,
ablaze, then moving across and down.

Today, in the window,
a crystal spins on a bit
of fishline, throwing off light

like netted koi, shiny ruptures
on the ceiling. My small daughter climbs up
its trembling ladder,

extends her small beautiful hand.
In the perfect center of the glass
there is resistance to the image: a room

too brightly lit, in the basement
of the old house of Detention,
where I taught the dazzling inconsistencies—

Pictures in the Mind—
under the Watch Commander's
electric map: its red neon eye–slits

blinking each time a door cracked
within the walls. The women
gravely scrawling on Rainbow

tablets: not graffiti, but poems wrenched
from the same desire to own something—
to tie the tourniquet of style,

the mind's three or four known
happy endings clamped tight
on the blood jet. Love poems to a pimp,

for example: she would never say
he beat her. No, he held her close,
he was "capable of love"—

he was like the elegy
written for the little one
whose mother tried to make her fly:

he would stay suspended in the air.
No one would see that child
screaming, step by step, along the gritty ledge.

If she'd lived, she might have become
the one who thought she wrote songs
like Billie Holiday, or the one

who plagiarized, week after week,
the poems of Langston Hughes.
Nobody writes anything that moves

across and down the face
of mortal anguish. That cutting tool
found in no book nor

in the exquisite, denatured vision
of Invention—page after page
of Pictures in the Mind—but

I taught it right after all.
There were images for her,
this mother

taking back the face she made—
with her bright, revisionist blade—
too ugly, too fat, too stupid
to be loved

and an image for that sudden spidery blood
on the tiles, somewhere the red eye
tracking my impulse
as I pushed open the warning door,

then stood back, catching
the baby at the window—
her open hands, the moving light

she holds at the source
but cannot still.

nominated by Sherod Santos

LEAVES THAT GROW INWARD

by SUSAN MITCHELL

from IRONWOOD

So you see, it was my favorite time
for waking, toward evening, when the lights came on
all together like candles on a child's cake.
I would yawn, as if just leaving a movie.
The better part of the day was over, no longer
a chance of doing anything worthwhile.
The relief of it. This was the hour
I took my bath as a child,
not always alone, sometimes with a friend, Clara,
whose left arm ended abruptly at the elbow,
as if she had managed to draw up
inside her the hand, its fingers, even
a small object the fingers had been holding
at the time this miracle occurred. If
I had known Hölderlin's poem about the leaves
that grow inward, I would have recited it
to her, *hängen einwärts die Blätter,*
as she splashed water in my face
with that budding stump of hers. Once
at this hour my mother plucked a snail

from watercress, a black glistening that sweated
across my palm. Clara held it too
with her eyes, the way I held her
in the school playground until all at once
I heard the train, still far away, that brought
my father from his office, its wind
blowing on the lights of our street.

Sometimes all my childhood burns like a fever,
even my mother's hand on my forehead
as she urges me to practice
the piano, as she tells me to drink the music
like blood, holding my cramped
fingers under running water
until somewhere in the street a child lets out
a long necklace of sounds, a crying
that gradually loosens itself
from whatever flesh has held it. It
is not easy, it is like pulling hairs
from the tenderest parts
of the body . . . Only, to tell the truth, there
never was a Clara, a point I might confess
to a psychiatrist. Instead,
I confess it to myself, waiting
for illumination, eyes closed,
but still seeing as if through leaves, through the sap
of my cells. . . . At school, there was
a girl like her, but her arm
terrified me. I withdrew
from it. Which is quite another
thing, isn't it? Though in the safety of my bath
she sometimes entered my life as a possibility
of future loss. So, you see,
I am not the person you thought I was,
the one you had grown comfortable with, maybe
even liked a little.
                    Liking,
our first grade teacher used to say, begins
with proximity, as before—waking

into a day already over, I heard
the highrise in which I live talking
to itself, moaning like the sea
or like someone stumbling in and out
of sleep. The building was neither happy nor sad,
but continuous, one of those
unending songs a child sings to itself.

The grief of my neighbors, the grief of all
the neighbors I have ever had is
another story, the secret
lint a child digs from its navel
while its fingers age in the bath. What
would it have been like to be the one who played
with Clara, whooping down on the neighborhood
bakery, mouth stuffed with strudel, not caring
if my tongue scorched and blistered? What would it
have been like to hold
the sticks of dog shit, the purified chalk
they scrawled their names with? At the edges
of memory, Clara glimmers, beckoning
as if into a forest. Striped with desires
more bruising than prison bars, she leans out of
herself, toward a flashing on the pavement,
toward snow greened with dog piss.
                                    Well, life
is better now, and sometimes I consume
four movies in a day, surprised, as I drift
to the street, it's dark outside too, surprised
to see people waiting to see what I have just seen.
This is the hour when two men
kiss in the elevator, a long kiss,
which stops only as an old woman gets on,
then they hold hands. Half asleep,
I hear them kissing and the sky
darkening, washing out to the Hudson
where the freighters kneel in the sailors' shadows
and kids tripping on acid come
to watch the men knotting
and unknotting in their ecstasies.

Even from here I follow their brief spurts
of pleasure, the tides of clouds, until I feel
far away as someone drifting in a boat
or waving from a train a paper
hat, while the dark snails of my flesh slide
toward some heaven of their own.

nominated by David Wojahn

WHAT THE SHADOW KNOWS

fiction by SANDIE CASTLE

from EXQUISITE CORPSE

HE WAS ONE OF those men who prided himself on understandin women. He said, "I know them inside out." He sounded like an asshole ta her but she was much too tired ta tell 'im and he'd stopped listenin weeks ago anyway. He would bring books ta the house by the dozens, mostly about socialism and the women's movement. One day when he came ta visit she was drawin a picture of a man who had a single hook where his hand shoulda been and it was reachin for somethin clean off the page. When he asked her about the significance of the image, she said, "It don't mean nothin."

The next time he stopped by he was actin all excited. He said, "I brought you a wonderful present, you're gonna *love* it, I promise." Lookin really tickled with himself, he handed her a book called *Trotsky on Art and Literature*. All she could do was sigh in disappointment. What she really wanted was a television. He said, "Look, you don't understand what this is, this guy is great, he'll show you just where you're coming from. I think that's just what this country needs, more art from the working class and I for one want to encourage your creativity." Oh Christ, she thought, just what I need and God knows I always wanted one. She used it to prop her window open.

Now whenever he came by she would complain about a clock tickin. He became annoyed with this after a while and attributed the

388

noise to her preoccupation with self. He said, "You have too much imagination." He asked ta see more drawings but she refused ta show him, they'd gotten so strange that she didn't like seein them herself.

While standin in front of her mirror, he said, "You know a lot of people have told me lately that I look like Che Guevara." She was watchin him stroke his mustache. "What do you think?" he said, striking a pose. She laughed, replyin quickly, "Henry Higgins." "What?" Then repeatin herself with painful exactness, "Henry Higgins." He walked away pretendin he hadn't understood.

He was fascinated by her poor white background, strewn with prostitution and drug addiction. She was tryin ta figure out why anybody with a college degree would feel like a hero for makin a conscious decision to work in a factory. She had never been fascinated by factory workers and knew damn well she never would be. The only hero she'd ever had was Peter Pan. "Now there's somebody fascinatin," she'd say. She had always loved the androgynous quality of his nature and the clothes he wore. She was convinced that Peter could fly simply because he'd never looked between his legs. Sometimes she wished she hadn't, today was one of those. She had a backache and her head hurt and not bein able ta fly still depressed her from time ta time. She confided all of this ta the man layin next ta her, who professed ta be solely concerned with the human condition.

Now this here man was real busy at the moment tryin to get laid so he hastily reminded her that people somewhere right now, at this very moment, were fallin down dead in the streets from hunger. It was another "count your blessings" lecture. By now she realized she was gettin her period and wondered if she should use a sanitary napkin or a tampon, she felt empty and inserted a regular. He was not amused by her earthiness as she licked the blood from her fingers. She was fully aware that this made it taste much better. She wondered if this habit of hers would be discussed with his therapist. Imaginin the conversation gave her a great deal of pleasure. However, she was not pleased by the fact that he was payin some guy fifty bucks an hour ta listen ta the same shit she had ta hear for nothin. Some guy who never slept with him and his goddamn politics, who she was sure had never believed in Peter Pan. His patient hadn't given her so much as an orgasm and she knew that this wouldn't ever be the topic of any conversation they had.

Tonight *the patient* was angry because she could not come up with anything sufficiently warped or freaky in her past to satisfy him. He said, "There must be something you left out, just think about it for a minute."

She tried ta remember some incident which he might find arousin but this whole thing was startin ta get on her nerves. "I just can't," she said. "That's your whole problem," he said, "you just repress things." She asked again if he heard a clock tickin. He just shook his head.

The only complaint she'd ever voiced to his face was that he was not a good cunt eater. This distressed him ta no end. He was so bitter about it that ta get back at her he said quite smugly, "Real women are responsible for their own orgasms." She did in fact think about this and then took a woman as her lover, she felt much better and told him so. He did not appreciate her interpretation of responsibility, he told her that lesbianism was a dangerous form of political separatism and sexually immature. He suggested she grow up.

The tone of his voice changed as he ran his hand along her thigh. He began talkin about the last demonstration he had been to. By the time he got ta the part about the folksinger he was hard. She wondered whether it would help things if she played Cuban music on the record player and covered the bed with propaganda pamphlets.

He rubbed her breasts roughly and told her that she did not deserve to have such a nice body because she never exercised and drank and smoked too much. She thought about this and lit a cigarette. He accused her of bein cruel and manipulative. As he positioned himself above her, he said, "you use your sex as a weapon." She put her cigarette out and blew him. When he came he wrapped his hands around her hair and pulled her head so close she was afraid she'd smother or choke ta death. She swallowed hard and thought she tasted metal. She had performed like a good machine and for this it was hard ta forgive her. The accusation from time ta time was that she was too professional.

As soon as he recovered he began ta talk about the problems connected with oral gratification, mumbled something about people always havin high expectations, thinkin things always have to be reciprocal. It was the "thought that counts" theory. She heard the clock tickin again, this time it was much louder. She decided not ta mention it. She went ta brush her teeth, he followed her. Standin in the doorway watchin her spit into the sink, he began tellin her how much he loved her. She lit another cigarette and started fillin the tub with water. He was capable of workin himself up ta quite an emotional pitch without her assistance so she chose ta ignore him.

He was cryin now and sayin that she had completely misunderstood his motives for bein with her. The only thing she thought a person needed a motive for was murder. She lowered her body until her ears were underwater. Now he was screamin that she was an ungrateful, calloused and ignorant bitch and one day she would regret this and understand that he had only tried ta help her, but then he added that it would be too late. She closed her eyes tightly and thought about her mother.

By the time she started dryin herself, he had calmed down completely. "After all," he said, "you're just a victim. What could I expect? Just a helpless victim of a classist capitalistic society, reared with the wrong set of values, however honest." Of course he would forgive her, he would even say he was sorry. "There now," he said, kissing her on the top of her head, "isn't this better than fighting?" He was actually smilin. He reminded her cheerfully that after the revolution things would be different. She was sick ta the stomach at the thought of it. She let the water our of the tub and, applyin her eyeliner ever so carefully, agreed. He chattered away in the background while she studied herself in the mirror. She was glad her eyes were green, she was glad that this was over.

He said he would call in the mornin so they could examine what had happened. She walked into the bedroom with him trailin behind her. Now he was talkin about the positive energy of anger. She handed him his lunch box and said, "Have a good session." She could tell he was feelin great as he left, he was whistlin.

She laid in bed for an hour smokin, masturbatin, readin. It was the latest book he'd left, entitled *Understanding Fascism*. She kept readin little sections aloud and laughin. Che Guevara, indeed! She got up, washed her hands and threw the book in the trash can. She began ta dress as if she were on a mission. Pullin on tights and blouse, caressin suede boots that she'd saved for a special occasion. She felt ten years younger already. She went in search of scissors, cut her hair as short as possible, pulled the tampon out, stuck it into a vase and watched it bloom. The blood trickled down her leg. She could hear her mother's voice sayin over and over, "You'll never grow up, you'll never grow up. I just don't understand it. What's wrong with you? NEVER NEVER NEVER NEVER!" The clock began tickin so loudly that the voice disappeared. She knew she had to hurry. The belly of the crocodile hadn't ever seemed smaller than now. Removin the book from the window, she stood on the ledge, took a deep breath and jumped. She hoped Tiger Lily would remember her. And never–never land? Why it had never looked better.

nominated by Ted Wilentz

LIFE MOVES OUTSIDE

fiction by BARBARA EINZIG

from LIFE MOVES OUTSIDE (Burning Deck)

WHEN I AWOKE in the morning there I heard cries outside, individual, passionate, detached. They entered my sleep as if calling or tapping, calling and tapping, indifferent or sad. Immediately some mundane texture, the sound of an alarm bell, the smell of coffee, entered also. So I located those cries in between being awake and sleeping, such that when I heard them again each morning I felt as though touching a sheet, a sheet familiar and endlessly clean, endlessly washed and waving in the wind, that was connected to the bed I slept on, fitted loosely over my body, naked beneath it. It was what kept me warm, along with the other layers which I perceived, hearing the cries, as being of incalculable weight, the weight of what I woke into.

The word for "here" merges with the word for "now," the word for "there" with that for "earlier" or "later."

The sky was lit up from behind by the sun, which is rising up now in this morning. The ground is a moist and dark place that will dry out by noon and then will again moisten and fall into a semidarkness, into deep red and yellow and orange as the sun sets in the west. So for the morning a pale blue yellow or red (watch and see) maybe even white, for noon bright take dark blue and the golden maple leaves looked up to against it, but leaves not pasted there, the blueness is above, referred to as the vault of space.

393

That squirrel moving through the green red and yellow leaves, some of which have already fallen and some of which are growing close to the ground, moves in an impervious, cautious, and impulsive way. In front of him golden leaves, suspended from an invisible branch, dance in a silent wind, as I am seeing the whole through glass.

The seam of the ability to move one's glance.

The flowers are orchids, white, in time each one opens. They are sweet, rare, and held on the stem at fixed intervals, determined by the kind of plant.

Telling what moment by moment now amounted to his own story, the former political prisoner is interviewed:

Describe your thoughts in the Ilyushin–62 as you were being flown to an unknown destination.

I had never before flown in an Ilyushin–62, and for that reason alone the flight should have been memorable. But I was in a state of shock from the moment I learned of my release and so for this reason I existed as might a person who has no internal life. I would eat when they served me. I answered questions about the weather posed by the guard who sat alongside me.

As the woman sitting down on the bus straightened her skirt, the child was sure she was about to hear the stranger's story.

"Cold this morning.   Nobody ought to be out of bed this early.   Where are you going?" She paused for a long time between the things she said.

The seat held no holes to retreat into, no doors to close.

"School." That seemed broad and vague.

"Waste of time." And she leaned back, putting her shopping bag down, settling in.

So she wasn't going to tell a story, the girl thought with relief. And the straightening of the skirt had been not the prologue to her narrative but only an assertiveness, an occupation of space in a definite way. She was not the kind, then, who used stories to make herself comfortable.

Mutual facing away appears early on in the pair formation process of gulls, when both partners are not yet fully used to each other and may be seized with an impulse to attack or flee from each other. In these Herring Gulls, facing away or head flagging is an important appeasement ceremony.

The river is full and heavy and flowing. I think about oil when I look at it, though I am sure no oil is in it. Things are so hot they burn the eyes to see, and in water sky condenses as a blue or platinum powder, which is in a liquid form, but thick and shifting.

In "the zone" of a Soviet film, claiming to be science fiction, functioning philosophically and politically, northern creatures occurred in a southern climate.

They travel in flocks and packs and gangs, tracing a figure eight in a brittle geography.

"Something's eating her."

"She's out of her mind with grief."

"O the pain—it's something terrible."

Those sounds you are making have got to be worse than birdcalls, rasping. There is a tone on the phone that sounds like that. It is black plastic and hard. The redeeming light of Vermeer is famous and consoling. How rare it is in this landscape that has always been known for its extraordinary light, but of a different sort—revelatory, blinding, nothing to read a letter by.

The baby, how many days old, lets out a cry. The baby is beginning to look around while in her mother's arms, to not just be still there like a doll or toy, like a thing collapsed in on itself, feeling so intensely, core of flower, its own nature, its own body (all the internal movements rippling over the face and passing in a spasm or stiffness through the tiny perfect body of the newborn) but perching on the mother's arm, post of joy and safety, looking all about. The baby is told the name of her city and her county and her state and her country.

The window is open, sunlight is bright on the keys that wear letters as if they were hats. Suddenly the number, dollar, percentage signs and ampersand take on a peaceful existence there. There is one red key, on it the number one, above it an exclamation mark.

Their mood is no longer contagious. As after a close death, the world is empty, free, yet the shapes in sunlight retain their ability to obstruct or to be touched or to dance in slow motion, shadows on an ever-recurring wall. A curious dignity comes about, the beginning bars of a music, chords of things that do not match but lie there next to each other anyway, their very discordance a form of humility.

Memory is involved he said in knowing one's every need is not being actively denied but simply is wanting, as a plant in light, the shoulders of the growing girl cycling down the street in light, or a character trait is wanting. First she wobbled but now she cleanly drives forward, strongly leaning with her machine. Those are pedal pushers and this the fashion of speech, getting up and going to bed the sentence they neatly said being what happens in between.

Full stops. I knew she was trying to tell me something, and I tried to help her through my coaxing expression which in this case had to seem uninterested but not preoccupied, a feat for sailors and for saints.

Illuminating their most beautiful object they find it casts shadows. These shadows they find distracting. The shadows make them lose their sense of what the object is about. For they like to talk about the object, and how can they go on talking if they have lost their sense. They paint the wall black to lessen or erase the shadows.

The basketball players had seven seconds to get their three points to win the game, and, isolated in their intensity, they were emblems, pure, moving on the court.

He spoke of the professional athletes as a different species.

First, there must be a special respiratory organ, the lungs, affording an immense extent of internal surface, covered by a vascular network, through which the blood flows in innumerable minute streamlets, only separated by an extremely thin membrane from the atmospheric air that has been inhaled; secondly, there must be such an arrangement of the circulating system that fresh blood may be continually driven through the lungs and then onward to the general system; and thirdly, there must be provision for the frequent and regular change of air contained in the lungs.

After leaving the family, young ostriches, still in the monochrome brown plumage of immaturity, form small wandering flocks. They are able to travel at speeds of up to sixty miles per hour, but are nevertheless captured, as they run in circles.

We were repairing the costumes of the dancers. I was searching for holes and tears caused by the stress of the dancers' bodies within the costumes.

Many go fast on the freeway, and many have died; it is accepted that many more will, that conversation will be limited to what and who is inside the car, the "interior" of which may be upholstered with a velour-like fabric or may be coming apart at the seams. The inside of the car has an intensity unmatched by the other environments they dwell in, and they fill it with music but mostly with noise, brought in on waves projected through the air.

It is accepted that vegetation planted by the freeway will be stunted, will grow in a perpetual weather of the freeway's exhaust. The dependence on oil and the vulnerability to its price fluctuations is lamented as weather. That we will quickly move from here to there with nothing on the way is a "fact of life."

Many think these things, but many do not dream of what they think of, but of something held in the hands like jellyfish, inner life raw or yellow. Holding it in shells, in the hands, such naked flesh suddenly experienced, as if photographed or filmed, entirely forgotten, swallowed whole.

They had two-by-fours and half-decayed decorative square logs, like railroad ties but smaller, and all of this stacked as in a lumber yard but in the store feeling more like an archive, under the roof extending into things like the housewares section and he, who had recently worked for a living with the same materials, looked at the stickers that had been placed, little price tags on each piece of wood, and said: "Isn't that funny the way they put those stickers on, like they were cups."

This was a strange situation, to fall in and out of relation, the way a summer umbrella does to the helpfulness of its shade as fall throws the shadows of clouds over and over it, and it sits solidly planted in its aluminum holder. The terror of all this is so dull that it has virtually disappeared: life appears pleasant, and full of pleasures. Not many of them are secret or treasured, it is true, all of them almost are worn, taken out of the closet, valued, possibly counted, certainly displayed.

Median strip and the runners along it. Broad trees, cars swift, relentless. Often it is mentioned that a person behind the wheel acquires the qualities of his or her machine. A person who would not think of challenging someone on foot, who would smile uncertainly and even imagine the other one's name, insists on right of way, forgetting. I skip over you, I throw a rock, shout the rhymes out, the other girls do too. And the adult activities have the counterpoint of remembered children's games, which serve as waiting room, paradigm, playground, stage set, the flower of time.

Brevity like an axe frees them: the prince cuts his way with no difficulty through the briars of stone.

The young trunks of the citrus trees are painted white or wrapped in rags to keep them from burning in the sun.

Her whole family seems to be made up of tortured souls, who have no reason for being tortured. The apparent semblance of a balanced mind, the phrase "peace of mind" which it once seemed meaningful to question, now appears to have fled.

When she first began writing it was an intensification of feeling. It was a setting of the world of her own family into a larger world. This world, this larger one, was vague and amorphous, and had no known history. When she had the opportunity to attend lectures on world civilization, she ditched them. She was too involved in her emotions and her sexuality to see straight, and found a kind of rightness in living in the following of this passion, which she deemed living passionately.

Thousands of pairs of gannets breed on the island, their photographically accurate memory enabling each bird to find its own nest again after leaving to feed.

I would then be. My mouth over his, his over mine. My mouth over his over mine. Against. When we lift up and shake the blanket in making the bed, it settles down this way. When the air is dry in the dark, raising the covers in getting into the bed, sparks fly sudden, small and white.

Those colors are what one calls primary. To ripen in Russian is to turn in color, and we often use color to judge, judiciously, whether a fruit is ripe. Will it taste good, sweet, soft, yielding and at the same time not be over-ripe, be past its peak, gone, soft, spoiled?

When the flock of birds, of geese, lifts off, they seem to agree on this movement, though a few stragglers, in disciplined form even so, join up with the vast main group, a kind of punctuation, or modifying phrase.

Sunlight. Clean air. The sticker said that survival is a basic human right. There is a soundbox that still works inside the stuffed animal, the leopard whose green eyes glow in the dark.

We call that kind of a marble cat's-eye.

The next day they named the place Acaghcemea, *the meaning of which is given as "a pyramidal form of anything which moves, such as an ant hill."*

In the city she had the distinct sensation, while lying in bed at night, that parts of her mind were orbiting round her head, that she could not contain all that had happened to her. She walked next to this extra, partial body of her own experience, trying to recognize it as her own, or to see it as a discrete entity, or to feel some closeness or relation.

She continually turned to him for reassurance that she was "alright."

What does the mind do, does it digest and eat things. Many animals, he said, have no time to think of anything but eating.

Now those birds, whose feathers are stippled grey and white, almost black and white in this shrouded over light coming through a dense cloud of a sky, overcast, these birds are females I suppose and that one with the orange chest must be the male. They are both busy eating. There are two on the feeder and one is waiting.

The birds aren't sure if the sound of the typewriter is safe. They decide not and leave.

He said he felt human privacy to be a small thing against his first felt violation of the privacy of animals while in the far north. They are white to hide them in the snow, simple as that. Or the privacy of the so-called inanimate world, she flattened herself against the wall to watch him enter without being seen. Atomic privacy wrenched too, bumper stickers saying split wood not atoms. Waste of the plants makes the ocean water warm. This true story bores her, for she has heard it before, living as she does in a family, though with her own phone.

Living as you do. You would then be. Your ear here, tying knots in the supposed calm blue (turquoise, mint, shallow) waters of my intent. Conversation like snorkelling may be an easy tourist sport, and that area, roped off for our observation, seemingly not to be spoiled or harvested, is in truth, or as they say, reality, and on closer examination, cleared every morning of those sea plants and animals not thought by the hotels to be pretty, meaning now "pleasing to the eye," though the original sense of the word, on closer investigation, is found to be "tricky," "cunning," "full of wiles."

The bird outside the window on the new bird feeder that clings directly to the glass could not be too shy still I moved slowly and softly to avoid startling her, dull colored and perched erectly without relaxing whether because in the open at the feeder or whether this is the way birds eat I do not know but at each mouthful the bird straightened itself up and consumed with deliberation.

Masturbation before the mirror heightened the silver quality of the mirror, the way the surface seemed to be brushed on over the glass, or behind it.

He remained convinced through the twenties that writing was at its best a primal instinctive thing like love, and he kept trying to get at the primalcy with a whirl of words as if writing were a physical thing like swimming or running and one simply poured on the muscle power.

This typewriter, while certainly bulky, is a good deal lighter than my previous one. You can tell the date of the typewriter by whether it is rounded. If it is rounded chances are it is the older model. If it is almost plump, almost circular, it is the oldest model which we call A. Then the model with the soft curves is B, and the sleek, elliptical model C, and this latest model, with no curves, has the console look.

Probably for ages after the civilization of man commenced, the still waters of ponds and lakes were the only mirrors.

Although he often felt the boredom of life, in an empty Paris, it was by fulfilling his vocation and by hard work that he was so well able gradually to dissolve the loved one in a broader reality that he ended by forgetting his suffering and feeling it only as if it were a disease of the heart.

The leaves of this tree are like broad fronds, but the tree is covered with them, down to the trunk. It resembles slightly the avocado, but clearly has no fruit, and one wonders, from where it stands, if it was planted or is actually a weed. However we leave it standing.

The peacock was brought to Europe by a mighty conqueror, a man who made history. In its natural habitat it is extremely shy, and only in places where the natives hold it sacred does it become more trusting.

Mean people abound. Senses of humor. Knives. Do not break me. The writing has changed fundamentally, from description, lasso, to request, direction, the hand moving out instead of in. Lasso: a long light but strong rope usually of hemp or strips of hide used with a running noose for catching livestock or with or without the noose for picketing grazing animals.

Tristan Tzara: I detest artifice and lies. I detest language which is only an artifice of thought. I detest thought which is a lie of living matter; life moves outside of all hypocrisy, hypothesis; it's a lie that we have accepted as a starting point for the others.

The black crow doesn't know how to settle on the green palm, whose fronds sway, brilliance, violence, sunlight, under his heavy flapping body that wants to set down on a solid thing.

nominated by Burning Deck

MAKING A GREAT SPACE SMALL

by GREG PAPE

from QUARRY WEST

The sun is going down. A few miles
to the east on Navajo land the sheep scatter
and the people spit in the dust when the bombers
fly low making a great space small.
Last night snow filled the crevices
and the inner basin of the peaks. Frost
blackened the stems and leaves and broke
the necks of the marigolds. Now the wind
has died down. The sky is a dusty blue
streaked with contrails—the fear of a nation
at work in the sky. Down here curled seed heads
of grama grass are lighting up like candles
in the late sun, as they've done since before
there were Octobers. Now a flicker hammers
a juniper in the distance and the piñons
glisten with voices of small birds. I feel
a fall sun on my face and hands, a breath
of ice at my neck.

We say the sun is going down
and know it's not true. The truth is
we're turning away. If I know anything,
I know this: this is my body—ice, wind,
this light mending the grass, birdsong,
the spit in the dust, this argument that goes on.

nominated by Patricia Goedicke, Garrett Kaoru Hongo and Jim Simmerman

A LITTLE DEATH

by ARTHUR SMITH

from CRAZYHORSE

Anyone almost anywhere on the walkway could have
    heard it—I did—
That boom-like, intermittent grunting
    pained with effort, resonating suddenly like a foghorn
Through the late-summer, Sunday afternoon drowse
    of the Knoxville City Zoo.

Here, I thought, was an animal
    so overwhelmed
The most it could hope for was to bellow into being
    that intensity—those waves mounting, even then
Bearing it away. A group already ringed
    the tortoise pen,

Where earlier, leaning over a barrier of logs, patting,
    and then more boldly
Stroking the larger of the two, his fatherly, reptilian neck
    craning—distended, really, upward,
Tolerantly, it seemed—I had reckoned
    him old,

So old, in fact, that crowding
    back around the pen,
I expected to find him dead or, worse, still living,
    convulsed
With those horribly irreversible last spasms for air.

He was "dying," to be sure, clambered up
  and balanced—to say the least—precariously on
The other's high-humped shell,
  his stump-like front feet extended forward,
Grasping, as they were able, the other's weathered carapace,
  for leverage,

His own neck dangling, gaze floating
  vacantly downward,
And his mouth agape, saliva
  swaying on short, thick threads only inches
From the other's bony face. And,
  all along,

The noise. It wasn't pretty
Though it was soon over—
This "little death" referred to in our youth,
  snickeringly,

As "makin' bacon," back when all knowledge
Belonged, by fiat, to the young, but here witnessed
  in the frank
Generation of matter, all amenities
  beside the fact—

The male beached on his own bulk, panting, less than
  tolerant, now,
Of the heavy-handed petting,
And the female, unencumbered again,
  scooting rather

Indifferently toward the mud-bracketed pond
  tattered with froth-pads
Of algae, immersing herself as far as the shallow water
Would allow.

nominated by William Matthews

WHAT SHE HAD BELIEVED ALL HER LIFE

by ALBERTO RÍOS

from IRONWOOD

Sometime in the night she became afraid
Of noise—loud at first, but then any
So that even the smallest motions of a cat
Unrecognized became noise, and she
Grew smaller, into the folds of the strong sheets,
Like men into the cave-like mines for copper.
As she was shrinking she became as afraid
Of disappearing as she was afraid of noise
The other way, and she wished now
   Only to stay perfectly in between,
   To live there decently
   Suspended better than any carnival trick.
But she could not balance, and whimpered
A loud sound in that moment of falling.
Together they won her this time,
Noise and pain, away and toward.
How this sound could come from inside,
Betraying what she had believed all her life,
That inside at least was a private place, hers,
   As now she heard a noise that would not stop,
   The leopards of the inside forest,
   The spiders that are darkest, all surfacing,
She could not understand, she could not.

And pain, it should not fit there.
She had taken the care to eat too much
For all the days of her tiny breathing
So that nothing more should fit.
   This surprise, this surprise,
   Like a party inside among her organs,
   But before she could fix herself up,
   Before she could plan what to wear.

nominated by Dorianne Laux

FLIP CARDS

by ROBERT POPE

from THE GEORGIA REVIEW

In the spring of my ninth year, I invested fifty cents—then two weeks' allowance—in baseball cards. At that time, baseball cards came one to a pack, a penny a pack, with a slice of dusted pink bubble gum stuck in to scent the card. The wrappers were waxed paper, yellow and red and blue; the cards were stiff and rectangular, each with a bright hero on one side and his vital statistics on the other. The bubble gum itself was a marvel, the scent tuned to a perfect pitch—too sickeningly sweet for an adult, it had an almost aphrodisiac effect on a child. You could shove a wad of it in the side of your mouth and pretend it was chewing tobacco. And baseball players then had great names: Peewee Reese, Dusty Rhodes, Whitey Ford—they seemed to be the realization of everything in which we believed.

I recall the woman behind the counter the day I bought my fifty baseball cards, a reddish-blonde woman with red cheeks and knuckles. I believe she had sharp eyes, the eyes of a natural betrayer. As soon as I left the store, she called my parents so they could be stewing over the profligacy of their oldest boy, making dire predictions about his future. (When I think of the excitement these days about whether a teen-age girl should have to tell her parents she's having an abortion, I really wonder about what that woman did. If she's alive today, and I hope she is, I imagine her as a stiff-necked Republican.)

Those were better days, some will say. Maybe, but I learned pretty quickly that I would have to pursue my interests independent of my parents, and, if necessary, in secrecy. My life would have been much thinner if I had listened just once more than I did. I respected my parents, even feared my father, but life is there for the taking, and only the fool of Ecclesiastes—the one who folds his hands and gnaws at his own flesh—really wants to refuse what is offered.

I had already been practicing with some cards I had borrowed from my friend Danny, and I had discovered that I had an innate talent for flip cards. On my way home from the candy store, I tore off those bright wrappers, my head filled to pounding with the scent of bubble gum, and gathered my cards together, inspecting each one as I chewed rigorously. I found a couple of boys stomping a mud puddle and gave them something like half of the pink slabs, threw away a few more, stuffed a couple in my shirt pocket, and so on—you see, I was not after the bubble gum. This was my parents' error. They thought I had blown two weeks' allowance on the gum!

I headed for the school yard right away. No one was there yet, so I practiced awhile. Saturday mornings, eight or nine fellows would gather for flip cards, and I wanted to be ready. My form was both studied and natural, tight and loose. I'd hold the baseball card lightly, lightly, my four fingers along the top, the tip of my thumb stiff on the bottom edge. In practice, I'd hold it up to the sky to make sure I had a lengthwise rectangle of cardboard perfectly parallel to an imaginary line deep inside the earth, a line I could feel through my feet. By the time the others showed up, I could find that line the way some singers can find a C every time, on time, on demand. I'd bring my hand down another line, perpendicular to the one inside the earth and running up one side of my body, and release the card at a point along that line. The speed of my bent arm, not my hand, and the point of release, determined the distance. If I snapped my wrist at all, it was for extra distance and a *chance* of greater accuracy.

There were two games you could play. I had no patience for *Heads or Tails*, which could have been played just as easily with pennies, because it was too exclusively a game of chance, not native to the cards themselves, a matter of matching with no tricks of skill. My game was *Tops*. It demanded accuracy. It demanded patience and verve. And, of course, luck. Such a game could sustain our mutual belief, in those days, that skill was lucky (which it is) and that luck was skillful (which it is). We had an implicit, unstated belief that those upon whom luck descended had coaxed it down upon themselves through desire or beauty or poise—something indefinable, unimaginable. We believed in the gods, and the gods had their heroes.

Let me put it this way: I liked flip cards because the god of flip cards saw something in me he liked. I played flip cards maniacally for the weeks of the sport's duration—too few—because when I played flip cards I felt favored, graced. I won. I won and won and won. And this is the reason why we do the things we do: because we can. Because we are given to doing them. Let me be more specific. By the end of the first day's round of playing, I had doubled my cards. I now had one hundred flip cards, and, more important, I was a dominant figure—a player, as we say, in the field. I was someone to be reckoned with. And reckon I did, for by the end of that brief season, I had filled two shoeboxes with seven hundred baseball cards, bound with rubber bands in bundles of twenty-five or fifty, all of them smelling faintly of that insane, oh irrational, bubble gum.

I could flip my card and land it on another card every time if I wanted to, and only missed on purpose, to throw the other guy off, to fill him with foolish hopes and dreams. The first card tossed out onto an empty field was always a statement of pure whimsy, a voice calling out across an echoing canyon, at once proud, egotistic and humble, vain, absurd. The second card was the opponent's voice in that wilderness of one. It could say, *Let the game roll on*. It could say, *You die*. It could say, *I know who I am, you take the first shot, the first prisoner*. As the cards piled one on the other, the game grew more intense, more dramatic until one player lost his nerve, lost his eye, lost his cards. How I remember going to my knees, scooping up the take, arranging that fat stack of cards, tapping them on the ground to line them up. I carried a supply of rubber bands so I could snap one around the stack and drop it at my feet without missing a game, a breath. As long as I could land my card on top of another card, I was in the game, and more often than not, I was in the game until the end.

Well, on that first flip-card afternoon, when I came home randy as a young billy goat, I somehow knew enough to hide my cards under the porch. I brushed my hands together, smelled that bubble gum on them, and went inside to find my parents leaning over me with

410

astonishment. This, this is our son? they seemed to ask. This fellow who spends his money on bubble gum? Can it be that we have slaved to feed and clothe him, and this is how the rascal has repaid us? They were beyond anger—or before it, I'm not sure which. They kept asking me the same questions over and over, but they could see the unregenerate idiot in my eyes. They sensed the power, the success that informed my respectful silence as I continued chawing that wad of gum, my baseball hat askew.

I sympathize with my parents now—perhaps I did even then—but the fact remains that they simply did not understand what it took to make it in the world into which I had come, at age nine, a decade after the second war, guiltless as a baby. Oh, I was ashamed of myself, to be sure, but I had no intention of changing. In fact, I waited for my chance to take out the garbage that night so I could smuggle the cards back inside and fondle them, count them, smell them, read the mysteries printed on their backs.

When I mentioned my friend Danny, many pleasant associations with him all came rushing back together. Right away, however, I know what I want to tell you about first. We lived in Fort Monroe, Virginia, but Danny's family was from Chicago. This fact alone startled me in those days, though I can hardly say why. I had already lived in Africa, and in Paris too—so why should the idea of Chicago seem so unusual? Because it conjured a life I could not imagine actually getting to live—you know, a big-shouldered life. I knew certain things about Chicago: gangsters, tough laborers, factories, baseball, and music (though I didn't know what kind at the time). For some reason, I liked the Chicago White Sox, and I make no apologies for this.

Here is what Chicago came to mean to me. The apartment in which Danny lived was strange and alluring, a den where the principles of the life I had so far lived no longer held. Right on the floor beside the stereo, the very first time I went to Danny's house, I saw a record-album cover on which Eartha Kitt—wearing nothing but a white fur of some kind, her leg exposed to the thigh—looked directly at me. Of course she struck me as beautiful and forbidden—she was black and half-naked!—but then her voice poured through the rooms, and I knew I had never been so stung in my life. In my house, it was hymns all the time, sung by my mother as she worked. Here, it was Eartha Kitt, rich, black and funky—a word I had never heard in those days—and Danny's mother and father not only permitted it, they enjoyed it. They acted as if it might be the most natural thing in the world to have that album cover and that voice in their living room. It hurt my heart, I can tell you.

Danny's house lacked the order I had always known. Nothing looked *placed*. The couch and the chair might have walked into his living room and settled in whatever spot felt most comfortable. The colors were vivid, and warm, and clashing, and then Danny's generous mother came in humming along with the music. They were darker, almost swarthy, blunter, hairier than my family, with thick, dark eyebrows and black hair. Danny's father's large, oval head protruded naked through his hair, and he always wore a satisfied look, his lids half-closed. A big man but never bullish. I remember one day Danny's mother had been cleaning the house, and she dropped into the couch, just let her legs give way and dropped completely relaxed from the shoulders down through her legs, which were spread thoughtlessly wide. She gave the room an animal presence. And then, a few minutes later, as Danny and I sat on the living-room rug playing Clue, his father came sweeping into the room serenading us all on a monstrously large accordion, something wild and mournful. I felt half drunk in his house.

Danny collected things: stamps, coins, and military patches. He started me on my own collections. We would go to the military dry cleaners and ask for the patches they had snipped from uniforms to replace with fresh ones, and then we would save the patches our fathers brought home, and soon we had over four hundred different patches between us, beautiful things. We would trade them, laying them out on the floor and admiring the bright colors. And Danny had games, plenty of them, and odd things, like a Dick Tracy detection kit. Together we developed wild fantasies, perhaps the last really elaborate pretend games I would play in my childhood. Often we went back through the woods behind his apartment to the little river that ran toward the ocean, and we followed it to the Civil War bunker in the hill that rose along its banks. With stolen flashlights, we explored those darkened, empty rooms, never telling anyone because it was all too obvious that what we did was dangerous and forbidden.

He was in my class at school, and we were together so much of the time that I think of Danny and that time and place at once. I had other friends, of course, but casual friends with whom I played at

412

war, or whatever ideas made themselves felt in that world of impulse. Rosey, who lived upstairs and was two years older—in my sister's class—had a crush on me. It seemed so odd then to find this out. When my sister told me, in front of Rosey, that she had seen my name written all over Rosey's schoolbook covers, Rosey claimed it was another boy with my same name. I felt flattered, though I did not really have a crush on Rosey. I favored a girl in my own class, Helen, who always wore white or red boots to school and had long white-blonde hair. Rosey was stout and sweet and pathetic. I couldn't understand why she would like a boy two years younger than she was.

Rosey had an uncle in show business. He was an actor, she told us, and one afternoon we watched a gangster movie on television just because her uncle was in it. Just before he came on, she said, "OK, get ready." Three or four gangsters in oversized suits and fedoras were planning something really nasty in a hotel room. A knock came at the door. The gangsters swiveled their heads like wolves toward the sound, went for their pistols. Someone threw the door open.

"That's him!" screamed Rosey. "That's my uncle!"

It was a good thing she shouted quickly, because her uncle, a skinny fellow, went down in a dramatic leap and twist, his hands clutching his chest. The last thing we saw of her uncle was a shot of the soles of his shoes, his body spread out long behind them. It took about forty-five seconds. My sister and I tried not to laugh, but we failed at last, and Rosey didn't care. She had an uncle in show business—what else mattered?

Sometimes I'd walk through my back yard up to the hard-packed dirt path that ran along the seawall just to look out over the ocean. The seawall dropped straight down about fifty yards, with a chain-link net protruding halfway down to catch children like me who couldn't help but lean way out over the chains hung between posts that were supposed to keep people back. I could walk down this path and reach the beach, where hermit crabs scuttled under rocks or into holes in the sand, leaving little zigzag patterns behind them. Down by the rocks, a boy from school was building a raft, and he worked on it the entire year I lived in Fort Monroe, Virginia. I don't know if he ever sailed away, but I do know that he and a friend once had an egg fight on the beach. The admission price was as many eggs as you could steal, and my sister and I showed up with a carton of twelve we had taken from our refrigerator. We were all so excited that something so exotic was being staged on our beach.

The ocean was a constant presence that year, making itself felt most during Hurricane Hazel. My father covered every window in the house while Danny and I sailed down the sidewalks on our bicycles, our arms spread wide, holding our jackets up like sails. The wind drove us, bore us away from home, and we pedaled back into it with cries of delight, our eyes watering, eager for the next wind ride. When we finally had to go inside, my father packed towels around the doorjambs and blocked the doors. He turned on the radio and we all sat down in the living room to ride out the storm, which made the sea come over the wall and splash onto the path and brought the tide into our back yard. It was like being on a ship, and we were all terrified. My two little brothers huddled into Mom, and my Dad sat smoking his pipe and listening to the radio. My sister and I watched him and noted his passive alarm and his absolute solidity. In my father's form we placed all our fears, and in this manner we weathered the storm.

Another time I became especially conscious of the ocean was once when a friend of my mother came over with her little boy, perhaps six years old, and I took him out in the back yard at her request to toss my new basketball with him. In a wild toss, the basketball went up the hill and onto the path, which was tilted slightly toward the sea. I made a dash after the ball, but it went over the side, bounced once on the edge of the net, and went out to sea. I watched it moving out swiftly on the waves, riding high as it went farther and farther from the land.

I did a terrible thing. To get to school, I had to walk down our long street and across a wide field. At school there were friends, but there were also dangerous characters who threw stones at girls, or threatened violence, or who smelled of death and sex. One such fellow accompanied me home one afternoon, his dark hair chopped off abruptly above his forehead. He had dark eyes, kept his hands in his pockets, and talked out the side of his mouth. He made me feel fear, though not specifically of him. It just so happened that this very day, on the edge of the field, we saw a green purse.

We stood beside the purse, and he said, "Pick it up." I picked it up, and he said, "Open it." I opened it and looked inside. I removed the green wallet and unsnapped it. I saw the girl's name. I knew her, though not well. She was in my grade, though not my class. "See if there's any money," he said. There were two dimes in the coin purse.

"Why don't you take them out?" he said. I took them out. "Just toss that purse over there. The wallet too." I did so. I walked home stiff with fear. I carried the dimes in my pocket, and felt them tinkling together.

We parted without words. When I got home and saw my father, I asked him if he would keep these two dimes for me. He looked curious, and asked me where I had gotten them. "I found them," I said. I was terrified. I wanted my father to press me right then, but I must have seemed strange. He was wearing his uniform.

"All right," my father said. He took the dimes and put them in his pocket. I was relieved, but still felt dread. I lay in my bed awhile, then went out back and leaned on the chains, looking into the ocean. I considered leaping in, though perhaps only into the safety net below. Then I considered leaping far enough that I would miss the safety net. Eventually I went home for dinner, which I ate in silence.

The next day at school, the teacher announced that the girl in the other second-grade class had lost her purse—a green purse, with a green wallet and two dimes. I wanted to call out. I wanted to die. I thought about nothing else the rest of the day. On the way home from school, I walked past the edge of the field, where I had thrown the purse and wallet into the woods. They were still there—shiny and green. For a few minutes I could not move. Then I looked around, picked them up, and carried them home, walking at a swift clip, fearful of ghosts.

When I got home, I asked my father for the two dimes I had given him the day before. His eyes were so green.

"Why?" he said. He could have said that the day before and spared me my shame, my terror. "What's going on, Bobby?"

"I have to return them," I said. I held out my hand.

"To whom?" he said.

"To the girl who lost her purse."

"When did she lose her purse?"

"Yesterday."

"How did you get these dimes?"

"I took them out of her purse."

"What did you do with the purse?"

"I threw it in the woods."

"Why did you throw it in the woods?"

"Because I took the dimes."

"You found the purse, took the dimes, and threw it in the woods?"

"Yes."

"And you didn't return it?"

"No."

"You stole the dimes?"

"Yes."

"What's wrong, Bob?" my mother said.

"Maybe you should tell your mother what's wrong."

"I found a purse on the edge of the field on the way home from school. I opened it and took two dimes out of the change purse, then I threw the wallet and the purse into the woods."

"Was the girl's name in the purse?"

"Yes."

"And you still threw it into the woods?"

"Yes."

This went on for at least two hours, and for one of those hours I was weeping quietly, my lips quivering. I felt exactly as my parents felt about me. It was a terrible, horrible thing to do. It was a sickening, vile thing to do. It was a sin, the thing I did. My father gave me back the two dimes and I put them in the wallet. They talked about the purse and looked inside repeatedly. Then they gave it back to me and the rest of the night was silence. I took it to school the next day and gave it to the teacher. I told her I found it on the edge of the field. She looked at me strangely as I turned back to my seat. The dread of that experience held me in its terrible claw for weeks.

I don't think I ever knew the name of the other boy, the boy who told me to do the thing. I never saw him again, though my sister said he once chased her home from school, throwing rocks at her and calling her strange names.

If this happened before I spent my fifty cents on bubble gum cards, it may have colored my parents' opinion of me. It may have heightened their fears. I was terrified of doing something bad like that. I knew what it felt like. It felt terrible. I do not like it even now. It reminds me of something else I did about that time. We used to ride our bicycles to the swimming pool. There were always dragonflies there, and a telephone that shocked me whenever I used it. There was also a hole in the bathroom wall. Once I looked through that hole and saw a woman undressing. She must have been in her late thirties or early forties. It gave me a strange sensation.

I only looked once. That wasn't what I thought of a moment ago, what the purse made me think of. In front of the swimming pool, outside the gates, where they checked between your toes for athlete's foot, was a small, round fishpond with a little fountain. Good-sized goldfish swam around inside, extravagant things with double tails. I would always try to catch them with my hands. One day I brought a large coffee mug with me, to see if I could catch one in it. On the first try, I scooped one out. It startled me so much to see the orange-gold life thrashing about inside that I dropped the cup. It broke on the side of the fishpond and the pieces fell on the cement walk around it. The fish lay on the wet concrete, flipping wildly. I felt very similar to the way I had felt when I stole the dimes and threw the purse back into the woods. It took nerve and resolve to touch that squirming life, but I picked it up, flipping and smacking in my hand, and dropped it back in the water.

We went to a chapel on the military base. It might have been Presbyterian or Episcopalian or nondenominational. It was orderly and bright. While my parents were in church, I went to Sunday School. There might have been thirty kids my age in the class. The woman who conducted the class, Mrs. Thompkins, seems intelligent in retrospect, and I responded to her intelligence, though she was also a little ecstatic. She said things to me that startled me. Once, when she talked with my parents in front of the church, she suddenly turned her dewy eyes on mine.

"Isn't it wonderful, Bobby?" she said, her blue eyes glistening, her mouth moving slightly. I didn't know what to say, though I wished I did. I would have given her a good answer. I agreed, basically, that it was wonderful, but what was *it*? What did she mean? Did she mean the sunny day? Did she mean the church? Did she mean our redemption through Christ? What did Mrs. Thompkins mean?

Her fervor surpassed the fervor of the children in her class, but she was a good woman. We liked her, but we could not keep up with her in the ecstasy category. One day she had us do a sentence prayer. In a sentence prayer, everyone in his turn adds a sentence of supplication or thanks. This day, she wanted us to think of everything for which we could be thankful. We had a lot for which we ought to have been thankful, but the situation struck our funnybone. All those second or third graders thanking God for something He had given them.

I was in the second row, perhaps the tenth child to add a sentence, and I thanked God for something standard, for the beautiful day, or for my parents, or for my friends. I don't remember what exactly. But the prayer began to break down. Halfway through, someone thanked God for squirt guns. Now, that might have been a sincere thought, but it was also funny. We got a great deal of pleasure out of squirt guns and yo-yos in those days, and the next person mentioned the yo-yos. It went downhill from there. Mrs. Thompkins turned red, but never raised her eyes, never forbade us our iniquity. Someone thanked God for Ghosty-Whoasty-Toasty-Mosties, and this trend took over. It was a travesty, to be sure, but it was also very funny. I fought my own urge to laugh, but laughter finally exploded from my lips. Those in the back, who didn't know Mrs. Thompkins so well, laughed unabashedly.

Mrs. Thompkins never said a word. Obviously hurt, she proceeded as if nothing at all had happened. Her attitude impressed me, even moved me, but the rest of the hour I just wanted to scream my laughter, and so when services were over we tore around the churchyard shrieking and laughing.

Mrs. Thompkins was godmother at my sister's confirmation. Elizabeth was dressed in white, and Mrs. Thompkins had bought her a white Bible. Elizabeth wore white gloves. Her hair was blonde. She looked so beautiful and solemn and happy I could not take my eyes off her. I loved her so very much, I admired her more than any other child I knew. She really enjoyed rituals. There were other girls there, but Elizabeth stood out as most beautiful and most lucky and most favored. If I could have spoken my mind then, I might actually have thanked God for my sister.

After her confirmation, we played sheep-and-wolves and steal-the-bacon. In these games, a great number of children form two opposing sides and do a great deal of running at each other, a great deal of stealing things and people, a great deal of screaming. We played on a wide green lawn beneath old, overhanging trees that speckled the sunlight with cool shade. Elizabeth played in her white dress. She was good at games. She ran fast and played hard. She had strong arms and legs. I think we all felt free to be mean and wild. It had been such a holy day already.

I remember another day at church. A holy magician came and showed us a red cloth heart, and when he dipped it in a bowl of sin, it came out black, and when he dipped it in a bowl of love, it came out white. He shook it in the air and it turned red again, and he put it back in his chest.

This was at the beginning of summer. Danny and I had gone down to the schoolyard with our back pockets crammed with baseball cards. By this time, I viewed my early practice and expertise as the work of a novice. Now, I had much greater flexibility in the matter of the card toss. I still believed the card must be held against the tips of the four fingers on the top and the tip of the thumb on the bottom edge, but my good right arm could now toss from the middle of my body or even, on occasion, from the extreme left. I had developed a nasty little wrist flick that did crazy things, and I didn't have to stand so straight. It had become a dance, and we all knew it.

I don't remember the exact day, but it must have been Saturday because later on, when we walked to the fishing pier, we hoisted up some workingman's minnow traps and set the minnows free. It was a day full of sunlight with a nice breeze coming off the sea, and yet I remember the day with some sadness, for that's when the all-too-brief season of flip cards came to an end. I did not know this then, as Danny and I and three other boys (only one whose name I remember—Corey) danced our final dance with the cards. I snapped my wrist and twisted, playing with the forms of the game, falling to my knees, snapping the rubber band around the take, up in time to flip my first card, next game.

I remember Corey because he had a great name and because he had never caught on to flipping the cards so they twirled lightly end-over-end. He still held fast to the belief that by holding on to a corner and zipping his card swift and flat he could buy greater accuracy. By the end of the last game, Corey was into me for ten baseball cards, which I had loaned him just so I could win the ones he'd already tossed, all he had left of the season. There must have been a hundred cards on the ground when his caught the wind wrong and lifted and slid beyond the pile. I realize now that if I'd let him win that day, the season might not have ended, but it would have been false. When he spun his card too hard, the season ended for real. The other two boys pumped and pumped, and their cards fluttered out until they lost their nerve. They would jerk at the last minute, say, and that was that. Then it was just Danny and I, and the other boys couldn't stand to watch. They began to wrestle, so Danny and I agreed to split the take. We gathered up what remained of a great season, a season of heroes.

We headed for Danny's house, and I left my cards there while we fixed ourselves a drink of Tom Collins mix on ice and pretended it was cocktails. Danny sneaked the flashlights out of the kitchen, and we headed out back through the woods. Before we reached the narrow river running toward the ocean, we came upon three older boys firing rifles in a little clearing. They had set a box in a tree and were filling it full of holes. We stood and watched a few minutes. The boys laughed and glanced at us. Then one of them, a large slab of a boy with orange floppy hair, went to get the box. He jerked his head at us so we'd come over, and when he opened the box, the bigger boys watched us and laughed. Inside was a brownish rabbit with holes torn in him and veins of blood sticking him to the sides like a web.

One of the boys took a look at me and Danny and said they needed a couple of bigger boxes. They all laughed at the idea, but the biggest one took a bead on Danny and we took off. We didn't look back. Our legs leaped and leaped and we didn't stop. We heard the rifles firing behind us and we didn't stop until we reached the black wall of the old Civil War bunker, and then Danny and I took our flashlights and went into one of the dark, gaping, cavelike doorways. We stood back inside the cold cement room looking out to see if we had been followed. Our breathing sounded loud in that dark room. After a while, I flicked on my flashlight and searched along the floor. A few beer bottles sat by the far wall; otherwise the room was empty. I found another doorway and we headed back inside. Our stomachs tingled as we followed the flashlight beams through that absolute dark. Once, we stopped and dared each other to turn off our lights. When we did, a darkness surrounded us that seemed to grow and grow. We might have been in outer space. We were blind.

"Don't say anything," I said.

"I won't," he said.

"This must be what it's like to be dead," said Danny.

"I don't know," I said. "Maybe."

We stood inside that darkness until we heard a sound, and then Danny flicked on his light, and so did I. Something with a tail moved from the beam and we tried to catch it again. It must have been a rat. We found a few more doors, and then, deep inside the hill, Danny wondered aloud if we could find our way out.

"Of course," I said, but my voice rang in the hollow room. We found three doorways.

"Which one should we take?" Danny whispered.

"We have to go back that way," I said. I didn't know I had lost my sense of direction. It was cold inside the hill.

"I think we went the wrong way," said Danny.

"So do I," I said. We stood looking at two doors, and we didn't know any longer which one to take.

"Maybe we'll find some old ammo in here," Danny said.

"Yeah," I said. We studied those two doors and listened to our breathing.

"Are you afraid?" Danny asked me.

"What's there to be afraid of?" I said. I wished he hadn't asked me.

We wandered through several more rooms, each no different than the one we had just left, no glimmering of light in any.

"Do you think we'll get lost?" Danny asked.

"No," I said. "I don't think we'll get lost."

"That's because we're already lost," said Danny, and then we laughed. We flashed the lights on each other. All I saw was Danny's laughing face, the eyebrows dark, almost meeting, the eyes dark and terrified. He must have seen it in my eyes too, so I shined the light up my face and made my eyes do funny horror things, and then so did Danny. We laughed and our laughter echoed, and we heard how small it was. We kept going through rooms, and our talk seemed hushed and breathless.

"Look," Danny said. We ran to it, a grayness, a movement of light on the dark. We ran following our flashlight beams, and then we stood outside, laughing and panting and trembling weakly. We dropped to our knees and laughed until we cried. When we finally got up and saw where we were it surprised us. There was only one doorway out that side of the hill, and we couldn't see the river anywhere. Ahead of us, an old, blackened factory stood vacant, many of its windows broken, and from the other side we could hear the faint voice of the river. A dirt road ran between us and the factory, but there was no one else around. We walked across the road and stood looking up at the factory, and then we collected a few rocks and broke a few windows, as high up as we could reach. When we heard voices from the other side, we ran.

We didn't really know where we were until we saw the pier. That's when we pulled up the minnow traps and set the minnows free. Then we headed down the road that ran past the candy store where I had bought my first bubble gum cards and we went back to Danny's house and played Monopoly the rest of the afternoon. About four or five o'clock, my parents called to tell me it was time to come home, so I got my half of the take and wandered back.

My parents were talking in the kitchen when I went in, and my brothers followed me back to my room. I got the two shoeboxes out and put the rest of my cards inside. My father came back down the hall and looked in.

"I thought I heard you come in," he said.

Then he saw what I had on my bed, and what my brothers were playing with.

"Where did you get those cards?" he said.

I looked back at my bed. There were over seven hundred cards being spread out, and I seemed to see them for the first time, their reality, as my brothers played with them on my bed. I looked back up at my father and felt it coming on.

"I won them," I said.

My father stared at the cards and his face became set and hard. He looked back at me with those bright green eyes. "Who did you win them from?"

"Friends."

"Where did you win them?"

"Different places. By the schoolyard."

"When?"

I shrugged. How could I tell him all the *whens*, or *wheres*, or *from whoms*? I told him the names of the boys who had been playing that day. His jaw became even more set, and his voice broke on me like a fist. "Take them back."

This confused me: "Take them where?"

"I want you to give them back to all the boys you won them from." He stared at me, his face growing harsher every moment. He must

422

have seen my astonishment, my obvious confusion. "I don't want to hear anything more about it," he said.

I didn't want to anger him. I didn't want to risk his backhand. I wanted to tell him that was not the way it worked. It? What was *it*? How could I have explained *it* to him?

"Do you understand me, boy?"

I lowered my head. I could not lie to my father, so I did not. I lowered my head, and I felt truly humbled, but I also let him think it meant I had heard and would obey. I would as soon have jumped off the seawall as return those cards.

I don't know what you know about the lure of the sea. I used to hear that if you stood too near the railroad track when the train went by, the urge to leap into the onrushing energy of the implacable machine would be too great to resist. It might have been the next day, it might have been later, but I was all by myself. My parents had left, and I had walked out back to stand on the hard-packed earth and lean on the chains and look out over the sea. I don't know how long I stood there either, but I remember leaning on those chains and rocking, my thoughts full of the sea. The sea had moved inside my head. I leaned and rocked on the chains, and then I was spinning.

I had fallen forward. My shoes had slipped on the dirt. I tried to catch myself but my feet flipped right over my head. I managed to hold on for a second, long enough to hear the ocean right beneath me, slapping and sucking at the seawall, then I plummeted. I seemed to drop a very long time, and then I hit the chain-link net hard. It dazed me, and I lay there at the bottom of a deep gray-green and rolling darkness. I saw little lights flashing here and there, like a town seen from out at sea, and then I was alive and shaking, trembling in the net. The knees of my pants had gone, and my knees were bloody, and my hands had been scraped raw. I must have tried to grab onto the wall as I fell, because a couple of nails were pulled away and bleeding. My head ached and I couldn't move for a while, but when I could I turned onto my belly and held onto the pole at the far edge of the net and looked beneath me at the slapping sucking ocean. I had difficulty getting my breath, but when I could I shouted from deep in my stomach.

I shouted for help repeatedly, and then I tried to call for my parents, but they were still away. After perhaps half an hour, I began to realize I would have to stay in the net until someone got home and happened to come outside and look for me. I couldn't hear anything but the ocean churning beneath me, and it went as far out as anyone could see. It wasn't until dusk that I heard my father's voice at last, above me on the seawall, and saw him leaning over, and then, beside him, my mother and my sister and my two little brothers. They stood at the top of what had become a dark gray pit. I couldn't say anything to them.

"Good God," my father said. My mother asked me if I was all right. My sister and brothers looked at me. My father disappeared, and in a few minutes he came back with a rope and tried to lower it, but it wouldn't quite reach, and I was too weak and shaky to try to stand and leap for it.

"I'll be right back, Bobby," he shouted. He looked frightened himself. He came back in fifteen minutes and stood above me until a small crane arrived. A man in a black slicker came down the cable and helped me sit on a crossbar, and they raised me up the wall. My mother put her arm around me while everyone looked at me very strangely, and then we went back inside the house.

I think it's important to tell you that I did not give back the baseball cards. I hid them from my parents for an incredible twenty years. When I was twenty-nine, in graduate school, having a hard time of it financially and watching the bottom of the peanut butter jar, I did a little research, attended a few flea markets and conventions. I found the exact worth of the wreckage of an American childhood. The baseball cards alone paid my tuition and bought books for a year. I'd say that was a good investment of fifty cents, and I hope the woman from the candy store is alive and reading this right now.

One memory leads to another, but I have to stop somewhere, and I have to leave you with an understanding of what this all means, don't I? Or are the details of the memory, the life as lived, sufficient unto themselves? Must I arrive at last to a final moral or political or literary statement? I must admit there is none, for the days of which you have read make no statements, possess no consciousness of their own except the kind you might expect from a small boy waking up one morning to discover he is alive, and that the light reflected on his ceiling has arrived from the sun playing off the great sea that called him in the voice of God, which is Silence. Something had dazzled me awake; did it not dazzle you? I saw only Truth because there was as yet no lie I knew. Could it be that love itself is not a sufficient argument for love? Must I say that such is how this literary hero lived, how he came to vision? Instead, I appeal that this is how one man came into his eyes, and what they received.

One day Danny and I were playing croquet, and while I was sticking a loosened wire wicket deeper into the earth, Danny took a back-swing, his foot on his own ball, hoping to knock mine into the sea. He caught me just above the eye. I fell howling and bleeding, and I still have the scar. When I woke up, everything had changed. We were somewhere else again. Nothing that had been familiar remained. I had to learn to get used to this, and I had to learn to do it more quickly. It was like a nightmare in which the rules are constantly changing. You have to be ready to see them, and to understand them. You had to be ready to move again and breathe. You had to think of it this way: I've come again, to another good place.

nominated by Rita Dove

SPECIAL MENTION

(The editors also wish to mention the following important works published by small presses last year. Listing is alphabetical by author's last name)

POETRY

Lunar Eclipse At A New England Aquarium—Julie Agoos (Partisan)

Ode on Carbon–14—Sandra Agricola (Georgia Review)

The Keeper of the Dead Motel—Agha Shahid Ali (Ironwood)

Biology—John Allman (New Directions)

Tracking The Transcendental Moose, VI—Nelson Bentley (Bellowing Ark)

My Cousin From Brazil—Ginger Bingham (Denver Quarterly)

Party—Joseph Edward Bolton (Crazyhorse)

In Memory of Benjamin E. Linder—Henry Braun (American Poetry Review)

Libyan Pantoum—Philip Dacey (Poetry Northwest)

Missed Chances—Stephen Dobyns (Antaeus)

Seizure—Lynn Emmanuel (Ohio Review)

Sensing The Enemy—Margaret Gibson (Michigan Quarterly Review)

Mother Pills—David Graham (Flume Press)

Meditations on a Skull Carved in Crystal—John Haines (Zyzzyva)

Prophecy—Donald Hall (Paris Review)

Ulysses Grant: His Prose—Michael Harper (Black Warrior Review)

Hands—Linda Hasselstrom (Barn Owl Books)

Self-Portrait—Conrad Hilberry (Other Wind Press)

Vespers—Brenda Hillman (Field)

Skinning A Deer—John Clellon Holmes (Staten Island Review)

A Christian on the Marsh—Andrew Hudgins (Ploughshares)

Coleen's Faith—Ray A. Young Bear (Wicazo Sa Review)
For L. C. Z., (1903–1986)—Paul Zimmer (Three Rivers Poetry Journal)

ESSAYS

What Henry Knew—Jean-Cristophe Agnew (Grand Street)
The Magazine Wars—Joe David Bellamy (Witness)
Beacons Burning Down—Bernard Cooper (Georgia Review)
The Seat of the Soul—Arthur C. Danto (Grand Street)
Embarrassed by Jane Austen—Thomas R. Edwards (Raritan)
Reading—Richard Ford (Antaeus)
Gertrude Stein—Elizabeth Hardwick (Threepenny Review)
Actual Field Conditions—James Kilgo (Georgia Review)
The Confinement of Free Verse—Brad Leithauser (New Criterion)
Literature As Pleasure, Pleasure As Literature—Joyce Carol Oates (Antaeus)
Our Dinners With Andre—Amy Schildhouse (Indiana Review)
Remembrance of Tenses Past—Lynne Sharon Schwartz (New England Review/Bread Loaf Quarterly)
Plate Glass—Richard Sennett (Raritan)
On Hunting—Eric Zencey (North American Review)

FICTION

Wild Sage—Phyllis Barber (Dialogue: A Journal of Mormon Thought)
Two Stories—Rick Bass (Southern Review)
The Life and Times of Major Fiction—Jonathan Baumbach (Fiction Collective)
The Musical Lady—Leslee Becker (New Letters)
Beggarman, Thief—Madison Smartt Bell (Crescent Review)
A World Like This—Helen Benedict (Ontario Review)
Dog—Pinckney Benedict (Ontario Review)
Edward and Jill—Robert Boswell (Georgia Review)
The Given—Beth Boyett (Crescent Review)
The Evershams' Willie—Hortense Calisher (Southwest Review)
Materia Prima—Mary Caponegro (Conjunctions)
The Hungarian Countess—Kelly Cherry (Fiction Network)

Little Night Creatures—J. Patrick Lewis (New England Review/
    Bread Loaf Quarterly)
Girls—John L'Heureux (Denver Quarterly)
Heirloom—Renee Manfredi (Cimarron Review)
King of Safety—Michael Martone (Crescent Review)
The Smoke of Invisible Fires—Jack Matthews (Bottom Dog Press)
The Hellraiser—Robert G. McBrearty (Mississippi Review)
Bodies At Sea—Erin McGraw (Georgia Review)
Second Hands—Kevin McIlvoy (Missouri Review)
True—Thom McNeal (Epoch)
Horses—Peter Meinke (New Letters)
Giving My Mother a Bath—Mary Jane Moffat (City of Roses, John
    Daniel)
Blue Car—Christina Murphy (Crescent Review)
How To Pursue A Silent Hat—Fred Nadis (Another Chicago Mag-
    azine)
Don't Worry About the Kids—Jay Neugeboren (Georgia Review)
Death etc.—Joyce Carol Oates (Mississippi Review)
Yarrow—Joyce Carol Oates (TriQuarterly)
The Keeper of Dogs—R. H. Ober (Alaska Quarterly Review)
Odyssey—Michael O'Rourke (Crosscurrents)
Trip to Da Nang—Robert L. Perea (Bilingual Review)
The Hummingbird—Micah Perks (Epoch)
The Paperbag—Robert Phillips (Boulevard)
On The Ocean—C. E. Poverman (Sonora Review)
Everyday Disorders—Francine Prose (Ploughshares)
A Run of Bad Luck—E. Annie Proulx (Ploughshares)
Wind—Ann Pyne (The Quarterly)
A Better Class of People—Clay Reynolds (Concho River Review)
Staying Under—Marjorie Sandor (Agni Review)
Blood—Jeanne Schinto (The New Renaissance)
from The Closest Possible Union—Joanna Scott (Missouri Review)
The Black Fugatos—Eve Shelnutt (Alabama Literary Review)
The Age of Grief—Jane Smiley (The Quarterly)
Sergeant—R. T. Smith (Cream City Review)
The Business Venture—Elizabeth Spencer (Southern Review)
Banana Boats—Mary Ann Taylor-Hall (Paris Review)
Doney Gal—Annabel Thomas (Ball State University Forum)
Girls and Horses—Jean Thompson (Epoch)
Catch You Later—Melanie Rae Thon (Ploughshares)

PRESSES FEATURED IN THE PUSHCART PRIZE EDITIONS (1976–1988)

Acts
Agni Review
Ahsahta Press
Ailanthus Press
Alcheringa/Ethnopoetics
Alice James Books
Amelia
American Literature
American PEN
American Poetry Review
American Scholar
The American Voice
Amnesty International
Anaesthesia Review
Another Chicago Magazine
Antaeus
Antioch Review
Apalachee Quarterly
Aphra
The Ark
Ascent
Aspen Leaves
Aspen Poetry Anthology
Assembling
Barlenmir House
Barnwood Press
The Bellingham Review

Beloit Poetry Journal
Bennington Review
Bilingual Review
Black American Literature
    Forum
Black Rooster
Black Scholar
Black Sparrow
Black Warrior Review
Blackwells Press
Bloomsbury Review
Blue Cloud Quarterly
Blue Wind Press
Bluefish
BOA Editions
Bookslinger Editions
Boxspring
Brown Journal of the Arts
Burning Deck Press
Caliban
California Quarterly
Calliopea Press
Canto
Capra Press
Cedar Rock
Center
Chariton Review

Charnel House
Chelsea
Chicago Review
Chouteau Review
Chowder Review
Cimarron Review
Cincinnati Poetry Review
City Lights Books
Clown War
CoEvolution Quarterly
Cold Mountain Press
Columbia: A Magazine of Poetry
    and Prose
Confluence Press
Confrontation
Conjunctions
Copper Canyon Press
Cosmic Information Agency
Crawl Out Your Window
Crazyhorse
Crescent Review
Cross Cultural Communications
Cross Currents
Cumberland Poetry Review
Curbstone Press
Cutbank
Dacotah Territory
Daedalus
Decatur House
December
Dragon Gate Inc.
Domestic Crude
Dreamworks
Dryad Press
Duck Down Press
Durak
East River Anthology
Ellis Press
Empty Bowl
Epoch
Exquisite Corpse
Fiction
Fiction Collective

Fiction International
Field
Firelands Art Review
Five Fingers Review
Five Trees Press
Frontiers: A Journal of Women
    Studies
Gallimaufry
Genre
The Georgia Review
Ghost Dance
Goddard Journal
David Godine, Publisher
Graham House Press
Grand Street
Granta
Graywolf Press
Greenfield Review
Greensboro Review
Guardian Press
Hard Pressed
Hermitage Press
Hills
Holmgangers Press
Holy Cow!
Home Planet News
Hudson Review
Icarus
Iguana Press
Indiana Review
Indiana Writes
Intermedia
Intro
Invisible City
Inwood Press
Iowa Review
Ironwood
Jam To-day
The Kanchenjuga Press
Kansas Quarterly
Kayak
Kelsey Street Press
Kenyon Review

Latitudes Press
Laughing Waters Press
L'Epervier Press
Liberation
Linquis
The Little Magazine
Living Hand Press
Living Poets Press
Logbridge-Rhodes
Lowlands Review
Lucille
Lynx House Press
Magic Circle Press
Malahat Review
Manroot
Massachusetts Review
Mho & Mho Works
Micah Publications
Michigan Quarterly
Milkweed Quarterly
The Minnesota Review
Mississippi Review
Missouri Review
Montana Gothic
Montana Review
Montemora
Mr. Cogito Press
MSS
Mulch Press
Nada Press
New America
The New Criterion
New Directions
New England Review and Bread
    Loaf Quarterly
New Letters
North American Review
North Atlantic Books
North Dakota Quarterly
North Point Press
Northern Lights
Northwest Review
O. ARS

Obsidian
Oconee Review
October
Ohio Review
Ontario Review
Open Places
Orca Press
Oyez Press
Painted Bride Quarterly
Paris Review
Parnassus: Poetry In Review
Partisan Review
Penca Books
Pentagram
Penumbra Press
Pequod
Persea: An International Review
Pipedream Press
Pitcairn Press
Ploughshares
Poet and Critic
Poetry
Poetry Northwest
Poetry Now
Prairie Schooner
Prescott Street Press
Promise of Learnings
Quarry West
The Quarterly
Quarterly West
Raccoon
Rainbow Press
Raritan A Quarterly Review
Red Cedar Review
Red Clay Books
Red Dust Press
Red Earth Press
Release Press
Revista Chicano-Riquena
River Styx
Rowan Tree Press
Russian *Samizdat*
Salmagundi

San Marcos Press
Sea Pen Press and Paper Mill
Seal Press
Seamark Press
Seattle Review
Second Coming Press
The Seventies Press
Sewanee Review
Shankpainter
Shantih
Shenandoah
A Shout In The Street
Sibyl-Child Press
Small Moon
The Smith
Some
The Sonora Review
Southern Poetry Review
Southern Review
Southwest Review
Spectrum
The Spirit That Moves Us
St. Andrews Press
Story Quarterly
Streetfare Journal
Stuart Wright, Publisher
Sulfur
Sun & Moon Press
Sun Press
Sunstone
Tar River Poetry
Telephone Books
Telescope
Temblor
Tendril
Texas Slough

13th Moon
THIS
Thorp Springs Press
Three Rivers Press
Threepenny Review
Thunder City Press
Thunder's Mouth Press
Toothpaste Press
Transatlantic Review
TriQuarterly
Truck Press
Tuumba Press
Undine
Unicorn Press
University of Pittsburgh Press
Unmuzzled Ox
Unspeakable Visions of the
    Individual
Vagabond
Virginia Quarterly
Wampeter Press
Washington Writers Workshop
Water Table
Western Humanities Review
Westigan Review
Wickwire Press
Wilmore City
Word Beat Press
Word-Smith
Wormwood Review
Writers Forum
Xanadu
Yale Review
Yardbird Reader
Y'Bird
ZYZZYVA

CONTRIBUTING SMALL PRESSES

(These presses made or received nominations for this edition of *The Pushcart Prize*. See the *International Directory of Little Magazines and Small Presses*, Dustbooks, Box 1056, Paradise, CA 95969, for subscription rates, manuscript requirements and a complete international listing of small presses.)

A

Acclaim Communications, P.O. Box 81085, Chicago, IL 60601

ACTS, 514 Guerrero St., San Francisco, CA 94110

Adam's Apple, Rte. 4, Box 263B, Mechanicsville, MD 20659

Agni Review, Boston University, Boston, MA 02215

The Agincourt Press, 65 Eckerson Rd., Harrington Park, NJ 07640

Ahsahta Press, Boise State University, 1910 University Dr., Boise, ID 83725

Albatross, 4014 S.W. 21st Rd., Gainesville, FL 32607

Alice James Books, 138 Mt. Auburn St., Cambridge, MA 02138

Amador Publishers, P.O. Box 12335, Albuquerque, NM 87195

American-Canadian Publishers, Inc., P.O. Box 4595, Santa Fe, NM 87502

American Poetry Review, 1616 Walnut St., Philadelphia, PA 19103

American Studies Press, Inc., 13511 Palmwood Lane, Tampa, FL 33624

The American Voice, Heyburn Bldg., Ste. 1215, Broadway at 4th Ave., Louisville, KY 40202

The Americas Review, see Arte Publico Press

The Amicus Journal, 122 East 42nd St., New York, NY 10168

Ampersand Press, Creative Writing Program, Roger Williams College, Bristol, RI 02809

Andrews (James) & Co., Inc., Publishing, 1942 Mt. Zion Dr., Golden, CO 80401

Anderson Press, 706 W. Davis, Ann Arbor, MI 48103

Another Chicago Magazine, Box 11223, Chicago, IL 60611

Antaeus, 26 W. 17th St., New York, NY 10011

Applezaba Press, P.O. Box 4134, Long Beach, CA 90804

Arrival, 48 Shattuck Sq., Ste. 194, Berkeley, CA 94704

Arte Publico Press, University of Houston, Houston, TX 77004

The Ashland Poetry Press, Ashland College, Ashland, OH 44805

Ashod Press, P.O. Box 1147, Madison Sq. Sta., New York, NY 10159

B

BOA Editions, Ltd., 92 Park Ave., Brockport, NY 14420

Baker Street Publications, P.O. Box 994, Metairie, LA 70004

Balcones, P.O. Box 50247, Austin, TX 78763

Bamberger Books, P.O. Box 1126, Flint, MI 48501

Bambook Publications, P.O. Box 1403, Weatherford, TX 76086

Barn Owl Books, Box 7727, Berkeley, CA 94707

Bauhan, William L., Publisher, Dublin, NH 03444

Bellingham Review, 412 N. State St., Bellingham, WA 98225

Beloit Poetry Journal, RFD 2, Box 154, Ellsworth, ME 04605

The Bench Press, 1355 Raintree Dr., Columbia, SC 29212

Biblia Candida, 4466 Winterville Rd., Spring Hill, FL 34608

Big Foot Press, 57 Seafield Lane, Bay Shore, NY 11706

Bilingual Review/Press, Hispanic Research Center, Arizona State Univ., Tempe, AZ 85287

BkMk Press, 5100 Rockhill Rd., Kansas City, MO 64110

Black Bear Publications, 1916 Lincoln St., Croyden, PA 19020

Black Buzzard Press, 4705 South 8th Rd., Arlington, VA 22204

Black Heron Press, P.O. Box 95676, Seattle, WA 98145

Black Mountain Review, c/o Lorien House, P.O. Box 1112, Black Mountain, NC 28711

Black Warrior Review, P.O. Box 2936, University, AL 35486

Blue Moon, 1209 W. Oregon, Urbana, IL 61801

Blueline, Blue Mountain Lake, NY 12812

Bottom Dog Press, c/o Firelands College, Huron, OH 44839

Breakthrough!, 192 Balsam Pl., Penticton, British Columbia, CAN-
ADA V2A 7V3
Brob House Books, P.O. Box 7829, Atlanta, GA 30309
Burning Deck, 71 Elmgrove Ave., Providence, RI 02906
'by george' Publications, P.O. Box 172, Mt. Horeb, WI 53572
Byline, P.O. Box 130596, Edmond, OK 73013

C

CCR Publications, 2745 Monterey Highway, #76, San Jose, CA 95111
Calliope, see Ampersand Press
Calyx, P.O. Box B, Corvallis, OR 97339
Candle Publishing, 101 S. W. Blvd, Ste. 210, P.O. Box 5009,
Sugarland, TX 77478
Capra Press, P.O. Box 2068, Santa Barbara, CA 93120
Cardinal Press, 76 N. Yorktown, Tulsa, OK 74110
Ceilidh, P.O. Box 6367, San Mateo, CA 94403
Celestial Arts, P.O. Box 7123, Berkeley, CA 94707
Centering/Years Press, ATL, EBH, Michigan State Univ., East
Lansing, MI 48824
The Chariton Review, Northeast Missouri State Univ., Kirksville,
MO 63501
Chelsea, Box 5880, Grand Central Sta., New York, NY 10163
Clinton St. Quarterly, Box 3588, Portland, OR 97208
Clothespin Fever Press, 5529 N. Figueroa, Los Angeles, CA 90042
Coastline Publishing Co., P.O. Box 223062, Carmel, Ca 93922
Coffee House Press, P.O. Box 10870, Minneapolis, MN 55458
Comet Halley, 1504 Robinson Ave. #4, San Diego, CA 92103
Commonwealth Press, Inc., 415 First St., Radford, VA 24141
Concho River Review, c/o English Dept., Angelo State Univ., San
Angelo, TX 76909
Cougar Books, P.O. Box 22246, Sacramento, CA 95822
Crazyhorse, University of Arkansas, Little Rock, ARK 72204
The Cream City Review, English Dept., P.O. Box 413, Univ. of
Wisconsin, Milwaukee, WI 53201
The Crescent Review, P.O. Box 15065, Winston-Salem, NC 27113
Cross-Cultural Communications, 239 Wynsum Ave., Merrick, NY
11566

D

Dacotah Territory Press, P.O. Box 931, Moorhead, MN 56560
John Daniel, Publisher, P.O. Box 21922, Santa Barbara, CA 93121
The Dog Ear Press, 19 Mason St., Brunswick, ME 04011
Dog River Review, see Trout Creek Press
Dolphin-Moon, P.O. Box 22262, Baltimore, MD 21203
Druid Press, 2724 Shades Crest Rd., Birmingham, AL 35216

E

Elghund Publishing Co., P.O. Box 158, Simpsonville, MD 21150
Embassy Hall Editions, 1630 University Ave., Ste. 42, Berkeley, CA 94703
Emperor New Press, 2808 Woodland Rd., Mobile, AL 36609
Emrys Journal, P.O. Box 8813, Greenville, SC 29604
Epoch, 251 Goldwin Smith Hall, Cornell University, Ithaca, NY 14853
Erie Street Press, 221 S. Clinton Ave., Oak Park, IL 60302
Eve Press, P.O. Box 1117, Brookline, MA 02146
Exquisite Corpse, Louisiana State University, Baton Rouge, LA 70803

F

Falling Water Press, P.O. Box 4554, Ann Arbor, MI 48106
Farmer's Market, P.O. Box 1272, Galesburg, IL 61402
Fiction, Inc., Dept. of English, City College of New York, New York, NY 10031
Fiction Collective, English Dept., Brooklyn College, Brooklyn, NY 11210
Fiction International, English Dept., San Diego State Univ., San Diego, CA 92182
The Fiction Review, P.O. Box 1508, Tempe, AZ 85281
Field, Rice Hall, Oberlin College, Oberlin, Oh 44074
Fireweed Press, P.O. Box 83970, Fairbanks, AK 99708
Five Fingers Review, 553–25th Ave., San Francisco, CA 94121

Fjord Press, P.O. Box 16501, Seattle, WA 98116

The Florida Review, English Dept., Univ. of Central Florida, Box 25000, Orlando, FL 32816

Flume Press, 644 Citrus Ave., Chico, CA 95926

Footwork, Passaic Co. Community College, College Blvd., Paterson, NJ 07509

G

GCT Inc., P.O. Box 6448, Mobile, AL 36660

Gallery Sail Review, see Embassy Hall Editions

Garden Way Publishing, Schoolhouse Rd., Pownal, VT 05261

Gargoyle Magazine/Paycock Press, O.O. Box 30906, Bethesda, MD 20814

Garric Press, P.O. Box 517, Glen Ellen, CA 95442

Gazelle Publications, 5580 Stanley Dr., Auburn, CA 95603

Georgia Review, University of Georgia, Athens, GA 30602

Gesture Press, 66 Tyrrel Ave., Toronto, Ontario, M6G 2G4, *CANADA*

Giants Play Well in the Drizzle, 326–A Fourth St., Brooklyn, NY 11215

Graywolf Press, P.O. Box 75006, St. Paul, MN 55175

Great Elm Press, RD 2, Box 37, Rexville, NY 14877

The Greenwood Press, 300 Broadway, San Francisco, CA 94133

Gynergy Books, 145 Pownal St., Box 132, Charlottetown, P.E.I. *CANADA* C1A 7K2

Gypsy, c/o B. Subraman, Box 283, HHB 2/3 ADA, APO New York 09110

H

The Haunted Journal, see Baker Street Publications

Hayotzer, The Jewish Folk Arts Soc., 11710 Hunters Lane, Rockville, MD 20852

Heart of the Lakes Publishing, 2989 Lodi Rd., P.O. Box 299, Interlaken, NY 14847

Helicon Nine, P.O. Box 22412, Kansas City, MO 62113

Hermitage Publishers, P.O. Box 410, Tenafly, NJ 07670

High Meadow Press, Middletown Springs, VT 05757

High Plains Literary Review, 180 Adams St., Ste. 250, Denver, CO 80206

Home Planet News, P.O. Box 415, Stuyvesant Sta., New York, NY 10009

Hoofstrikes, P.O. Box 106, Mount Pleasant, MI 48804

Human Kindness Foundation, Rte. 1, Box 201–N, Durham, NC 27705

Hutton Publications, P.O. Box 2377, Coeur d'Alene, ID 83814

I

Indiana Review, 316 N. Jordan Ave., Bloomington, IN 47405

International Publishers Co., Inc., 381 Park Ave. S, New York, NY 10016

Interstate, P.O. Box 7068, University Sta., Austin, TX 78713

Inverted-A, Inc., 401 Forrest Lane, Grand Prairie, TX 75051

Ion Books/Raccoon, 3387 Poplar Ave., Ste. 205, Memphis, TN 38111

Iowa Review, University of Iowa, Iowa City, IA 52242

Ironwood, P.O. Box 40907, Tucson, AZ 85717

Italica Press, 625 Main St., #641, New York, NY 10044

J

Jeffrey Pine Press, Ltd., see Prairie Journal Press

K

Kangaroo Court Publishing, 1505 State, Erie, PA 16501

Kelsey St. Press, P.O. Box 9235, Berkeley, CA 94709

Kenyette Productions, 1968 Rookwood Rd., Cleveland, OH 44112

Michael Kesend Publishing Ltd., 1025 Fifth Ave., New York, NY 10028

Kick it Over, P.O. Box 5811, Sta. A, Toronto, Ont., M5W 1P2, *CANADA*

The Kindred Spirit, Rt. 2, Box 111, St. John, KS 67576

Knights Press, P.O. Box 454, Pound Ridge, NY 10576

L

La Jolla Poets Press, P.O. Box 8638, La Jolla, CA 92038

Lactuca, c/o Mike Selender, P.O. Box 621, Suffern, NY 10901

Lake Street Review, Box 7188, Powderhorn Sta., Minneapolis, MN 55407

Lake View Press, P.O. Box 578279, Chicago, IL 60657

The Lapis Press, 2058 Broadway, Santa Monica, CA 90404

Late Knocking, P.O. Box 336, Forest Hill, MD 21050

Laughing Waters Press, 864–18th St., Boulder, CO 80302

Levite of Apache, 121 Twenty-fourth St., NW. Norman, OK 73069

The Lighthouse Press, 1308 Lewis, La Junta, CO 81050

Lincoln Springs Press, P.O. Box 267, Franklin Lakes, NJ 07417

LIPS, P.O. Box 1345, Montclair, NJ 07042

Logbridge-Rhodes, P.O. Box 3254, Durango, CO 81301

Lost and Found Times, Luna Bisonte Prods., 137 Leland Ave., Columbus, OH 43214

Lynx House Press, c/o 9305 S. E. Salmon Court, Portland, OR 97216

M

MIP Company, P.O. Box 27484, Minneapolis, MN 55427

The MacGuffin Schoolcraft College, 18600 Haggerty Rd., Livonia, MI 48152

The Massachusetts Review, Memorial Hall, Univ. of Massachusetts, Amherst, MA 01003

McPherson & Co., Publishers, P.O. Box 1126, Kingston, NY 12401

Mercury House, 300 Montgomery St., Ste.700, San Francisco, CA 94104

Merging Media, 516 Gallows Hill Rd., Cranford, NJ 07016

Mho & Mho Works, Box 33135, San Diego, CA 92103

Micah Publications, 255 Humphrey St., Marblehead, MA 01945

Mid-American Review, English Dept., Bowling Green State Univ., Bowling Green, OH 43403

Missouri Review, University of Missouri, Columbia, MO 65211

Mother's Hen, P.O. Box 5334, Berkeley, CA 94705

Mr. Cogito, U. C. Box 627, Pacific U, Forest Grove, OR 97116

MSS, SUNY, Binghampton, NY 13901

N

NBM Publishing Co., 35–53 70th St., Jackson Heights, NY 11372

NRG Magazine, 6735 S. E. 78th St., Portland, OR 97206

Naked Man, c/o M. Smetzer, English Dept., K. U., Lawrence, KS 66045

New England Review & Bread Loaf Quarterly, Middlebury College, Middlebury, VT 05753

New Poets Series, Inc., 541 Piccadilly Rd., Baltimore, MD 21204

New Rivers Press, 1602 Selby Ave., St. Paul, MN 55104

New Seed Press, P.O. Box 9488, Berkeley, CA 94709

North American Review, University of Northern Iowa, Cedar Falls, IA 50614

North Dakota Quarterly, Box 8237, Grand Forks, ND 58202

The Northwest Review, 369 PLC, Univ. of Oregon, Eugene, OR 97403

O

Ocean View Books, 95 First St., Los Altos, CA 94022

Oktoberfest, see Druid Press

Old Harbor Press, P.O. Box 97, Sitka, AK 99835

Ommation Press, 5548 N. Sawyer, Chicago, IL 60625

Ontario Review, 9 Honey Brook Dr., Princeton, NJ 08540

Open Hand Publishing, Inc., 600 E. Pine, Ste. 565, Seattle, WA 98122

Open Places, Stephens College, Columbia, MO 65215

Orchises Press, P.O. Box 20602, Alexandria, VA 22313

Oxford Magazine, Bachelor Hall, Miami Univ., Oxford, OH 45056

P

Pangloss Papers, Box 18917, Los Angeles, CA 90018

Papier-Mache Press, 34 Malaga Place East, Manhattan Beach, CA 90266

Paris Review, 541 E. 72nd St., New York, NY 10022

Pennypress, Inc., 1100 23rd Ave., East, Seattle, WA 98112

Permafrost, English Dept., Univ. of Alaska, Fairbanks, AK 99775

The Permanent Press, Sag Harbor, NY 11963

Pig in a Poke Press, P.O. Box 81925, Pittsburgh, PA 15217

Pig Iron Press, P.O. Box 237, Youngstown, OH 44501

Pineapple Press, Inc., P.O. Drawer 16008, Sarasota, FL 34239

The Place in the Woods, 3900 Glenwood Ave., Golden Valley, MN 55422

Ploughshares, Box 529, Cambridge, MA 02139

Poetry, 60 W. Walton St., Chicago, IL 60610

Poetry Northwest, University of Washington, Seattle, WA 98105

Poetry/LA, P.O. Box 84271, Los Angeles, CA 90073

The Porcupine's Quill, Inc., 68 Main St., Erin, Ont., N0B 1T0, *CANADA*

Postscript, 2919 Bayview Ave., Baldwin, NY 11510

Prairie Journal Press, P.O. Box G997, Sta. G, Calgary, Alberta, T3A 382 *CANADA*

Processed World, 41 Sutter St., #1829, San Francisco, CA 94104

Prophetic Voices, Heritage Trails Press, 94 Santa Maria Dr., Novato, CA 94947

Prospect Hill Press, 216 Wendover Rd., Baltimore, MD 21218

Puckerbrush Press, 76 Main St., Orono, ME 04473

Pudding Publications, 60 North Main St., Johnstown, OH 43031

Puerto Del Sol, College of Arts & Sciences, Box 3E, New Mexico State Univ., Las Cruces, NM 88001

Q

Quarry West, University of California, Santa Cruz, CA 95064

Quarry Press, P.O. Box 1061, Kingston, Ont., K7L 4Y5, *CANADA*

The Quarterly, 201 E. 50th St., New York, NY 10022

Quotidian Publishers, Box D, Delaware Water Gap, PA 18327

R

Raccoon, P.O. Box 111327, Memphis, TN 38111

Ragweed Press, Box 2023, Charlottetown, P.E.I., *CANADA* C1A 7N7

Rarach Press, 1005 Oakland Dr., Kalamazoo, MI 49008

Raritan, Rutgers Univ., 165 College Ave., New Brunswick, NJ 08903

Raw Dog Press, 128 Harvey Ave., Doylestown, PA 18901

Rhyme Time, see Hutton Publications
River Styx, 14 So. Euclid, St. Louis, MO 63108
Runaway Publications, Box 1172, Ashland, OR 97520

S

S.E.E. Publishing Co., 5605 Charlotte, Kansas City, MO 64110
Salmagundi, Skidmore College, Saratoga Springs, NY 12866
Samisdat, Box 129, Richford, VT 05476
Sands, P.O. Box 638, Addison, TX 75001
Lloyd Schmidt, Book Publisher, 326 Allen St., Brawley, CA 92227
SCORE, 491 Mandana Blvd., #3, Oakland, CA 94610
Scream Magazine, P.O. Box 10363, Raleigh, NC 27605
Seal Press, 3131 Western Ave. #410, Seattle, WA 98121
Second Coming Press, P.O. Box 31249, San Francisco, CA 94131
Seven Locks Press, P.O. Box 27, Cabin John, MD 20818
Shameless Hussy Press, Box 5540, Berkeley, CA 94705
Li Kung Shaw, Publisher, 2530 33rd Ave., San Francisco, CA 94116
Sheba Review, Inc., P.O. Box 1623, Jefferson City, MO 65102
Shenandoah, Box 722, Lexington, VA 24450
Sign of the Times, P.O. Box 70672, Seattle, WA 98107
Silver Wings, P.O. Box 1000, Pearblossom, CA 93553
Sinister Wisdom, P.O. Box 1308, Montpelier, VT 05602
Sonora Review, English Dept., Univ. of Arizona, Tucson, AZ 85721
Space and Time, 138 W. 70th St., Apt. 4B, New York, NY 10023
Spinsters/Aunt Lute Book Co., P.O. Box 410687, San Francisco,
    CA 94141
Spiraling Books, 12431 Camilla St., Whittier, CA 90601
Square One Publishers, P.O. Box 4385, Madison, WI 53711
Squibob Press, Inc., P.O. Box 421523, San Francisco, CA 94142
St. Andrews Review, St. Andrews College, Laurinburg, NC 28352
St. John's Publishing Co., 6824 Oaklawn Ave., Edina, MN 55435
Star Publications, 1211 W. 60th Terrace, Kansas City, MO 64113
Starlight Press, Box 3102, Long Island City, NY 11103
Starwind, Box 98, Ripley, OH 45167
State Street Press, Box 278, Brockport, NY 14420
Streetfare Journal, P.O. Box 880274, San Francisco, CA 94188
Stone Country, P.O. Box 132, Menemsha, MA 02552
Stormline Press, Inc., P.O. Box 593, Urbana, IL 61801

Story Quarterly, P.O. Box 1416, Northbrook, IL 60065

Studia Hispanica, P.O. Box 7304, University Sta., Austin, TX 78713

Sudden Jungle Press, P.O. Box 310, Colorado Springs, CO 80901

Sulfur, Eastern Michigan University, Ypsilanti, MI 48197

The Sun, 412 West Rosemary St., Chapel Hill, NC 27514

Sunrust Magazine, Dawn Valley Press, Box 58, New Wilmington, PA 16142

Swallow's Tale Press, 736 Greenwillow Run, Wesley Chapel, FL 34249

Sweet Forever Publishing, P.O. Box 1000, Eastsound, WA 98245

Synergetic Press, P.O. Box 689, Oracle, AZ 85623

Synergy, Publishers, P.O. Box 18268, Denver, CO 80218

T

T.M.H. Press, 4000 Hawthorne, #5, Dallas, TX 75219

The Threepenny Review, P.O. Box 9131, Berkeley, CA 94709

Thunder City Press, P.O. Box 600574, Houston, TX 77260

Thunder's Mouth Press, 93–99 Greene St., Ste. 2A, New York, NY 10012

Timberline Press, P.O. Box 327, Fulton, MO 65251

Timely Books, P.O. Box 267, New Milford, CT 06776

Toledo Poets Center Press, English Dept., 32 Scott House, Univ. of Toledo, Toledo, OH 43606

Tool Box, 14445 E. 7–Mile, Detroit, MI 48205

Treetop Panorama, R Rt. 1, Box 160, Payson, IL 62360

Triglav Press, 1181 Pine Grove Ave., Atlanta, GA 30319

TriQuarterly, 2020 Ridge Ave., Evanston, IL 60208

Trout Creek Press, 5976 Billings Rd., Parksdale, OR 97041

2 AM Magazine, P.O. Box 50444, Chicago, IL 60650

U

US 1 Worksheets, 21 Lake Dr., Roosevelt, NJ 08555

University of Massachusetts Press, P.O. Box 429, Amherst, MA 01004

University of Pittsburgh Press, 127 N. Bellefield Ave., Pittsburgh, PA 15260

V

The Vampire Journal, see Baker Street Publications
Vocabulary, P.O. Box 1347, Sta. F, Toronto, *CANADA* M4Y 2V9

W

Walrus, Mills College, 500 MacArthur Blvd., Oakland, CA 94613
Water Row Press, P.O. Box 438, Sudbury, MA 01776
Waterfront Press, 52 Maple Ave., Maplewood, NJ 07040
Wayland Press, 25 North Cody Court, Lakewood, CO 80226
The Weekly, 1931 Second Ave., Seattle, WA 98101
West Anglia Publications, P.O. Box 2683, LaJolla, CA 92038
Westgate, 8 Bernstein Blvd., Center Moriches, NY 11934
Western Humanities Review, University of Utah, Salt Lake City,
    UT 84112
Wet Editions, Box 2045, Times Sq. Sta., New York, NY 10036
Whale Publishing Co., P.O. Box 21696, St. Louis, MO 63109
What, P.O. Box 338, Sta. J, Toronto, Ont., M4J 4Y8, *CANADA*
The William & Mary Review, College of William & Mary, Wil-
    liamsburg, VA 23185
Williwaw, P.O. Box 607, Brockport, NY 14420
The Word Works, P.O. Box 42164, Washington, DC 20015
Wordwrights Canada, P.O. Box 456, Sta. O, Toronto, Ont., M4A
    2P2, *CANADA*
The Wormwood Review, P.O. Box 8840, Stockton, CA 95208
Writer's Info, see Hutton Publications

Y

Yellow Silk, P.O. Box 6374, Albany, CA 94706

Z

Zeke Publishing Co., 56A Bowdoin St., Malden, MA 02148
ZYZZYVA, 21 Sutter St., Ste. 1400, San Francisco, CA 94104

INDEX

The following is a listing in alphabetical order by author's last name of works reprinted in the first thirteen *Pushcart Prize* editions.

CONTRIBUTORS' NOTES

LEE K. ABBOTT has published three short story collections, most recently from G. P. Putnam's.

SANDRA ALCOSSER teaches at San Diego State University and is the author of *A Fish To Feed All Hunger*.

JOAN ALESHIRE's books include *Cloud Train* (1982) and *This Far* (1987) both from *The Quarterly Review of Literature*.

JENNIFER ATKINSON has poems and essays in recent issues of *The Iowa Review*, *The Reaper*, and *Fine Madness*.

RICK BASS is the author of *The Watch*, forthcoming from Norton, and *Oil Notes*, due from Seymour Lawrence. This is his first published story.

BECKY BIRTHA lives in Philadelphia and has published books with Frog-In-The-Wall press and most recently with Seal Press.

EAVAN BOLAND lives in Dublin. Her new book of poems, *The Journey*, is just out from Carcanet/Arlen.

MARIANNE BORUCH teaches at Purdue and is the author of *A View from the Gazebo* (Wesleyan).

MICHAEL BURKARD's *Fictions From The Self* is just out from Norton.

SANDIE CASTLE is a poet and playwright from Baltimore.

GERALD COSTANZO heads the Carnegie-Mellon University Press and previously appeared in *Pushcart Prize X*.

CARL DENNIS teaches English at SUNY-Buffalo. His latest book is *The Outskirts of Troy* (Morrow, 1988).

LAURIE DUESING has published in Five Fingers Review and elsewhere.

STEPHEN DUNN's seventh collection of poetry, *Between Angels*, will be published by Norton soon.

BARBARA EINZIG is the author of books from Membrane and The Figures presses. She also translates from Russian.

DAVID FERRY is the author of a study of Wordsworth and several books of poetry.

RICHARD FORD authored *The Sportswriter* and *Rock Springs.* He previously appeared in *Pushcart Prize XI*.

TESS GALLAGHER is the author of a poetry collection from Graywolf, an essay collection from the University of Michigan Press, and a story collection from Harper and Row.

REGINALD GIBBONS is editor of *TriQuarterly*.

C. S. GODSHALK is at work on a novel set in Borneo and is the author of *Anna*, a memoir (New York State Historical Association).

ALBERT GOLDBARTH teaches at Wichita State University. His most recent book is *Arts & Sciences*.

VICTORIA HALLERMAN teaches children's poetry in the New York City public schools and has published in *Poetry, Southern Poetry Review* and elsewhere.

JOY HARJO is the author of *Secrets from The Center of the World* (Peregrine Smith Books).

EHUD HAVAZELET's first collection of stories, *What Is It Then Between Us?* was just published by Scribners.

SEAMUS HEANEY contributed "The Impact of Translation" in last year's *Pushcart Prize*. He lives in Dublin.

EDWARD HIRSCH has published two poetry collections with Knopf. He teaches at The University of Houston.

JANE HIRSHFIELD lives in Mill Valley, California and has published in *The New Yorker, The Atlantic*, and elsewhere. Her second book is just out from Wesleyan.

MARIE HOWE is the author of *The Good Thief*, just out from Persea. She lives in Cambridge.

MARK JARMAN's *Far and Away* was published by Carnegie-Mellon University Press. He teaches at Vanderbilt University.

LAURA JENSEN's poetry collection, *Shelter*, is available from Dragon Gate. She lives in Tacoma, Washington.

DAVE KELLY is the author of poetry collections from Steps Inside Press and Nebraska Review Press.

WILLIAM KITTREDGE wrote *We Are Not In This Together* (Graywolf, 1984). His story "Agriculture" appeared in *Pushcart Prize X*.

YUSEF KOMUNYAKAA's *Dien Cai Dau* is just out from Wesleyan.

MELISSA LENTRICCHIA's short stories have appeared in *Kenyon Review, Raritan*, and *Antaeus*, among other literary journals. She teaches at Duke.

THOMAS LUX's most recent collection is from Hougton Mifflin. He teaches at Sarah Lawrence College.

DAVID ZANE MAIROWITZ lives in France. His short fiction has appeared in *New Directions, Partisan Review, TriQuarterly* and elsewhere.

DAN MASTERSON is at work on his third book, *Poems of Forest, Field and Pond.*

LYNNE MCFALL's story is from her first novel, *The One True Story of the World,* for which she received a Stegner Fellowship.

HEATHER MCHUGH lives in Eastport, Maine and is the author of two collections from Wesleyan University Press.

LEONARD MICHAELS is the author of *Going Places, I Would Have Saved Them If I Could* and *The Men's Club.*

LESLIE ADRIENNE MILLER lives in Houston and has published poetry in *The Georgia Review, Antioch Review* and *Chelsea.*

SUSAN MITCHELL's first book was *The Water Inside The Water.* She teaches at Florida-Atlantic University.

CAROL MUSKE has published four poetry collections. A novel, *Dear Digby,* is due from Viking in 1989.

SHARON OLDS published *The Gold Cell* with Knopf in 1987. She lives in New York City.

GREG PAPE is the author of three poetry collections. A fourth collection, *Storm Pattern,* is just completed.

ROBERT POPE's writings have appeared in *Crazyhorse, The Antioch Review* and elsewhere.

FRANCINE PROSE is the author most recently of *Women and Children First.*

MARK RICHARD has worked as a commercial fisherman, radio announcer, reporter, private investigator and bartender. His first short story collection will be published by Knopf.

ALBERTO RIOS won a Guggenheim Fellowship in 1988. Sheep Meadow Press has just issued his most recent collection, *The Lime Orchard Woman.*

LEON ROOKE's *Shakespeare's Dog* won Canada's top literary award, The Governor General's Award. He lives in Victoria B.C.

MARJORIE SANDOR has appeared twice in *Best American Short Stories.* Her story collection, *A Night of Music,* is due soon from Ecco Press.

DENNIS SCHMITZ lives in Sacramento. His new book, *Eden,* is soon to come from the University of Illinois Press.

LAWRENCE SHAINBERG has just completed a novel, *Memories of Amnesia.* He is also the author of *One On One* (Holt).

EVE SHELNUTT's third collection of short stories was recently published by Black Sparrow. She teaches at Ohio University.

ARTHUR SMITH is the author of *Elegy on Independence Day* (University of Pittsburgh Press).

CHRIS SPAIN is a Stegner Fellow at Stanford University.

SARA SULERI was born in Karachi, Pakistan. She now teaches at Yale and is co-editor of *The Yale Journal of Criticism*.

CHARLES WRIGHT's *Zone Journals* has just been published by Farrar, Straus & Giroux.

FOR THE BEST IN PAPERBACKS, LOOK FOR THE

In every corner of the world, on every subject under the sun, Penguin represents quality and variety—the very best in publishing today.

For complete information about books available from Penguin—including Pelicans, Puffins, Peregrines, and Penguin Classics—and how to order them, write to us at the appropriate address below. Please note that for copyright reasons the selection of books varies from country to country.

In the United Kingdom: For a complete list of books available from Penguin in the U.K., please write to *Dept E.P., Penguin Books Ltd, Harmondsworth, Middlesex, UB7 0DA.*

In the United States: For a complete list of books available from Penguin in the U.S., please write to *Dept BA, Penguin,* Box 999, Bergenfield, New Jersey 07621-0999.

In Canada: For a complete list of books available from Penguin in Canada, please write to *Penguin Books Canada Ltd, 2801 John Street, Markham, Ontario L3R 1B4.*

In Australia: For a complete list of books available from Penguin in Australia, please write to the *Marketing Department, Penguin Books Australia Ltd, P.O. Box 257, Ringwood, Victoria 3134.*

In New Zealand: For a complete list of books available from Penguin in New Zealand, please write to the *Marketing Department, Penguin Books (NZ) Ltd, Private Bag, Takapuna, Auckland 9.*

In India: For a complete list of books available from Penguin, please write to *Penguin Overseas Ltd, 706 Eros Apartments, 56 Nehru Place, New Delhi, 110019.*

In Holland: For a complete list of books available from Penguin in Holland, please write to *Penguin Books Nederland B.V., Postbus 195, NL–1380AD Weesp, Netherlands.*

In Germany: For a complete list of books available from Penguin, please write to *Penguin Books Ltd, Friedrichstrasse 10–12, D–6000 Frankfurt Main 1, Federal Republic of Germany.*

In Spain: For a complete list of books available from Penguin in Spain, please write to *Longman Penguin España, Calle San Nicolas 15, E–28013 Madrid, Spain.*

In Japan: For a complete list of books available from Penguin in Japan, please write to *Longman Penguin Japan Co Ltd, Yamaguchi Building, 2-12-9 Kanda Jimbocho, Chiyuoda-Ku, Tokyo 101, Japan.*

FOR THE BEST LITERATURE, LOOK FOR THE

☐ THE BOOK AND THE BROTHERHOOD
Iris Murdoch

Many years ago Gerard Hernshaw and his friends banded together to finance a political and philosophical book by a monomaniacal Marxist genius. Now opinions have changed, and support for the book comes at the price of moral indignation; the resulting disagreements lead to passion, hatred, a duel, murder, and a suicide pact.　　　　　*602 pages　　ISBN: 0-14-010470-4*　**$8.95**

☐ GRAVITY'S RAINBOW
Thomas Pynchon

Thomas Pynchon's classic antihero is Tyrone Slothrop, an American lieutenant in London whose body anticipates German rocket launchings. Surely one of the most important works of fiction produced in the twentieth century, *Gravity's Rainbow* is a complex and awesome novel in the great tradition of James Joyce's *Ulysses*.　　　　　*768 pages　　ISBN: 0-14-010661-8*　**$10.95**

☐ FIFTH BUSINESS
Robertson Davies

The first novel in the celebrated "Deptford Trilogy," which also includes *The Manticore* and *World of Wonders*, *Fifth Business* stands alone as the story of a rational man who discovers that the marvelous is only another aspect of the real.　　　　　*266 pages　　ISBN: 0-14-004387-X*　**$4.95**

☐ WHITE NOISE
Don DeLillo

Jack Gladney, a professor of Hitler Studies in Middle America, and his fourth wife, Babette, navigate the usual rocky passages of family life in the television age. Then, their lives are threatened by an "airborne toxic event"—a more urgent and menacing version of the "white noise" of transmissions that typically engulfs them.　　　　　*326 pages　　ISBN: 0-14-007702-2*　**$7.95**

You can find all these books at your local bookstore, or use this handy coupon for ordering:

Penguin Books By Mail
Dept. BA　Box 999
Bergenfield, NJ 07621-0999

Please send me the above title(s). I am enclosing ＿＿＿＿＿＿＿＿＿＿＿＿＿
(please add sales tax if appropriate and $3.00 to cover postage and handling). Send check or money order—no CODs. Please allow four weeks for shipping. We cannot ship to post office boxes or addresses outside the USA. *Prices subject to change without notice.*

Ms./Mrs./Mr. ＿＿＿＿＿＿＿＿＿＿＿＿＿＿＿＿＿＿＿＿＿＿＿＿＿＿＿＿＿＿＿

Address ＿＿＿＿＿＿＿＿＿＿＿＿＿＿＿＿＿＿＿＿＿＿＿＿＿＿＿＿＿＿＿＿＿

City/State ＿＿＿＿＿＿＿＿＿＿＿＿＿＿＿＿＿＿＿＿ Zip ＿＿＿＿＿＿＿＿＿

Sales tax:　CA: 6.5%　NY: 8.25%　NJ: 6%　PA: 6%　TN: 5.5%

FOR THE BEST LITERATURE, LOOK FOR THE

☐ **A SPORT OF NATURE**
Nadine Gordimer

Hillela, Nadine Gordimer's "sport of nature," is seductive and intuitively gifted at life. Casting herself adrift from her family at seventeen, she lives among political exiles on an East African beach, marries a black revolutionary, and ultimately plays a heroic role in the overthrow of apartheid.

354 pages   ISBN: 0-14-008470-3 $7.95

☐ **THE COUNTERLIFE**
Philip Roth

By far Philip Roth's most radical work of fiction, *The Counterlife* is a book of conflicting perspectives and points of view about people living out dreams of renewal and escape. Illuminating these lives is the skeptical, enveloping intelligence of the novelist Nathan Zuckerman, who calculates the price and examines the results of his characters' struggles for a change of personal fortune.

372 pages   ISBN: 0-14-009769-4 $4.95

☐ **THE MONKEY'S WRENCH**
Primo Levi

Through the mesmerizing tales told by two characters—one, a construction worker/philosopher who has built towers and bridges in India and Alaska; the other, a writer/chemist, rigger of words and molecules—Primo Levi celebrates the joys of work and the art of storytelling.

174 pages   ISBN: 0-14-010357-0 $6.95

☐ **IRONWEED**
William Kennedy

"Riding up the winding road of Saint Agnes Cemetery in the back of the rattling old truck, Francis Phelan became aware that the dead, even more than the living, settled down in neighborhoods." So begins William Kennedy's Pulitzer-Prize winning novel about an ex-ballplayer, part-time gravedigger, and full-time drunk, whose return to the haunts of his youth arouses the ghosts of his past and present.   228 pages   ISBN: 0-14-007020-6   **$6.95**

☐ **THE COMEDIANS**
Graham Greene

Set in Haiti under Duvalier's dictatorship, *The Comedians* is a story about the committed and the uncommitted. Actors with no control over their destiny, they play their parts in the foreground; experience love affairs rather than love; have enthusiasms but not faith; and if they die, they die like Mr. Jones, by accident.

288 pages   ISBN: 0-14-002766-1 $4.95

FOR THE BEST LITERATURE, LOOK FOR THE

☐ **THE LAST SONG OF MANUEL SENDERO**
Ariel Dorfman

In an unnamed country, in a time that might be now, the son of Manuel Sendero refuses to be born, beginning a revolution where generations of the future wait for a world without victims or oppressors.

464 pages   ISBN: 0-14-008896-2   **$7.95**

☐ **THE BOOK OF LAUGHTER AND FORGETTING**
Milan Kundera

In this collection of stories and sketches, Kundera addresses themes including sex and love, poetry and music, sadness and the power of laughter. "*The Book of Laughter and Forgetting* calls itself a novel," writes John Leonard of *The New York Times*, "although it is part fairly tale, part literary criticism, part political tract, part musicology, part autobiography. It can call itself whatever it wants to, because the whole is genius."

240 pages   ISBN: 0-14-009693-0   **$6.95**

☐ **TIRRA LIRRA BY THE RIVER**
Jessica Anderson

Winner of the Miles Franklin Award, Australia's most prestigious literary prize, *Tirra Lirra by the River* is the story of a woman's seventy-year search for the place where she truly belongs. Nora Porteous's series of escapes takes her from a small Australia town to the suburbs of Sydney to London, where she seems finally to become the woman she always wanted to be.

142 pages   ISBN: 0-14-006945-3   **$4.95**

☐ **LOVE UNKNOWN**
A. N. Wilson

In their sweetly wild youth, Monica, Belinda, and Richeldis shared a bachelor-girl flat and became friends for life. Now, twenty years later, A. N. Wilson charts the intersecting lives of the three women through the perilous waters of love, marriage, and adultery in this wry and moving modern comedy of manners.

202 pages   ISBN: 0-14-010190-X   **$6.95**

☐ **THE WELL**
Elizabeth Jolley

Against the stark beauty of the Australian farmlands, Elizabeth Jolley portrays an eccentric, affectionate relationship between the two women—Hester, a lonely spinster, and Katherine, a young orphan. Their pleasant, satisfyingly simple life is nearly perfect until a dark stranger invades their world in a most horrifying way.

176 pages   ISBN: 0-14-008901-2   **$6.95**